I0733048

ALSO BY D.T. NEAL

The Wolfshadow Trilogy
Saamaanthaa
The Happening
Norm

Other Wolfshadow Books
Lupinia:
The Selected Poems
of Polly Drinkwater, 2007–2015

Novels
Chosen

Novellas
Relict
Summerville
The Day of the Nightfish

SUCKAGE

SUCKAGE

D.T. Neal

NOSETOUCH PRESS

CHICAGO | PITTSBURGH

Suckage
Special Edition
© 2013 by D. T. Neal. All Rights Reserved.

ISBN-13: 978-1-944286-27-9

Published by Nosetouch Press
www.nosetouchpress.com

For more information about bulk purchases,
please contact Nosetouch Press at info@nosetouchpress.com.

Cataloging-in-Publication Data

Names: Neal, D.T., author.
Title: Suckage / D.T. Neal
Description: Chicago, IL : Nosetouch Press [2013]
Identifiers: ISBN: 9781944286279 (special edition paperback)
Subjects: LCSH: Horror—Fiction. | Vampires—Fiction. | GSAFD: Horror fiction. | BISAC: FICTION / Horror.

Cover & interior designed by
Christine M. Scott, Clever Crow Consulting and Design
www.clevercrow.com

The text for this book was set in Adobe Garamond Pro.

For victims of vampires everywhere.

Prologue

I'm there—not telling you where—and I've got my hand on the stake, my other hand on the mallet, arm raised, poised to strike, and there's always that moment, that pause before the plunge, because you know what's coming, you're sure of it: the splash of blood in your face, the howling, the shrieking, the rending, the last words, the dying, the death, the ashes, the dust.

It comes like clockwork carnage, and, before that blow falls, you go through that moment of hesitation, and ask yourself: "Is this worth it?"

Do you have any idea how hard it is for a mosquito? How elemental the compulsion is that she—and the ones that bite you are always she—because she needs that blood meal, the protein for her eggs, that she risks her very life to get it?

There are the dragonflies, the birds, the bats.

There are spiderwebs and car windshields.

And there's us, the swatters: the slayers.

Lazy fliers, they make their desperate pilgrimage on windless nights for blood, a constant quest. Most people don't think about it; they just swat at them.

Me, I think about it, and I still swat them.

Cry me a river, Bloodsucker.

Swat. You're dead.

Nobody likes mosquitoes.

Why would you?

They're pests. They're nuisances. They're parasites.

Who could possibly like a parasite? Who, indeed?

Nobody likes parasites, but everybody loves vampires. Why is that, do you think? The immortality? The hypnotic gaze? The good taste? The money? The power?

People just love their walking corpses. And that's all a vampire really is: an exquisite corpse.

That's what I tell myself, and then the hammer falls, as inexorable as an avalanche, as unstoppable as a landslide.

You think that it's the end, but it's only the beginning.

CHAPTER 1

Right now, I'm talking to the girl. Her name is Clementine— swear, they're all named Clementine these days, or Sarah, Emily, or Olivia. What happened 20 years ago to compel moms and dads to all give their kids the same names? Why did they all suddenly decide that they just had to name their daughters that? How did that even happen? Aren't they disappointed to find that everybody else had the same idea?

I know because I'm sitting here talking to Clementine, this blue-eyed, overtanned blond girl swilling an orange juice smoothie, telling me a story with waves of her hands, and I'm thinking "Another goddamned Clementine?"

Not saying this, of course. My work requires the proper discretion— I really have to mind what I say, keep it quarantined from what I'm actually thinking.

Clementine doesn't notice. She's talking about cats.

She loves cats.

She has three of them.

Shelter cats. Rescue cats.

One is a tortoiseshell cat named "Snitch." One is an orange tabby named "Sneaky." The other is a Russian Blue named "Boots." I knew what a tabby was, and she explained the other two to me, at length.

She's wearing skin-tight orange leggings, has gilt bronze sandals, and this pink, I don't know, Indian-themed blouse that has swirls and patterns on it, and a couple of big bracelets at her wrists, and she's got a pair of Ray-Ban Wayfarers perched on her head as she's talking. She's blissfully blond, with that happy-go-lucky tan and green nail polish I commented on when I first started talking to her—she called it "Mint Squint" and I liked that.

I like her. She's a nice girl. She cares about stuff. You can just see it. She deserves better than this. I don't know why I picked her. I could have talked to anybody. That's the thing; eventually, everybody just becomes another body.

It's not like *she* will even care.

I bring them to Iris because she likes women. She doesn't say she does, but she always wants women, so I gather from it that she prefers women.

Maybe they taste better. I don't know.

So, Clementine's still talking, and I'm almost done with my coffee, and I'm figuring out what to do next.

It pisses me off that I even have to do this. I mean, Iris should be doing this herself. Why am I the one who has to go out trolling like this? She's the one with the problem, not me. Why do I have to fetch for her?

It's not fair. Nothing's fair.

"You know what, Clementine? It's getting late," I said. "I should let you go."

Clementine looked genuinely put out, which showed up on her face as a pout, a toss of her hair and a furtive look, like she's trying to figure out how she blew it, how something that seemed to be going along so well suddenly went off the rails.

It's not you; it's me.

"Really? That's too bad."

Yeah, so, I'm good-looking. Women like me. Gay guys like me. People who like good-looking guys like me.

I don't know what it is—the combination of being tall and a kind of bland manliness that passes for Hollywood handsome these days, maybe. I know one thing: it's my looks, not my personality. I don't think I have much of a personality—I'm a beatific blend of silent smugness and ironic attitude, maybe. Maybe they think I'm dumb, I don't know. But because I'm easy on the eyes, people pay attention, accept the rest of me.

I sometimes think that's what drew Iris to me, but honestly don't think the mossy tombstone of her heart could possibly be moved by something as mundane and human as beauty. She's moved way beyond that.

I force a smile, and Clementine doesn't even notice; they never do.

"I hope you and your cats find what you're looking for," I said.

Clementine can't believe that I'm not taking her with me. I can just see it. She wants an overnight, wants to wake up in my bed, to have breakfast at Kookies and talk about lame stuff like we were a proper morning-after couple.

Again, with experience, I can just tell.

"Let me at least give you my number," she said, waiting for me to take out my phone. I slip mine out and take down her digits.

"Got it," I said, putting the phone away.

She smiles at me, those pretty, straight teeth bright against that round face. She's young—mid-20s, tops. Not wrinkled yet, not old. No trace of death on her: she's vital and alive. Pretty, even, in that Chicago Pretty kind of way—that kind of meaty face and broad hips, an easy smile and eyeshadowed gaze.

Midwestern chic. Wholesome as fuck, suburban sexy.

"Maybe I'll see you around, Nate," she said.

"Sure," I said, shaking her offered hand. She's got soft hands, and she gives my hand a nice long squeeze, her fingertips lightly touching my palm as our hands part. Clementine would like to have me over. Clementine would like to do things to me. And, were this a date or even a hookup, I'd let her. But it's not.

She doesn't even guess that I've just saved her life.

CHAPTER 2

Iris is pissed off when she finds out that I didn't bring her a snack. Iris always has to have somebody waiting for her when she wakes up. I just show up at her place as the sun goes down, and I wait, knowing full well that she's not going to be happy.

She rises the moment the sun dips below the horizon, appears before me in a cloud of mist, assuming solid form, and she gives me a "What the Fuck?" look with her radiant indigo eyes. That might sound contradictory, but her dark eyes do project a deadly radiance, like the corona around an eclipse.

Those eyes are deadlier than anything I have ever known. You look into those eyes, and you're lost. You ever hear that expression about losing yourself in someone's eyes? Iris has those eyes. Vampires have those eyes.

I never meet her gaze; not anymore. I'm too afraid to look.

She has a pointy nose and a long face and thick, soft, black hair. She's deathly pale, which is always the case when she wakes up, since she always wakes up hungry. She's a curvy, juicy little thing, and even manages a stretch when she rises.

Iris looks old—no, let me rephrase that: Iris looks classical. She looks like she's about 20 years old, but she's way, way older than that. Iris looks like she belongs in a painting on a wall. I know, because I've seen the paintings (we'll talk about those later, I promise).

There is just something about her features that speak to European antiquity, of a bygone world, where your dad could still be a knight, where your mom could end up on a pyre for being a heretic, where your sisters could have been thrown into fast-flowing rivers in burlap sacks for being witches.

Hers was the face of a young Renaissance woman of beauty and uncertain ancestry—Franco-Italian, Anglo-Swiss, Teutonic-Iberian, Romano-Turkish. Something like that, a blended nonspecific European beauty, a hybrid history from a region that had been long in contention between feuding forces, where city-states fought empires for the same patches of land that had caused the Romans and the Celts to contend with one another, where Visigoths and Ostrogoths ran from Huns, where Byzantine cataphracts hunted down Phrygians, or Scythians, or Stygians; I sometimes lose track.

Iris was beautiful, but it was a different beauty from the women of today. It was a bygone beauty that had no proper place in this world. Iris belonged in museums, in fine restaurants, in embassies, in opera houses—she did not belong in malls or department stores. Iris did not belong in the suburbs.

It would have been easy to see Iris in an embroidered green velvet gown, pouring poison from a bejeweled ring into a goblet, serving it up to a lover or a lord without so much as batting an eyelash over those resplendent eyes of hers. Iris belonged to crueler, wilder times, where bravos prowled the streets, where stilettos punctuated sentences, and precious life hung precariously on opportunities taken, and whole nations threw their lot behind the whims of kings.

I long wondered when she'd seen her last sunrise, what had that world been, and how she faced today with that deep knowledge of the past. I'd ask her about it, and she'd just laugh, thinking I was a fool for asking. But for an American, a people unburdened by introspection and awareness of history, it was something that made me curious. She'd speak of Venice and Siena like she was talking about Cleveland or Buffalo, with this casual kind of disregard, and I wanted to know more. I wanted to know everything.

There just wasn't much that could move her these days. But hunger? That got her attention. The sharp gaze comes when she sees that I haven't brought her anything.

"Well?" she asked. She was wearing a black silk gown, sleeveless, with long leather gloves. She wore black knee boots, heeled, pointy-toed, and had a belt of diamond and gold at her waist, and a brooch positively crusted with diamonds, a spider brooch, with a big, round, red ruby for its body. The brooch alone was worth a human life, the way it sparkled, diamond-eyed.

"Well, what?" I replied.

"I'm hungry, Nate," she said.

"So, go out and hunt," I said. "It's what you're supposed to do."

"I want you to bring me something. I'm hungry."

Something.

That's how she sees us: we're all just a bunch of somethings to Iris.

I remember when I first ran into her. It was total chance. I was up late, at an all-night diner in the city—Maestro's—and she came in with a bunch of Goths from Own, the prime Goth bar in the city, where the 80s had never died.

I was eating a bacon burger, just minding my own business. I'd had a breakup with Hillary Edmund, my girlfriend of the past three years—she'd been getting her degree in architecture, I'd been dithering around indefinitely with my thesis in art history. I don't even want to go into my thing with Hillary, but I was right, she was wrong, and we were finished. She dumped me flat out, said I would never be serious about anything, starting and ending with our relationship.

I ate with abandon, filling the empty space in my heart with bites of burger; if the way to a man's heart was through his stomach, in my view, the way to mend a broken heart was to eat a goddamned bacon burger. Fuck it.

And then Iris just flew in with these Goth crows. Even with them, she stood out, because she was different. It's just one of those weirdnesses with Goths—the boys are skinny, and the girls aren't. Go figure. But Iris looked different among those preening Goth girls. Despite her curvy build, there was a predatory feel to her, she radiated a feral hunger. She looked like trouble. She looked like danger. I remember half-thinking that, even then, at first glance. I should have known better. But how can you really prepare for it? Nobody just walks up and says "Hey, I'm a vampire. Want to go somewhere?"

Nobody says that, not even the vampires. Frankly, I'd have more respect for them if they showed that kind of candor. But vampires are all about the con, the seduction. They lead you on as they lead you in, and then you're stuck by the time they're ready to feed.

Iris was wearing a pink ensemble—a pink flapper dress is what it looked like, with ripped pink stockings and pink heels. She wore a pink shawl, and had a clattering stack of pink plastic bracelets up her slender wrists, and a long, pink scarf that looked like gossamer, and pink finger-less gloves that looked like they were lace. She was wearing pink-rimmed sunglasses, which just looked idiotic at that hour, even more bizarre than her pink outfit. She was ridiculously pink.

I watched them settle into a booth while I ate one of my fries, and noticed how Iris's black hair was blacker than all the other kids' clothes, and how nicely it complemented her absurdly pink attire.

And she saw me notice.

That moment, in retrospect, fills me with dread. The turn of her head, her seeing me, in this flutter of chattering black around her, that pause, the noticing. She saw me, she smiled: a wry turn of her mouth, black lipstick, a hint of dimples—a parenthetical to that amused expression.

Even then, I should have noticed: her face was more rough-hewn than the whey-faced babies around her—there was an uncompromising, pan-European angularity to it that was an undead giveaway. She was not some American bon vivant; she was European. A young woman from the Old Country, far, far from home. I could not guess where, or if countries even existed when she was born. It was just a sense, an intuition. Maybe it was my background in art history, but looking at her, I saw a work of art, clear as daylight. I saw a masterpiece.

I rolled my eyes at her and looked away, went back to my late night meal and brooding.

Hillary had great big eyes, brown and beautiful. I missed those eyes, and her great big smile, and big teeth, even. She smiled majestically. Crazy as a bedbug, but what an incandescent smile she had. I missed Hillary's big mouth, her big smile, her great big kisses. When she came, the rafters shook. Car alarms went off. Hillary was a screamer.

"Hey," Iris said. She was standing there. I hadn't seen her approach. It was always that way with her—she was silent as a ghost, quick as death. She'd just show up, she'd just be there, like she'd been there all along, like she belonged there.

"Hey," I said. She extended a gloved hand.

"I'm Iris," she said. "Iris Augenblick."

I could not place the accent, the barest hint of something, that aroma of antiquity. Nobody talked like Iris, nobody sounded like her.

"Nathan Sharp," I said. I shook her hand. The gloves were soft and supple, but her grip was strong, like steel. She held my hand a moment in her firm grasp before releasing me.

"Sharp," she said. "What a great name."

"Thanks," I said.

"Mind if I join you?" she asked.

I nodded at her bevy of Goths, who were watching with undisguised disdain. I mean, I could taste their contempt. Seriously, every chalk-faced one of them was filled with loathing for me. There was something else in their gaze—envy, perhaps. Resentment. I didn't know what I'd done to deserve it.

"Would they mind?" I asked.

She glanced over her shoulder, scoffed, turned her attention back to me. Something in that movement, the finality of it, made everything else around me seem to recede; it was like we were alone together.

"They're nothing."

"Alright," I said. I had taken one of those little "booths for two," anyway. Iris slid into the seat across from me, still wearing those sunglasses.

"Want a fry?" I asked. Not that she looked like she needed them, curvy as she was, but she just looked hungry to me. I didn't know any better.

"Not hungry," she said. "You're really handsome, Nathan."

"Nate," I said. "Only my mom calls me Nathan."

"You're really handsome, Nate," Iris said.

"Thanks," I said, taking a bite out of my sandwich. Fuck it, I was hungry and heartbroken. I had earned my midnight meal.

She perched her chin on her hand. Her face, what I could see of it, was so fucking pale it bordered on luminescent. She had an oval face that would have been comfortable on a curio carved from ivory.

"Sunglasses at night," I said. "Like the song."

"What song?" she asked.

"'Sunglasses At Night,'" I said. "Corey Hart, I think. A long time ago. Ancient history."

Me saying that made her smile to herself, her private joke. Of course it was me sounding like an idiot, not knowing. What was a song from the '80s to a woman who had been alive for centuries? I didn't know that, yet, couldn't fathom that little smile, what it meant.

"Never heard of him," she said. "Does it bother you?"

"A little," I said. "Just kinda pointless, don't you think?"

She smiled, again, that turn of her lip, the dimples. She was a charming creature when she wanted to be. The crowning idiocy of it all was that she looked younger than I was, so it put me off my game. I felt like I was the voice of maturity, talking to this younger woman, never guessing just how thoroughly the tables were turned.

"You mean an affectation?" she asked.

"Something like that," I said. The Goths had ordered their food, but they were still watching us, scowling. "Like wearing pink."

"Oh, this?" she asked, laughing. Her laugh was high and lilting, kind of charming when contrasted with her enigmatic flapper femme fatale bearing. "I was making a statement."

"And what statement was that?" I asked.

"That Goth need not be black," she said. "In fact, that masters of the form can be any color they choose, but only a true master of Goth... or mistress...can wear pink like they mean it. Really, it's all a joke. The Visigoths would have eaten these plump little ptarmigans for supper."

I didn't give a city rat's ass about the Gothic subculture; they were simply another urban adornment, one of those things you just saw, like the Gothic couple snogging on the El, or the Goth working behind the counter at the record store, giving you the Evil Eye because you caucused as "norm" to them.

Whatever.

"Wow," I said, completely unimpressed.

"In the South, the color of Goth is green," Iris said. "Not that anybody knows that. The Goths down there wear black, too, just like up here. But in the South, Goth is green. Because plants overtake everything down there—not just the kudzu, either. You find old towns completely overgrown by the green. It's ever-present—the heat, the plants, the swamps. You can't ever escape the green, Nature run rampant. Green. Sultry. Overpowering. Southern. You can smell it, the decay, can feel it in the heat and in the darkness."

I hadn't given that any thought, wasn't entirely sure what she was talking about.

"The way the vines creep over statues, up walls. You feel like if you stood in one place long enough, the vines would grow over you, too," she said. "Everything in the South lives in the shadow of that green. Whether forests or swamps or in fields. You can't escape the reality that Man has only so much purchase on that land—a generation without people there, and the green would overtake all of it, and there would be only ruin, garlanded in green. No one would ever know people lived there at all."

"Creepy," I said.

"Yes," she said. "Creepy. Creepy like a vine."

She just sat there a moment, letting the words die, while I thought about it for a stray second or two, imagined old slave plantations and mansions overgrown with green, thick foliage, rusting farm implements, wanton and listless, slovenly, horrible—the scent of growth and life and death on the wind, of rot and reconstruction.

Yes, I suppose I could see it.

"Then again," I said. "With global warming, maybe brown should be the new color of Goth, cuz everything's drying up. Never-ending drought. Wildfires."

Iris didn't like the mention of fires. I could see it register on her face, the barest hint of something, a remembrance.

Iris was icily sexy, there was no denying that. She absolutely was, but the thing was, I could afford to not be impressed by Iris, because I was used to women coming to me and talking to me. It's what happened.

What I couldn't get my head around was Hillary dumping me. I mean, what the hell was that even about? She just flat-out dropped me, said we weren't progressing, as if there were some kind of, I don't know, list of things we were supposed to have done. Maybe she had been irked that I'd not married her by then? I don't know.

Hillary was uptight, she was always like that. It was her thing. I'd given up a pile of friendships over the years, chasing around with Hillary. She was all I'd had left, in the end.

But she'd dumped me. Said I had no substance. I'd never, ever been dumped before. I'd dumped plenty of women, but never had I been on the receiving end of it. It hurt. My whole heart ached. She had crushed me, and I didn't even know what I had done wrong, how I had failed her. I only knew that I had, and only because of what she had done, in cutting me loose.

No substance? What did that even mean?

It wasn't necessarily enough to make me empathic for the list of romantic casualties I'd assembled over the years, but it still fucking hurt. Pain mattered any time you felt it.

"You're in pain," Iris said. "I could see that from across the room. Your heart's been hobbled."

"Hobbled," I said. "That's a funny word."

She smiled in her fleeting way, like she was humoring me once again. Iris was hot, but it was the coldest heat I'd ever seen a woman throw off by way of a vibe. It was this complete self-possession she had, this sense of worldliness, having seen absolutely all that one could have seen in the world. She may have been jaded, weary, or titillated behind that mask-like façade she wore. But while I couldn't quite see into her, she could most definitely see into me.

"She isn't worth your pain," she said. "They never are. I've seen it a thousand times, and it's always the same. No one is worth all of that pain."

I looked up from my plate, into the face of the sunglassed apparition across from me. She just held that neutral expression, like she was a statue. I mean, her face didn't move when she did not speak. Never having sat with a vampire before, I had no frame of reference for this, that supernatural stillness. But there it was, staring me right in the face, as plain as Doris Day. Death was staring me in the face, and I didn't recognize her for what she was.

"You don't know," I said.

"I know," she said. "I really do."

And then she took off her sunglasses, just slowly lifted them and put them down on the table in a smooth and sensuous motion. And then I saw her eyes, those luminous indigo orbs.

It's hard for somebody who didn't know her to understand the power of her eyes. She had them dressed up with fake eyelashes, mascara, and they were impeccably made up with shades of eyeshadow and hints of silvery glitter like moondust.

But the eyes themselves were these pools of utter darkness—a luminous, inky darkness—they gave up exactly nothing, and yet were dauntingly deep. They were like an endless well, and you knew several things: that there was water in that well, somewhere, and that something monstrous lived in that water, and that thing in the depths was looking up at you, but you couldn't quite see it—you only knew that it was down there, and that it was staring at you, seeing through you with the hungriest eyes.

It was a gaze that was inscrutable and nakedly revealing—the eyes of a perfect predator. Gazing into her eyes, I saw nothing else around me, forgot myself: sound, light, love, hope, life itself—they all receded before that gaze.

"Forget about her," Iris said, and I did. "Why don't we go someplace?"

And I thought it was a great idea. I would go anywhere with her, so long as I could go there with her.

Iris. My Iris. Hillary Who?

So, we walked out of there, and her Gothlings whined like whipped dogs, but she stayed them with a curt wave of her hand, and she and I went outside, where the autumn chill had only now just started to touch the air.

She took my hand in hers, and we walked down the street, looking ridiculous—me tall and skinny-handsome in my Western shirt and worn jeans and navy blue Top-Siders, and Iris clacking along in her heels, this lovely-curvy little specter in pale, dusty pink, barely coming up to my chest. People looked at us as we walked by, but I could hardly care. We were beautiful, we were together. Not a soul in the city could touch us.

She took us to this little park, one of the many half-assed parks in the city that counted as green spaces, but were hardly more than horticultural hiccups. This one was a handful of trees, a couple of benches that were bracketed to "bum-proof" them, so derelicts couldn't comfortably sleep upon them, and an old stone thumb of a water fountain. This park was a brick-and-concrete trapezoid within the city. I saw the brass plaque for it: Augenblick Park. I didn't think about that at that moment, what that even meant; I didn't think about anything.

We just sat down, and I saw a rat scamper by in the shadows. And then another. And then another. A little rat parade. Iris saw them, smiled.

"Don't mind them," she said. "They won't bite."

"What about you?" I asked.

"No promises," she said, biting me.

CHAPTER 3

Only those of you in relationships with vampires can possibly understand what I felt at that time. Iris was amazing, she was wonderful, she was perfect. She was everything I needed and could possibly desire in a woman.

That first bite sent me off into this euphoric state. Hillary became a ghost in a heartbeat, dead and buried, lost in the endless shadow of Iris's eyes.

Looking at it with some semblance of objectivity, yeah, it was messed up. She was a fucking vampire. I knew that the moment she bit me, but the ramifications of it were lost to me in the heady expanse of that moment. At the risk of sounding like a self-help or addict in recovery, when you're in that moment, you are transported, and nothing else matters.

Absolutely everything sang with color, everything signified.

I'd walk down the street and the trees looked like they were laced with neon. The ground radiated light. The sky crackled. Life throbbed through me, which made sense in retrospect—it was passing through me and into Iris, by way of my blood, but at the time, in the thick of it, it felt like nothing I'd ever experienced before.

I suppose I was in love, but "love" doesn't even frame that emotional state properly. I understood, with lymphocytic clarity, what my purpose was:

I existed to make Iris happy.

In our angst- and anomie-ridden world, you can't know how therapeutic having so clear and unambiguous a purpose like that was. What Iris wanted, I provided. Anything she needed. Had she needed me to step off a bridge, I would have done so without hesitation back then.

But she hadn't needed me the way she needed her victims. I suppose I'm fortunate in that regard, because if she had, I'd have been dead, just another casualty to her endless appetite.

No, she needed me as she needed an extra set of hands, an extra set of eyes, someone to mind things in the day, while she slept. If she was

Batgirl, then I was Alfred, the butler, making sure everything in her world was right.

I didn't think of it that way back then, or even recognize it. All I knew is that Iris's happiness was what made me happy.

Does it really help to lay out everything I did in that time, the empty years, the wasted time, the lost life? Would that give insight into why I did what I did in that time, in the "honeymoon phase" of my service to Iris?

No. I did a good job. I was a good dog. I served Iris without question for five years. She rewarded me with tastes of her blood, which gave me brief power and fleeting supernatural resistance to harm. She allowed me to sit in on her feeds, she fed on me—never enough to kill me, of course—but enough to feel the intoxicating sting of her kiss.

I was her pet.

And that's ultimately what I was to her, what all of her minions were ever to her, once she started having them.

Sit.

Heel.

Stay.

Fetch.

Good boy.

A dog.

And, I suppose, my exemplary service to her is what actually let me slip out from under her spell. I think Iris began to take me for granted at some point. Maybe she always did. I can't really know for sure, because it had never been my place to know, and Iris hadn't wanted me to know, and she never shared.

All I do know is that, while early on, she'd bite me and send me off in that blissful state, or look at me with those cavernous eyes of hers and enthrall me, or she'd give me a bit of her blood and let me taste a fraction of that power she possessed—but, over time, she stopped doing those things. The feedings became fewer, and she'd not make me look her in the eye to forget everything I ever was.

She just stopped doing it, and slowly, in time, I came out from under, back to my senses. Five years older than I had been. I'd met her at 25, and now I was 30 years old. That's incredible to me, that span of lost time. I just remember looking at a calendar and seeing that five years had gone by, and feeling a sense of wonder, sorrow, and amazement. Where had those years gone? Where had I gone?

There was only Iris. First, last, and always, there was only her. So narrow had my focus been, so limited had been my vision, that Iris was all that I knew and all that I loved and all that I lived for. What friends I had become like ghosts, vanished from my life. My world had collapsed in on itself, was sucked dry by Iris, who had taken whatever I was and turned it to something she could make use of, had me shelve the rest of who I was, the parts that didn't fit or didn't matter, the "useless" parts of who I was that weren't valuable to Iris.

That was what vampires did to you. They took lives and they took life, and never changed. There was something terribly alienating about it, watching yourself grow older while they looked exactly as they did when you first crossed paths with them. She was this petite beauty, dark-haired and indigo-eyed, the European confection I had fallen for to begin with, not a day older, and I had aged. What the fuck?

Don't let anybody tell you differently: there is a world of difference between being in your 20s and being in your 30s. When you're a 20-something, you can pretend you're an adult somewhat better than when you were a teenager—bigger, better toys, more complicated games.

But you turned 30, and suddenly you were thrust into adulthood, and you had to start thinking about stuff, had to start being serious, had to begin maybe doing something with your life, whether it meant starting a family, or getting a real job, or in some way doing something that was important to you, making your mark, one way or another.

What was I doing in those years? I was serving Iris. I was waiting on her hand and motherfucking foot, doing what I could to make her life easier, happier, more trouble-free. And that's all I was doing. Forget the thesis, forget my future. Forget everything.

And, for her, it was like it was the most natural thing in the world. Of course, for her, yeah, it was—it was a game she'd been playing for centuries, with companion after companion. I didn't think about it that much then, but I became aware of it, that sense that I was just another in a series of acquisitions for her, one of many who had entered into her service over the years.

If mortality was what defined humanity, was central to the human condition, in being freed from those bonds, vampires immediately stepped out of the confines that hemmed in the rest of us, and in so doing, lost touch with everything that made us who we were. There isn't some big moral lesson in this; it simply was how they were.

I was still young, but not as young as I had been, and Iris was the same. Iris was always the same. There's no way to account for it, but I could see it, and it would become more pronounced as the years went by—I'd get ever older and weaker, and Iris would be exactly as she'd always been, this young, pretty, black-haired thing, girly-gorgeous, pale and precious.

Iris was changeless.

Iris was immortal.

I don't know why she'd loosened the leash that had held me fast. Maybe she thought she didn't need to keep me reined in, that where I had been in thrall, now I was merely in love, and that would sustain things indefinitely.

Or maybe Iris wanted to have me be more than just her thrall. Maybe she wanted a friend who could confide in her, and not simply slavishly obey her without question.

Even vampires need friends, right?

The point is that, eventually, I woke up from the stupor, came back to my senses, and when that happened—and it was a gradual, erosive process—what I had with Iris could no longer stand as it once had. I'd sleptwalked through several years in her service, so when I came out of it, there was a cold and shocking awareness that closed in on me. A sudden sobriety, a sense of clarity.

Turning 30 will do that to you. You wake the hell up and think that you could keep on going this way for the rest of your days. For Iris, a decade was an eyeblink. Five years was less than nothing. It simply didn't matter to her, this infinitesimal wrinkle in space-time that was Nathan Sharp. I was just another link in the ever-growing chain from where she had come from to where she was, now.

As I gradually woke from that stupor, I'd ask questions of her, would try to sound her out. Iris was a terrible storyteller, had absolutely no gift for it, but I would still manage to pry things out of her from time to time. I remember asking her on the eve of her 499th year, when she was thinking about it, decided to talk about it a little.

"I never know whether to count my birthdate as part of my life, or whether my moment of unlife is the more logical starting point," Iris said. "What do you think, Nate?"

I had no answer. What she wanted was the right answer, of course. "Does it matter? You were made when you were 20, right?"

She nodded. We sat in her living room, a kind of salon she had, one of the only adorned places of her lair. She had donated most of her possessions to the Augenblick Museum, which, as near as I could tell, were collections of her personal effects accumulated over the past 500 years—furniture, clothing, jewelry, armor, weapons, art. She'd bought the property shortly after the Great Chicago Fire, so the museum had been there since 1871, so, for the last 141 years, members of the "Augenblick Family" (bizarrely, only Iris, in one of her incarnations) had contributed to it.

"What I'm saying is that you are either 500 years old, or you are 520 years old, right?" I said. "You were born in 1492 and made in 1512. So, what difference do those 20 years make?"

Iris treated me to one of her "Nate, you're an idiot but I forgive you anyway" smiles. "Those first 20 years were very different for me, Nate," Iris said. "I had my life mapped out for me, you know. It's how it was done back then. I was a *cortigiana onesta*. A courtesan, before you ask."

"A prostitute?" I asked.

Iris just looked at me sadly. "It's too complicated to explain to you, Nate. Americans don't know anything about love, or the complexities of it. You're all a bunch of children, groping around in the dark. At any rate, my sire could not hope to be without me, could not bear to see me grow old and die, so he bit me."

"Who was he?"

"No one you would know, Nate," Iris said. She loved being cryptic like that. Imagine that, a vampire being cryptic.

"I had hoped to make myself a force to be reckoned with as a courtesan. That had been my world," Iris said. "And he had come along and changed that."

"Did you know he was a vampire?"

"Of course I knew," Iris said. "Not at first, but I knew. It's pretty easy to tell, when you do what I do. He intended to take me away from Venice, away from all of the intrigues. He told me that he could see the trouble that was brewing in Europe, yearned for better for me, took me away from the stink of the canals and the constant plagues and the war and poisonings. I went because I had no choice. He had compelled me. I wrote my family and told them of my travels, as we went from city to city throughout Europe, as he freelanced his way from war to war. The poor thing was quite in love with me, and for me, a child the way you are a child to me, I didn't know any better. I was vain, and the prospect of always being beautiful? To a young courtesan in Venice, at the brink of the clash between the Old World and the New World, before the French Disease had yet ravaged Italy? How could I turn that down? He took me away from all of it. He had been a Varangian, was old before I'd known him."

I didn't know what a Varangian was, had to look it up. They were Vikings, basically. Vikings who had settled in Russia, who pimped themselves out to the Byzantines as hired muscle, as part of the Varangian Guard, who protected Byzantine Emperors.

"So, it's your 500th birthday," I said.

"There is no way to commemorate it," Iris said. "You cannot honor an unlife. It is a meaningless moment in time—to us, what matters is surviving, the span of time. A newborn vampire is as mindless and meaningless a thing as you could hope to be. No one listens to the counsel of infants. No one pays them any mind at all. I became my sire's companion. We left Venice well ahead of the monstrous plague of 1575, which killed all of my family—had my sire not made me, I surely would have died then, an old woman, useless and wasted, one of the 50,000 who had met their end in that plague. Instead, I saw my 100th year of unlife in 1612, in Moscow, of all places, my sire hunting Cossacks in the night, while I hunted behind closed doors, a confection to draw in hapless lords. We were quite a team in those days, he and I—steel and satin, he used to say. He with sword, and me with pillows and perfume and winsome words. I would gather intelligences, and he would act upon them. He was always passionate about politics, at least in those days."

"Who is he?" I asked again.

"No one you would know, Nate," Iris said again. "Don't wrinkle that pretty face of yours with worry. We have such history, my sire and I. I followed in his train for 250 years, then I was determined to be shut of him, and his endless wars. I'd never known someone like him, this dashing warrior prince, a mercenary soldier who fought beneath a moonlit standard. The Nightlord, they knew him as, in so many languages: *Pán Noci, Gospodin Noch, Domnul de Noapte, Senhor da Noite, Panem Nocy, Herre Natten, Señor de la Noche, Gece Efendisi, Arglwydd y Nos, Dominus Noctis.*"

To hear her say those names, in all of those languages, was strangely beautiful. Antiquity on her lips, living history.

"I owed him my unlife, but to be forever in the shadow of the Nightlord? It was not a place for me," Iris said, looking far away, to a place that had long predated my own life. "I was not content to be part of his retinue, to travel from battlefield to battlefield, campaign to campaign. In those days, there was so much war. I left him for the New World in 1762, when he'd been busy pounding Prussians into jelly, earning Catherine's favor wherever and however he could. I think he was in love with her, perhaps had designs on her—the Everlasting Empress. Can you imagine? I suppose I was jealous, despite my resentment in riding in his wake all those years. I had planned it all very carefully. Let him have his empress; I would build my own world, far from him."

"Catherine the Great?" I asked. I didn't know shit about history, but even I had heard about some of those rulers. You didn't earn "the Great" without being kind of awesome, right?

"Yes," Iris said, and I could see that it still bugged her a bit. "He stayed with her until she died, in 1796. I always wonder why he did not turn her. I wonder if she ever suspected? At any rate, he chose her over me, and I had a 34-year head start on him, before he recognized the enormity of his error in letting me go."

"But you left him," I said.

Iris's eyes turned away from whenever they were, and were back in the here and now, on me. Her eyes were hard as gemstones in that moment, before she composed herself.

"It doesn't matter," Iris said. "I don't expect you to understand, Nate. I was just a courtesan; she was an empress. Never mind that I would have been a greater ruler than she, that I had known more of war and politics and diplomacy than she could hope to have, that I would have made a better empress. To him, I was what I had always been in his eyes: a child."

I could see that it embittered her in some way, this memory, and seeing her petrified pain caused me pain, even though I could feel that same envy she had felt, that sense of being captive to someone—something—greater than myself.

"I've already said too much," Iris said. "You need to get me something to eat. I have a powerful thirst, Nate."

She'd had it lucky—her "Nightlord" had just taken a fancy to her and turned her. That seemed damned gentlemanly compared with what I'd experienced. He'd obviously loved her and had turned her out of love, wanted to preserve her beauty forever, maybe wanted their love to last forever. That was romantic and put my own relationship with Iris in context.

She didn't give a shit about me; I was just a means to an end. She needed stuff done, and I was there to do those things. It was a utilitarian relationship.

It didn't feel good to be in that place.

-X-

Iris was was pissed that I hadn't delivered her any food. She pouted, she sulked. When she got hungry, she'd get restive that way, petulant.

"I'm just tired of delivering people to you," I said.

It was the truth. I was sick of it. Sick of all of it by then.

"But I need you to, Nate," she said. "Do you know what's out there? Other vampires. Werewolves. Werewolves, Nate. Do you know what a werewolf does when it catches a vampire?"

I had never seen a werewolf, didn't even know they existed. I just shook my head.

"It's messy, Nate," she said. "Werewolves are terribly messy."

"I thought vampires were, you know, top of the heap," I said. Sometimes, when Iris was peevish, it helped to distract her with conversation.

"Yes and no," she said. "Look, we're connected, but werewolves are wild cards. I don't even want to talk about it. You were supposed to bring me something to eat and you didn't."

"But my point is that you could go out and get it yourself," I said. "You don't need me."

"I do need you," she said. "If you loved me you'd do this."

"If you loved me, you'd not ask me to do it," I said.

She sat down, clutched her knees. We lived in her place. Some old building that had survived the Great Chicago Fire, a square stone structure, four floors. She talked about that enough times, saying that it wasn't the cow, it wasn't a couple of drunkards; it was the damned vampire hunters, trying to purify the city. That she'd founded the museum to spite them, in a way, creating a monument to her own immortality.

"Fire purifies," she said. "It's what they always say. Back in the day, Chicago was lousy with vampires. Ever since the World's Fair put it on the map. It was wonderful. The place was teeming with people, and the locomotives coming and going. You could just smell the blood, wherever you went. People everywhere. Prey everywhere. The Fire was a reaction. It was retaliation. I don't really remember the details. I was just living here, and I saw it. I knew something was happening. It was dreadful, devastating. All those people, fleeing toward the river, toward the lake. That's what happens sometimes."

"It was a long time ago," I said. "And you used to hunt. I mean, what the fuck?"

"Get me something, Nate," she said. "I'm starving."

She liked to feed on at least one person each night. So, you do the math. It's over 1800 people. And here's the deal: Iris wasn't a sipper; she was a guzzler. Not entirely true—she sipped me back in the day, but that was because she'd already fed that night. But she chugged people, drank them right down. She swigged people the way frat boys swig beer.

I had been witness to over 1800 murders. I had been an accessory to them. And with her lately having me fetch people for her, it was worse: I was a Judas goat, now.

And anybody who knows dick about vampires understands that if someone dies from a vampire's bite will come back as a fucking vampire, right? And Iris didn't want the competition, wouldn't tolerate something like that. Some vampires build little gangs around themselves, but to Iris, it was a matter of more mouths to feed, and she was lazy about that. She fed herself, and herself only. Kept her operation small. She could afford to do this because she was older than almost all of the other vampires in Chicago, and so, personally, she was powerful enough to tear them limb-from-limb if they crossed her. But it was more than this—she just didn't like the hassle of dealing with the others. Iris kept things intimate, where she could pay attention to the details. But not too many details.

That meant putting me on body patrol. That's what really fucking began to gall me. I'd been companion, confidante, bait, butler, and undertaker. She'd kill'em, and I'd have to deal with disposing of them. What the fuck, right?

What made it even more annoying was that she was particular about it. She'd sit there and supervise me doing it. She'd have me lop off the head of the victim, saying that was most important of all. Then she'd have me cremate the body. And then the head. Like separate fires, because she said if the ashes weren't carefully scattered, a vampire could come back. And she didn't want a body being found, because it would mean the police would investigate.

Conveniently enough, she owned a crematorium, so we'd drive there, and she'd have me burn the body after hours, and we'd get that all handled, and then she'd supervise while I scattered the ashes, making sure they were done in two separate places. Only then was she satisfied.

More than 1800 times we did this.

1800 lives.

That's the thing: early on, I was so under her spell that I did it willingly, without hesitation or reservation. You know, the whole "Yes, Master" kind of thing like you see in the movies? I lived that.

That carried me through the majority of the killings—it sounds awful, but it's the truth of it: love makes you do scary things, and love isn't only blind; makes you deaf and dumb, too.

After that, she could perhaps sense my dis-ease over this, and then she'd dangle out the prospect of making me into a vampire, too. I mean, any vampire groupie is going to tell you that this is the dream of any minion. You want that gold card, you want in the club. And she'd hint that she'd do that for me, one day, once the time was right, once I was ready. And that held me for about a year and a half. After that point, it was becoming a fucking slog.

Because I really started to feel bad for everybody she killed. Her fey voracity was appalling. That hunger never, ever went away. She'd look at me, sometimes, while she was feeding, just gnawing on their necks while the victims would moan in bliss. And I'd just watch, cold inside, envious of the victims, and afraid for them. We'd even talk about it sometimes.

"They don't feel any pain," Iris said, while I was shoveling ashes from the oven, piling them in a bucket. "They feel something more intense than anything they've felt in their entire lives. The ultimate ecstasy. You know how it feels, Nate."

"It's still murder," I said.

She mock-pouted.

"Poor Nate. A little late in the day for morality, don't you think?"

"Just saying," I said, shoveling. She would always just sit there, would never help. I knew where I stood in the scheme of things by then.

"The strong take what they want from the weak," Iris said. "It's nature's way. It's ironic, really—you're culling the human herd. Or helping me, anyway. You're taking out the dim girls who fall for a pretty face. The girls who are easily flattered, who don't listen to their more cautious natures, the ones who think that looks matter. The shallow, empty-headed little consumer vessels who would likely squander their paychecks on liposuction and lip jobs in a few years, anyway."

As an immoral immortal, Iris had nothing but withering contempt for aging. She always found it amusing, the beauty industry. She wore makeup sometimes to disguise her pallor, but it was only a practical move, undertaken with more than a little irony on her part.

Iris walked up to me, her face transforming, her voice cold. When this happened, she became something far from beautiful.

"Get me something, Nate. Or am I going to have to make do with you?"

She snarled at me, bared her fangs. When she was hungry, they would get very long. It bothered me, like in movies, how, so often, film makers would make the second incisors into fangs, when it was really the canines that were fangs. ·

You need look only at any mammalian predator to see it—the incisors were really just placeholders to keep the big guns, the canines, in proper position. Sure, the incisors had a role, but that role was more like scissors, snipping off bites of flesh, not puncturing, which was the province of the canines. A lengthened incisor was ludicrous, compared with the raw, carnal efficacy of a lengthened canine, which would let the predator lock onto their prey, sinking their teeth into them.

Triangular, spearlike, the canines were where the action was, where biting was concerned. You talk about sinking your teeth in to something, and you're talking about the canines.

But movie vampires of the last 30 years, if they had teeth at all, too often had those tidy little incisor fangs. I wondered why that was, and decided that, at some point, someone in the movie industry decided that having those pert incisor fangs let actors appear pretty without the protrusion of speech-impeding qualities of long fangs. The old Hammer movies never skimped on that—they did fangs right.

Rightly or wrongly, I traced the lineage of the incisor fang to *The Lost Boys*.

Early on, I would watch every vampire movie I could, because I wanted to see what they got right, and what they got wrong, since I was living the vampiric American Dream. But I saw that other movies would adopt the incisor fangs in the wake of that movie.

Iris had only scorn for *The Lost Boys*, meandering in while I watched it, scoffing as she treated it to a moment of her attention. I told Iris about it, and she just shrugged. She could care less. She almost never watched movies; they were as irrelevant to her as anything else.

"That movie is nonsense. You can't go back from vampirism," she said. "There is no room in the coffin for tourists, no respite from our unquenchable thirst. You either are, or you aren't. You're either in, or you're out. They wouldn't be able to cure it; there is no cure."

But I tell you: when she got hungry, those fangs grew, and spittle would fly from her lips as she'd angrily pace about, her eyes flashing brightly, going from that lustrous dark blue to an incandescent orange.

"I have to do everything myself," she said.

"I'm only saying that you could do this," I replied. "So you don't get out of practice."

"Out of practice?" she said, as if she couldn't even believe I'd been so bold as to gainsay her. "How old am I?"

"Old," I said. "Really old."

She walked up to me, rested a hand on my arm. It was like cold stone. "How old?"

She gripped my arm tighter. I couldn't even hope to pry my arm free.

"Fucking 500 years old," I said. "You're hurting me."

"Go get me something to eat," she said, shoving me away. I tumbled across the room, falling squarely on my ass. "Don't make me ask again."

"You didn't ask," I said, getting up, dusting myself off. "You never do."

She gazed at me in the dark, her eyes glowing that malevolent red-orange. For someone so petite, she could loom, and in the shadows of her lair, she did.

The clarity of that moment struck me, how fleeting my own life was, how inconsequential it was in relation to hers. She would use me until she'd used me up, until she had no use for me. And then my successor would be scooping up the ashes of me with a shovel, and that dance of death would continue.

I turned around and went out the front door.

Her place was a tidy brownstone that had a wall around it, and a garden within the wall, although in her case, this was strictly ornamental. Iris could give a fuck about flowers. What grew there were thick, thorny, unkempt roses. It was deliberate. The roses formed a kind of barrier. So did the colored glass that decorated the top of that outer wall. Sharp shards of it, all sorts of colors. If somebody was careless across that wall, they'd cut their hands. If they landed on the inside of the wall, they'd get mired in the roses, which formed an interlocking thicket of thorns. And if anybody managed to drag themselves out of that, there was Iris, waiting for them, smelling their spilled blood.

She said it only happened once, in 1910. An anarchist had slipped onto her property. She had been a visible enough member of the American aristocracy in Chicago that this anarchist had thought of dispatching her—propaganda of the deed, they called it—today, it would likely be referred to as terrorism.

At any rate, the man, a young Ukrainian, had thrown a mat over the top of the wall, and had jumped into her garden, only to find himself caught by her rosebushes. He had brought a knife with him, and had cut himself free, but not without rending his dark clothes and bloodying himself.

To hear her tell it, the blood-scent of the man wafted her way and she knew exactly where he was. She could see so well in the dark, after all. And she waited for him in the shadows, watching him struggle. She waited until he got free, then confronted him.

Iris has no ear for dialogue, so she'd never tell me what the man said, only that he had been badly frightened, and she'd given him cause to be more frightened, still, and she drank his blood beneath the light of the gibbous moon.

I went out the front gate, slamming it shut. I had a whole floor to myself, not that this meant much of anything, except that it was rent-free. My only job per se was day trading some of her investment portfolio, which was considerable.

That was another infuriating quality of the vampire—they were usually rich. There were some who were so stupid or jaded that they were unable to appreciate material things, but the brute force of their own immortality all but ensured that many of them were able to enjoy actually watching their investments mature over time. With infinite time, even paupers could become princes.

She had a foundation set up in her name around 1901 or 1902, the Augenblick Foundation, which she used to keep her considerable assets flowing smoothly and seamlessly. She had always arranged to have another "descendent" of hers inherit her fortune, and kept it going in perpetuity.

But what did she do with it? Nothing. She'd invest when it suited her—like the crematorium, obviously. She invested in a huge range of blue chip stocks, diversified and leveraged to ride out the inevitable upswings and downturns of the market. By and large, however, she did not do much with her money. She certainly didn't buy things. Her place was dreadfully empty, with her life's possessions largely consigned to the Augenblick Museum.

I'd asked her about that, and she'd said that she'd long since grown past the need for opulence. Almost everything she had left was in the basement of her place.

"When was the last time you donated to the Augenblick Museum?" I asked, wondering if she'd tell me or not.

"1995," Iris said. "It's not really the same, anymore. What matters is antiquity. I've shared all of the relics I care to share, to be honest. What's left is for me, and me alone."

I'd been seven years old in 1995. That kind of weirded me out. I think my school had arranged a field trip to the Augenblick Museum when I was 10 years old.

I told her as much, and she just accepted that with the faintest amusement, a very vampiric kind of reaction.

"That's funny," she said. "Little Nate, seeing my life, without knowing it was my life. Without knowing that our paths would cross."

It was weird. My school usually managed a trip to the Augenblick about every three years, so I think I'd been there three times. It was one of those semi-worthless field trips the school would offer to show off some civic or cultural thing of significance. Of course, it was very strange to me, thinking that I had seen Iris before knowing her. There had been a handful of paintings of her there. Had I been, perhaps, primed to fall for her? The significance of the trips to the museum were lost on me, my childish self was more occupied with flirting with a girl, or punching a boy, not paying attention to whatever they had told me at the museum.

It made me want to go to the museum again, to look through it with this knowledge. I brought that up to Iris, who shook her head.

"Honestly, Nate, why would I even do that? I left those things to the Museum because I was over them. I don't need to see them. For me, the stories I have with them will always be with me. I don't gain a thing seeing my own possessions in a museum. But you are welcome to go."

"Oh, but you could tell me stories about them," I said.

Iris shook her head again. "There are no stories to tell, Nate. Nothing you could appreciate. You wouldn't know the players, wouldn't know anything I was relating."

"But I want to know you," I said, almost plaintive.

Her home looked like a giant crypt, really. It was empty. Room after room, simply empty and dark. She had her token presence in the living room, where she sometimes held court with some of the vampiric notables of the city, the underworld, as I saw them. But beyond that, nothing.

My floor was the only breath of life to the place, where I'd use some of my profits from the day trading to purchase a few things— a futon, some lights, a television, a fridge, food. In truth, though, there was precious little to leave behind.

Man cannot live on blood alone.

—✗—

CHAPTER 5

It wasn't unreasonable of me to suggest that she feed herself: she'd gotten so lazy. She was better-suited to the task, was built for it, and she knew what she had to do, but for some reason, with me in the mix, she didn't want to do it. She just delegated, relied on me to do the heavy lifting, the hunting, the dreadful parts of her endless nightlife.

What really pissed me off is that other vampires would see me. I'd recognize them, and they'd recognize me. Sly glances from them, mocking, as if to say "Look! There's Augenblick's toy boy, fetching her another victim."

That's what I really was—delivery boy. It pissed me off.

They wouldn't mess with me, because they knew that I was protected, and, at least in theory, that Iris could stomp them into dust if they crossed her minion.

At the same time, I still got pissed off.

I dug out my phone and texted Clementine.

NateSharpie: Clementine? We met earlier.

ClemDash: Hi!

NateSharpie: Wnt to get 2gether someplace?

ClemDash: Sure! Whre?

NateSharpie: L'Strega's? I'll be there in 30min.

ClemDash: K.

I put my phone away. Easy as that. I picked L'Strega because the place reeked of garlic, and that'd keep Iris the hell away from it if she was inclined to rove. The place was festooned with it—clusters of it, hanging from hooks. I remembered it from before. Hillary and I used to like going there.

The thought of Hillary brought me a bit of pain: I hadn't thought about her for years. Five years felt like forever when you were in the service of the undead.

I went down the street, hands in my pockets, full of thought. It realized belatedly that I was wearing the same stuff I'd been wearing earlier, but oh, well. I'd sneak back to Iris's in the morning, when she was sleeping.

Did you know that I never saw where Iris slept? She always kept that from me, said she had "trust issues" and that it was safer for me not to know. I would comb the place, looking for her lair, but I never found it. Forget the movies, where you just turn a candlestick and presto, there's the vampire. She hid, and I never could find out where she went.

I should point out that everything you know about vampires is true—they really can turn into bats, or wolves, or mist, even—garlic pisses them off, and they don't cast reflections. The thing with the Cross, that's more a product of the times. Like these days, it's hard to find a vampire that actually believes in much of anything, let alone God. Iris would get philosophical about it.

"Would a kind and benevolent God have created us?" she asked. "And, if He did not, then are we outside of His power? In which case, He is not omnipotent. Either He is all-powerful and all-benevolent, or else He is not all-powerful, and/or is not benevolent. Our existence points to this, Nate."

I had seen Iris deal with a fundamentalist preacher once. There had been some kind of protest downtown, and the preacher had a great big Cross he was bearing, talking about how people were all going to be damned, how they had perverted the meaning of Christmas, which had nothing to do with shopping. He harangued pedestrians in the shadow of that great Cross, using a small microphone and speaker setup he had.

The man had been preaching up a storm, and Iris and I walked up and she stood there, listening to him, her face unreadable. I watched it with some interest, because I wondered whether it would affect her. I mean, it was one big-ass Cross, hewn from what looked like railroad ties.

The preacher had shoe polish-black hair, side parted in a kind of hair helmet, wore a black suit with a black raincoat and a black necktie. His shoes were black oxfords, worn but carefully polished. He looked like a holy hitchhiker on some spiritual superhighway.

And opposite him was Iris, petite and dazzling in her white fur coat and matching fur hat in which she'd set a diamond-shaped ruby brooch. She'd let her dark hair spill on her shoulders, and wore black leather heeled boots with pointy toes.

What a pair they made, this holy man in black, and this unholy woman in white, regarding one another across a moral chasm, with me in the middle as her escort, her chaperone, in a gray wool peacoat and sneakers.

Seeing us, seeing her, the man stopped his free-form sermonizing and held out a tract, a Xeroxed pamphlet that asked us if we were ready for the end of days?

Iris nodded and I took one.

The man seemed to know there was something unusual about Iris, for she had that way about her. I won't say it's an "aura," but there was a presence to her that far outstripped her actual physicality. You could just feel that otherness, that sense of being exposed to something more than human when in her company.

Vampires all had this mojo, this vibe that would command hearts and minds, like there was a spotlight on them, even when there wasn't. People noticed. You felt it, a captivation.

"Are you a demon?" he asked. "Come to haunt my steps, Unclean?"

"I have seen you before," she said. "You always come out in dark times. Like rats, you come and gnaw and gnaw. You have to. Your teeth grow long without something to chew on. You long for human tinder for your holy fires. You are the spawn of Savonarola. I saw your great-great-great-great-grandfather burn in Florence. It took so very long. You would make a pyre for this world, and call it 'Heaven.'"

"I have nothing to fear before Almighty God, Demon," the man said. And he gestured to the great Cross.

Iris just smiled at him, a ghastly grin that chilled the air around us, bit off some of my soul. I had never seen Iris look this way, and knew that it was her drawing from something in her past.

"You speak of profanity and obscenity as if you understand it," she said. "Let me show you what it really means."

And she moved quicker than I could see, just a blur and the Cross was shattered. It actually exploded into four pieces, in a cascade of splinters, and she was at the man's neck, drinking from it. The man let out a strangled wail, too shocked to even move to defend himself. This all took place in seconds, before even the onlookers could see what had happened.

I was right at the center of it, and it had happened faster than I could see. One minute they were having words, and the next moment, bedlam.

Then Iris was at my arm and whisking me away, while the man's acolytes surrounded their fallen prophet, who was howling and choking, spitting up blood, his handbills flying around him like over-sized confetti.

It all happened so quickly.

We rounded the corner of Tiffany's, basked in the shadow, while people ran to see what had happened to the street preacher. Iris was wiping her mouth with a tissue, tossing it in the trash.

In the shadows, just off of Michigan Avenue, she leaned against the wall and laughed to herself, pale face half-lit by the hustle and bustle of the Magnificent Mile, the other half of her wrapped in shadow, her mouth damp with the man's blood, her fangs dimpling her lower lip. Uncertain, I laughed with her.

Where we were, the milling travelers and tourists flowed like a sea, north and south, oblivious multitudes, while we, the conspirators, shared our laughter.

"That was brazen," she said. "But I couldn't resist. It's almost worth it, you know."

"What is?"

"Earning their wrath," she said. "It's always the same. Their dance is an old one, but it's the same plodding steps they always take, the same tired hymns they sing."

She held out a hand, and I gave her the handbill, and she scanned it, grinning, gave it back to me.

"I've given that man a whole new purpose in life. He should thank me, when we meet again."

I felt a stab of jealousy.

"Did you make him?" I asked. She shook her head.

"Just a sip, Nate," she said. "He knows, now. I have enlightened him."

"How so?"

"He was content to proselytize at a streetcorner," she said. "To conjure up demons and damnation with his wagging false prophet's tongue. But now I've changed all of that for him, given him something tangible to fret over. He'll become a vampire hunter, now."

"Aren't you worried about that?" I asked.

Iris looked at me like I was an idiot, as ever. Of course, why should she worry? She'd faced countless vampire hunters in her past, I was sure. She'd seen it all, hadn't she?

"They will come as they always do, Nate," Iris said. "Under the light of the day, hammers in hand, holy water, and they will seek to root me out and kill me. The way they always do. And I'll be ready for them, the way that I always have been. Do you know that I used to be afraid of them, back in the day? Of course, how could I not be? Back then, people believed in us, and would prepare themselves accordingly. If a neighbor claimed that their cow had been bitten by a vampire, they'd not think twice before forming a mob and chasing down that vampire and staking them. No questions asked, beyond 'Where?' and 'When?' But today? Nobody believes in us, even when we're right in front of their faces."

I peeked around the corner, saw people talking and gesturing, arguing. Saw a police officer there, people talking. What were those people thinking? All they could attest to was that the preacher had been attacked by a woman. Or, perhaps worse, maybe they remembered only me, the lanky man walking with her. The shattering of the Cross had perhaps drawn their gaze. I couldn't be sure, but nobody was seeing us.

"Today, even when it happens, people don't believe it. Had I told you I was a vampire before I showed you I was one, would you have believed in me, Nate? Of course not. You would have thought I was insane," Iris said, reapplying her lipstick. Red, of course. "Today, even the believers don't believe—that is to say, even the faith that they have is shallow compared with older days, when monsters loomed just out of reach of the campfire or the candleflame."

I didn't understand. Did she want them to hunt her? Was she so empty and bored that she would create her own peril to liven her nights? She seemed to know what I was thinking, took my arm in hers and walked us back into the crowds on Michigan Avenue, window-shopping.

"You welcome those attacks?"

Iris stroked my face, a gentle gesture, despite the chill in her fingertips that came through even the gloves she wore.

"We go way back," Iris said. "What makes me laugh is when someone faces true evil for the first time, comes face to face with it, and they think that they are the first people to make that discovery, the first ones to know it; but they're not. They're just the latest ticketholders in a very long line. And I've seen it all before. I've seen every shade of moral outrage, tasted every sin, heard it all before, Nate. There are no surprises for me, because people are unimaginative; they act in predictable ways. That preacher will round up some hunters and they will come for me, you will see. Assuming you are still in my employ, of course."

"You're not worried?"

"Not at all," Iris said. "A vampire hunter's weakness is greater than his mortality. You might think that mortality is their biggest vulnerability—that I am quick and strong and possess many powers that far outshine anything a mortal can bring to bear. But the biggest weakness of a vampire hunter is his very humanity, that sense of righteous indignation, even that bit of compassion he probably feels for my plight. Violating the sensibilities of the moral is easy. It's easy to upend a righteous man, to drive him to do reckless things."

I gazed into the store windows, at the beheaded mannequins that modeled fine clothing and the latest fashions, found their white bodies haunting and familiar, became very aware of it, the preponderance of bodies in the windows, those mannequins, missing heads, arms, legs. There was a carnality to it all that I had not seen before, and, perhaps drawn into it by Iris and her talking, I could see it in ways that I had not seen before. Death was all around us, in a way, with the mannequins as mutilated corpses on display. What was I seeing? What was I thinking?

I tried to shake that grim image from my head, turned my attention back to Iris, my small and beautiful lovely mistress, arm in mine.

"Besides, I've got you to protect me, don't I?" she said, giving my arm a squeeze. "You wouldn't let anything hurt your Iris."

She was right about that. I wouldn't. And she was right about the man. He did take up the hunt. It took him three years, but he did find us. I don't know how he did it, but he and his acolytes dogged our steps, and Iris seemed entirely unafraid and amused by her little game, the tiny war she'd begun. She had nothing to worry about, but I certainly did, for I was out in the midst of it, and his minions thought I was one of the undead, too.

They didn't even remember that I had been with her on that night; all eyes had been on her. But they had seen me hunting and had followed me to Iris's home.

And the man had reappeared by day, with three of his most zealous disciples, I presumed, and they'd broken into Iris's house by the dawn's early light. I heard it. I'd been in my room, at my computer, when I heard it.

They'd broken in through a back door that led into the alley behind Iris's building. I peeked out the window and saw them hacking their way through the rosebush bramble. The man, a young blond woman, and two tall, blond, young men. They were using machetes to cut through the brambles.

"Iris," I said, running through the house. "Iris. They're here, Iris."

But there was no sign of her, for she had gone to her secret place to hide from the sun.

"Iris!"

I didn't know what I was supposed to do. That's not entirely true; I knew what I was supposed to do, but not exactly how I'd do it. It was situations like this that she had intended for me all along, why she kept me alive.

First, I thought about calling the police and reporting trespassers. But I didn't necessarily want police attention. Not in a situation like this. Because, for all I knew, I would take the fall for Iris—something I would have gladly done back then.

And, I knew that she would have no sympathy for me, for I guess I had been careless, that they had even followed me to her lair. In her view, it was my fault. My mess, I had to clean up. Never mind that she had provoked this reprisal with her actions.

The fearless vampire killers had bloodied themselves on the brambles, and were now tramping around the grounds, trying to find a way in. To their credit, they went toward the basement, going, they felt, straight to the source. There was an external entry to the basement, although I didn't think Iris was actually down there, because I had looked.

They had brought a great bolt cutter and made short work of the lock on that door, opening it. Three of them went down into the basement, while a fourth, the blond girl, stayed behind to keep watch.

That was my opportunity. I grabbed a baseball bat, an old Louisville Slugger I had from when I was a kid, and a padlock. Then I snuck outside, crept my way up to the girl, who was pacing around in front of the open storm doors. She was carrying a crossbow.

I didn't want to get tacked to the wall of Iris's lair, so I waited for the girl to have her back to me in her pacing, before I ran at her and took a swing, catching her in the back of the head with a clonk. She went down with a yelp. I hadn't quite knocked her out, had just stunned her. She was a big girl, strong.

Then I tossed her down into the basement and slammed the heavy storm doors, locking them with the fresh padlock.

It was the easiest thing I could think of doing.

I picked up the crossbow and went to the alley door and shut that. We'd have to work on that. Maybe put a statue in the alcove or something, something to block it. Something only Iris could move.

The vampire hunters made a muted racket, banging on the storm doors, which were thick metal, and the sound was much less evident than they likely thought. They had walked into a trap. I found this out later.

Iris had put all sorts of traps in her dwelling. She was nothing if not cautious, and the basement trap was one of her favorites. She let me see it, later. There was a coffin in there, in a corner, and nothing else. That basement was, in fact, a kind of crypt. It had once been a coal cellar, long ago. And she'd kept it for just this purpose. The thick cement walls were all but soundproof, and when those doors closed, there was no way out, as she'd had another of her minions (before my time) brick up the one door that had led to the place.

Those vampire hunters had thrown open the coffin, stakes in hand, only to find a letter from Iris printed there:

SEE YOU SOON.

I could hear them calling in the dark, but their voices were tiny and distant. I could hear them fishing out their cell phones, but Iris had prepared for that, too: no reception in that dreadful cellar. I could hear them cursing. They kept hammering at the doors, but they were just too thick.

Satisfied that I'd handled things to the best of my ability, I walked the grounds to ensure nobody else was sneaking about, and then went back inside. I put the crossbow in my room and went back to my day trading, before getting sleepy and taking a nap. Having been long accustomed to Iris's schedule, I would try to get sleep during the day, since I'd usually be kept busy in the evening.

I could still hear the vampire hunters calling out through the ductwork of the building, but was confident nobody else could. A neighbor put on some Bob Marley and was blaring it while giving his car a final autumn wash before winter kicked in.

I woke up with a start at sunset, to see Iris standing there, watching me. She did that a lot, and it was always unnerving. I mean, who does that, just stands there, looking at you while you sleep? It would be creepy if anybody did it; but to have a vampire do it? Even worse.

"Hey, Nate," she said. "Looks like we don't have to go out for dinner, after all."

"Nope," I said.

"Do you want to watch?" she asked. "I know you kind of like it."

"What are you going to do?" I asked.

"Something fun," she said. "You can't really watch, anyway. But you can listen."

She nodded to the ductwork.

"Why can't I watch?" I asked.

"You'd only be in the way," she said, touching my face with her cold hand. And then she vanished, dissolved into mist and flew down the ductwork.

I heard the preacher exclaim, then heard a scuffle and a crash.

Then another crash.

Then the girl screamed. Then another crash.

Then silence.

And moaning.

Then more silence.

Then Iris speaking, her voice oddly distorted through the ductwork.

"I've left you a little present, Preacher."

And then Iris was back beside me, wiping her mouth with a napkin. She was smiling to herself, something she did a lot.

"What is it?"

"It's nothing," she said.

"No, really," I asked.

Her face was flushed, now, and she was momentarily warm. She always glowed after feeding.

"I killed the girl," she said. "Drank her down. So, you know, three days from now, she's going to become a vampire. Unless, of course, they kill her. Let's see how much they love her, what they decide to do."

"Wow," I said. "That's so cold."

"Do you think so? I left them some water, so they'd be able to drink. I want them fasting, but I don't want them dying of thirst down there."

I nodded, unsure if she was joking or whether she was serious.

"What about the guys?"

"They're next," she said. "Tomorrow. And the next day."

I wondered what the preacher would do. Iris went upstairs, while I listened to the men come to. Iris had pounded them into senselessness. When they discovered the condition of the girl, whose name was Gudrun, I gathered, from what the preacher said, crying out, there was much dismay, as Iris had intended.

"The creature bit her, Dick," one of them said. "She's dead."

"My Lord," Dick said. I'm assuming it was Dick, anyway. "Forgive me."

There was a hammering sound, and one of the other guys cried out. Another one was simply crying.

"Jesus," I said. "He staked her."

I went upstairs and told Iris, who was dressed to go out, by the look of things, wearing a purple dress and black velvet heeled knee boots.

"Yeah?" she asked, somewhat surprised. "Maybe he's made of sterner stuff than I imagined."

She patted my arm and went out that night. I wasn't invited to come along, so there I was, listening to the men, who were hammering at the doors, trying to get free. One of them was praying, and the others joined in.

The moral thing, the human thing, would have been to release the men from their prison. I knew this as I knew sunlight from darkness, but at that time, to have acted in that fashion would have cost me Iris, may have cost me my life, and most certainly my life with Iris. I was in a dark place in those days, entirely captive to Iris. To have freed those men would have upended all that I had in place. A servant I was to Iris, but she was eternal and all-powerful; you cannot know the temptation of such company. For all of the Victorian quivers and qualms about the vampire's nature, I belonged with her, belonged to her; I could no more act against her wishes than I could have stopped breathing. And, sad to say, I loved her then, and knew that those men were there to harm her—and whether or not they would actually be able to inflict harm on Iris, I wanted to ensure that they were not able to do so. And that meant keeping them locked within her trap.

The second night, Iris visited them again, and took another one. And, again, Dick the Preacher staked him. And the third night. And, once again, he staked him. Then he was alone down there, and I listened to their exchange through the vents, like it was some kind of radio play.

Iris congratulated him. "You're really a ruthless cock, aren't you, Dick?"

"I will not play your sick games, Monster," he said. "I am unafraid of you."

"What a pity," she said. "You should be."

And (she later told me) that she removed the stakes from the hearts of his acolytes, and the other assorted vampire hunting gear, and left Dick the Preacher down there with his stricken companions.

"That won't work, will it?" I asked. "I mean, he staked them before they even became vampires. Like, I dunno, vampiric abortion?"

Iris shrugged. "Let's see what happens."

Dick the Preacher prayed and prayed and prayed, and his prayers were answered, but perhaps not the way he intended, as his acolytes, indeed, rose.

"Daddy," Gudrun said. "I'm cold."

And Dick the Preacher screamed, and there was a horrible rending sound, and then there was silence. I glanced over at Iris, who was sitting there, arms folded, just listening absently. She saw me looking at her and gave a noncommittal shrug, by way of her eyebrows.

"My, that was interesting," she said, in just about the most bored voice I'd ever heard.

"What do we do about them?" I asked. I was more than a little peevish that they'd all enjoyed her kiss, had all been giving her dark gift, something I had yet to receive.

"I thought about sending them after their benighted congregation," she said. "But what I'd rather do is just have you take them out into the sunlight tomorrow. Can you do that for me, Nate?"

"Whatever you want," I said.

"And the preacher, too," she said. "I'd love for him to wake up and savor his own damnation for all time, although I doubt his daughter left much of him."

Then she changed her mind, and had Gudrun come out of the vault, and had the other two remain in there. It was an easy thing for her to do, as their sire, the command she had over them, as effortless as anything else she did, this force of will she possessed.

Gudrun was covered in her father's blood, still wearing her black commando sweater and black pants. There was a hole in her sweater where the stake had been. Her eyes were wild. She looked at me with undisguised, orange-eyed bloodlust.

"Gudrun," Iris said. "This is Nate. Nate's with me. You're not to harm him, not to feed upon him. Not to touch him. Do you understand me?"

Gudrun nodded.

"I do have an important mission for you, Gudrun," Iris said.

"What would you have me do?" Gudrun asked, her eyes still on me as she paced back and forth.

"I want you to go back to your church and kill every last member of your congregation," Iris said. "Can you do that?"

"For you, anything," Gudrun said, her fangs long and shiny white. Her blond hair, which had been in a neat ponytail when she'd come to Iris's place, was now wild and unkempt, a spray of blond that gave her a leonine visage to go with her flatly luminescent eyes.

Iris directed her to go, and off Gudrun flew, becoming a bat before my eyes. It was marvelous and ghastly all at once. Iris watched my reaction with ironic amusement, and then made a motion like she was dusting her hands.

"Now," Iris said. "Come morning, I want you to dispose of the others. Put them in the sun. And then scatter the ashes in my garden."

I did what I was told.

In the morning, I went to the storm door and unlocked it. I'd brought some rope with me, and I threw the doors open, went down into the vault.

It was dark and the air was heavy with the scent of spilled blood and fouler things. I coughed into my hand and hunted around in the dark for the bloodsuckers. I had never in my life actually hunted down a vampire. There was a world of difference between serving one and hunting one. I felt frightened, uncertain.

That's the weird thing about it—I'd been intimately acquainted with Iris, had seen and experienced nearly everything a mortal can possibly face when confronted with the undead, but in that vault, in that moment, I saw there was a lot still to learn.

I was still just a man.

I saw no sign of the bodies. The two sons of Dick the Preacher weren't there. I saw what was left of Dick. He was crumpled in a corner, mangled, in a dreadful position, a look of contorted wonder on his face, his neck gnawed nearly to ragged oblivion. There were fang bites all over him, a profligate number, and not a lick of blood remained to him. He was the ghastliest white I'd ever seen. There was no blood on him or in him.

I hooked the rope around his leg and dragged him into the sunlight. The sun scalded his corpse and the thing flared into light, throwing off sparks and fire that consumed the body in moments, leaving only some ash behind, which I dutifully scattered.

All this time, she'd been having me hack up the bodies and serve them up in her crematorium, when I only apparently needed to leave them in the sun to let Nature take care of it? What the fuck?

I went back down into the basement, flicking on a flashlight, hoping to find the others. Where had they gone? I kicked around down there, unable to find them, wondering in an acid splash of jealousy if Iris had taken them under her bat wing after all, but then, seeing the coffin, I knew where they had to be, and wanted to laugh—what better place to hide a body than a coffin?

Sure enough, when I threw open the thing, there they were, the two burly brothers, packed in there like a couple of smoked kippers.

I'd never before seen a vampire sleeping—as I'd said, Iris never showed me where she took her rest. The brothers had slept heel to toe, in order to fit, and one of them was looking up at me, unblinking, fanged mouth agape.

Those eyes. It was hard to look away from them, but I did, giving myself a smack in the face to clear my head. Always, always avoid the eyes. Everybody fucking knew this; I knew it, and I still got distracted.

They weren't moving. They were silent and motionless. They were undead. Well, duh, right? Undead. They'd be young forever. Their sister,

Gudrun, would live forever, would stay young and beautiful for all time, in her square-jawed, big-shouldered Teutonic way. But never again would disease or age ravage her. She'd be picture-perfect until the end of time.

That was something that never made sense to me, and yet, there it was—vampires never cast reflections in mirrors. I have no idea why this is, and when I'd ask Iris about it, she'd just give one of her "who gives a fuck?" shrugs.

But it always made me wonder—were vampires simply figments of our imaginations? Is that why they never had reflections? The old convention was perhaps that the absence of a soul meant they'd cast no reflection, but did vampires actually lack souls? If a soul was an animating spirit, then they had one, because they were animated spirits. If a soul was a gift from God, a source of goodness and grace, then I suppose not. Whatever the case, you couldn't see one in a mirror. It was bizarre.

I closed the lid of the coffin, sat on it a moment.

Did Iris sleep in a coffin? Where did she go by day? She had to be somewhere on the premises.

I leaned in and gave the coffin a push along the dusty ground. It ground and slid against the earth.

Reaching the stairs into the basement, I worked like hell to get that heavy coffin up, thumping along, afraid of awakening the occupants, unsure of what I'd do if they did arise.

At last, I reached the top of the steps and switched my position from pushing to pulling, and then dragged the coffin a ways in the gravel, until it was in the sun.

Then I went back to the vault and closed the doors. Then I went back to the coffin and grabbed the lid, making sure I was on the side with the hinges.

Taking a deep breath, I threw open the lid, bathed the coffin in sunlight. Instantly, the brothers came to life, howling, hissing, snarling, flailing. One of them jumped out of the coffin and, awash in red and green fire, threw open the doors to the storm cellar and ran back down into the sheltering dark, leaving a trail of acrid smoke behind him. The other one was less fortunate, and had run off into Iris's garden, vainly trying to find shelter from the sun.

He'd made it about halfway there, this ghastly flaming scarecrow, when his legs actually snapped beneath him and he fell, clawing his way along the ground, blood boiling, skin curling like paper in a roaring fireplace, glowing like an ember. I got up from behind the coffin and walked alongside the thing, which glanced up at me with hateful, ghoulish eyes that had all but slipped free of the skull that held them. It reached for me, one skeletal hand pawing at my sneaker before breaking into a dusty puff.

In moments, the thing was gone, leaving only a man-shape on the gravel that I carefully swept away, my hands shaking, sweat running down my face. I'd never seen anything like that.

Of course, I was frustrated that his brother had managed to take refuge back in the cellar. It was stuff like this that really bothered me, like my service to Iris—I was always stuck with the messes. It wasn't fair that I was expected to deal with the vampires that she made. She should have handled it.

Instead, I had to trek back down into the basement, flashlight in hand, the beam very visible thanks to the smoke the last son of Dick the Preacher had left behind.

He was in the shadows, as far from the doorway as he could get. I could see his eyes glowing orange in the dark. I shined the light on him, and his face was horrible, all burned and scarred. He looked like a burn victim, his fanged face sneering.

"You," he hissed. "You're him."

"I'm him," I said, not sure what he meant by that.

"I'm thirsty," he said.

"I'm sorry," I said.

"I prayed for deliverance," he said. "It didn't come."

"Maybe this was it," I said, feeling sympathy for this poor young man, who had only done what his father had bade him to do.

Honor Thy Father.

"Does this look like deliverance?" he hissed at me, trying to draw my eye, hands tipped in ragged claws that clutched at gravel on the ground.

There was no way I was venturing out of that sunbeam to get at that bloodsucker. And, in those moments, you could see the movement of the sun, could actually see it tracking in a way that I'd not paid attention to for awhile, since usually daytime was downtime for me, I'd not paid attention so much, anymore.

"I didn't deserve this," he said, slurring his words around his fangs.

"Nobody does," I said.

"I killed my own father," I said.

"I know," I said.

"It hurts," he said, clutching himself. "It burns."

"Just walk into the light," I said. "It'll all be over. I mean, I'm sorry about what happened. She did this to you."

"Your mistress," he said, slurring. "My mistress. Unholy creature. The Devil's."

The sun kept traveling, working its way up the steps, one by one. I retreated along its path, stayed in the light, feared the shadow, and the specter in the darkness that gazed at me with undisguised hunger and lust.

"I'm thirsty," he said, crawling toward me. I kept not looking at him directly. I would not fall for that one.

"Do you know what you have ahead of you?" I asked. "An endless lifetime, feeding. Drinking blood, man. A damned creature of darkness, for all time."

"I am here to do the Devil's work," he said. "God has forsaken me."

The vampire wailed a little bit, still crawling toward me. I was unsure if he was stalking me, or if I was reaching him, somehow. I just kept backing up the steps.

"It doesn't have to be this way," I said. "Just step into the light, and it'll all be over for you. You'll go to Heaven."

I didn't believe in Heaven, but the vampire certainly did, and I could see the pain his transformation had brought to him, the contradiction it had thrust into his face, the reality of his condition contrasted with all that he had known in life.

"Not anymore," he said. "Not as a murderer."

"God will forgive you," I said. "It wasn't your fault; it's her fault. You were just a victim of her evil."

The creature hovered just out of the light, eyes aflame, arms spread, fingers splayed. He looked ravaged, his clothes shredded, his skin sundered. He reached for me, and I stayed out of his reach.

"You honestly want to pass up the opportunity for Salvation, and lead an unlife of eternal Damnation?" I asked him.

I was halfway up the steps, while he stayed in the shadows, hovering, gnashing his teeth. I could see the war for what was left of his soul, this newborn thing, this vampire new to unlife, still weighed down with his passing life.

"If you don't step into the sun, it's like you're granting her victory," I said. "It's like you're just handing your soul over to her. The noble thing, the human thing, is to end it before it gets any worse."

"Or what?" he hissed.

"Or, I lock you in here, and she comes," I said. "And she'll take you away from yourself. You'll be her slave, for all time. Like me."

Saying that, I shuddered inside, for I knew what I was talking about. It was such a weird place for me occupy, trying to persuade a newly-minted vampire to step into the light, to sacrifice himself and, in so doing, take that last little bit of what had made him a man and throwing it in Iris's face, to not grant her a final triumph over him.

"You always did what you were told," I said. "You did what your father told you, thought what he told you to think. This is the same. She made you what you became. Are you going to just take that? Following your father led you into this crypt, to this fate. Are you going to keep following, or are you going to take a step for yourself, for the first time in your life?"

The residue of that man, what was left of him, heard my words, thought about what I'd said, gazed at me without comment. Ghastlier than anything I had ever seen, this ruined revenant gave real thought to what I had said. There was an irony in it for me, for this man had what I'd always wanted—Iris had given him the gift she withheld from me. In my own moment of weakness, I thought of giving myself to this creature, knowing full well that he would drain me dry, that I would become a vampire, like I had always wanted—well, not always; like I had wanted in my time of service to Iris.

One step into the shadows, and it would be done. He would feed on me, and I would rise a vampire. But I also knew that Iris would be terribly disappointed in me if that happened, and I couldn't bear that. She would have thought less of me, had I taken that step.

It was an odd thing to think about, but somehow, withholding her gift to me was, in its backhanded way, a sign of some measure of regard Iris had for me. That's how I saw it. She was fairly profligate in her feeding, and to her, it meant less than nothing. She took lives the way you'd take mints from a candy bowl—with as much consideration and reflection.

That she spared me could have meant that, despite herself, I meant something to her. Maybe something that she had not been in touch with for centuries. There was the contrast of this newly-made vampiric ruin in the shadows near me, and my own hard beating heart. He had meant nothing to Iris, and she'd taken his life, had sent his sister on a seek-and-destroy mission. But maybe she actually valued something about me, which was why she spared me.

I hadn't really thought that before, but seeing the undead desolation of the preacher's son stalking me made me think that.

Perhaps, in her ineffable way, this was some kind of test Iris had fashioned for me, without clueing me that it was, in fact, a test. She'd be the last one to even admit to any of this, but I chose to see it that way.

This was a test.

This was only a test.

"Come get me," I said, holding out my arms. "You want me? Come on, then."

Snarling, he leaped at me, impossibly, inhumanly quick, this vision of fangs and clawed nails, ravaged face, blistered flesh and baleful gaze. He grabbed at me, but his inexperience was his undoing, his hunger and greed overtaking him as he toppled me backward, onto the safety of the ground, instead of dragging me into the shadows of the vault with him. And, falling backward, I flipped him over me, which sent him tumbling into the scorching rays of the sun.

He howled and jabbered as he burned, and I threw the vault doors shut. He begged for forgiveness to his father, and whether he was talking to God or his dead dad, I'll never know, for he was gone in moments, the sun having finished what it started, leaving only smoke and ash where once there had been something that had been a man.

I sat down with a gasp, rubbing my forehead, my hands shaking. The silence of the garden, the city sounds in the distance, the world grinding on, the breeze in the trees—all of it mixed together to make me both profoundly glad to be alive, and also horrified at what I'd just faced, that such monstrosity could exist in a world so beautiful, and that I was in service to it, whether I admitted to that or not.

Getting to my feet, I dusted myself off and walked around Iris's lair, this hollow home that had housed her for over a century, imagined Iris living there amid the ashes of the Great Fire, untouched by the blaze, unfazed. That was Iris, though—untouched and untouchable.

I went back inside and collapsed on my bed, slept until Iris woke me, not by doing anything, but just by standing there, at the foot of my bed. I awoke with a start, and she was there, as she so often was.

"Rough day?" she asked, wearing a gorgeous dress of white silk, trimmed with a white fur collar. She was adorned in gold jewelry, emeralds and gold, and her hair was lustrous and shiny. Except for her pallor, she looked like a movie star, saw my awe at the sight of her and merely smiled, a beatific burgundy.

"Don't ever have me to do that again," I said.

"I'm hungry, Nate," she said. "Go get me something to eat."

And I did. Despite everything, I did. I brought her back a mouthy babe I'd picked up at Slice, the boutique pizza place that sold gourmet pizzas at obscene, by-the-slice prices. Her name was Ambrosia Mac-Ready, this plump number who had been noshing on a gorgonzola, pine nut and heirloom apple pizza when I'd lured her away from her food with a promise of something tastier to eat.

Iris took her the minute we got through the door, parting the woman's pile of permed red hair to get at her neck, drinking her down, staring at me while she fed on her victim. It was just me there, and that horrid sucking sound as Iris fed, and Miss MacReady cried out in ecstasy, legs buckling, spilling out of her clogs, collapsing to the floor.

Seeing me make to leave the room, Iris paused in her feeding, her mouth smeared red with Ambrosia's blood, letting Ambrosia fall to the hardwood floor, holding only one of her chubby arms by the wrist.

"What is it, Nate?" she asked.

"I hate watching you eat," I said. "It's gross."

Ambrosia moaned.

"Ah, poor Nate," Iris said. "I'm sorry this is grossing you out, Darling."

She bit down on Ambrosia's wrist, pointedly staring at me some more while she fed. It was creepy, alright? Fucking creepy. There was the sheer act of it, to be sure—this vampire, killing this human woman who I had lured away from her gourmet pizza to die at the hands of my vampiric mistress. It was a layer cake of red velvet suckage, to be sure.

"You should let her live," I said.

"Fat chance," Iris said, pausing again in her feeding, her eyes glittery in the dark, enjoying herself.

Ambrosia moaned again, weaker, now. Her life was hanging in the balance. Iris considered it, looking ghoulish with the blood on her face, contrasted with her white gown.

"Nate, Darling," Iris said. "If I let this woman live, she'd probably report you to the police. They'd come after you. She knows where we live. Well, where you live."

"You could mess with her head, make her forget this place," I said. "Make her forget everything."

Iris seemed to consider it for a second, but I knew she was only humoring me. When you were with somebody that long, you could simply tell.

"But I don't want to," Iris said. "I want to finish her. Do you know how unjust it is for us—and by 'us' I mean 'me'—that we must feed this way? How infernal a joke that is, that we are blessed with strength and immortality, with power and powers that you could not even imagine, and yet, every night, we have to feed? What cruel irony that is, what a crude mockery of life are we that we must drink blood to continue?"

"Not my fault," I said.

"Of course not, Nate," Iris said, contemplating Ambrosia's fingers, several of which were covered with rings. Her fingers squirmed as what was left of Ambrosia's consciousness fought for control. She murmured from the floor, her denim miniskirt riding up on her hips, her muffin top spilling beneath her blouse. I saw a hint of a belly button ring, a loop of silver peeking out from the folds of flesh. "But what a cruel irony—and do you know something else? If I didn't feed, I still wouldn't die. Do you know that? Immortality is immortality—I am eternal, but I still must feed. So, in truth, it's a choice we make, because as we feed, we grow strong, we remain beautiful. And I am beautiful, aren't I?"

She said this without a lick of irony, bloody-mouthed, eyes aflame, fangs bared, holding Ambrosia's arm like it was a handbag.

"Yes," I said, hating myself for saying it. She was beautiful. She was the most beautiful thing I had ever known in my short life, and the most horrible.

"We choose this, Nate," Iris said. "I want to be beautiful and enchanting forever. I don't want to be a shriveled, horrible wretch. So, I feed, even when, in truth, I don't actually have to. It's a quality of unlife issue."

She bit down on Ambrosia again, drank deep from her, and I saw Ambrosia shudder with delight, deep in the throes of that horrible euphoria that accompanied the bite of the vampire, in some horrible parody of predation, where the prey actually relished succumbing to the predator.

"She wants this," Iris said. "She wants me to take her into death."

"Spare her," I said.

Iris looked at me, wryly grinning at me. "Sweet Nate, you're too far into the game for conscience, My Love."

And she sank her fangs into Ambrosia's wrist again, and drank her to death, and I didn't do a thing, just stood there, rooted to the spot, for I had made the mistake of looking Iris in the eye, and she had willed me to stand immobile, to watch her feed, to drink that woman into oblivion, until she'd tossed down her lifeless limb at last, drained her white, and licked her face clean.

Now, having just fed, her pallor changed, and she radiated pinkish warmth once more, and could pass more readily for human, albeit an exceptional specimen, dazzling and charming, intoxicating.

Iris walked over and touched my face with her hand, now warm to the touch.

"I love that you still care, Nate," she said. "I love that you are compromised by your love for me, and I love that you bleed for my victims."

"Do you love me?" I asked. It was a painful thing to even ask of her, an ache that I hated feeling, and hated expressing.

"Of course you are loved," Iris said. "What a silly thing to ask of me. Do you think I would suffer your company a moment beyond what I wished if I didn't care for you, Nate? You know me better than most, and know exactly what I feel for my victims. That I allow you in my company, have continued to do so, that should speak everything about you and me."

She reached out and held me to her, and kissed me, my diminutive demon, little Iris. And kissing her, I could taste Ambrosia's blood on her lips, and I kissed her, just the same.

CHAPTER 6

I was not free.

That came directly to mind when I reached L'Strega, with its garlic hanging from the beams and all. Black paint and white linen, cushioned seats of dark red. The smell of the food cooking inside was intoxicating. I hadn't had anything with garlic in it for years. I had forgotten how much I'd missed it, but then, one forgets a lot of things when living with a vampire, starting first with oneself.

I got a booth in the back and a text from Clementine: she was on her way.

While waiting, I got a Stella and nursed that, told the attentive waiters that someone would be coming shortly. Watching the waiters and waitresses do their service industrial dance, I got a call from Iris, of course.

"Where are you?" she asked.

"Out," I said.

"I'm hungry, Nate," she said.

"So am I," I said.

"Bring me something savory," she said.

"I think you need to get something yourself," I said.

The silence on the line made me think she didn't like the sound of that so much, as I knew she wouldn't. Iris didn't ever like assertiveness.

"Are you dumping me, Nate?" she asked. "Is that what this is?"

"Yes," I said.

Because it was. I was cutting her loose.

I could hear her silent on the line, thinking, parsing, assessing, evaluating. Wheels turning, gears grinding.

"You. Dumping ME?"

"That's right," I said.

"Are you out of your mind?" Iris asked.

"No," I said. "In fact, I think I'm maybe only now becoming sane."

Silence on the line.

I could hear clattering of plates and kitchen business somewhere behind me, the business of running a restaurant—that ordered, culinary chaos that created savory things and memorable experiences for patrons, and had done so for a long, long time. When had restaurants first come about? The idea of the restaurant went back to the Romans, with their *thermopolia*, where customers could get food and drinks, and to the ancient Chinese, who had all sorts of restaurants to feed their hungry citizens. Feed or go hungry, eat or be eaten. Drink and be merry. Everything meant something, if you paid close enough attention.

"Where are you?" she asked.

"I told you," I said. "Out."

"Are you on a date?" she asked.

"Yes," I said. It wasn't really quite a date; more like a hook-up. But Iris didn't need to know that.

"Nate," Iris said, in this patronizing tone she saved for special occasions like these, served it up chilled on a plate of pretension. "I don't think you really know what you're doing, here. You serve me. That's our deal."

The thought of it just pissed me off. I knew exactly what she thought of me.

"I'm changing the deal," I said. "We're done. I'm done."

"You're finished," she said. "You make me come after you, and it's not going to be pretty, Nate. You know this?"

"Try me," I said.

I'll be the first to admit that I was scared. Petrified. I mean, I had seen all of her, every facet of her character, or lack of character. Iris could snap me in half. She could suck me dry. I may not have known all of her secrets, but I knew more than most. I knew what I was up against, should I dare to stand against her. And what was I? Just a man.

Clementine appeared, and I hung up on Iris, turned off my ringer. That alone would infuriate her.

Clementine looked tan and lovely, wearing some big gold loop earrings and a nice sand-colored shawl minidress with lace-up gilt sandals. She smelled good. She had an ankle tattoo, an orange sun, surrounded by a wreath of flowers—roses.

"Hey," I said. "Wow, you got here fast."

"Did I?" Clementine asked. "It's not too far from here."

I was marveling at her tan, to be honest. She looked like one of those girls who laid out in the sun on a Saturday, like all day. That might seem commonplace to you, but for me, it was the picture of novelty. It would have been hard to find someone further from Iris than Clementine—from Creature of the Night to Sun Bunny.

Her voice was a little hoarse in the way that Lincoln Park girls, oh, let's be honest—Trixies—sometimes were. You would hear them in the night, calling out "Woo WOO!" to their Chads enough that I kind of thought of them as Woo Woo Girls. They'd be your buddies at the sports bar, bumping and grinding in the stands to Journey, prone to loudly, if atonally, singing along, a plastic cup of beer in hand as they swayed.

"I hope you're hungry," I said.

"Starved," Clementine said, nosing through the menu. She had on big golden bracelets that jangled as she moved. While she looked, I peeked at my phone. Of course, there were messages. I pocketed the phone.

The waiter turned up and I ordered us some garlic bread, and Clementine ordered an Amaretto Sour as her drink, and I got another Stella. I intended to enjoy myself tonight, Iris be damned.

Garlic bread arrived with melted cheese laid atop it like a bedspread, and Clementine and I happily crunched on it. She worked downtown at a real estate development firm, and, of course, asked me what I did. I told her that I simply day traded, which she liked, as it implied that I had money and was successful enough at it to be able to do that, or else I was rich enough that I didn't have to care.

She'd gotten spaghetti with meatballs, which she ate with gusto, while I had a slice of lasagna. The garlic taste throughout it was fantastic. I had really missed that. I'd missed a lot of things. Clementine's humanity, for example. I just listened to her talk, contributed where I could. I was a fairly adroit conversationalist, as my service to Iris demanded, but to be there talking to a woman on my own, without any ulterior motives, it was nice. It was human. I had not known how much I'd missed that.

There was no con, no trap waiting to be sprung; there was simply man and woman, enjoying each other's company. I liked being able to simply exist without worry about having to clean up a mess afterward, or having to account for one of Iris's moods.

"I'm totally going to hit Key West this summer," Clementine said. "I want to just chill out down there."

"Key West? Whatever for?" I asked.

"Why, have you been?"

"No," I said.

Clementine smiled at me, broad-faced, a big, meaty grin, her blue eyes pools of womanly warmth.

"We should totally go," she said. "I know a guy who has a place. We can rent it."

"And do what?" I asked.

"Sunbathe," Clementine said. "Drink. Bike around. Chill out with the chickens. You know."

The notion of sunbathing with Clementine made me almost want to laugh out loud. I had to be looking so pale these days, after my years with Iris.

"I think I'd need some sunblock," I said.

"Oh, for sure, Nate," Clementine said. "We'll have to put you in some SPF120 or something. Otherwise, you'll be Colonel Sanders."

"All that sun will make you wrinkly," I said. "Don't you worry about that?"

Clementine shrugged, spooled some spaghetti on her fork, speared a meatball, popped the whole thing into her wide mouth.

"Everything'll kill you if you're not careful," she said. "Give me some sun and some fun, and I'm good, Dude."

My phone buzzed in my pocket, a half-dozen more times. Iris was going to be fucking furious with me, but I let her. I was having a motherfucking date.

Clementine and I talked and ate and drank, and when we were done, she asked if I wanted to check out her place, and I did, and once there, hung out on her sofa.

Her condo was very bright and orange—she had an orange sofa, and a giant clock on one of the walls with orange numbers. Her coffeemaker was orange, all perky plastic. There was a white bowl on her kitchen table that was full of oranges.

"Wow, you seriously like orange," I said.

"I love orange," she said. I'm part Dutch. I'm all about orange."

She cut one of the oranges into slices, brought it over. They were very red inside.

"Blood oranges, from Valencia," she said. " That's in Spain."

"Thanks," I said, tasting it. It was delicious, very juicy-sweet. And so was Clementine, hiking up her minidress, revealing an orange V-string that blended so well with her tanned body—no trace of a tan line, I noticed, slipping off her panties as she straddled me a moment, kissing me tenderly on my lips, before she enthusiastically impaled herself on me.

And that was something I hadn't had for a long time, either. I couldn't even remember when. The animal urgency of it, the release. God, yes. I had been starving, and those very human appetites returned with a vengeance. We fucked six times that night, Clementine and me, her hoarse voice calling out as she came, her blue eyes gazing up at me in wonder and that faraway look women got when they were enjoying being fucked, something I had almost forgotten in my years with Iris. The way Hillary would look as she howled.

She came and came and came and came and I came with her until my crotch ached, feeling bruised, and nighttime became morning, and I was exhausted.

Clementine was asleep on her stomach, her arm draped across my chest. She was snoring softly, little short puffs of air between her lips, and I slid out, landing on the floor with a grunt.

I went to her fridge and saw she had a bunch of little bottles of Orangina. I took one out and shook it, opened it, and drank, sitting down on an orange chair, watching the sun rise. I checked my messages.

There were 11 messages on my phone. I felt a chill run through me, but played them, anyway.

"Nate, it's Iris…" delete.

"Where are you?" delete.

"Seriously, Nate…" delete.

"Are you fucking…" delete.

"Don't even…" delete.

"Nate, this is ridiculous…" delete.

"You son of a bitch…" delete.

"I'm going to…" delete.

"And you're not…" delete.

"If you even…" delete.

"Pick up, Nate…" delete.

I laughed to myself, drank Orangina, watched that big orange ball of fire rise over the lake, while Clementine slept beneath an orange blanket.

Clementine wasn't exceptional. She was simply human, like me.

And I had missed that.

Iris had been human, but certainly wasn't, anymore. She was only superficially human, now. Iris was faking it, doing what she had to in order to get by, to trick others into crossing paths with her, so that she could kill them, and drink their damned blood. This was her game, the nature of her unlife, her entire reason for being.

Whereas people were ultimately wired to breed and multiply, a vampire's only real priority was feeding. The purpose of a vampire was to drink blood. That was why it existed at all; everything else was secondary to that.

There was dread in my heart as I got dressed, wrote Clementine a little note, set it beneath a blood orange, using it as a paperweight.

Iris was going to kill me.

And that wasn't just a figure of speech; that was the simple truth of it.

I slipped out of there like a ghost, headed back to Iris's place—I didn't dare call it "home," because, in truth, it wasn't. It was just a place where I lived.

The brownstone looked like a tombstone as I went up to it, fearful of every shadow. The trees hung gloomily around it, the windows were dark. I went to the front gate, and found it open. I walked in, carefully closing it.

Inside the wall, nothing looked different, although everything was fraught with meaning to me—the curve of a rosebush bramble twining around a broken bird bath, a spray of gravel across one of the flagstones. I felt like a forensic investigator, trying to get a sense of what had happened here. There was no way of knowing.

I knew, however, that Iris had left open the gate, for me. That was as clear as the rising sun.

I went up the front steps to the entrance to her lair, and found this door, too, was just slightly ajar. Opening that, I went inside, into the gray dark of the first floor. The emptiness of the room made it feel more cryptlike than ever.

Inside, the silence of the place was even more potent than I remembered. After the cozy vitality of Clementine's orange-hued pleasure palace, Iris's building was cold and terrible.

Resisting an urge to call out Iris's name, because, of course, she'd be sleeping, now, I walked upstairs, to my room.

There, on the floor of my room, was a body, half-wrapped in my bed sheet. It was a young man, handsome, brunette, short-haired, robustly built. And quite dead. He had bitemarks at his neck, stared sightlessly at the ceiling.

Everything else was the same. I didn't know what I expected, but I didn't expect that.

Part of me wanted to say "See? You can hunt; you don't need me to do it."

But then the other part of me looked at the body on my floor and knew Iris was making some kind of passive-aggressive point with it.

The guy was dead, which meant, of course, in three days, he'd rise as one of the undead. The infection was already coursing through him.

That Iris had done this was just to be a bitch, like to extend to this nobody, this pretty stranger, what she refused to give to me.

In better times, I'd asked her why she didn't have a big group of vampires around her, a retinue like I'd seen with some of the other ones, who seemed to have entire entourages. It was about three years ago, and she'd been in an expansive mood, having just fed on twin Trixies we'd picked up at Spoke, a comedy club in Bucktown.

Having gorged herself on both of the twins, who were these tall redheads, Iris glowed with the stolen blood. I had been impressed at her two-timing them, feeding on both of the twins at the same time, but she'd blown that off, like it was something she did every day.

It had been summer, and Iris had worn a black cocktail dress that showed off her shoulders and her petite figure, heeled sandals on her feet that lent her about four inches of height she didn't otherwise have.

"I did try to make my own coven," Iris said. "It would have been around 1862. A Virginia plantation I had come to occupy, a home in Richmond. There wasn't anything for it; I just went there because a good vampire knows that war always makes for good feeding, and even then, I could tell which side was going to lose, and, as a vampire, you stick with the losing side in a war, and you will never go hungry."

"But you said you were tired of war," I said.

Iris held up a finger, stilling me with that single motion. "I said I was tired of following my sire in war after war. That's another matter entirely, Nate. Vampires love war. War throws civilization on its ear, creates all kinds of opportunities for us, opens doors as surely as it opens veins. Spilled blood? Carnage? Why wouldn't we love them? I volunteered as a night nurse, served admirably in that capacity in many battles. I was there for Antietam, for example, which, thankfully, ended at dusk, so I was able to tend to the dying without delay."

The image of Iris walking among the thousands of dead and dying on that bloody battlefield filled me with fear and loathing.

She watched my reaction with amusement.

"You asked me about why I am not surrounded by hungry mouths, Nate," Iris said. "And I'm telling you. At that time, in my 350th year of life, incredibly enough—isn't that incredible? There I was, walking those battlefields, having lived for 350 years already. Even at that time, the body count I had accumulated even then far dwarfed the losses on the battlefield. None of those soldiers could even imagine what walked among them, and I wasn't the only one, to be sure—there were plenty, but America was such a young country, I was one of the old ones, and I had the run of the place. It wasn't like Europe, when you had some real fossils roaming around, trying to run the world. In the United States, a vampire of 350 years might as well have been a goddess to those gap-toothed vagabonds who hunted in the shadows of your young country. I filled my home in Richmond—my husband had been killed at Shiloh—I filled it with vampires, turned the place into an ad hoc hospital for Confederate wounded. It was a successful enterprise, too, before the Confederates had put Richmond to the torch in 1865, trying to spoil the city for the Union army. Although, in my heart, I suppose that some of those among their numbers knew that there were vampires aplenty in the city, and wanted to be rid of us."

I thought of the chronology, since she had been in Chicago during the Great Fire. It made some sense. Burn the vampires, clear the streets for a time.

"Ironic that you fled one fire to land in another," I said.

"Yes, Nate," Iris said. "Fire tends to follow us, doesn't it? I did flee Richmond in the night, abandoned what I had built there, took my flock with me to Chicago, for by then, we knew the war was ending fast, and we had best settle someplace safer. Chicago seemed ideal. I'd drunk my fill in Richmond, and when it went up, the only sane response was to land someplace else. At the time, there were 20 of us, my girls, and we settled in this place you see right here. Isn't that funny? I still see them walking these halls. I took everything I had carried with me and rode through the battle lines, attended to by my small army of human bodyguards, Confederate soldiers who were in my thrall. And do you know what I did? As we neared the battle lines, we fed on my body-guards, until we were able to cross the lines in the dark and draw Union men to our ranks, and bind them to my will. And I had them escort us safely to Chicago, of course, feeding on those men as we neared our destination, as well, erasing our tracks, vanishing. It was an old trick I'd learned, feeding on your followers that way, a moveable feast, as your Hemingway would say, but no doubt in a way unlike anything he would have imagined. My men would give their lives for me, and every one of them did."

The memory of it stirred her, I could see, her fleeing ash and fire to settle in a safer place, in a manner that she had, no doubt, done hundreds of times before, in other settings.

"At any rate, we arrived in Chicago by 1866, in this very building," Iris said. "Me and my 20 daughters. They were beautiful, Nate. Every one of them, handpicked by me in my travels. Amanda, Lucinda, Ann, Caroline, Emma, Rachel, Charity, Rose, Narcissa, Charlotte, Emily, Diana, Prudence, Priscilla, Serena, Cassandra, Cornelia, Nelly, Lydia, and Ruth."

"A lot of mouths to feed," I said, using her own way of saying it, and she smiled, nodding.

"It was," she said. "I had accumulated them in my time in the States. In this country, back then, you needed some numbers, just for some measure of protection. It was something I had arranged. I had my men-folk companions, but I wanted to build my own kind of group, like what I'd seen in Europe. There, vampires rarely operated alone; you needed the numbers and the protection numbers brought. People were still so superstitious, and people died so readily—a vampire had only to worry about the sun, and other vampires. There was a logic to it, I assure you. So, with that many mouths to feed, we did what made sense to do: we built a brothel. Chicago was swarming with brothels back then, and it seemed a ready way of accessing the necessary flesh in plain sight. Can you believe it? I had men paying for the pleasure of being bitten by me and my girls."

The notion of Iris as a madam in 19th century Chicago amused me, although it was curious, too.

"You went back to what you knew best," I said.

She smiled, humoring me. "I made use of my knowledge, yes, to create that kind of sophisticated, sinful experience so sorely lacking in American cities. Never mind that we weren't actually having sex with them, that we were drinking their blood and muddling their minds to keep them coming back for more and more. With so much flesh and blood crossing my threshold, we had nothing but good fortune. I was already rich, and it made me even more money. We weren't in the Levee District; I had bribed and seduced the politicians needed to operate here without undue molestation, for a better class of client."

I had a hard time seeing this place as a brothel, even a bogus brothel. Iris seemed to understand that feeling I had.

"Oh, I hated tending to the patrons like that," Iris said. "But a night-life enterprise like a brothel? We were uniquely suited for the task, yes? My girls and I did very well for ourselves. Prudence and Priscilla were my oldest daughters—I know it's a conceit to call them that—but I had made them in 1765, my sweet twins, when we lived in Philadelphia. So, they were my lieutenants for the others, who were younger still. I let them administer it, while I just collected the money and ensured that nothing got out of hand."

"What was it called?"

"I called it the Carnival," Iris said. "You would have enjoyed it. I fully indulged myself with it, spared no expense. I suppose I might have been a little wistful for my beloved Venice. It had been centuries since I'd seen it, but I brought it to life in the Carnival. The theatricality of it, the splendor and decadence, it was gorgeous. Each of my girls wore a unique Carnival mask, at my own insistence. We catered to exclusive clientele, and while all of my girls were beautiful, there was a delightful mystery to the masquerade we held there. I hired musicians, staged plays, let artists adorn my walls with paintings, recreated the artful wickedness of Venice within these walls."

"A shame you didn't set up on Canal Street," I said.

"I had no interest in feeding the river rats," Iris said, and I wasn't sure whether she spoke figuratively or literally. "I had set up strict rules back then: no killings, or as few as we were able, and no marks, no signs of our feedings. We were to be a discreet place of sin."

"Did you wear a mask?" The idea of Iris in a mask intrigued me.

"I was Madam Moonlight," she said. "I still have the mask. At any rate, Carnival thrived for years. Despite the Great Fire—which cost me five of my daughters, incidentally: Ann, Charlotte, Emily, Rose, and Rachel—we endured and thrived. So many men in the city, in need of what they felt was a release. We certainly left them feeling spent. We were the toast of the World's Columbian Exposition in 1893, when absolutely everybody in the world wanted to come to this city. And don't you know that I felt that it was my destiny to be here, Nate?"

"Why?" I asked.

"Because it was celebrating Columbus's discovery of the New World in 1492, Darling," Iris said. "It had been 400 years ago, just like my birthday. Isn't that marvelous? What a birthday present for me it seemed. I took it as providence, in a way. Somewhere near 27 million people came to Chicago during the six-month run of that World's Fair, and represented 46 countries. We fed like fiends in the White City. My girls and I would travel beneath the electric lights with our clients, would arrange pilgrimages from the Carnival to Jackson Park, and would host clients of wealth and power and drank our fill, night after night. I saw Nikola Tesla shoot lightning from his fingertips, like a mad wizard, saw bellydancers seductively snakedance on an ersatz Cairo street, rode a Ferris Wheel, saw titanic German howitzers looming, simply monstrous cannons. I even saw Buffalo Bill and his Wild West Show, which was nearby. Six glorious months of it. After 400 years, to have this world of wonder at my doorstep, I felt it was all somehow meant for me."

Coming from anybody but Iris, I would have mocked the conceit of it, the presumption, but for her, I could see it as having that kind of significance.

"Like everything else, though, it came and went," Iris said. "I loved the World's Fair, had that feeling of something new, of modernity flexing its metallic wings and getting ready to grasp the world in its talons. I felt those things. But it ended, like everything ends. And Carnival, which had been a huge success, had enjoyed 27 years of uninterrupted prosperity, had run into a bit of a problem. We were a victim of our own success, Nate. And do you know why?"

I took a wild stab at it. "Because you're vampires?"

"Exactly," Iris said. "Our patrons loved us, were addicted to us—we had worked so carefully to build a stable of clients like that, had enriched ourselves on them, and our reputation had spread, accordingly. But the intimacy of relations between client and courtesan—and let's be honest, my girls were, in their clumsy way, courtesans—not like I had been, but an American approximation of it, and that relationship is an intimate one. Simply put, the clients aged, and all of my daughters did not. It could not be overlooked, even with our masks and machinations, after 27 years, think about it—a young man of 20 years of age frequents dear Cornelia for 27 years, and now that dear boy is 47 years of age, and Cornelia remains the lustrous 19 years of age she appeared to be when they first met. I could not keep up the deception without drawing on still more suspicion. Oh, to be sure, we put our lovely eyes to work and bent minds and hearts to our needs, but people still noticed. The women of Carnival were mysterious, ageless creatures who would steal a man's soul. Our reputation began to tarnish. I shut down the Carnival on October 31, 1893, the day after the end of the World's Fair. The Halloween Party to end all parties."

I imagined all of those odd "daughters" of Iris, masked and costumed, their patrons and clients among them, in a grand Victorian masquerade, a stone's throw from the next century.

"We were all of us rich," Iris said. "Me, most of all. And I broke up the Carnival, kicked all of my daughters out. They had lived under my roof long enough, understood how to make their way in the world. I think I did it at the right time—there comes a point in a vampire's life when you chafe beneath the scrutinizing eye of your sire, when you simply must strike out on your own. Priscilla and Prudence were nearly 130 years old, and were aching to bolt, and though I loved them dearly, I wanted them to go, just the same. It was well timed."

I wondered about these dearly departed daughters of Iris, where they were, what they were doing. Seeing this dead man in my bed, the memory of what Iris had told me, it all came back.

Maybe it was a gesture on her part intended to have me return to my custodial role—like "Look what I left you to clean up. So, clean it up, and all is forgiven."

That seemed more like Iris, more in character. Just that particular level of bitchiness that screamed "Iris."

So, I didn't do it. I didn't clean up her mess. I just left the guy there. My computer was there, untouched. I really had expected her to break it, to have tossed it out a window, or crush it into powder. But that hadn't happened, either. She was put out, but not off-put. It was hard to know what animated that empty spirit of hers. Maybe the novelty of my rebellion amused her, offered her an entertaining break in her routine.

I glanced at the dial of the clock in the corner of my computer screen. It was 9:35 a.m. I had hours until dusk, time to decide what to do.

The problem was that I wasn't sure. I had lived so long in Iris's shadow, it was hard to know what to do, where to go, and even who I was. I had become so used to handling everything she needed, it wasn't entirely sure anymore what I even needed. Think about somebody else's needs long enough and you invariably forget your own needs.

First, I checked my bank accounts. Iris didn't care about money anymore; it was as meaningless to her as anything else that kept us hapless mortals occupied. The money I'd managed to make was still there, enough to keep me going for a few years without suffering the living death of wage labor.

If Iris had really wanted me over a barrel, she'd have cleaned those out. Just to be safe, I moved the money I had to new accounts, ones she didn't know about. Fortune favored the prepared.

While I was pecking away on the keyboard, I would periodically glance at the dead guy in the room, laying there, eyes shut, a deceptively peaceful expression on his slack face. I felt jealousy, looking at that Eurotrashy man-slab on the floor.

"This is what she picks?"

Maybe it was part of it, like her showing she could do better. But no way was he better than me. He wasn't even as good-looking as I was, and I'm sure she probably just bit him to get him to shut up.

I'd seen her do that before, at Club Vertigo, where there was this babbly babe named Jennipher, who was wearing a silver wig, silver minidress, silver chunky knee boots, silver bangles (not actual silver, or there'd have been problems, I imagined), and even silver lipstick. She'd been enthralled by Iris and was talking about how cool Vertigo was, and how it probably had already jumped the shark, but in that moment, it was just perfect, and running into us there, how cool that was (this was when Iris would still go out with me on "dates"), and how her nail polish was called "Effusion" and Jennipher wondered why they had stopped naming things real colors, why they were always things like "Effusion" and "Epiphany" instead, and how that didn't mean anything, and now nothing meant anything, or everything meant something, which then meant that something was the new nothing, and then Iris just leaned into her neck and bit her, draining her right there by the light of the club, while I sat there and drank my Manhattan, nursing the ice, wondering if anybody had seen.

Iris actually let Jennipher's head hit the table, and she primly wiped her lips with a cocktail napkin. She glanced at me with a half-lit grin.

"I had to do something to shut her up, Nate," she said.

Then she got up and nodded to Jennipher.

"Take her."

So I picked her up, draped an arm around my shoulder like she was just passed out, and we got her out of there, Iris parting the crowd and me just keeping my poker face, carrying the corpse of a club girl, trying not to look like I was carrying dead weight.

Once out of there, Iris hailed a cab, and the three of us got in there, Iris telling the cabbie where to drop us off. It was a surreal ride: Iris on one side, checking her makeup, doing her lipstick, all aglow with Jennipher's blood, and Jennipher between us, dead, her head lolling on my side, naturally, dead eyes gazing at me beneath silver eyeshadow. And me, squirming, wondering if the cabbie noticed the bitemarks on the girl's neck, and whether he even cared. Iris was so blasé about her kills, anymore. This would've been a bit more than two years into our relationship, or whatever you wanted to call what we had. She just didn't care, didn't have to pretend to care. But I wondered what would happen to me if some police came along.

The cabbie dropped us off, made minimal conversation. He was a black man from Uganda, and maybe he saw this kind of thing all of the time back at home, but he asked no questions, and I paid the cabbie—another petty annoyance, but Iris didn't even lift a finger to cover it or to carry Jennipher; it was all on me.

A bloodsucker and a cheapskate.

We got out, I was carting Jennipher, and Iris just stayed in the cab.

"Take good care of her, Nate," she said. "I'm going out."

"What?"

She smiled at me, shut the door, and said something to the cabbie, who sped away. So, there I was, a dead girl on my arms, in the heart of Chicago. I felt a pang of heartache as Iris left me there, wondering where she was going. But she was always off doing vampire stuff, and I was never invited.

Not wanting to be standing there brooding with a dead body on my arm, I opened the door to get into Iris's place, and hefted Jennipher to my shoulder.

In a weird way, perhaps for the first time, I felt true sympathy for one of Iris's victims. Not like I hadn't necessarily felt it before, but with her, there was, I don't know, a sense of just how unjust and horrible Iris could be.

Sure, Jennipher'd been a chatterbox, but that didn't actually rate an undeath sentence. And what was worse was that Iris had left it for me to fix this, didn't even take responsibility for her actions. How did that make me feel?

I laid Jennipher down on my bed, and decided in that moment that I wasn't going to dispose of her the way Iris wanted me to; rather, I was going to let Jennipher live. Or not die. Whatever you want to call it when an undead victim revives.

The problem for me was that it was a net gain for Evil, I suppose. What was the morality of undeath? It was beyond the morality of Man, beneath the morality of God. But, in my heart, I thought it was unfair of Iris to simply end this girl's life that way. She was pretty, she was fun, she was at least somewhat intelligent.

She didn't deserve this. Who did?

But there was a world of difference between action and intention, and I had to find someplace to put her, for if I didn't do so, Iris would surely kill her when she got home, whenever that was.

So, I went to the garage behind our building and put Jennipher in the car with me. Iris had an old maroon MGB that she kept in the garage, and never, ever drove. A convertible, amusingly enough, which always struck my funny bone, a vampire cruising with the top down, which was even more amusing, because Iris didn't drive. So, rather, it was the car of her minion of that time, whoever that was.

I did a little research, and that car line was discontinued in 1980. Not that the car couldn't have been purchased since then, but my suspicion was that it was the vehicle of one of her playthings from that time. All that was left of him (and I'm assuming it was a him) was a pair of driving gloves in the glovebox. Whoever he was, he had big hands.

I'd asked her about him, and she said "Oh, nobody you would know."

Which irked me, because the whole fucking reason I was asking was because I didn't know, but Iris was always evasive like that. It was a scientific impossibility to get a straight answer out of Iris.

Anyway, I thought about driving Jennipher around town, finding a place for her, but then I decided that the garage was, perhaps, the perfect hiding place.

I wrapped Jennipher up in a blanket and popped her in the passenger seat, just reclined the seat and left her there. I thought of taking her to her place, but I didn't want to get caught carting a dead girl home.

I closed the garage and dusted off my hands, since the garage was pretty dusty. I only went in there to grab gardening tools. Gardening had become a bit of a hobby for me.

Having handled that to my satisfaction, I went back inside, played on my computer, wondered where Iris was. She got home hours later, right before dawn. I know because I stayed up.

She came in, aglow, so she'd likely fed again. I wondered in that moment if she had a group of minions, if I was maybe only one link in a chain.

"Cutting it close, aren't you?" I asked.

"Worried?" Iris asked.

"A little," I said. She took off a black fur coat she'd been wearing, tossed aside some shades she'd had on. She was always so light-sensitive, and would always have the shades on when sunrise was near. She wasn't wearing the same clothes she'd worn at Vertigo with me. Now she was in a black pencil skirt and charcoal blouse with a plunge neckline, and some black slingback heels.

"Did you take care of that girl?" she asked.

"Sure did," I said. She paused, gave me a quick look, those dark eyes raking me up and down.

"What did you do?" she asked.

"I handled it," I said. "Don't worry."

She walked up, patting the side of my face with her gloved hand.

"Where were you?" I asked.

"Out," she said. "With old friends."

"I thought this was your, you know, home," I said, feeling stupid.

"It is, Nate," she said. "It is."

And she kissed my cheek and turned to vapor, vanishing before my eyes. I tried following the mist, to see where she went, but we'd played that game so many times, I didn't know where she went, couldn't see where she'd gone.

That was the least of my worries, in truth. I was irked at the change of clothing. Where had she been? Who had she seen? She'd just tossed that fur coat, no doubt expecting me to pick it up and put it in one of her cavernous closets, so I picked it up and went through the pockets.

In the pockets was about a thousand dollars cash (which I pocketed) and a card that said ALEXEI on it in big, black letters. There was an address on it, too, on the other side.

The sun had come up, and it was quiet. I knew that Iris was asleep somewhere in the place.

I pocketed the card and hung up the fur coat, and stalked around the lair, from top to bottom, trying to find out where she went. It was a ritual of mine, but I could never see where she'd gone. I tried to imagine it as the Carnival, but could only see emptiness in this place.

I was tired from being up all night, and I resolved to look into this Alexei business after a nap.

CHAPTER 7

I awoke with a start around noon, having dreamed about Jennipher, imagining her in a silver half-mask at the Carnival. In the dream, she was crawling toward me in a silver v-string panties with a matching silver bra, her mouth bloody, her eyes silver as well. She'd crawled for me and bit my ankle, sucking my blood from there, talking while she was feeding, blood splashing everywhere, talking with her mouth full. I realized that they were all watching me, Iris's daughters, all of them masked, wearing robes, kimonos, gowns, dresses. The walls were red and black, running with blood, and there were bodies all around, and it looked like it might have been an orgy, only everybody was dead except for me.

Taking a shower to clear my head, I got dressed and pocketed the card and went looking for this Alexei. First stop was checking it out on the Net. There was no sign of it on the Net, although the street address put it in Ukrainian Village. So, I hopped a city bus and went out there to check it out.

I rode in the bus all the time. Having a part-time job finding victims/dinners for Iris, I was always trawling around—or is it trolling? I think that's one of those words that's migrating toward itself, like "lose" and "loose"—the evolution, or regression, of language. Anyway, I was always on buses and trains, trying to find just the right girl for Iris.

Depending on the route, you'd get different prey—close to the lake, the Trixies, all blond and professional (or freshly-scrubbed, ashy-eyed Midwestern chic), whereas further west you'd get the Latinas, or the blacks, or the Koreans, or, more recently, Indians and Pakistanis. Head toward certain 'hoods and you'd get the Goths and the Punk chicks and the Hipster babes. Iris didn't really have a preference, except that they be women, as I'd mentioned before.

I asked her about it, and she just shrugged.

"It hardly matters, right, Nate?" she said.

"It does to me," I said.

"They're easier to fetch," she said.

"You could fetch guys easily enough," I said.

She looked at me with her languid eyes, sizing up the depth and breadth of my challenge to her by daring to gainsay her even a bit.

"I've had my share," she said. "I like women better."

"But you're not gay," I said.

"No," she said, with a trace of vehemence.

"Mmm hmm," I said. I didn't believe her. I think she liked women more than men, and just wouldn't cop to it. Of course, if she liked them so much, why was she always killing them? Maybe she was trying to kill something in herself.

A key rule: Never try to psychoanalyze a vampire; you'll only make yourself crazy.

The bus I was on had several very fat women on it, and a pale girl in a red and white striped too-tight-tank and some skinny black leggings and chunky shoes. Her hair hung in plaits that looked like they'd been pressed with shoe polish or wax, and she had fake eyelashes on. She gave me an up-and-down glance while chewing on gum, her full lips colored plum and carefully traced with a mahogany pencil. She'd powdered her face very white.

I sat down in the back of the bus, favoring that, because I had long legs, and back there, you could stretch out if you had a corner seat.

Seeing the sun high overhead, I was pleased that nobody on the bus was a vampire. In service like mine, one found oneself appreciating things like that. Daytime was my downtime, when I didn't have to worry about a vampire coming and fucking with me.

I turned the card over in my hand.

Alexei.

The pale babe got off in Wicker Park, trotting off, while my bus headed south toward Ukrainian Village.

My stop came up, and I got off, by myself, and hunted around, looking at the street address on the card, trying to figure out the numbers in the Village.

The address led to an entirely nondescript building that had no sign on it. Cinder blocks and a flat roof and a heavy metal door on the front of it, painted maroon. There were no windows. I tried the front door, which was locked.

I walked around the entire building, and saw that it was completely windowless. There was a service entrance to the back, also painted maroon, like the writing on the card.

It was a fucking bunker. There was an empty lot beside it, fenced in. Just piles of dirt overgrown with weeds, and a razorwire fence that was festooned with stray bits of plastic shopping bag that flapped in the breeze. Part of the fence had been broken.

In fact, looking at it, it appeared to me that part of the fence had been ripped open. I put my hand on the spot where I thought it happened. For somebody in the vampire trade, even as "the help," it was pretty apparent. Something very strong had simply torn open that fence from inside.

Bending in the fence at the breach, I ducked my head and walked in.

There was something I noticed about the side of this building: no graffiti. No gang signs, nothing. Nobody touched it. There was just this naked expanse of gray cinderblock wall, a big, ripe, pristine urban canvas. The graffiti artists knew this was a bad place, a place to avoid. I imagined some of them being taught this in displays of calculated cruelty.

Walking around in the side lot, I saw lots of disturbed dirt that wasn't apparent from the sidewalk. Standing next to the wall of the building, I put my ear to it, heard nothing. I gave the wall a tap, and it sounded thick.

This time of day, anybody inside would be sleeping.

I tripped over a spraycan that was partly rusted. Picking it up, I saw it was flat black. Poor bastard probably never knew what hit him.

On a whim, I looked around. Nobody seemed to notice. The area had that watchful desolation that always seemed in evidence in poor areas—like nobody around, and yet some sense of eyes on you, anyway. There was a blinking blue police box on a telephone pole some distance away, but it couldn't see me where I was.

I shook up the can, popped the cap.

Then I spraypainted "BLOODSUCKERS!" in big, black letters along that bare wall, as big as I could do it. I put an arrow pointing to the entrance.

Stepping back from it, I looked at my handiwork, drying in the midday sun. That'd piss "Alexei" off, I was sure.

Then, I heard a growling behind me, and I turned to see a pit bull creeping toward me, head low, teeth bared. The thing had been stalking me, like the way a terrier will sneak up to a squirrel or something, before that final charge.

This thing was brown and white, and its eyes were full of canine menace. It just kept stepping toward me.

"Easy, boy," I said, feeling like a fool, because it was clear from the thing's posture and its gaze that there was nothing easy about this fucking dog. It was Alexei's dog. I could just see it in the thing's eyes, the malevolence. I was trespassing, after all.

I broke out into a full-body sweat, backing away from the muscled mutt. It wore a studded collar, even had dog tags. The thing wanted me to run. I imagined myself trying to, tripping on a rock and falling, devoured by the dog, while the locals maybe looked on.

"Fucking dog," I said, holding out the can of spraypaint. "You want some of this?"

The dog lunged at me, and I let go with the spraypaint, right in its face, in its open maw. The dog yelped and whimpered, its leap for me thrown off by my counterattack.

It pawed at its muzzle, its face ludicrously black, and I sprayed it again, and the dog yelped again and ran away from me, blinded for the moment by the pain and the paint.

I threw the can away and ran back out the way I came in, almost snagging myself on the fencing. I went out the alley and around the corner and came back to the sidewalk, admired my graffiti from afar.

It was childish and catty—but it was also terribly satisfying, because it would surely irk Iris's friend(s), whoever was in there. I thought about setting fire to the building, but thought I shouldn't add arson to my lengthy rapsheet in my head, not yet.

I wanted "Alexei" to appreciate this.

There was no question of going in that place; first off, I didn't know how to break and enter yet, and second, I was entirely unprepared to handle whatever was in there. I was so green back then.

Blackface the Dog howled and stumbled about, insensate. It couldn't see or smell me, and that was good enough. I got the hell out of there, before some cops got me for trespassing, vandalism and animal cruelty. Little did they know that what was behind that wall was something far, far worse.

I went back home, got myself a late lunch, strolled into Iris's place, did some late-afternoon day trading while noshing on my sub, and waited for Iris to awaken. I searched for unsolved murders and disappearances in Ukrainian Village, trying to find something. There were a number of them, but people vanished all the time in the city, and even a slacker like Iris knew better than to feed in her own neighborhood.

I also tried searching for Iris's "daughters," randomly googled their names, wondered if they had taken "Augenblick" as a surname. These were the ones who had, who I assumed were her daughters:

Amanda Augenblick.

Lucinda Augenblick.
Narcissa Augenblick.
Prudence Augenblick.
Priscilla Augenblick.
Serena Augenblick.

All of them had seats on the Executive Board of the Augenblick Foundation, with Iris as the Chair. I wondered where the other "daughters" had gone, what had happened to them. It appeared that Lucinda was the only one who actually lived in Chicago, and who appeared to be the curator for the Augenblick Museum, which I assumed to be just a front for her, a pretend job to occupy her time.

Still, I felt the urge to check it out, to see what the deal was, but doubted I'd actually find this child of Iris's. Vampires found you; you didn't find them.

I googled her, anyway, wanted to see what I could about Ms. Lucinda Augenblick. The pictures I saw showed a fox-faced young woman with long, pale blonde hair and high cheekbones that made me think that she might have been Scandinavian. She had a bit of an overbite and kissy lips. Her eyes were cornflower blue, and there was a cavernous cruelty in her gaze. In one of the pieces I saw, which showed her at her home, I saw a Venetian Carnival mask on her wall, in the background. It had a crackle finish of ivory and called to mind Saturn, with a plume of gilded cloth arranged at an angle at the top for the rings, but done in a way that made the rings look like they were a hat. There were little gold stars studding the cheeks of the mask like celestial freckles.

I found my gaze going from Lucinda to the mask, and back again. There was some corroboration to Iris's story, right there.

-X-

I dragged the Eurotrash man-slab down to the vault, got him the hell out of my living space. It was hard work, and I was pretty careless. I just heaved him over the balcony, let him crack on the hardwood floor below. Then I dragged him by his feet, not caring if his head bounced on the cement steps that led to the vault. Fuck him. I had other things on my mind.

The condition of a body mattered when it became a vampire. Everything you carried with you in life, you had with you in death, and in undeath. So, that embarrassing ankle tat, that beer belly, that mole you had would be with you forever if you lucked upon a vampire who decided to take a drink of you and got you in the club.

I was terrified to face Iris after our disagreement. I glanced at my watch. She'd be up in an hour or so. I went around her place, trying to find her, again, no trace, no sign. I didn't know what I would do if I found her. And I wasn't sure what she'd do when she found me.

The truth was that I really didn't have anywhere to go. My phone had texts from Clementine, wanting to get together. I didn't know what I should do.

But I knew that I had to face Iris.

One way or another, I had to.

Thinking back on the Jennipher thing, which was our first big disagreement, like my own kind of insurrection, I remembered sneaking back to the garage peeking in on Jennipher. It was day three, and she'd be coming to life at dusk, hungry as hell. I didn't want to be there when that happened. Or did I? Jennipher would bite me, would make me a vampire. She'd be too ravenous not to.

Lifting the blanket and looking at her body, I could see that her eyes were open, now, and I avoided her gaze. It was something some vampires did—they'd sleep with their eyes open, and if you got caught by their gaze, and you were alone, you'd just stand there, fixed, motionless, and would wait until the vampire awoke to bite you. Bad scene, nothing you wanted to get mixed up in. It was one of their many tricks.

She looked beautiful. Iris would be pissed that I'd fibbed about Jennipher. I put the blanket back over her. Let her come to unlife and go from there.

I went back inside and waited for Iris to rise, irked about the whole Alexei thing. I had to know who the hell he was.

Iris appeared in a veil of mist, coalesced out of her own fog, wearing a bright red dress and some heeled ankle boots.

"I'm hungry, Nate," she said. "What'd you bring me?"

"Who's 'Alexei?'" I asked.

She regarded me with ironic amusement, her beautiful face a mask of momentary mirth, unmoving, held for an inhumane beat that made me squirm, before the mind behind that ghastly masquerade chose to animate her visage once more. It was one of the most disconcerting things about vampires; when they did not choose to emote, or to appear to emote, their faces were lifeless.

"A friend."

I held up the card, turned it around in my hand for her to see. She just walked up and took it from me in a smooth motion. The way she moved, it could only be called "feline."

"An OLD friend," she said. "I hope you didn't do anything stupid, Nate."

"Not me," I said.

"Alexei doesn't like stupid," she said.

"His place looks like shit," I said. "He has no taste."

Iris smiled at me: this bland, wan upturning of her lips.

"He has a taste for other things."

Then it hit me. Of course. I felt particularly thick.

"He's the Nightlord. He's your sire."

Iris smiled, graced me with half a nod. "Yes. Took you long enough."

"Why won't you make me?" I asked.

Iris sat down, crossed her legs, slouched in my office chair, gave my keyboard an absent peck or two with a slender finger. She considered computers quaint.

"I remember when the first computers were built. Massive things, wound with tapes, filling whole rooms. This little toy has far more power than those machines of yore. How times change, eh? In a way, it's like how it is with us. With vampires. We are born in a moment in time, grow up and live with certain expectations, and then we depart from the world of men and become what we are. Only we become greater than what we were, stronger."

"What does that have to do with me?" I asked.

"You're not ready, yet, Nate," she said. "You really want to go through life like this? It's not for everybody. I don't think you have lived enough to face this. When I was your age, we had to grow up fast; life didn't offer us the cushiony experience you have. You are at 30 what I was at 12, Nate."

That just bugged me. She was having me do everything else; why not simply make me a vampire, too? At least let me have the benefits that came with the costs of it.

"I'm ready," I said. "I don't want to get old."

"I don't think you could handle it, Nate," she said. "I've been around for so long. You know what that is like?"

"Obviously not," I said.

"I saw the Sistine Chapel when it was first unveiled. Brand new."

Her face was like stone, just pale white, her fangs protruding as she spoke. She was hungry. I halfway hoped that she'd be hungry enough to have a go at me.

"You see people doing the same things, over and over again," Iris said. "You know that line about people not learning from history, being doomed to repeat it? That's how it goes. Over and over again, the same stupid people doing the same stupid things, the same failures of imagination and courage. The costumes change, the scenery, the smells, yeah, but it's still people. People aren't as ugly as they used to be—I'll give you that. They're cleaner by far, don't stink nearly as badly as they used to, and they live longer. Although they're fatter and softer, too. Back in my day, people knew what to do with a vampire when they found one. Today? People want to BE us. What does that say about you, about what you've become?"

"Of course we want to be you," I said. "You're ageless, you can do what you like. What's not to like about that? The freedom? The power?"

"It's an affliction, an addiction," she said. "You have no idea what you're talking about, what it's like."

She leaped at me and grabbed me in her arms, cold, like stone, and stronger than steel. She was shorter than me, but I knew she could snap me in half if she'd wanted to, could have thrown me through a wall.

She sank her teeth in my neck and drank from me. Iris seldom did this, anymore. The feeling of it is hard to describe—there's no real pain, actually—there's just a kind of moment when you realize that she's there, and she's lapping up your blood, just drawing it forth, and there's an ecstasy in it that paralyzes you with pleasure. The communion of vampire and victim is incredibly intimate, the taker and the taken. There are no words for it, only colors and textures. It is exquisite.

Iris licked the bite, which stopped the flow of blood, and tossed me away, dizzy, breathless. She'd gotten some color to her cheeks.

"That's what it's like," she said. "You're just meat to me, Nate. You're a blood meal. It's what it comes down to. I like you, so I suffer you to live, alright? But it's like that. Always."

There was a crash outside, and Iris looked at me, while I staggered to my feet, light-headed. The bliss from her bite was overwhelming, left me gasping. It had been awhile.

"What did you do?" she asked, as we went to the balcony that overlooked the garden in the back, toward the garage.

"Jennipher," I said.

"You told me you took care of her," Iris said, her voice croaky with reproach.

"Ohmigod," Jennipher said, holding her hands out in front of her, turning them this way and that. "Am I, like, undead?"

"Yes," Iris said. "Come over here."

"Iris!" Jennipher said, breaking into a toothy smile. "Nate! Hi, you guys! I just had the weirdest thing happen—I'm in a car, with a blanket on my head, right? And I woke up in there, and I'm fucking starving, and I'm like 'Dude, what are you doing in a strange car? In a strange garage?' And I don't even know! The last thing I remember was being at Vertigo with you guys, and I'm totally wearing the same outfit, and then I totally bite my tongue with my own teeth, and I'm like 'Ow!' and then I bonk my head on the dashboard of the car and I pop up in this gnarly garage that's totally dusty, and I'm standing there, but I can totally see in the dark—"

Iris turned to me. "You did this. You take care of it. Jennipher. JEN-NIPHER?"

"—and I'm like 'I don't know' and—"

"JENNIPHER!" Iris said, silencing her with an upraised hand. "This is Nate. Nate is mine. You are not to feed on him under any circumstances, okay?"

"Alright, Iris," Jennipher said. "See, I thought you guys were both vampires, but I see that you're totally the vamp, and Nate's just your boy, I see how that works. I need something like that, too, I guess, and I—"

Iris looked at me, shaking her head. "Stay away from Alexei. And handle this. I don't care how. She can't stay here."

Then Iris became a bat, and flew off the balcony. When Jennipher saw that, she was impressed.

"Whoa," Jennipher said. "She totally is like this vampire queen, right? Am I right? Nate, I'm totally starving. What do I do?"

That bugged me. Sure, I hadn't told Iris about Jennipher, but it sucked to have to be the one to walk her through Vampirism 101. But that's how it always went. Iris spills the blood, Nate brings the mop.

"I'll be right down," I said, grabbing a jacket.

I got downstairs and Jennipher was pacing around, biting her wrist—a little vampiric masturbation. She glanced at me, hid her arm behind her hand.

"Ohmigod! I totally have fangs," she said. I went to the garage and opened it, fired up the MG, which hadn't been driven awhile, and protested a bit. Then I put the top down on it and pulled out.

Jennipher hopped into the passenger seat with me, showing off her fangs to me.

"Look at these, Nate," she said, grinning at me. "Look at my fangs!"

"Yeah," I said. "I know."

"Totally," she said, shaking her head. "Ohmigod! Where's my reflection, Nate?"

I cruised out of the place in the MG, into the alley, careful not to go too fast until I could see clearly.

"Yeah, see, vampires don't cast reflections," I said.

"What? How'm I gonna get ready if I can't see myself?" Jennipher asked. "Not like I can't manage, because I'm really super good at that kind of thing, just looking great and all, but—"

"It's just one of those things," I said. "Part of your new nightlife. I don't make the rules."

I cruised out onto the street, glad I'd brought a windbreaker, as the air was chilly. Jennipher didn't notice. Vampires never felt the cold.

"How old are you?" I asked.

"Twenty-three, why?" she kept running her fingers over her fangs, periodically pricking them, sucking on the blood she spilled from them.

"Just curious," I said. "You're always going to be 23, now. Like for all time, you will be. As long as you exist."

Jennipher liked that, I could tell. The novelty of it, the prospect of everlasting life before being able to appreciate life, itself.

"That is wicked," she said. "Totally, totally wicked. We should stop by my place."

"Yeah, where is that?" I asked.

"Streeterville," she said, and started to give me directions, but I stopped her.

"I know where it is," I said. We headed south, me trying to explain the basics of vampirism to Jennipher, who, to her credit, listened and only interrupted a dozen times with questions or exclamations.

It gave me some satisfaction to have thwarted Iris, even a little bit, in the creation of Jennipher, who would make a disarming vampire. Nobody would even see her coming.

We got to her place, a nice condo in the heart of downtown, in a high-rise, and she keyed into her place.

"In the old days," I said. "Vampires had to be invited in by the rightful owners of the home. But in today's world of absentee landlords and what-not, it's kind of not so big of an issue, anymore. I don't know why that is—maybe it's kind of like how the Cross doesn't really work anymore, except on the really, really stupid vampires."

Jennipher's place was ultra-modern—lots of chrome and neon, angular leather furniture that looked like geometric planes that were sharp as razorblades. She told me to get comfortable while she changed. The view she had of downtown was insane.

"Jesus, what does this place cost?" I asked.

"A lot," she said. "My folks bought it for me."

"Wow," I said, standing close to the window, peering down. We were on the 40th floor. It was awesome. I never had money; this was money. Everything in Jennipher's place was nice—high-quality.

She came down in a pair of incredibly tight silver gilt jeans with a silver mesh tank top.

"You really like silver, huh?" I asked.

"Oh, you," she said. "This is just for clubbing. I want to be noticed. I want to sparkle."

She'd slipped on some silver slingback heels, and wasn't wearing her silver wig. Her hair was black, and she had a widow's peak. She'd brushed out her hair, which hung around her head in a sweet spray of looping curls.

"I'm starving," she said. "Just totally starving, now."

She actually went to the stainless steel fridge and opened it, looked in there, sighing, then closed it. She sat down across from me, her teeth very much in evidence, now, her eyes glowing a bit orange in the dark of her place. It would have been weird to be the only one breathing in the room, but I was so used to that by now.

"Tell me everything," she said. "Everything I need to know."

And I did, which took maybe a half hour. Because, let's be honest, there's really not that much you have to know, where being a vampire is concerned. Even kids get it; they understand.

It bugged me that Iris had, through her whole master/slave thing that vampires had with their victims, cock-blocked me with Jennipher. I was in the Friend Zone with her, because of what Iris had said about not biting me. It would take an act of willpower and sedition greater than I imagined Jennipher had in her to override Iris.

I warned Jennipher about other vampires, said they tended to be pretty fucking crazy and dangerous, and that there were turf wars that sometimes erupted between them. I warned her about the werewolves, although I'd never actually seen one of those, and wondered if Iris was really just fucking with me by bringing them up at all. I warned her about vampire hunters, and told her that she had to be sure her place was safe. I told her about how she could become a bat, or a wolf, or a mist, which she thought was "bitchin'" and she totally transformed into these things in front of me, one at a time, like trying on a new pair of shoes.

In a bit of cosmic irony, her wolf form was, of course, silvery. I told her as much, and she loved that. I told her that anybody she slew by her bite would rise in three days, as she had, as a vampire, and that she had to be very careful about that.

Then I told her about how she could die, because I felt like I owed that to her. Being a vampire would either be very hard or very easy for Jennipher. It could go either way, depending on her, and how she took to it.

"The stake to the heart puts you in suspension," I said. "It effectively kills you so long as the stake is in place. However, remove the stake, and you will come back. Decapitation will kill you, but, again, if your severed head is put back on your body, you will come back."

"For reals?" she asked.

"Totally," I said. "But if somebody's lopping off your head, I'll wager that they know what they're doing, and they won't make that mistake. Now, burning will destroy you, but get this—they have to burn the head and the body in separate places, and scatter the ashes. If that happens, you're fucking gone for good. Game Over. But, if, for some reason, they burn you in one place, and they don't scatter the ashes, you will come back."

"Cool," she said. "Trippy."

"I've never seen anybody come back like that, but Iris told me it's possible," I said. "Running water is supposed to hurt you, too, so don't be hopping in the shower anytime soon."

"I can't bathe?" she asked.

"Not that way," I said. "At least check before jumping in, okay? I don't know if that one's for real or not."

"So, like, if I get caught in a rainstorm?" she asked.

"That probably wouldn't be good," I said. "Look, I don't make the rules; I just know them."

Jennipher pouted toothily. "I love showers."

"I wouldn't go further than a sponge bath, if I were you," I said. "Garlic will repel you. You'll find that out, soon enough."

"Why does that even work?"

I didn't know, and Iris would never say. But garlic did repel vampires.

"Maybe it's got antioxidant properties that offend vampire allergies," I said. "I don't know."

Jennipher hopped up and went to her chromed kitchen. "I totally have garlic in here, Nate. Get me a clove?"

I walked in and grabbed one, a nice, white, chubby clove of it. Jennipher watched me, a look of growing revulsion on her face.

"Okay, so brandish it," she said, and I held it out, and she recoiled, hissing. "Fuck, yeah. Get that shit OUT of here."

I popped the clove in my pocket, and took the bag she had in her kitchen and put it out her front door. When it was gone, Jennipher heaved a sigh of relief.

"Boy, you weren't kidding," she said. "That stuff SUCKS."

The opportunity to be scientific about it intrigued me. "How did it make you feel?"

Jennipher laughed. "You sound like my therapist. Umm, bad. Afraid. Disgusted. Grossed-out. It burned, kinda. Like burnt toast, a bee sting, and an allergy attack at the same time."

"Wow," I said. My cell rang, and I peeked. It was Iris. I opened it. "Yeah?"

"Where are you?" she asked.

"With Jennipher," I said. "I'm showing her the ropes."

"Oh," Iris said. "We'll talk about that later. I need you to come home."

"Why?" I asked.

"Because I need you to come home," Iris said. "Now."

"Alright," I said, hanging up. "Look, I gotta go. Here's my number. Call me anytime you need advice or whatever. Usually, you can get away with one meal a night, if, um, you drain somebody completely. If you just drink people here and there, not fully draining them, like then you may need several. You remember what I said about your eyes? You can make people forget that you bit'em, if you have to. And your tongue will stop the bleeding, like when you bite somebody. I don't know why. Oh, and anybody you completely drain becomes a vampire in like three days. So, remember that, too."

Jennipher came up and gave me a hug, which was more than a little creepy, just because she was already all skinny-strong, vampire-strong. I'd told her about that, too. Now she could lift about a ton, which was incredible, given her thin build.

"You're the best, Nate," she said, her breath on my neck. She actually gave me a lingering kiss on the neck, but no teeth.

Parting, she smiled at me. "You'd better go, now."

"Yeah," I said. "Be careful out there, okay?"

"I will," she said, smiling at me in the dark, her orange eyes ablaze. I left her in the shadows and grabbed that bag o' garlic, took the elevator down, and tossed that in the back of the MG and got out of there, thinking about things as I headed back toward Iris's place.

I wondered how much of her humanity Jennipher would keep, when faced with the manifold temptations of vampirism, how long she would be herself, how soon she would succumb to the enervation of immortality. How long did anyone last? The nature of the nightlife was surely demanding enough, took a toll on the soul, but the longevity had to make one even more remote and disassociated from their own humanity. If being mortal was what made us human, and vampires transcended mortality, then, in one stroke, they had become other-than-human.

Right now, Jennipher was a newborn, basically, and so all of those human habits were there, the memories, the life she led before crossing paths with Iris. And maybe it was enough to sustain her in the normal course of a human lifespan. Or maybe it would not, since she was so young when she'd been made. Maybe there wasn't enough life to buttress her against the temptations of undeath. Perhaps the lack of life would, instead, make it easier for her to excel as a vampire. Time would tell.

Even Iris had to have been what passed for normal in the 16th century. Maybe she was as hard-edged back then as she is now. Or maybe she was a carefree young thing in the way Jennipher was.

What would vampires do at the end of the world? I mean, mankind was surely on cruise control toward its own extinction. What would vampires do? The logical choice seemed to be taking control of society, itself, to ensure a steady flow of blood. But if that was the case, maybe it had already happened. Maybe vampires already did run things from the shadows, and subtly directed the ebb and flow of human history to suit their ends. That was a weird thing to think about. They certainly had the time, and the dominant institution of my time, the corporation, was itself immortal—why wouldn't vampires create something in their own image? Powerful, selfish, parasitic, ruthless, amoral, immortal, psychopathic—the corporation was a perfect proxy for the vampire. I could just imagine how seamlessly a vampire could wend their way through a corporation, and what that could mean for humanity. I thought of Iris and her daughters and their foundation.

That thought gave me chills. Vampires wouldn't be content to just sit on the Earth until all humanity was consumed, or, worse, watch the Sun grow into a malevolent dying ball of fire that heat-pasteurized the planet and put an end to them.

No, they would want to get off the planet with us, somehow. If they took control of the world, of the culture, they would travel with us, wherever we went. Parasitic puppet masters.

I imagined the early mammals and surviving reptiles feeding on dinosaur corpses, not realizing that they were eating dinosaur tapeworms along with dinosaur meat. Tapeworms, going right down the gullet. Dinosaur tapeworms, but then, in time, becoming our own tapeworms. The passing of the torch, the adaptive nature of the parasite.

It was the same with vampires. Maybe vampires themselves were only a delivery system for the blood, the ichor that moved them. Perhaps the blood itself was what made them what they were, and the changes they experienced were simply the symptoms of the infection, which then intended to make them a better infection-delivery system.

The thought of that made me smile—it would not sit well with Iris's haughty self-conception, being an infection delivery system. And yet, it made its own kind of sense. The blood was their everything. Vampirism was malaria from Hell.

They were not predators, the way they liked to say they were; rather, they were parasites.

—X—

I got back to Iris's and parked the MG, went strolling in to see Iris standing there with this thuggish-looking man. Not a man, though—one of them. Another bloodsucker. He was impossibly broad-shouldered, and wore a black shirt and a burgundy suit with a crimson necktie. He had a very square head and had his long red-blond hair slicked back with liberal portions of product. He was horribly pale, and his face was so rough-hewn as to look like it was etched from a block of wood. He looked like curdled blood and Satan all at once, and he was smirking at me over stone-gray eyes that I avoided, lest they entrap me.

"This the guy?" the man asked. "You the guy who spray my dog? Who paint my wall?"

His accent was thickly Slavic. The man bore a gold signet ring on his thick pinky finger.

"Nate, this is Alexei," Iris said. "The man whose property you vandalized. My sire."

Now, I don't know how much experience you have with the living dead, but one thing that gets overlooked in all the vampire romanticism is that vampires are like flies in amber—they are truly creatures of their time, reflective of the moment that spawned them. Only "Nosferatu" really ever gets at this right, because people want vampires to always be suave and sleek and beautiful—always by the standards of the day.

And that's exactly where they go wrong, because when a vampire is made, they look like people did at that time. I don't know when vampirism first began, but if you had a caveman vampire, that fucker would look like a caveman for the rest of his undead life. Not saying you couldn't dress him in a suit like they did those actors in those caveman commercials—but he's still going to look like a caveman. Or those pix of people during the Civil War, where they all look so hard-bitten and haggard—you make somebody a vampire from then, and they're going to look like that.

Their faces and bodies show the times that spawned them. So, a woman made at the time of the Gibson Girl era is going to be a pudgy vampiress, see? All curves and double chins and massive lengths of hair. And so on.

They look different. Sure, they can compel you with their gaze, they can crack you in half with their limbs, but they—the old ones, anyway—look different. Depending on their origins, yeah, they look unusual.

Like Jennipher right now blended seamlessly into the world around her; nobody would think twice about her. But put Jennipher a thousand years into the future, or two thousand, or five thousand (assuming we aren't extinct by that time), or a million years—and she's going to look like an early 21st century human. While mankind would improve and evolve (ideally), vampires would remain exactly as they were at the time of the infection.

There was no evolution of vampirism.

I bring this up because Alexei looked OLD. I don't mean physically old—physically, he looked like he was perhaps in his early 30s. But the coarseness of his features, the brutish, chiseled nature of his face, itself concealed beneath a red beard that had twin streaks of white through it, and his slablike marble pallor, and the raw power that seemed to charge the air around him—all of these things communicated age to me.

And danger.

"I'd like you to apologize to Alexei, Nate," Iris said.

"His dog attacked me," I said.

"You were trespassing," Iris said. "Apologize, Nate."

"Sorry I painted on your wall," I said. "And painted your dog."

Alexei's face was immobile, this sort of sly half-grin on his face.

"Tell me, why you paint on my wall? I keep low profile in this town," Alexei said. "You try make trouble for Alexei?"

That fucking accent, the nasally tone of it. It was grating. This man had been around for centuries, and still hadn't purged his accent? Or perhaps he held onto it out of some sense of nostalgia for whatever it was that he was. This monstrous man was Iris's maker? He looked like the warrior that he had been, this Nightlord.

I wasn't sorry for what I had done; I already hated Alexei. And I think I knew why. I could feel it, could see in the way Iris hovered nearby.

"You made Iris," I said. "You're her sire, right?"

"Smart boy," Alexei said, glancing at Iris, who smiled like she'd just eaten something she didn't want to and had to tell the host it was delicious. "Not TOO smart, mind you; no one who crosses Alexei is too smart."

He remained seated, for he had nothing to prove to me. Alexei could probably lob me into outer space if he wanted to. I wondered how old he was. I was guessing a thousand years. I'd never seen such an old vampire before. The Nightlord. *Dominus de Nocte.*

"Dominus Noctis," Alexei said, making me jump. He'd read my mind.

A thousand years, and he held onto his accent. It was an affectation.

"Is not affectation, Child," Alexei said. "Is choice. I remember from whence I come. Always. Forget that, and you are like ship without rudder, adrift."

"Where did you come from?" I asked.

"Nate," Iris said. "This is about you, not Alexei."

"Iris," Alexei said. "You teach this pup lesson, yes?"

"Of course, Alexei," Iris said, and I could hear fear in her voice, could see it in the tightness of her posture, her deference toward him. For the first time, ever, I saw fear in her. Iris was never languid in her movements—there was always a kind of stiffness to her, like a spring wound too tight, which gave the appearance of stillness, but, upon closer examination, revealed that tightness, the tension.

"Right now," Alexei said, and before I could so much as blink, Iris struck me, a backhanded slap that sent me flying across the room. I mean, I spun around, spitting blood, and narrowly missed hitting my head on the opposing wall.

I collapsed to the ground, my head spinning, ears ringing, and Alexei was there to catch me before I fell, his fanged mouth right in my blurry field of vision.

"Because you are hers," Alexei said. "You live. Understand? That is only reason you live. I am Rus. I am Vampir."

I was like a leaf in his hands, a feather. Light, insubstantial. My legs felt far away, my feet felt like they were in another time zone. My mouth bled, my heart broke. Iris had never struck me before.

"But you ever, ever do anything like that again," Alexei said. "I tear you into tiny pieces. I make you one of mine and brick you into wall, let you starve for eternity, praying for death."

And he let me go with a curt shove that slammed me into the wall. Then, without appearing to move, he smoothed out his suit, and said something to Iris in Russian or Ukrainian, I couldn't tell. Something Slavic as hell that turned one's tongue into a rollercoaster.

I was a puddle against the wall, my ears still ringing from Iris's blow. I couldn't believe she'd struck me, without so much as a second thought, a hint of hesitation. In that ghastly moment, the two of them there, I felt incredible hatred.

So pissed off was I that I didn't even realize that Alexei had gone. He moved so quickly that he seemed to teleport. There was just a blur, and he was gone.

Iris just looked at me without a hint of emotion.

"I can't believe you would embarrass me like that," she said. "And with Alexei, of all people."

"I was jealous," I said.

"You haven't the right to be jealous," Iris said. "You haven't earned it."

She hadn't broken my jaw, but I would have a heckuva bruise. I spat blood, and could see that it distracted her, despite her effort to appear coolly indignant in front of me.

"What haven't I earned?" I asked. "I've only been your fucking servant. You won't even make me."

Iris didn't move, didn't breathe—she never breathed. "You don't want this, Nate."

"I told you I do," I said. "I don't know how many times I told you. You're going to just use me up, right? Like you did your others? Just watch me get too old to be useful, and then put me down when you're done with me?"

She didn't say anything, and that said so much. She couldn't pretend I wasn't right about her. I had her number. Iris was older than me by many centuries, but I had her number, all the same. Maybe it was because I was still human, could see it.

"How many flunkies have you had?"

"You're not a flunkie," Iris said. "You're my…companion."

"How many 'companions' have you had?" I asked.

"40," Iris said. "Are you happy to know that, Nate?"

I wondered who they all were, and whether Iris was as coldly aloof and indifferent to them as she was to me. It was hard to imagine.

"Being my companion is a lot of work," Iris said. "I know that, but look what you get? You get me."

Because I was good with numbers, I did the math in my head—I was guessing her companions had a shelf-life of about 13 years. Likely some lasted longer than others.

"I don't get you," I said. "I never will."

"No," she said. "You won't. You can't."

Iris walked over to me and crouched, there. She was wearing black hose and a black skirt and a prim red jacket with gold buttons that had tiny lions pressed into them. She took off a black leather glove she was wearing and slid a finger on her floor, mopping up my blood. Then she licked her finger until it was clean and white again. She repeated this, distracted a little, just mopping up my blood with her finger, without a word.

"That's disgusting," I said.

"That's life," Iris said. "You're sweet, Nate."

Any time a woman—even an undead one—told you that you were sweet, it was the kiss of death. To be "sweet" in the eyes of a woman meant that you were too nice, too whatever-it-was that a woman might find agreeable but not desirable. It really meant that you were somehow lacking in their eyes, but it made them feel bad to view you that way, so they'd label you "sweet" to make themselves feel better for not wanting you.

I knew right then what I had to do. It was just so apparent to me. Iris seemed to sense this, because she stopped sucking on her finger and she grabbed me by my shirt and held me close, in a kind of parody of Alexei's own move.

"Don't do anything stupid, Nate," she said. "Don't embarrass me. Ever again. Alexei is more powerful than you can even know. He's far, far beyond you."

I just hated that bond, that knowledge that Alexei had known Iris when she was human, that he had found something he liked in her centuries ago, and had claimed her for his own. Long, long ago.

"How did you meet him?" I asked. The pain of it was almost more than I could bear.

Iris let me go, put her glove back on, flexing her fingers.

"It doesn't matter."

"It matters to me," I said.

"But it doesn't matter to me, Nate," Iris said. "I told you, anyway. I was a courtesan. He met me in Venice."

She stood up.

"You told me, but you didn't tell me," I said. "Tell me, now. It's the least you can do, after nearly taking my head off."

"What would you have me say? He was a client. This dashing warrior prince whose reputation had preceded him. You see him. That red hair. That beard. Mercenaries and courtesans were two sides of the same coin in Italy—warriors and whores for hire. We had much in common, spoke the same language of sex and violence. While my courtesan sisters played with local talent, Alexei had come to Venice looking for me, I liked to think. He came to me by the light of the moon, the Nightlord. He had fed before seeing me, I realized that later, because his skin was warm, his flesh was pink. He did not want to frighten me. He called me 'Little Flower' and told me that the Turks were coming, would drive us all into the sea. We were all afraid of the Turks back then. Even joyful, playful Venice feared the ever-growing shadow of the Turk."

"You had said you knew what he was," I said.

"I did," Iris said. "The Nightlord was a mercenary knight of renown. A supernatural soldier, who only fought beneath the stars. His reputation was that he could not be defeated in battle, that he had some kind of pact with the Devil, or with Selene, by the light of the moon. He had come to me one night and had told me that he would take me out of this place, that I would never have to fear growing old and ugly, that the future could be mine, if I only had the courage to reach out and take it. He recounted his deeds of valor, that I might know who he was. He told me that he had been a young soldier who had been in the service of Byzantine Emperor Anastasius I, known as Dicorus. Alexei had fought in the Isaurian War as a youth, had distinguished himself in that campaign, and had served the Emperor faithfully until his death in 518, although, in 515, he had been taken by a vampire, and had kept his affliction secret from the Emperor and his peers."

"Who was his sire?"

"He was taken by an Ostrogoth witch by the name of Candra," Iris said. "He never told me much about her. I think it was not something he was proud of."

"That's it?"

"History's dead to me, Nate," Iris said. "Everything is."

"Even me?"

She didn't answer.

"Get yourself cleaned up, and find me something to eat. I'm starving," she said.

-X-

One evening, without warning, Iris came to me and told me to get dressed up. She drifted into my room, wearing a beautiful white silk sleeveless gown with a gray fur collar, had baubled gold bracelets at her wrists. She looked me over as I sat at my desk, posting on Facebook, and she spoke to me softly.

"Nate, I want you to put on something nice," she said. "Put on a jacket and a tie."

"Why?"

She looked at me like I'd slapped her in the face. Iris didn't like when I questioned her directives.

"We're going out to dinner," she said. "And I want you to look presentable."

I was just wearing one of my western shirts and jeans, was barefoot. "This isn't presentable?"

"No," she said. "Put on a nice shirt, a nice tie. Go, right now."

"What is this about? Am I getting made?" I asked.

Iris smiled to herself, but I could see that her mind was on something, that she was otherwise preoccupied. My curiosity piqued, I shut my laptop and I got dressed. I put on a gray pinstriped suit, something I never wore these days, but which Iris had gotten for me a few years before, when she needed me to look sharp. While I did this, Iris hovered nearby, watching me prepare. There was no pretense of privacy.

"We haven't been on a date in ages," I said. I was almost looking forward to it.

"It's not a date," Iris said. "Not that tie. Pick the blue one. The Prussian Blue one. Yes."

I put on my necktie, now genuinely wondering what was going on.

"What's the deal? Come on, don't keep me in suspense," I said.

"You'll see," Iris said.

"Is it a good thing?"

Iris smiled cryptically, spoke elliptically. "It's something."

When I got myself dressed to her satisfaction, she reached up and tousled my hair a bit, and took my arm in hers and walked me outside. She was very pale, had not yet fed.

"Don't you want to feed?" I asked, wondering why she hadn't bitched about me not bringing her a body or anything.

"Soon," Iris said, walking me through the garden, out the outer gate. Outside, curbside, was a limousine, waiting for us.

The driver, a strong-featured young man with a set jaw and thick hands like a construction worker, opened the door and held it for us. Iris slid into the back, and I followed in her wake. The driver shut the door and then took the wheel, proceeded to drive us.

I'd never had a limo waiting for me before, could only wonder what this was about.

"Are you going to tell me or just keep me in suspense?" I asked.

"We're going to dinner," Iris said. "We've been invited."

"By whom?"

"Alexei," Iris said, cocking an eyebrow at me.

My stomach clenched. "Alexei? Why?"

"Because you were stupid and you got his attention," Iris said. "Now that you have gotten his attention, he wants to get to know you. And please try to behave tonight. I won't have you embarrassing me in front of him."

Dinner with Alexei was about the last thing that I wanted to do. What I wanted to do was pull an action movie trick and take a roll-dive out the side of the limousine, but I knew that Iris would just grab me and take me there, regardless.

Still, my mind was swimming. Why the hell would Alexei want to meet me again, after browbeating me over my petty vandalism? He'd already threatened me. Was he trying to mend fences, or to further rub my nose in the dirt? I wasn't sure what to make of it, and I didn't like it.

We drove through the city, Iris in her own thoughts, opalescent in her white gown against the black leather seats, me fretting opposite her, wondering if I was dressed up for my own funeral.

The car delivered us to an opulent kind of food fortress with **КИОСК** written across the top in big letters of red and gold.

"Knock?" I said. "What's 'Knock?'"

"It's Kiosk," Iris said. "That's 'Kiosk' in Russian, Nate."

Kiosk, a West Side place that I'd never been to. Fucking wonderful. The chauffeur got us to the front of the place, and let us out, where we faced the building, itself. The walk-up was arched, leading to some thick doors. We made our way to it.

I fished out my phone, looked up the word on the fly.

"What are you doing?" Iris asked.

"I'm just seeing what this place is rated," I said.

"Don't embarrass me, Nate," Iris said. "Put that phone away. And turn off your ringer. I don't want you texting or anything during dinner."

"Dinner with Alexei," I said. "You guys don't eat."

As I navigated the reviews, I wondered if I was going to be the main course, here. Wouldn't that be rich?

The doorman, who was wearing red and gold livery with great golden buttons on his jacket, opened the door for us and ushered us in.

Inside, the place was radiant red and gold. Fucking everything.

"It says that 'kiosk' isn't even a Russian word," I said. "It's Persian."

"Shhh," Iris said. "We're in America, Nate. Nobody cares."

"Alexei cares," I said.

"He owns this place," Iris said. "Please just put the phone away and don't be stupid."

The wood in the place was dark, and there were competing scents in the air. I could smell strong women's perfume, hints of it, various scents clashing, and a scent of smoked meat somewhere, I couldn't identify, and tobacco and alcohol.

We were walked through the place, past diners in a great open banquet hall of deep green that paired with golden columns at the periphery, and which vaulted geometrically overhead in a lattice of dark, arched wood overhead, from which hung several large chandeliers. The chairs were dark wood and red leather, and the tables were plentiful and rectangular.

"This must be the kiosk," I whispered to Iris. "Like this room."

The place got four stars and five dollar signs, so it was an expensive proposition. At least Alexei wasn't being a cheapskate. The patrons all looked very Slavic, were eating and talking to each other, paid us no mind.

We were being led to a private dining room along a golden wall that was festooned with old paintings in old frames.

A door was opened, and we faced a room of blue, gold, and ivory, a great dark table, and Alexei with a pretty young woman with big eyes.

Seeing us enter, Alexei rose, seemed to cross the room without moving.

"Iris," he said. "Right on time."

He embraced her, kissed her cheeks. Then he clapped me on the shoulder, just the barest brush, but which would surely bruise me in the morning, almost knocked me over.

"And you, Boy," he said. "Come, sit. This is Oksana. She is my girl the way you are Iris's boy."

The table had thick candles on it, ivory, in golden candlesticks.

It would be only the four of us, it seemed, as Alexei took his place at the head of the table, Iris took hers at the other end, and I took my place opposite Oksana, who looked me over silently for a moment. I could smell her perfume from across the table, dizzingly strong.

She had sandy blonde hair and very large, very pale blue eyes, a strong nose, and broad, full lips. Her cheekbones were high and lent an impudent gracefulness to her bearing, although there was a hardness to her angel's eyes, too. She had worn a red dress and gold jewelry, and had not looked once at Iris.

I was acutely aware of being the only American in the room—never mind that Alexei and Iris had long since transcended nationality; their origins remained, and Oksana was apparently full Russian, herself.

"So, you are The Kid," Oksana said, in thickly accented English.

"The Kid?"

"He's mine, yes," Iris said.

Waiters in blue and white livery whisked into the room, filling our tiny glasses with vodka. Alexei gestured, nodded, and the glasses were held aloft.

I watched the vampires pretend to drink, while Oksana and I made our toasts and drank the stuff. I wasn't a big fan of vodka, personally. Alexei and Iris looked at one another from across the table, and, in that moment, I felt I was enmeshed in some bizarre, vampiric power game.

Soup was brought out, a mushroom broth for Oksana and me, and borscht for Alexei and Iris, which was ironic, since the borscht looked like bowls of blood, and, yet, neither of them would take a sip of it.

"Eat," Alexei said. "This feast for you, Children."

Iris gave the faintest guiding motion with her eyes, toward the soup, toward me. I could practically hear her chiding me about not embarrassing her. Pale as she was, having not fed, her eyes stood out all the more.

I tried the soup, and it was heavenly—rich with the savory flavor of several types of mushrooms within it. I wished for bread to sop it up with, since that was what I liked to do when I ate soup. A dark loaf of bread was brought out, set between Oksana and me, and I tore off a piece and dipped it at once, which seemed to amuse Alexei, who watched without comment.

Oksana spoke to me. "Alexei was not happy with you, Nathaniel."

"Nate," I said. "Just Nate."

She nodded. "He would know if you were jealous type."

"I suppose I am," I said.

Oksana leaned forward and nodded in Alexei's direction. "Aren't we all?"

"Why are we here tonight, Alexei?" Iris asked.

Alexei smiled at Iris, and it was an odd thing, seeing his ancient face break into that private, almost shy smile.

"I wanted to see you," Alexei said. "We wanted to see you."

"We?"

Alexei nodded to Oksana.

"I'm hungry, Alexei," Iris said. "Your summons came at an inopportune moment; and you told me not to feed."

"You are fasting," Alexei said. "We are fasting. It has been too long since we last controlled our appetites, yes?"

"What is the point?" Iris asked.

I finished the soup quicker than I thought I would, and the waiters came by and took the bowls, replaced them with some kind of meat dumplings. I followed Oksana's lead, cut mine in half, took a bite. It was delicious, subtly seasoned beef.

"Alexei will make me one day," Oksana said. "He has promised."

"How old are you?"

"25 years," Oksana said. "You?"

"29," I said.

"Old man," Oksana said with a smile. "Alexei said I should have full flower of womanhood at 28; he waits, will give me the gift in three years. You?"

I shook my head. "She won't make me."

Oksana play-pouted. "She not love you, Nate."

"And you think he loves you?" I asked, nodding to Alexei.

Oksana looked at Alexei with love-lust in her eyes, as clear as I'd ever seen it in a person, although it was an odd, hard love to my American eyes, a Russian love—mysterious, opportunistic, enigmatic, pragmatic, ruthless—it was a type of love I had not known, would never know.

"You think he really will make you?" I asked. "That he's not simply promising that to you as a way of stringing you along?"

"He will," Oksana said. "I trust him."

I looked over at Iris, who was enmeshed in conversation with Alexei at that moment in another language that sounded like Italian, but could have been something else.

"*Non voglio morire di fame,*" Iris said. "*Che sconfigge il punto di noi, Alexei.*"

"*Dobbiamo controllare i nostri appetiti, Iris,*" Alexei said. "*O dobbiamo essere schiavi di loro. Vuoi essere uno schiavo ai vostri appetiti?*"

Alexei nodded to us, watching us eat, as if what we were doing was somehow beneath him. I enjoyed food, liked to eat. I wondered how that felt to the vampires, that inability to eat actual food, having to subsist on blood. Maybe they felt the ecstasy of the feeding that we, the victims, felt; maybe it was all that they needed. And yet, to me, to have that same blood meal throughout eternity, that same blood price in the lives of victims—it seemed like its own kind of hell to me.

"You trust him?" I asked, as the waiters brought another course, an appetizer plate filled with lox and olives and piles of little pickles and another plate with some toasted triangles of black bread circling three tubs of caviar: one black, one red, one gold. Oksana dove right into that, smearing the gold onto one of the toast points.

"I do," Oksana said. "He is a kind and gentle master. Yours, not so much?"

I watched her eat the caviar, followed her lead. I'd never had caviar before, found the creamy, salty-savory-fishy taste of it almost overpowering, and yet, I was hungry, so I ate.

Iris looked at me from her position down the table from me, breathlessly pale, clearly ravenous, but unwilling to give Alexei the satisfaction of breaking, it would seem.

"Uh, she's great," I said, perhaps too quickly, as I saw Oksana smile to herself. No doubt she knew better. I wondered how Alexei managed his relationship with Oksana—were they lovers? It seemed to me that Alexei only had eyes, in truth, for Iris. But maybe there was something for Oksana in his withered heart.

"You like, Kid?" Alexei asked. "Eat, eat. Do not stop. This is feast."

"Very yummy," I said, which apparently delighted Alexei, who clapped his hands and laughed uproariously.

"Yummy," Alexei said. "Such an American word, childish music. Yummy. Is it yummy, Oksana?"

Oksana smiled at Alexei. "It is delicious, Master."

Iris looked at me, not at them, and gave me the faintest, most wry of smiles.

"We are to be the entertainment of this evening, Nate," Iris said.

"Yes," Alexei said. "Yes, indeed. Yummy."

I could not guess Alexei's game, could not understand where his head was at, but I wondered if this was something routine for Iris, enduring these sitdowns with Alexei.

"You'd really want to be one of them?" I said to Oksana.

"Don't we all?" Oksana asked. "To be 28 forever, in my full womanly radiance, for all time. Your mistress, he made her young. You can see, yes? Her unformed beauty. Beauty, yes, but the beauty of a girl intersecting with that of a woman, an uncertain crossroads, a kind of ambivalence, roads not completely traversed and roads not yet taken."

Iris did not like being appraised by Oksana, I could see, but held her tongue out of respect and perhaps even fear of Alexei, who watched it all through steepled fingers.

"It was different then," Alexei said. "Uncertainty abounded. I could not risk losing Iris, having seen her, having loved her."

The mere mention of it was embarrassing Iris, I could tell. I knew her, could read the signs on her face, as mask-like as she tried to make it.

"In Venice, it was a different world. Plagues seemed to hit that fair city every other year," Alexei said. "All those canals, all the rats. It was the rats, you know now, but back then, no one knew. I only knew that I did not want her to die, could not risk losing her. I gave her the gift in haste, perhaps, but without hesitation or regret. She would be safe, my Little Flower."

I noticed how Alexei spoke more eloquently, his broken Slavic-English disappearing as he recounted his past with Iris. I could only guess what odd game he played with her.

"I'm sure they don't want to hear about that, Alexei," Iris said.

"You see?" Oksana said. "How like a girl she is? The petulance? The pouting? He captured her in that moment, the young courtesan. A pressed flower for his collection. He waits for me, three more years, that I may fully become who I am."

To be so deliberate in that decision as alien and unfamiliar to me, that Oksana was, apparently, at peace with it. It spoke of a strange intimacy between them, a pact, perhaps, and one that he would as likely as not make good on.

It was a contrast to what I had with Iris, which was really more of nothing at all, in truth. It was service.

The waiters brought in Chicken Kiev, put the plates in front of us. I was already starting to feel full, but Alexei insisted that we fill our faces, while he and Iris looked on, pale as ghosts. The waiters did not react to this, were clearly well-trained, understood what was expected of them.

"And what are you, Oksana?" Iris asked. "If not a maidservant?"

"I am his lover," Oksana said. "I am the Master's chosen."

She said it with such pride, with a glint in her eye as she gazed boldly, fearlessly at Iris. I could sense this power, this confidence in her safety in the company of her master. This impudent young woman, who, alone in the city, the country, even the world, who had nothing to fear from Iris. I had never seen such a thing.

"You think you are the first," Iris said. "They always do. Have you told her about your others, Alexei?"

Alexei just smiled, unfazed, untouched by it. It was an old score between them, never settled.

"I was his masterpiece," Iris said. "He has never made one to equal, let alone exceed me. You are no exception, sweet Oksana. How many has it been, Alexei?"

"Who can say?" Alexei said. "Math not my strong suit."

"Nate is good at math," Iris said. "Aren't you, Nate?"

"I'm alright," I said, around a mouthful of the delicious Chicken Kiev.

"Alexei is over a thousand years old, Nate," Iris said. "He's tried to recreate me, I don't know, 50 times. He's had 50 brides in his lifetime. You, Oksana, will be the 51st bride of Alexei. Does that make you feel special?"

"He saves best for last," Oksana said, without missing a beat.

Iris smiled the coldest smile I'd ever seen her make. "We all thought that, you know. Even I, his crowning achievement, even I am not so vain as to think that I was his first, you know. He was 500 years old before our paths crossed. I was not his first."

"No," Alexei said. "True enough. What can I say? I am in love with beauty. I love it. Oksana, she is beautiful, yes?"

Iris wrinkled her nose. "In a rather Slavic sort of way, I suppose."

"Slavic women most beautiful in world," Alexei said. "The cheekbones, the eyes—both in terms of size, and shape, and color, the delicacy of the chin, the exquisite coloration of the hair. I would say if you took most beautiful women in world, line them up, the Slavic woman will prevail."

"Italian women," Iris said, but Alexei stopped her before she could say more.

"No," Alexei said. "Italian girls. The beauty of the Italian woman peaks by 20 years of age. It is true. An Italian woman from, say, 17 years of age to 20, is exquisite. There is no doubt of this. But Italian women, like a breed of racehorse that runs itself too hard, too early in the race, run themselves out prematurely. Rare is the Italian woman who can escape this fate. It's not that they are not beautiful; but a hardness creeps into the features of the Italian woman that is not there in their fullest flower of young beauty. The babyfat, if you will, softens the Italianate hardness that invariably comes. Italian women are made of marble. Iris is fortunate that I caught her when I did, before the hardness laid full claim to her."

It was an observation only someone like Alexei could make, because, to me, Iris always seemed hard, but I felt this was just a result of her great age.

"The hardness of life etches itself into the countenances of Italian women," Alexei said. "It is inevitable."

"It's called maturity," Iris said.

"No," Alexei said. "It is something other than that. I have seen and I have known. You, my sweet, I saved from that fate. You are preserved intact, and retain that singular beauty. Even if you'd been spared the plagues, had I waited even five years for you, you would have been gone, your beauty would have already flown. A Venetian dowager, a casualty to culture. But we digress."

Still more food was brought out, this time, a roast pheasant, which was served to us with scalded potatoes. Oksana again dug in, and I found myself following her lead.

"The Slavic woman is the eternal beauty," Alexei said. "They carry it with them over time, a long, luxurious ride as they come into their own, traveling in a kind of gilded carriage. In this day and age, where the ravages of smallpox are unknown, where death and war and disease are not visited daily upon them, the Slavic woman enjoys her long ride."

"I think of them as blunt objects," Iris said. "What of French women?"

"French women are hard from the outset," Alexei said. "They have a Gallic beauty that is all their own, but they enter into this world hard, and leave it harder. They enjoy themselves in spite of this hardness, but the French woman's beauty is a proud and courtly thing, not a delicate or dainty thing. French women are delightful creatures, but they are not Slavic women."

"And the Spanish?" Iris asked.

"No," Alexei said, with a wave of his hand. "I do not like them. I see them and see their Celtic forebears. I cannot see them without seeing the lost legacy of Rome, in truth. They were always the thorn in the side of the Empire, the Celtiberians—contentious, fractious, proud. No. They aspire to what the Slavic woman carries so easily, but they are pretenders to the throne."

Oksana smiled, raised her tiny glass of vodka in a toast to Alexei.

"To beauty," she said, nodded for me to raise my glass. I did, in turn.

"To beauty," I said. And we both drank. Waiters filled our little cups again.

"What of Arab women, Alexei? African women? Persian women? Indian women? Chinese women?" Iris asked. "All of them are prettier than your beloved Slavs."

"Voluptuous," Alexei said. "Radiant creatures, to be sure, but they lack the delicacy of Slavic beauty. They come from sunlit places, and I am Rus. And I am vampire. I know what I know, because I have seen it. I do not deny that there is beauty around this tiny world; I only say that, pound for pound and ounce for ounce, the greatest share of beautiful women—truly beautiful women as women—are the Slavic women."

"Sounds like selection bias to me," I said, holding up my cup of vodka. "To selection bias."

I downed the shot, feeling the vodka shoot through me. Oksana joined in on my toast, laughing, while Alexei looked me over.

"Beauty is in eye of beholder, yes? That is the cliché? Beauty is symmetry. Therein lies its magic. Slavic symmetry surpasses all others. Clean lines, drawn with the most delicate of touches. Even with trace of cruelty, which makes the angel's kiss of loveliness all the more precious, the bitter with the sweet."

Oksana toasted again, seemed determined to drink me under the table.

"To the bitter and to the sweet," she said, pounding down that shot. I matched her, now feeling drunk, myself. The waiters, like wraiths, appeared and filled our glasses. More food was brought out, a steak tartar, filling my nostrils with the pungent scent of it.

"*Elle est un enfant,*" Iris said. "*Vous vous leurrez pas nouveau, Alexei. Elle n'est pas moi. Elle ne sera pas moi. Elle ne sera jamais moi.*"

"I don't want to be you," Oksana said. "I don't even look like you."

"*I vy nikogda ne budete,*" Iris said. "*On lyubit tol'ko menya. Vy prosto napominaniye o tom, chto on ne mozhet imet'.*"

"*YA yego lyubvi,*" Oksana said. "*I on moy.*"

Iris just smiled, her fangs evident. The hunger was doing this to her, making her bestial. Indeed, boozy as I was, I could see Iris's beautiful mask slipping before this contest of wills between her and her sire, could see the monster emerging, the orange rimming her eyes, her ears lengthening, emerging from the black confines of her head in diabolical points. And the teeth, growing more evident.

"*Eithaf y gymysgedd gennych y tro hwn, Alexei,*" Iris said.

"*Ona ne voskhititel'nymi?*" Alexei said. "*YA znal, chto vam ponravit-sya yeye.*"

It was irking me, all of these foreign languages bouncing around. I assumed Oksana and Alexei were slinging Russian, thought I'd caught a whiff of French, had no idea what Iris had just slung at Alexei.

"You guys are so rude," I said. "Talking around me like I'm not even here."

"We're not talking about you, don't worry, Nate," Iris said.

"Iris is jealous," Oksana said. "She does not approve of me."

Alexei, for his part, looked the same, only pale. Such willpower, such reserve he possessed. He was making some kind of point with Iris, forcing her to sit in this way with him, while Oksana and I feasted.

"Try the steak, *Rebenok*," Alexei said. "It's 'yummy,' rest assured."

The steak was delicious, and I was embarrassed to say I was shoveling it in my mouth, while Oksana continued to match me, bite for bite and drink for drink, her beautiful eyes on me in this hard and challenging gaze.

I was getting wasted, for sure, which got my tongue wagging. "You know, for all of your accumulated years and experience, you vampires are the past, not the future."

"Do tell," Alexei said. "Enlighten me, *Rebenok.*"

"Cybernetics is the future of mankind," I said. "Not vampirism. Oh, sure, there's the ongoing vampirism of, say, late- or postindustrial capitalism, for sure, but the real human future is with the machine, not with the macabre. Man will inevitably merge with the machine. It's happening already, in its infant stages. But let's fast-forward a century, or, better yet, a millennium. You'll still be here, let's say, but what will people be? Cyborgs. People will be halfway to becoming machines, with casting aside their physical bodies in favor of machine parts that can be rebuilt and renewed and restored."

I took a swig of vodka, and my glass was refilled at once.

"Go on," Alexei said. Iris watched, ghost-like, her eyes on the waiters. She was ravenous.

"People will want this, the certainty of experience," I said. "To become machines is the way to immortality for those of us who are not you. In time, the parts that were human will wear out and be replaced, until, eventually, we will be completely machines. I can't say how long it will take, but the funny thing is that you guys will still be here to see this. And then you'll see that your meal ticket has left. Can you imagine that, being a vampire in a world of cyborgs? What an anachronism you'll be, standing there, undead flesh and blood, in a world of chrome and neon, thirsting for blood the way Iris is over there, but without a soul to feed upon."

Alexei considered it quietly, thoughtfully, nodding, and I took that to mean that I could continue, and I ran with it.

"Immortality you have, for now," I said. "But you must depend on your blood supply to ensure continuity. There is a cure for vampirism: no blood, no vampires. Unless you somehow change your menu, and drink something other than human blood. So, if I were you guys, I would be very focused on my supply chain, because without it, you're nothing. But that's exactly the problem, isn't it? Let's say we're in this hypothetical future, and you've got your human livestock—maybe you blow enough vampire smoke their way and convince these 'natural people,' the ones who refuse to be cyborgs, to continue to live and die the old way, the useful way to you. They'll be a minority, an odd, obsolete kind of humanity in the face of the emergent, metahuman cyborg majority. They'll be like the Amish are today, I imagine. And there won't be enough of them to feed you. So, then what do you do? Feed on each other, I suppose? The strong vampires preying on the weak, until you're down to the Last Vampire. What a sight that will be, yes? The last bloodsucker in a world of chrome and steel. A vestige."

Alexei smiled at this. "You are more thoughtful than I imagined, *Rebenok.*"

"I understand what you guys are," I said. "You're parasites, at heart. So, you'll either have to work like hell to prevent that cybernetic future from happening, to ensure a place at the table for you, or you will have to either transcend your hunger or change your diet to accommodate the new food. But there's hardly any romance in that, is there? Drinking lubricant or some kind of synaptic fluid instead of the bountiful blood you enjoy right now? One way or another, Man's on the way out—we'll either become extinct, or we'll evolve into cyborgs, and, eventually, inevitably, machines."

"You overestimate the appeal of the machine, Nate," Iris said. "Nobody will voluntarily become one."

"It's piecemeal," I said. "A gradual thing. An arm, here, a leg, there, a heart here. Over time, it will improve, and people, by their very natures, will want to live. If a new part enables them to do it, so much the better."

"There is another way," Alexei said. "We could encourage genetic research, improve the human species organically, so that your mechanical evolution-revolution does not occur. Create a better species of humanity."

"Ah," I said, full of vodka and scalded potatoes. "Better breeding for your livestock? That will appeal to some, but not to all. Biology is wonderful and miraculous, but technology is still going to be there, and the drive will remain. Over time, your prey population will diminish. If you take two sets of people, one of whom grows old and dies, the other which can continue indefinitely, who wins?"

"What about us, Nate?" Iris said. "Vampires have always been outnumbered by mortals."

"Historically, yes," I said. "But technology changes everything. It alters the equation. We'll end up with multiple species of humanity on the planet again—*Homo sapiens, Homo superior, Homo vampiricus, Homo cyberneticus*—then things will get very interesting. My money is on the cyborgs crowding you out and the other three variants going extinct. And that's just thinking about it in terms of competitive advantage, not throwing in actual volition and deliberate extermination. See, the first two will be parasitized by you, and the fourth will have nothing to fear from you, and will take advantage of your weakening the other two to do away with all three. Maybe it'll even be a situation where Sapiens wants to be able to compete with Superior and Cyberneticus, and so joins Cyberneticus. Superior will not be content to be livestock to you, and will see itself as having to either join Cyberneticus or die out on their own terms. And that will leave you starving, with sleepless man-machines hunting you down, doing away with you once and for all."

Alexei clapped his hands together. "Marvelous! You are most entertaining, *Rebenok*. Let's play your game a little, yes? Vampiricus—I love that conception, incidentally—we own majority of wealth in world. We are the keepers of Capital. Our immortality gives us this natural competitive advantage. Corporations, which we created, continue to function as intended, continue to draw wealth from world, to line our pockets. With this abundant capital, we drive progress. Your evolutionary nightmare fades, because we captains of corporate industry do not want it to happen, will not fund the emergent technologies that would encourage cybernetics to evolve. We encourage, say, biotechnology as an alternative approach, using genes instead of machines."

"It means that you end up handicapping our future for your own ends," I said.

"Whatever it takes," Iris said. "We won't allow ourselves to go extinct, Nate. There's simply too much at stake, where we're concerned. If choice is extinction or continuation of the species, then the choice is simple. We will not permit your technological terror from destroying the world as we know it. We won't come out and say this, won't reveal ourselves—rather, it will be something like how it is with solar or wind power these days. How it's always a technology that's just around the corner, the promise of the future, forever out of reach. We're like Big Oil in that regard—we can buy up the patents, shelve them, ensure that the only change that comes is the change that we want to bring about, the change that is advantageous to us. We're doing it already, Nate; we've been doing it for centuries."

"*YA khochu dyuyma,*" Oksana said. "*Alexei, ne zastavlyay menya zhdat'.*"

"Heaven help us from the vampire capitalists," I said. "The ultimate redundancy, the deadest of dead ends."

"You speak of the future as if anything were possible," Alexei said. "But what is possible is only what we permit to exist. That is difference. There will be no bloodless coup. We will not permit it to happen."

"We've been working for generations to help make people dumber, Nate," Iris said. "It just helps. It makes things easier for us, in the long run."

"No," I said, banging a hand on the table, which make Oksana giggle and caused the vampires to stop and look at me a moment. "You have a vested interest in our future as a species. Let's say your Human Stupefaction Plan works, and you've created the perfect human livestock—biological, dumb, pliable. Perfect walking blood banks to fuel your appetites and your immortality. But what does that mean for Vampiricus? You just stay here on the Earth, tending your human herds like shepherds until the Sun dies, and the world is destroyed?"

"That is long way away," Alexei said.

"True, but you'll still be here," I said. "You have to think about the future, and where you will be. And, for all of your capital assets and immortality, you will need Man to advance as a species so that you can advance with him and parasitize him. If you go the Iris route and turn us into livestock, then you're stuck here, on this planet, in this bloody, rustic backwater place. But to have a future, a real future that is meaningful, you should be encouraging us as a species to advance, so that we can get into space, so you can hitch rides with us to other planets, in time. The way to expand your stock of prey is to give us more habitats, rather than keeping us penned on this world. And that means technological advancements. See what I'm saying? You're hamstrung, either way, and, eventually, Cyberneticus wins."

Alexei smiled again, while waiters cleared the plates and brought out coffee and desserts.

"You bring up interesting point," Alexei said.

"Iris always thinks of you as a predator species," I said. "But you are, in truth, parasites, dependent, in a fashion, on the well-being of your hosts. If you are too efficient a predator, you become extinct. If you are too rapacious a parasite, you become extinct. You must work *with* Man to ensure your own survival."

I could see him thinking about it, working it out in his head.

"He is smart *mal'chik*, Iris," Alexei said. "Not so much the dullard as you imply."

Oksana was clearly peevish that I was getting attention from Alexei.

"I embrace Vampiricus," Oksana said. "The future."

"Vampiricus is the past," I said. "Everything about you speaks to the past. Certainly, the immortality gives you an endless hypothetical future, but the richness of your experience lies in the past. Alexei, who is the oldest vampire that you know?"

Alexei looked at me furtively, as if he was unwilling to reveal such secrets. "What is your point?"

"They are rooted entirely in their past," I said. "Yes, they may walk inexorably into the future, but there is still that length of chain forged in where they came from, who they were, and the long experience of the years. That chain is a heavy weight to bear."

"We bear it well enough," Iris said. "We are strong enough to do so."

"And you don't evolve," I said, draining the vodka again, only to have the cup refilled again by the ever-present waiters.

"We grow stronger," Iris said. "As we age, we become more powerful."

"But you don't change," I said. "Alexei is the same Alexei he always was, right? You're the same, Iris. If anything, the power that you gain makes you even less prone to change than ever, less likely to evolve. Because you don't have to. The power insulates you as surely as the immortality. No capacity, inclination, or requirement to change for vampires is a sure recipe for stagnation."

Oksana looked at Alexei for comment, while Iris's nails had become claws, as her hunger was increasingly apparent.

I ate some cranberries that were in balls of white powdered sugar. They looked like blood on the snow, were delicious—a very Russian blend of the bitter and the sweet.

"It's probably why you guys meddle with folks like Oksana and me," I said, around mouthfuls of the sweet. "You try to rekindle the dying embers within you, bring life back to those corpse bodies you have."

Alexei smiled, banished the waiters from the room with a snap of his fingers. "You have been more entertaining than I thought you would be, *Mal'chik*. You have given me things to think about. Now it is time for us to feed."

He nodded to Iris, who became a blur, appeared by my side, and grabbed me, spearing my neck with her teeth, drinking from me before I could even say another word. I could see Alexei with Oksana, feeding on her across the table, Oksana crying out, grabbing for him, while he pinned her arms at her sides and drank from her. The two of us, prey and protectors for our vampire masters, as the ecstasy of the moment overtook me.

Iris did not drink me down, not entirely. She left enough so that I could live, although I just about fainted, and Alexei picked Oksana up, her arm dangling limply.

Their color had returned, and Iris was able to appear more composed again, with me coursing through her.

"*È stata una serata più piacevole, Amato,*" Alexei said.

"*Ne pense rien de lui,*" Iris said. "*Tu sais que je vais.*"

I passed out, a velvet curtain claiming me.

-X-

I awoke to have Iris hovering over me, creepily, staring at me with unblinking eyes that betrayed not a lick of love, but only the mute, almost arachnid appraisal that filled me with dread.

"Do you have any idea how lucky you are not to be dead, Nate?" Iris asked.

I looked around, thirsty, weak. We were at her place. She'd put me on my bed. What a sight that would be, tiny Iris effortlessly carrying my tall self, dropping me on the bed. I would have loved to have seen it.

"Did I embarrass you?"

"No," Iris said. "You were you."

It was one of those Iris things that could have meant anything. She marinated herself in mystery.

"Alexei likes you, despite yourself," Iris said. "And Oksana is not used to being upstaged. Frankly, I rather liked that. I am sick to death of that little pet princess he has."

"He's going to make her," I said.

"I know," Iris said. "He's done that so many times. Alexei's a man. He falls for his little toys and promises them the world, gives them the gift and, eventually, tires of them, or they of him, and he goes on his merry way. Another century from now, there'll be another Oksana."

"Or another Iris," I said. I had to get water, was terribly thirsty.

"There will never be another Iris," she said. She was pink and warm, so I know that she had fed while I was unconscious. "There is nobody like me."

"Why do you go to those things, then?"

"Because I must," Iris said. "When Alexei gives a summons, I must attend."

"He loves you," I said. "It's very clear."

Talking about it obviously made Iris uncomfortable, because she did something she never did—she waited on me. In a blur, she vanished, only to reappear with a pitcher of icewater.

"You're thirsty, Darling," she said. "Drink."

I upended the pitcher, drank every drop.

"Alexei only remembers love," Iris said. "I think he makes his brides as an homage to that. You're right, in a sense, about him being rooted to the past like that. Alexei lives and breathes his past. He is the past. He is my past, too, of course. He tries to teach me lessons."

"Unlife lessons," I said, sucking on some ice cubes.

"Yes," she said. "He still thinks of me as his child bride. But that was such a long time ago, and I am far from that little courtesan he knew in Venice, just as this world is far from that place. Do you recall what you'd said during the dinner? Or were you too drunk?"

I remembered. One of my gifts was the ability to recall everything pretty well, whether drunk or sober.

"Yes, I remember," I said.

"I'm not going to be extinct," Iris said. "We live in a galaxy with at least 100 to 400 billion planets, 17 billion of them roughly the size of this one. Perhaps a fraction of them habitable in a way that you could imagine. And there are anywhere from 80 to 100 billion or more galaxies in the universe that we can see. So, how many planets are there, Nate?"

I did the math in my head.

"At least 10^{24} planets," I said. "That's a lot of damned planets."

"I want to see this world die. I want to stand on the last planet as the last star in the last galaxy dies. Can you even imagine that, Nate? All of those planets out there, all of those stars, one by one, dying out, fading away into oblivion. But I'd still be here. I'll see it. I'll see the night sky fade into everlasting black as those stars die, and I'll be on that last planet, with the last souls that had fled the dying universe, and I'll be there, feeding on the last of them. Who knows what I will be in such a distant time? Can you even imagine it?"

I admit that I couldn't, could not imagine Iris in that place, that distant time.

"I can't," I said. "It's beyond me."

"And I will have you to thank for it," she said. "As odd as that seems. You and your nonsense blathering at Kiosk. I want to survive. I want to leave this planet behind and travel to other places. If humanity fails to expand to other worlds, I want to be sure that we—vampires—do. You're right, you know: we do get stuck in our past. But I imagine these intergenerational starships, filled with crew, sustainable, and at the center of these ships, their vampire masters. We have all the time in the world—you are right about that. So, we create these ships, arks, after a fashion, seeded with a vampire at the heart of it, attended by their livestock crew, who are bound to serve their masters, and these ships travel through space to find other worlds. I see these ships scattering from the Earth like dandelion seeds. How marvelous is that?"

"Uh, it sounds terrible," I said, regretting that I'd put any kind of idea in Iris's head at all, let alone one as bad as this one.

"The ships can travel as slowly as they need to be, because, as you've said, we have all the time we need. The crew can live their whole lives on the ships. Generations, even. Until we find new worlds to lay claim to. It's an open question whether the crew actually knows their purpose. I would wrap it up in the nobility of exploration, without the hard truth of it being apparent to the crew. I mean, one would not want to be stuck on a ship with vampire hunters. You were right—there was a failure of imagination on my part. I will put money from the Augenblick Foundation to work on space exploration, while the true purpose will be creating the vessels I have described. Creating sustainable bioships that can contain us safely. And best of all, we can operate within them with impunity, protected from the sun by the ship, itself. A vampiric diaspora. And all because of you, Nate."

Oh, shit.

I could see her thinking about it, her undead imagination fired up at the prospect. Planets to colonize, lives to take. An intergalactic vampire empire, with them pulling the strings, behind the scenes, as ever, above and beyond it. An endless quest, immortal, irrevocable. Once the mechanism was in place, repeating it over and over again, finding new worlds, colonizing, parasitizing them, and moving onward and outward, until there were no places left to conquer, no worlds or lives left to claim.

It was a monstrous vision, and with immortality as its engine, an unstoppable one. With immortals, it wasn't a matter of if; it was a matter of when. All would resolve itself in the fullness of time. That was how the vampire got you. It was their ability to play to the long-term, to see the distant horizons, and know that, barring accident or injury, they would live to see it through. How many things on our own world had been undertaken at the whim of vampires? One could only guess, but they could move mountains with their capital and their long-range planning, and their complete indifference to morality and mortality.

"I will remember you, Nate," Iris said. "I'll promise you that, as well: when I am on that distant world, billions of years from now, powerful beyond measure, a goddess who may even have transcended her monumental thirst, I will remember you, will remember this moment we shared, when you actually inspired me to become more than what

I am. I know it's ironic—you? Inspire me? But you have, and you did, and I will remember it. Even when this planet is burned to a cinder by the dying Sun, when humanity itself is a long-forgotten dream, I will remember you."

"Wow," I said. "Yeah, see, that doesn't make me feel better."

"I know," Iris said, stroking my cheek with her momentarily-warm hand. "I know, Nate."

She vanished in a mist, floated out of sight just minutes before dawn, leaving me to face a bloody sunrise that lit overhanging clouds, turning them shades of magenta, orange, and gold, as night gave way to day.

For now, anyway, life would go on.

CHAPTER 12

Having made enough inquiries of Iris about her past sometimes led to her just talking to me about it out of the blue, because, I was sure, how could I not find everything about her as fascinating as she found herself?

"It was easier back then," Iris said. "Not the travel part; that was always a challenge, and you had to be so careful, just because people knew about vampires back then. But there was so much room in America. And people kept coming. When the emigrations to this country were in full swing, that was a great time for vampirism."

Now, with most people, you'd just have to wait and they'd keep going, but Iris would just fall silent, still as a statue, so I'd have to sound her out, keep her going.

"And?"

"And nothing," Iris said. "It was a great time. God, the Puritans...."

And she chuckled to herself, shaking her head.

"What about them?" I asked.

"They were something," she said.

"You knew them?" I asked.

Iris shrugged. "I wasn't on the Mayflower, in case you were paying attention. And I missed the Salem Witch Trials, sadly. When I first arrived, mostly, I just kept to myself and let my husband tend land for me and, well, you know, take in lodgers. I had to be very careful, not let people know about me. I had left Europe because I'd gotten tired of the competition, of the wars. Wars are almost too good for vampirism—you end up with too many other vampires, everybody chasing the same prey. I went to the New World for a fresh start, away from Alexei, who was busy fighting in the Seven Years' War. I'd been content to settle in Boston, but the Great Fire that spring had me fleeing to Philadelphia."

It was weird, thinking that so much history had passed before Iris's eyes, and how unfazed by it she really was.

"Did you see the Founding Fathers?" I asked.

"Of course," she said. "Hamilton was a martinet. He was so painfully aware of his origins, he was always trying to compensate for them. I never met any of them. Your country knows nothing of itself, Nate. No proper suffering. Sure, there is suffering, but those oceans inoculated you against history, and you were blind to the agony of your slaves, to the slaughter of the Indians. It's still true. That's why it's such fertile ground for us. Nobody notices or even gives a damn, and even if they do, they don't necessarily know what to do. It's so easy here. Your nation was founded in blood, so it's only natural that a vampire should welcome it as a hunting ground."

She came over and sat next to me, rested a cold arm on me, looked into my eyes. Back then, I'd happily gaze into her eyes, lose myself in those sparkling things. I am convinced that I was able to do her dirty work for so long on account of those eyes, which would consume me and claim me, put me in that euphoric and forgetful state. I imagined myself in a courtroom, trying to recount my crimes, and just drawing an affable blank.

That would be from her eyes, her sepulchral stare.

I glanced at the clock on my computer. She'd be up soon. I'd have to find her. She'd be plenty pissed about me ditching her last night. I had combed through the building so many times. I went back to the basement, flashlight in hand, searching. The basement was where she kept most of her stuff, the accumulations of the centuries.

The basement was a museum unto itself, and it killed me that she kept nearly everything she had left down there, that whoever had been her minion before me (I'm only assuming it was the guy before me, Mr. Bighands) had moved her stuff into this basement. There were paintings of her through the centuries. I lined them up in a row. Those indigo eyes of hers gazing darkly from the canvas. There were 14 portraits, with the last one appearing to have been done around 1928.

It haunted me to see some of the greatest painters of all time taking brush and paint to Iris. It's difficult to adequately convey the horror this series invoked, but I'll try to explain it, anyway.

First, there was the obvious thing, which is that these men, over a span of over 400 years, all painted Iris. To see the same woman through the eyes of 14 master painters, themselves likely unaware of exactly who they were painting per se—I could only assume that they did not know what she was. There was this. Each painting was ineluctably Iris.

Second, there was the vanity of it, that she had so enjoyed herself as to hire or conspire to hire the hands of 14 masters to render her. Any one of the portraits on their own was of unfathomable value—she should have been honored to have any one of them paint her. But to have all of them do so? And always a portrait, a remembrance of herself.

Third, there was something else, the arrogance and hubris of the project, in that Iris considered herself worthy of so many portraits from so many great painters, that she was such a great subject as the warrant this treatment. I found that particularly repellant, because I felt I knew Iris more than most, and I could say that while she was beautiful, she was only Iris.

Fourth, there was the effortless presumption of it—either with Alexei's money or her own, Iris indulging her whim by commissioning works of herself as she traveled the world, completely free, rich beyond measure, able to enjoy the fruits of her monstrosity with patronage as she traveled the world without care or concern. I suppose I envied her that.

Finally, there was the horror of these masterpieces sitting in her basement, unseen by the world, that she had this magnificent private collection of paintings that was easily worth hundreds of millions of dollars, and they simply sat in her basement, unseen by anyone, even by Iris, herself. There was a dreadful diminishment in that act that was so very Iris.

Iris was not an artist. She was not artistic. No doubt she had pretensions of herself as being artistic, but there was, despite her training as a courtesan (which may have allowed her to speak to the pleasures of art, itself), an artlessness to Iris that set my teeth on edge. I was not an artist, myself, but I still took umbrage at Iris and her posturing in a way that I could not fully articulate. Being able to pay a great painter to paint you did not ennoble you, the subject. In my view, Iris should have paid the artists extra for the privilege of having them paint her. Frankly, I don't even know how they were able to look into her eyes and not stand insensate before a blank canvas. Or maybe Iris reined in her mesmerizing gaze in those moments, so that the painters could accomplish the task she had set to them.

I hated her all the more for it, as I gazed at the paintings, lined up by year.

There was a portrait of her by Titian, circa 1513. That was the oldest, her done up in her Venetian finery, a beautiful yellow-green gown, her breasts exposed, the very portrait of a young and beautiful courtesan— matchless, ageless, angelic harlot that she was. A newborn vampire, scarcely a year old, bright-eyed and lascivious and prideful in her bearing, like a young goddess, and her eyes captured perfectly with pigment, that blend of luminescent darkness, the indigo and the black conspiring to entrance and seduce as she perches on a bed.

There was a sketch of her by DaVinci from 1515. Incredible, but true—he captured her in action, gazing at him, a fan in her hand, the detail on her face and a hint of her clothing, a beautiful gown. A great deal of attention paid to her hand holding the fan, an almost clinical eye. Her look is impish, almost playful, and conveys an emotion I'd not known from Iris, a sly flirtation. I can't know if it was actually there, or if DaVinci placed it there in spite of her. Her hair is down, lustrously rendered.

A Raphael from 1518. Gorgeous, sensuously decadent sits Iris in a gray gown, her Carnival mask in hand, resting across her breast. The richness of the technique creates a reality to her, her form made flesh, ready to walk from the canvas. Raphael may have had some inkling of who Iris was, for the painting had a darkness to it, a dark, dark green forming the background, almost consuming her.

A Dürer from 1523. Iris gazed out at me from the confines of a marble terrace, wearing a richly-detailed green gown, posed in a three-quarter position with her hands beautifully detailed, like a couple of white doves. Her expression was almost sternly sensual, a pillow beneath her and Venice visible through a window, at night, a distant dream.

A Tintoretto from 1563. This painting spoke of turmoil and upheaval, perhaps Iris saying farewell to Venice, or preparing to. There is a hectic dynamism to this portrait of her, a sense of preoccupation as she sits gazing out from a garlanded balcony, the moonlit banner of Alexei draped around her, a sword and pike nearby. Her look is preoccupied, inward-facing, and it appears that a storm is coming, a feeling of movement and wind, of breathlessness.

Those 16th century portraits reflected, to me, Iris in her vampiric youth: enamored of her immortality, fascinated by her own ageless beauty, and, perhaps, indulged by Alexei, who wanted to pamper, flatter, and please his courtesan princess.

A Caravaggio from 1606. One of the most fascinating of her portraits, for this one was rendered on a very dark field, with Iris erotically presented, her white skin absolutely luminous as she crouches beside an overturned basket of rotting fruit that is rendered with such detail, you can almost pick up the whiff of decay. But most shocking of all is Iris holding a rat in her hand, stroking it like it was a pet. Only the rat is dead, you can see, and Iris grins luridly, with bloodied lips. There are other rats in the shadows, just hints of them. It is monstrous and beautiful at once. He had captured her utterly.

A Rembrandt from 1641. Iris dressed in linen, the cloth textured and rippled, and, for whatever reason, Iris had not fed, and appeared nearly as pale as the ivory gown she wore. It could have been a bridal gown or a burial vestment. She sits at a table, beside a plate with a wedge of yellow cheese and some black olives, untouched, a silver utensil nearby. There is an empty bowl nearby. For whatever reason, there is sorrow in it, and Iris looks out from the canvas with a measureless gaze. It is an intimate and haunting portrait.

A Vermeer from 1659. It is Iris with a book, sitting in a chair. It is incredibly dark and intimate, a single candle offering some light that plays on her skin with the lustrous, vitreous treatment Vermeer was known for. She is wreathed in shadow, but her eyes are luminous, and there is an incredible stillness in the portrait. He may or may not have known this, but he has captured undeath perfectly—she is equidistant from life and death, animate and completely still.

The 17th century paintings reflected perhaps something else, the change in her, or the death of her—death in the sense of whatever it was that she had been in life had finally died by the time of the Vermeer. How long did it take a person to die, when they would not die?

I found no 18th century portraits, making me wonder what was going on with Iris, whether she'd moved beyond her casual vanity or was preoccupied with serving Alexei in his campaigns. The gap created a sense of transition between who she was, and what she would become.

A Goya from 1807. A semi-nude portrait of Iris, ivory-skinned, her eyes challenging from the canvas. She's wrapped herself in beads—a handful of green and gold beads wrapped around her wrist, calling to mind a rosary. She has a necklace of black beads twined around her neck, and the necklace plunges into her cleavage, which is only barely concealed by a sheer silk gown of chartreuse. Her hair is up, and there is something playful in her gaze.

A Delacroix from 1860. This one shows Iris in a graveyard, holding court before a group of ghouls, ghosts, and rats. She is dressed as Persephone, in a golden gown, and stands before a statue of Hades, himself, who is represented on a great tombstone. The rats form a kind of sea—they squirm and writhe on the ground, atop some of the graves. The ghouls stand around her, seven courtiers, looks of undead adoration in their eyes, their skin shades of blue and gray. The ghosts are supplicants, and there are nine of them. It is a strange painting, yet vibrant. I can only imagine Iris having Delacroix paint this scene for her, commissioning him to do it.

A Whistler from 1888. This one is a full-length portrait of Iris, beautifully rendered in her wearing a gown of red and black, a patterned thing of zigzags that pools at her bare feet. She's standing on a Persian rug. In her hand, almost as an afterthought, is her Venetian Carnival mask, the crescent moon face of it a bluish—white juxtaposition to the vibrant red and black on the dress. The background is a dusty yellow, almost amber color, and there can be seen some candles in the foreground. She is very pale for this portrait, has clearly not fed before it, and her eyes are luminous and piercing, though her expression is a mask as surely as the one she carries.

A Fantin-Latour from 1893. Iris sits at a table with a vase of white roses, hands resting on the table, near some flatware and a plate upon which sits a pomegranate and three oranges. A great goblet of blood-like wine sits close at hand, indeed, one of Iris's hands rests on the stem of the glass. She has fed in this one, it appears, for her color is rosy, although, despite her eternally youthful face, there is darkness in those eyes of hers, and age. She wears a great black hat on her head, adorned with a red plume, and wears a dress of black that has golden pinstripes that follow her contours. Just barely visible in the shot, to one side, beyond the vase of flowers, sits a skull, facing Iris. You almost don't see it, as it's resting amid a rumpled bit of tablecloth, as if it, and the vase of roses were something Iris swept aside to make room for the other things. Her gaze commands in the portrait, draws you to her. I have seen that look.

Her 19th century portraits told a different story, of Iris ascendant, establishing herself beyond the confines of her sire, as a vampire in her own right. There was something to that, a change from the pretty girl of those early portraits—the woman-thing portrayed by these painters was an undead empress, having learned to have her way with the world after three centuries.

A Modigliani from 1919. This was the only portrait of Iris where she wore her mask, and if I had not known it was her, I might not have known. She's reclining, nude, on an angular sofa, wearing her Carnival mask, which gazes coldly at me, that crescent moon, hints of indigo in the sinister eyeholes, the pursed lips of the smirking moon both haughty and wanton. Her body is drawn in elongated detail, the curves rendered sinuously, smooth strokes caressing her frame, juxtaposed by her paleness. There is an invitation in her pose, of course, but the mask haunts and challenges. I can very easily imagine her inviting a lover to her, only to remove the mask and feed.

A de Lempicka from 1928. This last portrait of Iris shows her looking out at an angle, the indigo of her eyes fully radiantly expressed, her flesh pink, her young face impudent and seductive beneath her wave of black hair, upon which sits a shell hat like what the flappers would have worn. She's mostly nude, pale breasts apparent beneath a garland of emerald gown that is half off her body, while in the background, an abstracted urban landscape looms—towering buildings like tombstones, in a way. Her gaze is worldly and otherworldly, its hypnotic nature perfectly expressed. She holds a peacock feather in one hand, as if she were brushing it against her own face. She is both powerfully present and missing in action—a demigoddess in a daydream.

The 20th century portraits are the last ones in her collection of portraits, and the last two reflect an almost alien Iris, one who has moved even further from whatever it was that she was in prior centuries. She faces Modernity already having moved far beyond it, into some netherworld of caprice and complete liberty from the confines of mortality and morality. There is decadence and something ineffable in those last two paintings. In a way, Iris has become a brand by then—she has become Iris™ at last.

I wanted to take the paintings, put them on display, but Iris had forbade taking the stuff from her basement without her permission, for some reason she would not make explicit, but I kept after her.

"These are wonderful, Iris," I said. "This collection is worth hundreds of millions of dollars. You should have these on display."

"They're mine," Iris said. "And don't you understand, Nate? They're all me. You've seen them. They're all authentic, and they're all of me. At the time, I just did it out of a sense of fun, a little game I played. I had the money, I commissioned works. It was satisfying for a courtesan from Venice to have risen so high that I could indulge myself that way. I held onto them as mementos."

"Mementos," I said, wanting to scream. "These are masterpieces."

"They're mine," she said. "How could I explain how everyone from Titian to Tamara de Lempicka had a go at me with the brush? There would be only two responses: one is that they are fakes; and two, it would advertise to the world that an immortal walks among them. They are so demonstrably me. Each one of them captured me perfectly, in their way."

"Why should you care?" I asked. "Why don't you at least have them on display in here?"

Iris shrugged. "I'm over it, Nate. I enjoyed each of them in their day, but their day is past. They are mine, and I can do with them what I like. I choose to keep them in storage. Besides, if I did put them on display at, say, the Augenblick—there are immortals who might take umbrage at my hubris, at so nakedly presenting myself to the world as exactly what I am. They might destroy them."

"So, you're afraid," I said.

"At least here with me, I know that they are safe," Iris said. "No one will take them, no one will see them and ask complicated questions. I am not out to complicate my life, Darling. I'm here to simplify it. And keeping those portraits here keeps everything simple, the way I need it to be."

The basement wasn't damp, thankfully, so the condition of the things was good. I took solace in that, at least. But my head still reeled at the magnitude of the treasure she held hostage in her basement, and the breadth of her uncaring.

You might think I simply saw the paintings as a massive payday—14 paintings by some of the greatest painters in the world. As a set, inestimable in value; piecemeal, worth many hundreds of millions of dollars.

But I didn't. For me, it was this wonderful waltz with history; each painting was itself a dance between subject and artist, and Iris had danced with some of the best, a dance that had taken place over 400 years. The series itself was kind of a work of art, a transcendent thing. Of course, leave it to Iris to not fully appreciate it, or to see it as something irrelevant to, what, exactly? Her privacy? Her ability to hunt and feed unimpeded?

The monstrosity of that lack of vision gnawed at me, it festered. How could somebody do something like that? How could they simply fail to appreciate something as wonderful and amazing as that?

Maybe I was just being very human in all of this. Maybe she had moved beyond mundane mortality, the tyranny of the temporal, and was in this Spartan, Stoic place where vanities such as adornment and beauty were simple trivialities, beneath her consideration.

Or maybe she was simply an addict, unable to see anything of value beyond the beating of her victims' hearts, beyond her next blood meal. Maybe it was as simple as that. I didn't know, couldn't comprehend it.

After all, I was only human.

I would rummage through her basement, look at the wonders and treasures she had not yet seen fit to add to the Augenblick Museum, could not understand why these things that remained here were locked away in that basement. Why would she keep them there, and not share them with a world that would never know her, could neither understand nor appreciate her, at least the way that I did?

I turned, and she was there, gazing at me with orange eyes, the lone light in the basement back-lighting her.

"What are you doing down here?" she asked.

"Looking for you," I said.

"I'm not down here," she said.

"Are you done playing around? I'm hungry, Nate."

"I told you," I said. "You need to do this."

She was wearing a black dress, a black jacket, black gloves, black knee boots—everything was leather, creaking and supple. She'd accessorized with a crimson scarf that wound around her neck three times and traveled down the front of her.

"Did you like the present I left you?" she asked.

"Not so much," I said.

"Where is he?" she asked.

"The vault," I said. "Why won't you make me? The way you keep making everybody else, I'm feeling left out."

She walked toward me, boots clacking. I was trapped in the basement, eyeball to eyeball with an antiquarian abyss.

"I'm not going to make you, Nate," she said. "Why would I even do that?"

"Because you love me?" I asked.

Iris smiled, an indulgence, the shadowy reflection of an emotion long since dead in her, likely dead for over 400 years, now. That ghost of a grin chilled me to my bones, delivered in the dark of that basement.

"You're infinitely more useful to me alive, Nate," she said. "I'm not going to have to keep justifying this to you. You'd go from being My Nate to Nate the Vampire, a competitor."

The way she said it, it was like it was a joke. That hurt. I'd be a great vampire, I just knew it.

"I'd be your protégé," I said. "You could be my mentor."

"You'd be just another mouth to feed, Nate," she said.

"We'd be a team," I said. "We'd be stronger together like that."

Iris walked up to me, arms folded across her chest. "We're already a team, Nate. We've got both day and night covered, living and dead. See? We're symbiotic. This is our deal, Nate: I'm the vampire, and you're my servant. My minion, if you like. It's what we've done. It's what I've always done. I've been doing this for five centuries, Nate. I know how this is done. What you're trying to do is like when a fan tries to join a band they love—it never quite works out."

"Worked for Sid Vicious and Henry Rollins," I said, muttering, looking at my shoes. I wouldn't meet her gaze. I refused to.

"Not very well, I imagine," she said, like she even knew what she was talking about. The pop culture was immaterial and pointless to Iris. "You're my companion, Nate. You're always going to be my companion."

"Until I'm too old to be of any use to you, anymore, right?"

Iris sighed. "This always happens, you know? I've had variations of this conversation around 40 times. It's happened a little quicker with you. Most of my men, I got a good 10-20 years out of them before they buckled. You're buckling faster, Nate."

"I'm not buckling," I said.

"Maybe it's the whole culture-on-fast-forward thing," Iris said. "Have you noticed that? How everything moves faster, now? People are made of softer stuff; shoddy, hasty workmanship or something."

Who hasn't noticed that? For Iris, the most obvious things in the world were sometimes presented as grand revelations.

"Workmanship," I said, wanting to spit. "We have higher expectations of the world around us, I think. That's what it is."

"An overdeveloped sense of entitlement, I think," Iris said. "You want the world, and when you can't have it, you pout and sulk and complain. In older times, people were grateful for what they had, were content with their lot in life, and they knew their betters when they saw them."

To hear a "back in my day" lecture from Iris was almost too much to bear. All of it was galling.

"Maybe I just want to be more than an accessory," I said.

"Maybe you're burning out faster than the others," she said. "Maybe I need somebody new. Maybe a woman, this time. Women take orders better than men, anyway."

She just watched me silently a moment, gauging my emotions, my reaction. Of course, the prospect of being kicked to the curb by Iris haunted and terrified me. I hated even thinking of it. It was one thing for me to walk out in a huff, but it was another for her to cut me off.

Were I to stop mattering to her, I would be nothing more than meat. That chilled me all over again. Right now, I was useful to her, so I had some slight value. The moment that stopped, though, I was simply a meal for her, and, with her track record, she'd decide my fate in a moment, and waste not a thought about it.

I had calculated once how many people Iris had killed in her long unlife. She tended to take anywhere from one to three victims nightly. By my estimation, that meant she'd killed over 100,000 to possibly as many as over 500,000 people over the past 500 years. That frightened me. To someone with that much blood on her hands, what was another life to her? It was nothing. I was nothing.

I thought it was part of her testing me, trying to goad me back into the harness, to prove myself worthy of her. It was one of her games, something I so often fell for. But to be aware of the game was to avoid being played by it, right? That's what I told myself, anyway.

"Go ahead," I said. "Find someone new."

I went to move past her, and she grabbed my arm, stopped me in my tracks.

"I don't want someone new," she said. "I'm hungry, Nate."

In that moment, her holding me fast, effortlessly with that lone out-stretched arm, her hand as hard as diamond, I was terrified of her. She could feed on me if she wanted to. I don't think I could even hope to stop her. Not strong enough, not nearly fast enough. Not ruthless enough.

"I want to be appreciated," I said.

"Of course you're appreciated," Iris said. "It goes without saying."

"No, it doesn't," I said. "You just accept what I do, you take and you take and you never, ever give back."

Iris seemed almost hurt by that accusation. Her face assumed a wrinkle or two of concern with all the conviction of stage actress.

"I let you live here, rent-free. I give you some play money. You don't have to have a job, slaving yourself to death, dying by the minute on the clock. I've showed you a world that anybody would kill to be a part of, Nate. That's hardly nothing."

I pried my arm free of her hand. It took two hands to get free, and I knew I only got free because she chose to allow me to. She could have torn off my arm like it was a breadstick, had she wanted to.

"It's nothing," I said.

"I'm a vampire, Nate," she said. "It's what I do. It's what I've always done. Mortals always think like this, it's always 'me me me' with you. But you have to understand how utterly banal your life is to me: I have seen it all before. I really have. I've seen the full range of human behavior. You think you're capable of anything, but there's only so much you can do as a human being. Do you know that? You can be good, you can be bad. You can be sane, you can be insane. That's your sandbox, Nate. You all play in that same sandbox known as 'Human Nature.' It's not an infinite place. There's only so much you can do within that sandbox."

"It's not a sandbox," I said. "You make it seem so mundane."

Iris laughed, high-toned, mocking. "It is mundane, Nate. Free will is seen as, what, exactly? The capacity to make your own destiny? But look around you. This world, as grand as it is, remains a finite place. You lead finite lives within this finite space. Limited time, limited space. Your life passes by in a flash. And you're going to tell me that anything is possible in these narrow confines of existence? Wishful thinking, Nate."

"Make me one of you," I said. I could not let that go. "Let me cross into that infinite place with you."

Iris almost looked sad. Despite her perpetual youth, her indigo eyes spoke volumes, a haunting maturity in them, an ancient wisdom that belied their ersatz youthfulness. They were eyes that had seen centuries of human existence, had seen humanity in all of its beauty and its ugliness. Although she looked like a girl, that girl had died long ago. The woman she became was dead as well. What remained was only a ghost of the life she had once led.

"There is only so much you can do as a species," Iris said. "I know nobody likes to say that, or think that, but there is only so much available to you. The continuum you have is between those points of duality—good to bad, happy to sad, sane to insane, success to failure, lucky to unlucky, true to false, beautiful to ugly, love to hate, healthy to sick, young to old, alive to dead, and so on. There are steps between those poles, you fall somewhere between them, but there are only so many steps. I see this because I'm outside of your world. I'm undead. I'm inhuman. I can see it."

I almost felt there was sympathy in her, a tiny glimmer of it beneath the weight of the years. Seeing that hint of something in her made me want to relieve her pain. I loved her still, would suffer any agony to avoid seeing her hurt.

"There is only so much space between those two points, Nate," Iris said. "Only so much room, so much moral real estate to develop. You live within the margins of mortality, and tell yourself that anything's possible. You can choose your path, of course, but you cannot choose whether or not you're on a path at all; you can't transcend existence, itself. Existence means choices, and choices mean duality, and duality means limitation."

"Let me transcend this life," I said, reaching out for her. "Make me one of you. Let me put the lie to you."

"You're not ready," Iris said. "And you never will be, Nate."

-X-

CHAPTER 13

I don't know why she stopped hunting.

Since I knew her, she'd just go out and do her thing, and come back, usually with a victim, and would have me clean up afterward. Then she started bringing me out on her hunts, like her wingman, and, at the time, I thought maybe she was showing me how it was done, like she'd taken me under her bat wing or something, as preparation for me becoming a made man. But, as time wore on, I guess she just had me there as bait.

And then, for some reason, she'd just have me go out on my own and bring somebody back for her. The first time she did that, I didn't understand, but she just said "I don't feel like going out tonight. You bring me someone here, Nate?"

"It's a lot easier for you," I said. "You're made for this."

"It's so much harder than you think it is," she said. "You have no idea."

"I have some idea," I said. "I mean, I've seen you do it. You just pick somebody out, mesmerize them, and presto!"

She looked at me with mute displeasure, a downturn of her lips. Like I was the village idiot, and she was having to explain something painfully obvious.

"I'm asking you to do me a favor, Nate," she said. "Just find a girl, and bring her here. That's all I'm asking."

"But why won't you go out? How is tonight different from last night?" I asked.

"It just is," she said. "Are you going to help me or not? Sometimes I think you don't even care about me, Nate."

I sat down next to her, and she looked at me with those big eyes of hers, and I did what I had taken to doing, which is to look at her lips when I talked to her, instead of her eyes. I learned that early on. Another safe place is the forehead—you can look at somebody's forehead and it looks like you're looking at them, but you're not.

"Did somebody hurt you?" I asked.

"It's not like that," she said.

"Well, what is it like?"

Iris put her hand on my arm and held it there. "I don't want to hunt anymore. I want to feed, but I'm tired of hunting. The thrill of the hunt is gone for me."

She'd been hunting for five centuries. Five fucking centuries. And on my watch, she decides she doesn't want to hunt anymore? What kind of rotten luck is that?

"I'm not a killer," I said.

"I'm not asking you to kill anybody," Iris said. "I'm just saying that you bring them here. I'll handle the rest."

"Except for cleanup," I said.

"Except for cleanup," Iris said.

And she sent me off in pursuit of prey for her. That first one I got for her was a girl named Sunshine, weirdly enough. Maddy Sunshine. She had gleeful brown curls that dangled in front of her eyes and she had this impish smile. Maybe a little chubby, but she was nice, and was very flattered that I took an apparent interest in her.

I talked her up for a few hours at Club Dread, and then asked her if she wanted to come back to my place, and, of course, she said she would, and we hopped a CTA bus back, while Maddy told me about her classes, and how she was going to be a lawyer one day, like environmental law, she thought, and while she was talking, I just had this terrible feeling in my stomach, because I was setting her up.

And I flaked out. I told Maddy when we got to the place that my roommate was in tonight, and wasn't supposed to be, so could I get her number and maybe we could hook up some other time. She was flummoxed by this, couldn't understand what she'd done wrong, was stammering and confused and off-put, and I just called her a cab and got her the hell out of there.

I was afraid of Iris being pissed about it, but I was also relieved that I had balked, honestly.

I couldn't do it. I couldn't just lead somebody to the slaughter like that. And I went back in, and there was Iris, sitting around in her living room. She was actually on the same sofa she'd been on when I'd first gone out for her. She was just lying there, staring at the ceiling, like she hadn't moved an inch. Did vampires get depressed?

She turned her head, looked at me gravely.

"Well?"

"I couldn't do it," I said.

Iris sat up, just smoothly pivoted into an upright position. She could move strangely that way if she wanted. A kind of unnatural gracefulness that was always disarming when revealed.

"You don't care a bit about me, do you?"

I sat down next to her, put my arm around her, which she shrugged off.

"You want me to die," she said. "I'll die, Nate. Is that what you want?"

"No, of course not," I said. "But you're the hunter, not me. And you won't die, am I right?"

Iris bit her lip, stared at me, through me.

"I might as well be dead," she said. "Far, far worse than dead."

I imagined Iris in that situation, a revenant, withered, clawlike hands, mummified flesh, ossified, endless thirst.

"Not my problem," I said.

She looked at me, gave me this stricken look, those cold eyes upon me, puncturing me. "I can't do it anymore. I won't."

Again, it made no sense to me, since she'd gone hunting the night before, and I hadn't sensed anything amiss with her. She hadn't brought me with her that night.

My mistress vampire had an eating disorder, for God's sake. That's beginning to be what it felt like, that same kind of bullshit.

"What happened to you?" I asked. "Please, tell me."

"You wouldn't understand," she said. "Listen, Nate. Get me someone. I'm hungry."

Then she grabbed my face in her ice-cold hands and gazed into my eyes, and I fell into the indigo abyss of her stare, as she spoke to me, far, far away, and she told me to get her something to eat, and I went out with that rattling in my skull, the echo of her suggestion…"Fetch! Fetch! Fetch!"

She bit her wrist and she fed me some of her blood, the nourishing elixir, the ichor of immortality, which, when given to minions, could temporarily impart some of the vampire's power to them—speed, strength, resilience, healing, senses—it was the ultimate tonic, the panacea to life's complications. Better than any drug, it energized me, flowed through me, made me feel, however fleetingly, what it was like to be a vampire, maybe. Just a taste.

And like some kind of sleepwalker, I was adrift in the city, hunting, now, for real. I don't even remember the name of that poor girl. She had an upturned nose and jackal's eyes and brown hair, was rail-thin yet shapely, had snaggle teeth and shook charmingly when she laughed. She smelled like patchouli, wore almost no jewelry, except for a ring on her pinky finger, an onyx ring, and she wore dusty tan corduroys and a knit top the color of autumn leaves, and we talked and I was on autopilot the entire time, so strong was Iris's command, and I walked this girl back to Iris's place and the girl was like "Wow, this place is FAB!" and she turned in her clogs and there was Iris standing there, smiling, and the girl was like "Whoa, you own this?" and Iris was on her in a heartbeat, that fast, and she just sank her teeth in the girl's neck and sucked her dry.

And while Iris was doing this, feeding on her, the girl's back to me, Iris gazed at me, her eyes aflame with orange as they always would be when she was in that angry/hungry place, and the girl moaning, her fists opening and closing rhythmically, her sandals coming off her feet as I realized that Iris was holding her off the ground.

Just like that, the girl was finished, Iris was through with her, and she just let go of her, let her fall to the ground, while Iris took out a lace handkerchief and wiped her mouth.

"See?" Iris said, the girl's blood warming up her face a bit. "Now was it that difficult, Nate?"

I walked around the girl's body, while Iris tidied up. The girl had fallen forward, was laying there on her stomach, her arms splayed behind her, her face actually half on the floor, propped up by her nose, her blank eyes staring at the floor. Not a drop of blood had been spilled. Iris had gorged herself.

"She felt no pain," Iris said. "Only pleasure. You know what it feels like, don't you, Nate?"

"Now what?" I asked, feeling bad for the girl, feeling numb, too. I took the ring off her finger. Starved of fluids, it came right off. I put it in my pocket.

"We get rid of her," Iris said. "I mean, three days, and she's like me. So, I've got this place that's just right."

And she had me put the girl in the trunk of the MG, and we drove to Iris's crematorium, and then the grisly work began. The place was in Cicero, and it was both ugly and nondescript. It was just this unassuming, horrible building.

"It's an incinerator," she said. "Pets and such. Makes things so much easier."

She wanted me to lop off the girl's head, throw that in first. That was horrible enough. She just handed me a machete, this old nicked thing with a sharp, sharp blade. It looked old.

"What the hell is this?"

"It's a machete," she said.

"I am not cutting off her head," I said. "My god, Iris."

I wondered how many of her minions had used that machete before me. I imagined the big-handed guy from before using it.

Iris just folded her arms, looking at me. "What? There's no blood in her. Not a drop. What are you worried about?"

The girl's body was pale. She still had that baffled expression on her face, mouth agape, eyes blank and wide. I gagged a little. It was hard to imagine her animating in a few days, growing fangs, becoming a monster like Iris.

It's a hard thing to really convey, that sense of ambient monstrosity, like sharing a room with one of the living dead. They occupy this space you understand as human, but within the boundaries of that space, they are anything but human. It's very intimidating. And when one of them is pissed at you, it's even worse, really. Iris just stood there, not breathing, just silent, inscrutable, unknowable, unreachable, and unstoppable.

"Are you going to do this for me or what?" she asked.

"Is this what your other guys did for you?" I asked.

"Of course," she said, like it was the most natural thing in the world, like I was the one being unreasonable, here. The tone set my teeth on edge. "There is a balance, here, Nate. I have to feed, and each time I feed, I infect someone. I can't go around spawning vampires everywhere I go; that'll get me in all sorts of trouble."

"So why kill people at all? Why not have a stable of, you know, people to feed on?" I asked.

Iris shrugged. "I tried that years ago. A long, long time ago. One big happy family, right? Me and my livestock?"

I knew she was talking about people, not cattle. Iris never, ever fed on animals. The mere mention of it made her wrinkle her pointy nose in disgust, as if it were beneath her, or, somehow, obscene. This from a vampire.

"Yeah? So?"

"So, I did it before," she said. "It just gets too complicated. People get jealous, and, over time, they run out of steam, and some of them get infected, and then it's just a lot of work, and then I'm busy putting out fires everywhere. I've tried it, and it doesn't work. I've done it all sorts of ways, like had people scattered around a city, and I just take sips, but I tell you, then I'm busy commuting around town for my meals, and that gets old so fast, you have no idea, Nate. I'm just hustling around town, and before I know it, dawn's coming and I have to race home. This way works better—I just get my meal and then I have the rest of the night free."

"To do what?"

"Whatever I want," she said.

It was purely a matter of convenience to her. That made its own kind of creepy sense. For Iris, I could easily see her inconvenience being a matter of life and death for others. It was entirely her. It was all about her, all the time.

I looked at the girl, who just gaped silently up at us. I couldn't believe her face had been frozen in that expression like that. It was horrible, this baffled dead girl.

Iris followed my gaze down to her, then back to me, arms still folded.

"Do it. Just put an end to it. She was an acid casualty, anyway, Nate. Nobody's going to miss her."

"Her family will," I said.

"That's about it," Iris said. "And when they die, that'll be that. It's like that, you know. You're all just blinks of the eye—you're born, you come into focus with your life, and, over time, you begin to blur. Even the people who know you best don't truly know you, and you just start to blur, until you don't even know yourself, anymore. Nobody can really know you, and, in time, people's perceptions of you—if they remember you at all—take on a life of their own. Kind of like a ghost, really. We're all ghosts, Nate. This girl's no more real than you or me. There are probably, I don't know, 80,000 women on the planet who are alike enough to her as to pass as her sister, or even as her. Sure, maybe the details are different, but so what? A hundred years, it'll be like she was never here—maybe even less, depending on who she was. And a thousand years later, it'll have been like she never existed at all. In ten thousand years (and probably sooner), humanity will be extinct, so what does it fucking matter if you lop the head off this fucking corpse, Nate? Just do it."

"You do it," I said, setting the machete down. "If it's no big deal, you do it."

She took the machete and lopped off the girl's head with one smooth stroke. Just parted her head from her body like she was slicing a melon. The machete stuck in the table.

"Once again, is that so hard, Nate? I'm thinking you're maybe too soft for this work," she said, poking me in the chest with a finger that felt like a knife. "Too soft."

"It's not that," I said. "I just think she doesn't need to die."

"She's dead already, Nate," Iris said. "She's fucking dead. I killed her. Deal with it."

Just to drive the point home, she picked up the girl's head and tossed it into the oven, which she had turned on.

"But she could come back, if you're really fucking stupid and careless," Iris said. "So don't be. Keep the ashes in separate places, and scatter them."

She shut the door on the oven and cranked it up, leaning against the door of it, arms folded, looking at me with eyes like a spider's. I squirmed under her gaze.

"Maybe I misjudged you, Nate," she said. "I've got an idea: maybe we visit Hillary? Would you like that?"

"Don't hurt her," I said.

"Why? You still care about her?"

"I just don't want to see her on this table," I said.

"Don't you want some kind of revenge?" Iris asked. "We could do that. Hell, I could bite her and we could brick her up in a wall, to suffer for eternity. That's kind of old-school, but I've seen it done enough times. You know what that means?"

"No," I said.

"Eternal torment," Iris said. "Stuck and starving, about as close to Hell as a vampire can actually get. I could've done that to Headless, here, if I'd wanted."

I could not look at the bloodless, headless corpse. I couldn't bring myself to do it.

"This is easier, Nate," Iris said. "So much easier. One cut, two ovens, two bins of ashes, and that's that."

"I can't do it," I said, knowing that I was basically giving myself a death sentence by saying it.

"You can, Nate," Iris said. "C'mon, you eat meat, right? It's just like that. There are guys who render meat all day long."

"Yeah, but I'm not one of them," I said. "She was a person, not meat."

"Meh," Iris said. "Everybody's meat. When the head's done, take the ashes out and put them in that jar over there. Then put the rest of her in there, run it through that cycle. When that's done, put the ashes in the other jar. Then take them and scatter them. Two different places. Understand?"

"Wait, are you leaving me here?"

Iris nodded.

"Turn off the ovens when you're done, and the lights. I'll leave the keys here. Don't forget to lock up. Oh, and put the machete in that locker over there."

I was peevish; she was leaving me cleanup duty once again.

She became mist before I could offer a complaint, and I knew better than to complain about it, so I just put Patchouli in the oven, and then put the ashes in one of the jars, belatedly realizing that I had forgotten to clean out the original ashes. I had put them all in one container. I'd already screwed it up.

Turning off the ovens, I put away the machete and turned out the lights, and took the jar of ash with me, and locked the door.

Right from the start, I'd screwed up. It wasn't my fault; she shouldn't have entrusted me to this kind of work. I didn't know what kind of work I should be entrusted to, but this wasn't it.

Instead, I took the jar of ash, sad that this comparatively tiny amount of ash had once been Patchouli. Then I went home and put the jar of ash in a corner of my room. I wanted to see what would happen, if Iris was right about it.

Iris came back in the early hours, asked me if I'd taken care of everything. I nodded, and she disappeared in the bowels of her lair, as she always did.

Two nights later, the jar spilled over, and out came the ash, which swirled and assumed a human form, gradually becoming a horribly scarred and wrinkled gray wraith that had been Patchouli, who looked like a sheet of wax paper that had been crumpled, only to be unrolled again. I watched this, transfixed, the gradual filling in of the ash, the layers of flesh like the repapering of a hornet's nest, the same shade of gray, the assumption of the form, nails like chips of mica, and white fangs, coming together out of the detritus that she had been, in swirls of ash.

She rose, eyes like twin orange flames, her fangs long, this ghastly scarecrow version of herself, filling out, assuming the lean form she'd had in life.

"Whoaaaaaaaaaaaaaaaaaaaaaaaaaaaaaaaaaa," she said, drawing it out, like the groan of a banshee. She gazed at her hands and flexed them, her nails like claws. She looked horrible. Then she saw me gaping at her, and ran for me, a chimplike scuttling along the ground by her arms.

I ran out of my room, and into Iris, who was standing there, wearing a gray pencil skirt and a bright red wrap blouse and a black derby hat.

"Nate," she said. "Nate, Nate, Nate."

Patchouli saw Iris and hissed, the very image of malice, fangs bared.

"Not this one," Iris said. "Not for you. I should let you, but, no. He's mine. Get out of here. Don't come back."

Patchouli cowered before Iris, her jack o'-lantern eyes ablaze with hunger, fear, anger, lust, loathing, dread. All blended together in this undead emotional gumbo.

Then Patchouli became mist and wafted out of there, passing through me as she went. Cold and horrible, she fled.

"That's what happens when you don't scatter the ashes, Nate," Iris said. "You told me you had it handled. You lied to me."

"If you want something right, you just have to do it yourself," I said.

"Or get better help," Iris said. "I hope you're happy, Nate. You've just unleashed an evil upon the world. That girl is going to infect the first person she corners. And the next, and the next, until she's whole again, and has her wits, and can make more informed decisions."

I wasn't about to take anything from her.

"You infected her, not me," I said.

"You failed to properly dispose of her," Iris said. "It was your responsibility."

"She's not medical waste," I said.

"Your fault," Iris said.

It was impossible to argue with Iris. It really was.

"Not my fault," I said.

"It never is," she said. "Nate, here's the deal: either you fetch me food, or I kick you out. And that's me being generous. Here's what I'll really do: I'll feed on you, and then toss you in the oven, and you'll not be coming out of there like your hippy-dippy gal pal. And then I'll find somebody else, and she'll do what I want, and she won't let me down."

"Everybody lets you down, sooner or later," I said. "Right?"

She smiled a bit. "Yeah, that's true. You wait long enough, and it happens. Either the heart fails, or the mind fails, or the body fails, or the soul fails. But nobody's let me down quite as speedily as you have, Nate."

It was sort of ambiguous to me how she felt about that. I thought maybe on one hand it aggravated her, but on the other, it kind of intrigued her. Had I simply done a moral swan-dive right out of the gates, she would have perhaps been disappointed, or bored, or both.

Somehow, my passive-aggressive insurrection had tickled her fancy. Maybe none of her companions had given her as much trouble as me, or maybe not the same way. I couldn't be sure, and she sure wasn't telling.

"You are in my service," Iris said. "That implies a certain obligation to me."

"Sure," I said. "But I was really hoping you'd make me a vampire."

She just blew that off the way she always did. Immaterial. Irrelevant.

"I didn't want to just be your damned slave," I said.

Iris patted the side of my face with her hand. It could as easily have been a slap that would have taken my head off. Her fingertips felt cold and hard against my warm skin. She chose to be gentle, and that level of restraint did nothing to disguise the power she contained in her petite frame.

"I'm being kind as it is, Nate," she said. "I'm fond of you, so I'm tolerating this insubordination. The fact is, you are either with me or against me in this. You're either on my team, or you're off it. Another dose of duality for you, Darling. I simply cannot have it any other way. Because I'll admit to a certain fondness for you, you can just walk out that door and never come back, and I'll let you go. I actually will. I'll find someone else, and you'll live your short little human life, doing your mundane human little things, have yourself a family, grow old and die."

"But before you die, I'll pay you a visit, just for old times' sake. I'll come by and you'll see me and you'll recognize me, because I'll look exactly like I'm looking right now—I'll have not aged a day, Nate. And you'll be an old man. Knowing you, probably wearing a bow tie and a straw hat and a seersucker suit. Something quaint. And I'll ask you if it was all worth it, if you enjoyed your time away from me. Your youth spent, your candle burning low, you'll probably be bitter at having been left behind, at missing out on the wonders you would have enjoyed in my company all those years. You'll wonder if it was all worth it. And I'll kiss you on the cheek and tell you that it was good to know you, and you'll go to your grave not knowing if I was telling the truth or lying to you, because I'm that good. And I'll get you a nice bouquet of roses for your funeral—red, of course, or maybe white. And I'll be exactly as I've been, as I have always been. I haven't been to a funeral in so many years, Nate. But I'll go to yours, I promise."

It was the only time she ever promised me anything.

—X—

The biggest problem with being a vampire's minion is that people eventually notice. Police, especially. The vampire doesn't have to care, can afford not to, but eventually, people start to notice when this otherwise unassuming guy, if, you know, rather handsome, and he'll be seen with Ashleigh or Mylyssa or Emilee and then the next thing you know, those people who saw him with Mylyssa at Quandary will tell the authorities that they last saw her leave with this guy, and, over time, police start collecting stories and accounts, and then a composite sketch starts to emerge, this profile, like this guy who looks sorta like me, and then I have to do things like grow my hair longer, or bleach it, or dye it, just to change it up a little, so I don't look like the guy who they're looking for.

And I get that this is probably yet another thing that Iris wants, like she wants me to take the heat, to be the suspect, the Person of Interest, because in so doing, it keeps her hands clean. Never mind that she's the one who is actually doing the killing, here. Yes, I'm an accessory to murder, if you want to be technical, but Iris is the one doing the killing, not me—she's the perpetrator; I'm merely her accomplice.

And, yes, I know that the moral thing to do would be to go to the police and tell them about her, or to try to drive a stake in her heart and be done with it. But I wasn't in that place, yet. I still loved her.

Not like this would persuade any police office worth his badge. Never mind that they're not going to find any bodies.

The cop on the beat, the one tracking all those disappearances, is Detective Lincoln Davis of the Chicago Special Crimes Unit. I know this because he's the one who would give quotes in the newspaper when they would make the periodic inquiries as to whether a serial killer was operating in Chicago, and just how many girls had disappeared over the last few years.

Detective Davis is a tall, broad-built black man, middle-aged, who has bowling ball shoulders that call to mind a boxer. He's bald and dark-skinned, with a mustache that's gunmetal gray. He has a bulletin board with a lot of little pictures on it, and there's that composite picture, that creepy sketch. They always give the composite sketch these creepy killer's eyes, and those eyes are so not mine. My eyes might be, I don't know, mysterious, but they're not creepy like that.

And then Detective Davis coughs up surveillance camera images, like grainy things that show me with one of the missing girls, tells me that he's homing in on the suspect, and then I have this on the television and showed Iris, who just watched without interest.

"Huh," she said.

"Huh," I said. "This is me they're showing. I'm a suspect. I mean, they haven't found me, yet, but they sure as hell will."

Iris watched Davis talk. "Yeah, the surveillance cameras are annoying, aren't they? Not like I really have to worry about them, but, you know. They are absolutely everywhere, anymore."

"I have to worry about them," I said. "I still do."

It's only a matter of time. Someone will recognize me, say "Hey, that looks kinda like Nathan Sharp, don't you think?"

"You can tell them you're the minion of a vampire," Iris said. "Just tell the truth, and that'll guarantee you a lifetime of psychiatric treatment. Maybe a book deal. A memoir."

"Yeah, right," I said. That is exactly what I'd do. I'd sing a song of the vampire I'd been in service to, and would get myself locked up and drugged up, and the irony of it would be that I'd be telling the damned truth, and nobody would believe me. I could even imagine Iris visiting me. I could be her Renfield.

"It's not my fault that you weren't careful," she said.

"I thought I was," I said. "None of the shots they have are too good."

But it wasn't terribly reassuring. Sooner or later, someone was going to find me, or come for me, or recognize me, and then I didn't know what would happen. Or maybe I did know. The one thing that saved me was that the bodies they did find weren't ones that Iris had anything to do with; they were unrelated to the rash of disappearances.

"New plan," Iris said. "Target tourists."

"Tourists?"

She nodded. "They're from out of town, they're clueless. Yeah. Nab them."

"Again, this wouldn't even be an issue if you would just do it," I said.

"But you're just so good at it, Nate," she said.

"Why don't you hit Wisconsin, or Indiana?" I asked.

Iris didn't like that one bit, wrinkled her nose in mute disapproval.

"Commute? No way," she said.

So there I was, on Navy Pier, trolling for Iris. People everywhere, milling, coming here because it's where they assumed they were supposed to go, shopping, consuming, packing the promenade. I just walked around, got the feel for the place. I never went there, but between that, Millennium Park, and the Magnificent Mile, there would be almost no better place to find tourists.

I was preternaturally aware of the security cameras. I noted those as I cased those haunts, without trying to be obvious about it. I had on a White Sox baseball cap jammed low on my head (figuring I'd throw a little misdirection their way—I was a Cubs fan). I caught a ride on the Ferris Wheel, wondering what I was going to do. Iris was just being lazy.

That's really what it was. She was being a goddamned slacker vampire. And that pissed me off. It wasn't fair. She was holding out on me and was also being a fucking slacker.

As my dissatisfaction with the arrangement grew, I had taken to getting Iris uglier and nastier girls as her meals. She had definite preferences, and then I thought "You know what? Let me do my own unnatural selection, and if she complains, let her go do this herself."

So, I'd decided to bring her mean girls, crazy girls—or, ideally, both—real rotten apples from the bottom of the barrel, the very worst I could find, the very worst personalities. They were happy enough to go with me, some even asked what I saw in them, and I would always just say "Potential."

Iris didn't like it one bit, but beggars could hardly be choosers. She didn't complain, although she was terribly displeased with my selections. As a minion, you get a sense of your master's moods, and her lack of enthusiasm was apparent when presented with the latest bitch queen I'd procured for her. I took real satisfaction in that.

Passive-aggressive? Sure, guilty as charged. But so fucking what? I had to do something. Sure, maybe I could have left, but back then, I still held out the hope that Iris would turn me. I really did still hope for that.

Then, one night, there was Joliette. I saw her at Joey Patrone's, at the bar. Joliette was a classic good body/bad face kind of gal, sullenly nursing her beer. I sat next to her, scoping her out on the sly. She had an upturned nose with cavernous nostrils, thick, wormy lips, little pig eyes, and curly hair that she'd grown into a red-blond mane. She was wearing skin-tight denim leggings and some glossy fuck-me four-inch heels, and a pink fuzzy sweater than showed off an amazing rack.

"Hey," I said.

"Yeah?" she said, looking at me down the end of that nose. Her face looked like a bat's, especially head-on.

"You look like somebody," I said.

She laughed, this bitter carping sound, like somebody stomping on an accordion.

"Is that right?"

I nodded.

"Who?"

"Nobody you would know," I said.

"I might," she said. "You look like somebody, too, Pretty Boy."

"You think?" I asked.

"You look like a skinny version of that asshole actor who chewed out that guy," she said. "Patrick Bateman?"

"Christian Bale," I said. "Patrick Bateman was a character he played."

"I don't think so," she said. "What's your name, Bateman?"

"Nate," I said.

"Joliette," she said, holding out her hand. I shook it. "Buy me another beer, Nateman?"

"Sure," I said, and got her another Goose Island, which was what she was drinking. While we waited, Joliette turned on the stool toward me. She really did have a great body. She could see me scoping her out.

"You like that?" she said, touching her thigh.

"You look very fit," I said.

"I dance," she said. "I'm a dancer."

Her beer came, and she drank it, took a long pull from the bottle while I processed that. Like what kind of dancer? An exotic dancer? She couldn't be ballet, not with a face like that. I couldn't imagine.

"Right now, you're wondering if I'm an exotic dancer," she said. "See, that just bugs me, like you say you're a dancer, and that's what people immediately think. That fucking sucks."

I cleared my throat. "I wasn't thinking that. I was wondering if you were tap or jazz or ballet."

"Yeah, right," she said. "It sucks. I'm really good. But with this face? It means I'm never going to be in the front. They put me in the back. Squash a hat down on my head. I grew my hair long like this so it can kind of disguise it when I'm up onstage. Fucking choreographers."

"Shouldn't you be in New York?" I asked.

"It's because of this that I'm here," she said, pointing a hitch-hiker's thumb to her face. "Nobody can say it outright—nobody can say 'Gee, Joliette, you are really, really good, but my god, you're ugly.' They never, ever say it. So they come up with bullshit, talk about how thankful they are that I tried out, but that I'm not what they need right now, or that they'll call me, only they never do. It's such bullshit. Everything's bullshit."

"Wow," I said. She was one bitter babe. I wonder if her blood would taste as bitter to Iris. I hoped it would. I almost laughed out loud, imagining Iris doing a spit-take as she bit into Joliette.

"For awhile, I even thought about plastic surgery," she said. "Get myself a Hollywood nose, maybe belt-sand my cheekbones and pave chin. Something. But then I just got pissed off. Talent should be evident, don't you think? It should be apparent and undeniable. It should just steamroll the opposition. Instead, people's biases just come into the mix, and they don't see past the surface. My mom told me I was beautiful. She always did. And I believed her, at least until I got a clue."

I didn't know what to say, what I could or even should say. She'd be perfect for Iris's nightly meal. I hoped she gave Iris a tummy ache.

"Yeah, Pretty Boy," she said, watching me stew. "You've never had that problem. Pretty people get whatever they want. They get promotions they don't deserve, they become pop stars, they get movie deals, they get book deals—I remember reading somewhere that publishers actually pay attention to that, like if you've got a pretty face, they want that on the back of the books in hopes of getting more sales. How fucked is that? You really can judge a book by its cover."

"We still have problems," I said. "We have people resenting us because we're pretty. Just another pretty face."

Joliette sneered in her beer, rolled her eyes. She was mouth-puckeringly bitter. She'd be perfect.

"You look like Wonder Woman," I said. She snorted.

"What, my body?" she said. "Yeah. You want to know a secret, Pretty Boy? I AM Wonder Woman."

She polished off her beer, set it on the bar with a clank.

"I think you're alright," I said.

Joliette looked at me a moment before replying.

"Yeah? I almost think you do."

"I mean, you call me Pretty Boy, right? So, you're judging me by my appearance, too," I said. "People usually think you're dumb if you're pretty—or, you know, handsome. There's a flip side to that."

"Oh, cry me a river," Joliette said. "Boo fucking hoo."

"It's true," he said. "People get distracted and don't see the real you."

"Hah!" Joliette said. "Look, Nate, you want to go somewhere and hash this out properly? That's why you're even talking to me, isn't it?"

"Sure," I said, paying our tabs.

We walked out of there, Joliette clacking along, nearly as tall as me in her heels.

"Where are we going?" she asked.

"My place," I said.

"It's my body, isn't it?" she asked. "I've never had trouble picking up guys, you know."

Her body was magnificent—great, long legs, firm, sculpted thighs, nice ass, an almost waspish waist that swelled up to a taut-yet-full bosom. Toned arms. Everything looked sharp. She had incredible lines, knew how to fucking move. She was, in a word, stacked. Everything was perfection until that face, which was just a case study in the biomechanics of beauty, or the lack of it, and bad geometry brought her beauty to a screeching halt.

Her face was a case of too much yielding too little. Her lips were too big, her nose was too big, her eyes were too big. The nose was a dead end, but her lips, high cheekbones, and eyes alone would have given her a striking, earthy attractiveness, if you squinted. But altogether, it was just too much.

I wondered what she'd be like as a vampire. She'd be able to get around that. Those overlarge blue eyes of hers would tack guys to the wall.

"You really dance professionally?" I asked.

"Yeah, is that so hard to believe?" she replied.

"No," I said. "But you actually make money?"

"Not so much," she said. "I work as a physical trainer, too."

"Ah," I said.

I hailed a cab, which came up and got us. The driver was Pakistani, this very dark-skinned fellow with a bald head. I told him where we were going.

"Oooh, Moneybags," Joliette said. "Rich and pretty? My lucky night. That's another thing that bugs me, you know."

"What?"

She sat back against the seat of the cab, crossed her leg toward me.

"How easy it is to make it when you're already rich. Or come from money. They always try to downplay it—like Movie Star X had to stay at a motel once, or Writer Y lived in a studio apartment for a few months, so they craft this rags-to-riches story about them, like they had to eat pork and beans for dinner one time, so they know how rough it is. But the truth is, they went to Princeton, and their dad's an art critic for the *New Yorker*, and their mom's a talent scout for William Morris, or they come from a wealthy Italian family and went to school with Paris Hilton. And you think that didn't play a huge factor in them starting their own art gallery? Or landing a crucial acting gig, or becoming a pop star, or that kind of thing? It's always behind those stories, those people who make it. Like of course Llewellyn Brace becomes a Hollywood A-lister—she's Hollywood royalty already, has an actress mom and a director dad. All of them. It's a conspiracy of nepotism, connections, and favoritism. But what galls me is that they all retrofit it—"

"Retrofit?"

"You know, they scrub it, whitewash it, camouflage it," she said. "Try to make it out like they made it all by themselves. Ivan Carver thinks he changes his name from that of his famous relative to prove it that he can make it on his own, and not ride on the family name? You can't tell me that, stage name or not, that Family Name didn't open boodles of doors for him. His famous relative could have told him just where to go, who to see. Or, because they're all a bunch of kiss asses in Hollywood, maybe they're like 'Oh, shit, Famous Name's nutball nephew's coming to the audition—greenlight him, would you?' and it happens. And then a star is born. For all the Horatio Alger bullshit, you want to know the truth?"

"Sure," I said. "Tell me the truth."

"Nearly everybody who's somebody comes from somewhere," Joliette said. "There's always an angle. I used to entertain myself, trying to find the angle. Until it started to bum me out, because you'd see it over and over again. I call it 'Pedigree.' You just take a given celebrity, a star, and you can trace their lineage. Like if somebody's risen too quickly, too young—say, a book deal at 23, or a starring role in a movie at an early age—that kind of thing, it immediately triggers my warning bells."

"What about Arthur Bunko," I said, naming a famous young star who had rising meteorically in recent years, was kind of a triple threat—actor, writer, director.

"Mom and dad went to Stanford," Joliette said. "Mom's a poet and a novelist. Dad's a math professor at a top school. You think him writing a book is some kind of reach for him? They knew people, he knew people, he's pretty, and it happened. It's not based on his acting chops, believe me—I mean, I saw 'Sinkers,' for fuck's sake. Don't tell me he's a great actor. He's affable and pretty, sure, and maybe squarely out of his mind, but he's not a great actor. And then he gets into Harvard, Yale, all those schools? Why? Because he's 'Arthur Bunko' now—he's practically his own brand."

"You seem to have it all worked out," I said.

"I fucking do," she said. "Boy, do I ever. What's funny is how hard they try to cover it up, or downplay it, and how much the media just plays along. Just once I'd like to see a celebrity say 'I came from money, my folks knew exactly the right people, pulled the right strings, got me to the head of the line, and that's what made me a star.' But nobody ever says that, because they know then everybody would hate them, would resent the hell out of them. So, they have their publicist make some touching rags-to-riches story to snooker the public into thinking that they're alright. The key thing, the only thing that matters, is getting noticed—having the right people notice you makes all the difference. As a dancer, believe me, I know this. Nobody can tell me otherwise, because I've seen it. You get noticed, and you win. The rest of us just wallow in obscurity."

"I would think talent would win out," I said.

"You know, you would, sure. Everybody likes to think that—but it doesn't," she said. "Talent doesn't carry the day. Getting noticed is what does it. Having the connections is what makes it happen. It's so fucking corrupt. The line about 'it's not what you know, it's who you know'—that's the truest truism ever, Pretty Boy."

"You sound bitter," I said.

"Of course I am," she said. "You know the shelf life of a dancer? I'm 29—that's geriatric by dancer standards."

"So why do it?" I asked.

"Because I love it," she said. "Why do anything? Why be anything? Do what you love, be what you love. Life's too short to be anything less than happy."

She looked pissed when she said that.

"And yet, you don't seem too happy," I said.

She laughed, this sardonic snort that welled up from deep inside her.

"Now you know my pain," she said. "I love to dance, have always loved dancing, but with this face, I'm never, ever going to make it as a dancer."

"I don't know," I said. "Onstage, strong features probably show up just fine. Maybe better than normal."

I thought of the old Greek theatrical masks, how outsized their expressions were, but I wasn't about to tell Joliette that.

"Yeah, right," she said.

We reached Iris's place, and I realized that I liked the company of humans, had missed it. Iris only masqueraded as a human being—she had long since lost that part of herself that could be called human. Even as bitter as Joliette was, it was a refreshingly human flavor when contrasted with the cold and haughty contempt of Iris.

I paid the cabbie and we got out, Joliette whistling. "Rich Boy. I totally knew it. You have that blown-away kind of don't-give-a-fuckism that reeks of Rich Boy. You're not Captain Howdy, are you?"

"Captain Howdy" was the nickname for me, for the mysterious charmer who was fond of Western-style shirts who'd pick up gals and make 'em disappear. Captain Howdy was the appellation for this suspected serial killer.

"Not me," I said, grateful that I was wearing a black turtleneck that night, and not one of my Western shirts.

"Seriously, you live here?" she asked.

"More or less," I said, keying in.

Joliette laughed.

"Well, fuck me," she said. I intended to do just that.

Iris appeared behind her, coalescing out of the mist. She looked up at me, over Joliette's shoulder.

"I'm sorry," I said.

"For what?" Joliette asked, as Iris clamped onto her neck. Joliette gasped, her big eyes rolling back in her head as Iris drank her dead, pinning her with her arms, her pale hands dimpling Joliette's flesh, while Joliette worked moaned and sighed, overcome.

Iris looked at me as she fed, her eyes lit with that faraway look she'd get when she drank blood that called to mind the look in a woman's eyes when she came, that sense of transportation to something altogether wonderful. Christ, did I ever miss that.

In moments, Iris had sucked her dry, and she let her fall to the ground, wiping her mouth with a handkerchief.

"What?" she said.

"Nothing," I said. "I didn't expect you out here."

"You took long enough," Iris said. "I got tired of sitting around."

I went over to Joliette, picked her up, brushed gravel off her. Iris looked on.

"Another looker," she said. "Marvelous, Nate. Are you fucking with me? I didn't even want to look at her. Did you notice that?"

I didn't even want to look at Iris. And I wasn't going to dispose of Joliette's body, either. She watched me cart her indoors, and appeared in front of me.

"Oh, no," she said. "No more of that bullshit, Nate. You take her to the crematorium, and you light her up. Get it done."

In death, there was a kind of peace to Joliette's face that had been lacking in life—the anger lines were smoothed, the bitterness was absent. She was at peace. Her life's struggle ended with Iris Augenblick.

I went to say something else to Iris, but she was gone. She'd fed; that was all she cared about. She had moved on.

"I'm sorry," I said to Joliette's corpse.

I took Joliette home. I got her address from her license, and took her home. She lived in Logan Square, so she wasn't so terribly far away. Her place was a loft, and it was tiny. There was a mirror on one wall, and a barré. I felt bad for her—she'd never be able to watch herself again. I laid her down on her bed and closed the shades.

She had a fish in a tank, and I fed the fish, watched it swim around in there, not knowing the type.

I held a kind of private vigil for Joliette, stayed at her place for three days, watched her reflection gradually fade from the mirrors, as the infection took hold of her. I ate some of her food, drank her beer, listened as some of her friends left messages on her answering machine, wondering where she was, watched the television report on the goings on in the city.

I'd turned off my ringer, which had to have bugged Iris, because I know she was calling, trying to find out where I had gone, but I wasn't going to answer, just let it go to voicemail, let Iris stew. Let her go outside and get something to eat on her own, instead of me playing fetch for her.

There were photographs of Joliette on the wall, black and white images, sensuously shot, herself in a kind of white bodice, gazing out a window. High-contrast kind of stuff, and with her body turned, the planes of her face were somewhat lessened, and she looked almost lovely.

Iris kept calling, of course, wanting to know where the fuck I was, but I just let her leave a voicemail message. She left three. Each time, her half-dead voice leaving the same kind of message: "Hey. It's me. I'm just calling to see where you are."

More or less, the same thing.

I didn't return her calls.

The third night, Joliette rose from the dead.

"Holy fuck," she said, clutching her head, shaking out her mane of red-blond hair. She bit her big lips with her fangs. "What the fuck are these?"

"Fangs," I said.

"Pretty Boy? What the fuck?"

She looked at me with orange eyes, just the feral glow they got, what all vampires got in the dark, those fucking eyes. Joliette tugged at her fangs with her fingers.

"Nate, what the hell?"

I held out an arm. "Bite me."

She scoffed, sneered at me, those fangs sticking out, but she saw the veins in my arm, and she was on me in a second, grabbing my arm and biting me at the wrist. It had been awhile since Iris had bitten me, and while I can't say I'd forgotten how it felt, I had missed it, the rapture of it, that ecstatic entropy of a vampire's kiss.

A newborn, she was strong, but inexperienced, and I pried my arm loose from her after she'd had a good taste.

"My fucking god," she said, my blood running down her chin. "I'm a vampire."

"Yeah," I said. "It's been going around."

"Fuck," she said, trying to catch a look of herself in the mirror. She gazed at the mirror, then at herself, and at the mirror, and then at me. "Where the fuck am I, Nate?"

"You're here," I said, touching her shoulder with a poke of my finger. "But not there. I don't even know why that happens. Nobody does."

She walked over to the mirror and held her hand out to the glass, pressed her hand against it, moved it this way and that.

"It's not possible," she said.

"None of it is, right? I wouldn't sweat it," I said.

"You are Captain Howdy, you fucker," she said.

She still had my blood on her chin, and I got a tissue, handed it to her. She looked at me without comprehension, then licked the blood off her face.

I wasn't sure what to tell her. I didn't want to tell her about Iris, because after Patchouli and Jennipher, I didn't think Iris would take kindly to yet another vampire appearing as a result of her hunting.

Gazing at Joliette in the shadows, I decided that vampirism agreed with her—she didn't look ugly so much anymore, more strange and exotic. Somehow, the angles of her face worked well in the shadows.

"I'm a vampire," she said. "I'm a motherfucking vampire?"

"Yeah," I said. "You sure are."

"Who did it?" she asked.

"I can't tell you that," I said.

"What, are you like their pimp or something, Pretty Boy?" she asked.

I shook my head. "Look, I gotta go. You stay out of the sun, and try to be discreet. Anybody you drain completely, you can infect. Don't forget that."

She put herself between me and the door, moving with preternatural speed. "No, no, no. You're not going anywhere, Nateman. You tell me who did this to me."

"Her name is Iris," I said. "She's very old. You do not want to mess with her. She's as likely to kill you as not, if you cross her."

Joliette went into her bedroom and got herself some jeans and a tee shirt, put on some boots. Having tasted me a bit, her fangs had receded somewhat, her eyes returned to their natural color.

"I want to meet her," Joliette said.

"Terrible idea," I said, glancing at my cell phone messages. "She'll kill you. Seriously. I'm in bad enough trouble as it is by letting you return."

Joliette grabbed my cell phone, put her number in there.

"You fucking call me, Nateman," she said. "What am I supposed to do, here?"

"Do what you like," I said. "You need to feed."

"I'm a vegetarian," she said.

"Not anymore," I replied. "About every few days, you'll need to feed. You'll see. Anybody you kill will rise up like you, three days later, unless you do something about it. That means cutting off their heads and burning them in separate places and scattering the ashes."

"Motherfucking serial killer," Joliette said. "That's what I'll be."

"You don't have to be," I said. "You could just drain a bunch of people just a little bit, so they don't die."

Joliette turned her hands this way and that. "I'm dead."

"Undead," I said. "Totally different. You're gonna live forever, now."

"Fuck me," Joliette said. "Like, fuuuuuuuck."

She sprang on me again, knocking me to the floor, her fanged face in mine, looking at me with those big blue eyes, again ringed with bright orange.

"I'm hungry, Nate," she said, taking another bite on me, this time at the neck. She was fucking strong, and I arched my back, trying to pry her off, even as the bliss from her bite was overtaking me. I could feel her inside me, the way Iris used to be, could feel Joliette in my head, could taste her passion, her bitterness and venom. If Iris was a cold mountain, inscrutable and unknowable, Joliette was a raging forest fire, full of noise and malicious movement.

I pushed her off me, with more than a little difficulty, as I was weakened by her feeding off of me.

"No more," I said, pushing her off, dizzy. "Jesus."

"You're mine, Nateman," she said. "Fuck, yeah, you are."

And I could feel her coiled around my soul like a pale and luminous python, with opalescent scales. I got up, hand to my head.

"I have to go," I said, leaning against the door.

Joliette just sat there on the floor, grinning at me. "You can go, but you're not leaving, Nateman. You'll be back. And I'll be ready for you. The turn of the screwed."

There was a huskiness to her voice that hadn't been there before—her voice had been brassy, but now, that brass was tarnished. The darkness of the infection had done it.

I didn't want to leave. I wanted to stay there with her. The infernal nature of the vampire's kiss bound the victim to the vampire. It was as straightforward as that, a likely side effect of the affliction. Iris had long since given up on feeding on me that way, when she was sure of my loyalty—besides, I liked to think she was perhaps afraid of killing me, just because of the greatness of her appetite.

Not trusting Joliette to an embrace, I backed out of there, told her I'd call her, and went into the hall, which was moving beneath my feet. I don't know how much of my blood Joliette had taken, but I was thirsty and dizzy, my head was pounding, my heart was beating hard. I sweated, barely able to keep my footing. My skin tingled, my limbs were leaden.

I went down the hall, half-leaning on one wall as I made it to the elevator. I could have let Joliette take me; she would have made me into a vampire. It was weird to think that, after wanting Iris to make me one for so long, here was this opportunity to be sired by Joliette, and I refused it.

What was that all about?

Was it simply because I "belonged" to Iris? Or maybe I wasn't as ready as I had once thought I was for it? I don't know.

I walked down the street, weak as a kitten, the ground spinning. I looked drunk. And, lucky me, a police cruiser came up and two young cops, big beefy guys, one white, one black, they asked me where I was going, I told them I was going home, and they said I looked like I could use a ride, and that's how I ended up in the back of a cruiser. They just got me, took me by the arms and helped me in the back, where I passed out.

I woke up in jail, desperately thirsty, head ringing. I wasn't in a cell with other unfortunates; I was in a cell all by myself.

"Water," I croaked. "Anybody have water?"

The door opened, and in came Detective Lincoln Davis, carrying a cup of water in one hand, a pitcher in the other, and a thick folder under his arm.

"Captain Howdy?" he asked.

"Huh?"

"You Captain Howdy?" he asked.

"I'm Nate Sharp," I said.

"I know who you are," he said. "But who are you?"

Davis sat down, slid the cup of water toward me. I took it and guzzled it down. Water never tasted so sweet. I needed more, tapped the empty cup on the table. Davis poured another cup for me, and I drank it down.

"I need a doctor," I said, my hands shaking.

"Who did that to your neck?" Davis asked.

I touched my neck. There were two puncture wounds there. And, of course, the ones on my forearm. I showed Davis those.

"Yeah, we saw those," he said. "Who did that?"

"I didn't see them," I said.

"This some kind of Satanic vampire sex cult or something? Is that what it is, Boy?"

"I was attacked," I said.

Davis looked even bigger in person than he did on television. He looked like he could bench press me. He leaned forward in his seat, gazed intently at me.

"You Captain Howdy?"

"I don't know what you mean," I asked.

"Do you know who Captain Howdy is?" he asked. "You gotta know that, Son."

I nodded. "I'm really, really thirsty. I need a doctor."

"Doctor's on his way," Davis said. "Paramedics, more like. Here's the thing: you look like Captain Howdy."

He gestured to this thick file folder he had on his desk. "I've got a lot of witness reports, I've got cameras. There are cameras at some of the clubs. Café Fenris. Quandary. Fiendish. The Billy Club. Smirk. Wink. Fling's."

He held up a grainy photograph of me taking a girl somewhere, just walking. It looked kind of like me. Not definitively so, but close enough.

Davis read from a sheet of paper. "Tall guy, skinny, good-looking. I could go on."

The light from the room hurt my eyes, and I was desperately thirsty. I could feel my heart pounding in my chest. Was I infected?

"Do I get my phone call? Am I under arrest?"

"We got you for public intoxication," he said. "That's what we got you for, until you tell me something that makes a whole lot more sense."

"A vampire bit me," I said.

"Yeah," Davis said. "I got that."

"No, for real," I said. "Vampires are real."

"Mmm hmm," Davis said. He held up a picture of a girl. It was somebody. What was her name? I couldn't remember. "You know this girl?"

"No," I said.

"She's Madison Van De Kamp," he said. "Of the Van De Kamp family fortune. She went missing a year ago, Howdy. I've got you with her the night she disappeared."

He held up a copy of a cell phone picture, and there was Madison and me in the picture, beaming. We were at Fiendish. Everything was red.

"Is that you?" he asked.

"Looks like," I said.

"Is that you?" he asked.

"I think so," I said. "I was pretty wasted."

"Oh, so you do remember?"

I was thinking maybe I needed a lawyer, but I was still so sludgy, it was hard to think.

"I'm saying that it looks like me, yeah," I said. "But I don't remember that girl."

"She vanished," Davis said. "Last fall. Some of her friends said she was last seen with a tall, handsome, skinny guy."

"That narrows it down," I said.

Davis put a bunch of things on the table, nodded to them. "Sure, it's all circumstantial, right? No bodies, just vanished people. But I'm telling you right now—I think you're Captain Howdy. When my boys brought you in, I almost spat out my coffee, got it on my nice shirt, here. I've been looking for you for awhile, and here you are, dropped right in my lap."

"I'm not this guy," I said. "I'm not 'Captain Howdy.' I was attacked tonight, and I need medical attention. You think I'm making this up?"

"I think you're a pervert," Davis said. "I think you got caught in some kind of Satanic vampire sex cult thing, Man. That's what I think."

He put a blank sheet of paper and a pencil in front of me.

"Why don't you just confess? Make it easier on yourself."

He got up.

"I need more water," I said, having nearly emptied the pitcher. "Please, please, please, water?"

"We'll see about that," Davis said. He walked out, leaving me with pictures on the table, pictures with me in them.

I wrote on the piece of paper:

I AM NOT CAPTAIN HOWDY. I was attacked by something tonight, something that bit me and drained my blood. I am in urgent need of medical attention, and it'll be pretty clear if a doctor examines me that I am in need of a blood transfusion or something, because something, and I'm not saying what, bit me and sucked my blood. Detective Lincoln Davis tried to extract a confession out of me in the absence of legal counsel present, but what I really need is immediate medical attention. I'm a victim, here, not a suspect. Something attacked me. Something with teeth and a thirst for blood.

I signed it, then laid my head on the table. I didn't even look at the photographs on the table, didn't want to see. After awhile, Davis came in with another pitcher of ice water, which he set on the table, just out of reach. Sweating, shaking, I leaned forward and grabbed it, drinking right from the pitcher, guzzling down the water, while Davis read what I'd written.

"Bullshit," he said. "You're him. You're Howdy, Pardner."

I drank the entire pitcher of water, set the pitcher down.

"Who's 'Alexei?'" Davis asked, holding up the card.

"You'd better ask Alexei that," I said.

"You gay, Sport?"

"No," I said.

"We sent a cruiser to this address," Davis said. "They said nothing was there. An old, empty building, nothing else."

"They didn't go inside, did they?" I said.

"They didn't find anything," he said.

I wondered how Alexei did that. Maybe he mindfucked the cops. That would be easy enough for a vampire to do.

"We sent a cruiser to your place, too," Davis said. "Nice place. A bit, I don't know, Spartan? What are you doing, living in that big old empty place all by yourself, Howdy? Thing is, that place is titled to a 'Ms. Iris Augenblick.' But she wasn't home when we came over. We took your computer, Kid. And we found a body in the basement."

He slid a picture of that guy, the dead guy Iris had left in my room, the one I'd put in the vault. There he was, dead, drained of blood, puncture marks at the neck.

"You know this guy?" he asked.

"No," I said, feeling completely fucked, now. Goddamned Iris. Where was she?

The bright side of talking to Davis while feeling so rotten is that I couldn't tip how nervous I was, because I already looked like shit. Sweating, shaking, pale as a ghost. He just looked me in the eye, a smile playing at the corners of his lips.

"Where's Ms. Augenblick?" Davis asked. "Did you murder her, too? Take her residence as your own? We searched through that place, top to bottom, and we didn't find her. We did find evidence that the man you killed had been in your bed."

"Yeah?"

"Yeah," Davis said. "We can just keep holding you, Boy. Because right now, you're my prime suspect. And we've got a dead man in your basement, drained of motherfucking blood. You want to tell me about that?"

"I don't know anything about it."

"We got your fingerprints on the lock and doors to that basement. That holding cell, if you will. Forensics found blood in there, too. Is that where you take 'em?"

"I didn't take anybody anywhere," I said.

Davis stroked his moustache, just composed himself a bit, pausing. "Son, you have a body in your basement. We have your prints on that basement door. We've got you living in this fucking place that doesn't belong to you. Here's what I think: you killed Ms. Augenblick and made her place your lair. That building's old—it's more than paid for. You hunker down there and do your day trading to pay for it, while at night, you hunt down people and you fucking murder them. Enough bullshit, Howdy. Come clean."

"I didn't murder that guy," I said. "I don't even know who he is. I didn't even know he was there. You're just trying to set me up."

"I don't even need to do that," Davis said. "Nathan Sharp, aka, Captain Howdy, the Vampire Killer. You know the newspapers will run hard with that."

"This has got to be illegal," I said. "I want my phone call."

"Who you gonna call?"

Who would I call? That was a good question. It had to be Iris. I had to call her.

Davis slid the phone my way, and I dialed Iris. It rang twice, and then she picked up.

"Yeah?" she said. "What is it, Nate? *Now* you call me?"

"Iris," I said. "I'm in jail. They think I'm Captain Howdy."

"You *are* Captain Howdy," she said, making me cringe.

"I need help," I said. "They found a body in the basement."

"Not my problem," Iris said. "I'm sorry, Nate."

"Iris, what?"

"You're on your own on this," she said. "I can't help you."

"Can't you at least send a lawyer down here? They're trying to pin a murder on me—"

"Several murders and disappearances," Davis said, smiling at me.

"Please get me a lawyer," I said. "I need help."

"See how you like it," Iris said.

Then she hung up on me.

I just stared at the phone, incredulous, while Davis watched. I put the phone down.

"Weren't you supposed to give me some privacy for my call?" I asked.

"Meh. Supreme Court's been chilling out on that kind of stuff, Boy. So, 'Iris' didn't pull through for you, huh?"

I shook my head.

"Funny how that works," Davis said. "Well, how about we just keep you here until we get a confession out of you? After the doctor sees you, of course."

I just rested my head on the table. My head felt like a bowling ball crossed with a balloon—light as a feather yet weighing a ton. My heart pounded in my chest even as it sank like a stone. I was a dead man.

-X-

Dr. Stiles was this older guy with salt-and-pepper hair and a very tan face, and he looked at me with coolly clinical eyes. Drew a little blood, examined the bite marks, and recommended I get about two pints of blood immediately.

He chided Detective Davis for keeping me as long as he did. They took me to Grace Memorial Hospital, where I was restrained in the bed with a two-police officer guard detail, while they gave me back some blood.

I just lay in the hospital bed, weak as a kitten, while the blood got back into me. Davis came in and sat down across from me. He fished out a packet of chewing gum (Wrigley's Double Mint) and popped two pieces in his mouth.

"Dr. Stiles thinks the bite marks are for real," he said. "Doesn't think they're self-inflicted. The blood lab will have some results in about 48 hours. How are you feeling, Champ?"

"Thirsty," I said, although I was feeling better, now that blood was getting back into me.

"You want me to call the nurse, Cap'n?" he asked.

"I'm not Captain Howdy," I said.

"Sure, sure," Davis said. "I get it. But here's the thing: until you tell me how that body ended up in your basement, you are. We've had well over a thousand people disappear in this fine city over the course of the last five years. Now, I know, to you, that doesn't mean jack—but in a metropolitan area of, what, 10 million people? That means that—"

"A tiny fraction," I said.

Davis smiled. "Yeah, that many people gone missing? It's a god-damned epidemic of disappearances."

"People come and go, Detective Davis," I said.

"Not that many people," Davis said. "I mean, we're talking 'poof'—they're gone. Nobody's seen 'em since. Now, you seem like a good kid, but maybe you're all Ted Bundy, you know what I mean? All shiny teeth and perfect hair? They say some serial killers, the really sharp ones, they can charm the sparkle off of diamonds."

"I haven't killed anybody," I said. "Not a one. You can polygraph me if you like."

"Mmm," Davis said. "Don't think I haven't thought of that, Boy. But, see, that doesn't mean a damned thing, either, now does it? You can spoof a polygraph. You put enough icewater in those veins, and you can spoof it. That what you are, a spoofer?"

"Am I being interrogated some more, Detective Davis?" I asked. "I've had a rough day."

"It's gonna get rougher," Davis said. "A whole lot rougher."

His cell phone rang, and Davis scooped it up, never breaking his basilisk gaze on me. "Davis. What is it?"

Then his face cracked. "What? Are you sure?"

I watched, wondering what the hell he'd heard. Maybe Iris had pulled through for me after all? It was possible.

"No," Davis said. "That doesn't make any goddamned sense. He was dead. The report had him as dead. I'm saying we had guys there that said he was dead."

Then I guessed it: the guy, the one Iris had left for me, the chew toy—he'd come back. I could just imagine the coroner or mortician or whoever it was who handled the bodies like that, them choking when they saw that guy sit up. Lord knows how it actually happened.

"Alright, well you keep him there, you hear me? I'll be down there in 20 minutes," Davis said, hanging up.

"Everything alright, Detective Davis?"

Davis glowered at me, shook his head. "Doesn't make any goddamned sense. That stiff we pulled from your basement is apparently alive. He got up. Now you tell me what the hell's going on, Cap'n."

"He's a vampire," I said. "He's a goddamned vampire. How many times do I have to tell you this?"

I gestured to my neck, which was bandaged, now, and to my wrist.

"Like hell he is," Davis said. "You tell me how he got there, Cap'n."

"She bit him," I said. What the hell did I have to lose? "Iris bit him and put him down there."

"Iris," Davis said. "Augenblick?"

"That's the one," I said. "Look, you can get her number off my phone. Give her a call, she'll set you straight."

Why not? Seemed like the simplest way to get my ass out of dodge. I know you think I'm probably a rotten guy, but fuck you, alright? I had to deal with a lot that night.

Davis pointed at me, his finger like a wooden peg. "We're not done here, Cap'n. Not even close."

I laid back in my bed, rang for the nurse, put my arms over my head. I felt good for the first time that night. The nurse came in, a pretty young woman with thick eyebrows and black hair. A Latina, by the look of her.

"Sir?" she asked.

"Water," I said. *"Por favor."*

CHAPTER 17

Chew Toy had served admirably. The guy had said that he'd met Iris at Café Blanche, and they'd hit it off, had gone to her place, and that was the last thing he'd remembered, because he'd been drunk. He'd awakened at the Coroner's, on the table, and that was that. My name didn't even come up.

Not that it mattered—Detective Davis released me. He came in, his eyes glazed like fine pottery, and he tells the duty officer that I wasn't implicated in the Captain Howdy case, that I was a dead end.

It had to make him seethe, somewhere, deep inside his mind, but I knew what happened. He'd called Iris, had arranged a visit, and she'd royally mindfucked him. I know it, I sympathize—I've been there. I know what she can do with those eyes. She can just stare into you, and you—the you that you knew—just vanishes. Like a steamroller to the prefrontal lobe, she just smooths out the wrinkles, and then what you thought you knew, you didn't know anymore.

And like that, I was released. It had nothing to do with me—I know this. Iris didn't help anybody but Iris. It was how she operated. But, by being in her shadow, I benefited from it. And in covering her own tracks, she covered mine.

This didn't mean I was in any less danger than I was before; hell, if anything, I was in more danger. But at least it meant I wasn't going to be pegged as Captain Howdy, at least not by Detective Lincoln Davis.

The Chicago Police Department released me and no charges were pressed. I got away.

Fully charged with borrowed blood, my laptop tucked under my arm, I went back to Iris's feeling fitter than I'd felt in days. I keyed in and sauntered right into the place, only to see Iris standing there with a few of her friends—vampire friends. Like four of them. One of them being Alexei, looking like he'd walked out of one of those paintings Iris had in her basement.

They must have been having one of those serious vampire talks in the living room. Or the unliving room, more like.

I looked at the other vampires—one was an Asian guy in a black suit with a red shirt and a black tie, with long hair, all shiny. And the other was a Latino woman, short and curvy with black hair that sprayed around her head. They had all stopped talking when I'd come in. I knew they were all bloodsuckers the moment I saw them. You can just tell. Vampires exude that whole vibe, like spiritual pollution.

"Hey, Nate," Iris said. "We were just talking about you."

"That can't be good," I said.

"Is no good," Alexei said. "You make trouble for Iris. For me. For all of us."

The Latina didn't say a word. Her eyes were dark brown, but I avoided them. I didn't look any of them in the eye for more than a second.

"You make trouble for us all," the Asian said. "Stupid boy."

Iris walked over and put her arm around me. "Nate means well. He just makes mistakes. He's simple."

She actually tousled my hair with a cold hand. I wondered what I was looking at. Were these the dominant vampires of Chicagoland? Was this some kind of coven? Or was that reserved only for witches? Iris had used that term before, but I didn't know if it was right or not. What did you call a group of vampires? It sounded like the setup for a punch line.

"I'm not simple," I said. "I just got caught by the police."

"Stupid boy," Alexei said. "We should tear you to bits and feed you to the fish, you know that? Iris is the only one keeping you alive."

I hated Alexei with every breath, and he could feel it, just looked at me, orange eyes ablaze, face completely composed. Vampires could win any staredown, not just because of their hypnotic eyes, either, but because of their undeadpan expressions.

"The police come to my place. My place. Again. They ask questions," Alexei said, his thick necktie pumping as he spoke. "Ask questions of Alexei."

The Latina just watched me. Not a word spoken. She had such broad hips, it was hard to imagine her as a vampire—what did you think of with vampires? Skinny bitches, right? Always skinny bitches. I'm not saying the Latin was plump, but she was most definitely curvy. Voluptuous, even. She'd clearly been made at a time when a fuller-figured woman was the norm. There it was, as ever, the thumbprint of the times that spawned them.

"The balance we maintain in the city is precarious," the Asian said. "Delicate. An interconnected web of give and take. We hunt carefully in our respective areas. Chinatown and Midway are mine. Rosamunda has the West Side. Alexei, the Northwest Side. Iris and Lucinda share the lakeshore and the north shore. Constance has the South Side."

I looked around, not seeing the representative of the South Side, nor seeing Lucinda.

"They're late," the Asian said. "The point is, we maintain a very delicate balance. And you're upsetting the balance, Nathan. You keep loosing vampires on the city, you're upsetting that balance. Between us, and only counting ourselves, not our respective organizations, we take nearly 2000 lives a year, and that requires care, caution, and discretion."

Constance came in, this tall black woman in a one-piece denim jumpsuit, with goddess-like curves, impossibly tall, almond-colored eyes, her hair a delicate network of braids that hung around her head. She looked to be Creole to my eyes, possible Afro-Cuban. I immediately wondered what her history was, where she'd come from.

"Where is he? Where's Captain Howdy Doody?"

The Latina nodded to me, and Constance looked at me. "This skinny boy's the one been causing all the trouble? He's a big twig."

She walked up to me, and we were eye-to-eye. She was that tall. She was beautiful, looked like she was made out of chestnut. She looked to be in her 20s, but I knew she was far older. It just showed. Vampires were immortal, but they still somehow showed their age.

Iris was the oldest, except for Alexei. I could just tell that, too, from the deference they showed her. Vampires did respect age, for, among immortals, longevity counted. Age was power. Age implied survival, knowledge, skill, and experience, and vampires understood what that meant, valued those things. Age meant power in the vampiric hierarchy, both in terms of actual raw power and in perceptual power. To the vampire, that which didn't kill you really did make you stronger.

"Iris says you're worth saving," Constance said. "You want to tell us in your own words exactly why?"

I didn't like having to justify my existence to the vampires. They all just stood there, waiting, motionless, silent, listening.

"I like being alive," I said.

"You like being alive," Constance said. "You gotta do better than that."

"I want Iris to be happy," I said. "I have been so careful. I just had a bad night, that's all."

They scoffed in their various ways. I got the unnerving sense that my life was most definitely hanging in the balance, here, that I was facing a kind of tribunal.

Alexei spoke first.

"Live or die? He make trouble, we decide right here, right now," he said. He jabbed a downward-facing thumb.

I couldn't believe my life was being decided like this, on an up or down vote by a handful of goddamned vampires.

The Asian gave a thumbs' down. What the fuck? I didn't even know the guy. The Latina gave a thumbs' up. So did Constance. What the hell was this all about? My life hanging in the balance, based purely on Iris's whim?

Iris sighed. "I know you think he's an idiot, Alexei, and not worth the trouble. But we all have our favored minions, don't we? We all have people who get us through the tough times? Nate is that for me. He grounds me. I can't really express it properly in words, but he does. Yes, he's an idiot, yes, he is far more trouble than he's worth, yes, I do so much for him and get next to nothing in return, yes, he is an incredible, unrelenting pain in the ass, but he also centers me. His nearly endless human imperfections keep me in touch with what I was in a myriad of ways. His petty nature, his shortsightedness, his vindictiveness, his jealousy, his selfishness, his thoughtlessness, his sense of entitlement—all of those things help remind me of who I used to be. We all know how easy it is to lose oneself in this world. As time passes, we lose sight of those things. Nate is my anchor."

She gave a thumbs' up.

Alexei let out a disgusted hiss. "Of course. Mawkish nonsense. Women. My fucking god. This one should die. He make nothing but trouble. You find new minion."

"I'm keeping him," Iris said. "He's mine."

Then goddamned Alexei stood up. His blocklike face was a mask of stony hatred. For me. This bearded barbarian bastard, who looked like he would have been comfortable at the prow of a Viking longship, this man who would have ridden Cossacks down, this man who gazed at me with complete disgust, my enemy.

To think that I owed my life to Iris, that only her regard for me stayed Alexei from tearing me to bits, it was almost more than I could bear. I felt glad to be alive, and grateful to be under Iris's protection.

"You make mistake, Iris. This one should die."

"He's mine," Iris said again.

Alexei threw his hand up, got up, walked past me, disgusted. The Asian had already vanished, while the Latina became a bat and fluttered away. Only Constance remained.

"You're living on borrowed time, Junior," Constance said. "You keep that in mind, now. Iris, you need to keep that boy on a leash."

Iris smiled, embraced Constance. Vampire hugs were easily the most fake things you could ever see. Because vampires weren't givers; they were all takers, every last one of them, and hugging was all about giving, not taking—nobody took a hug. A hug was something given, was one of the simplest, most wonderful gestures of human affection people could share.

So, when vampires hugged, it was just incredibly awkward and wrong-seeming. It was like two porcupines hugging or something. Creatures unused to giving, and unwilling to give. All upper torso, and nothing else. Their hearts weren't into it. How could they be? Their hearts didn't beat.

Still, I understood that Iris had vouched for me in some fashion with the rest of the vampire mafia, and had saved my life. How I had transgressed wasn't entirely clear to me, except that it involved a rawer, more naked expression of power than the vampires were typically willing to exert. I wondered how much of the city's infrastructure the vampires had compromised. How many aldermen, how many city officials, how many police officers and ward bosses were in some way, shape, and form beholden to the vampires?

Iris watched Constance strut out the door, then turned to me.

"Once again, you embarrassed me, Nate. What are you trying to do? Are you trying to make me look bad in front of the others? Is that what you're trying to do? Because you're succeeding admirably."

I didn't have anything to say in my defense, because there was both nothing to defend, and nothing I could say. I owed her my life.

"You spared me," I said. "I don't even know what I did wrong."

"You inconvenienced Alexei," Iris said. "He was very angry, Nate. That's the second time you've bothered him. Don't let there be a third time. You have no idea how powerful he is. And don't get me started about Woo. Woo is mighty. They all are, in their ways."

I resolved in that moment to kill Alexei.

Admittedly, someone pissing you off was not a valid reason to want to snuff them, but in the case of vampires, it most definitely was. I fucking hated him. I hated that he was Iris's sire, hated that he hated me, hated that he was such a prick. I wondered if he'd been an asshole his entire, long life, if his sire had seen him and decided that an asshole like that deserved immortality.

I couldn't even count the ways that I hated him, except that his loathing of me was such a perfect reason to take him out. I was going to kill him. It was as simple as that.

Alexei would die. I would kill Alexei, or die trying. Now you think "How can skinny Nate Sharp take out Alexei the Ancient Vampire?"

Just watch me.

Iris sniffed at me a little, running her nose near my neck.

"Who did this to you? Who drained you, Nate?"

I was not going to sell out Joliette. It was not even a consideration. The opalescent python wound around my soul gave me a squeeze.

"Nobody," I said.

"Tell me, Nate," Iris said. "Who bit you?"

"I didn't see them," I said.

A tiny lie, and Iris could sniff it out. Iris lived in lies, swam in deception.

"Tell me," she said. "I want to know who, because you have to understand that it's not done, Nate. Nobody touches another's minions. It's not done. So, who did it?"

"Cleo," I said. "Her name was Cleo."

I could see Iris cycling through the vampire rolodex of her mind, drawing a blank. "I don't know any Cleo. What'd she look like?"

"Like a vampire," I said. "She was a blur. She was from Wisconsin. She said it was payback or something."

Iris paced around a little, thinking about it. "Cleo, Cleo, Cleo…."

"Yeah," I said. I couldn't believe I was jerking Iris around, but it felt pretty good, I have to say, after so many years of being jerked around by her. Yes, I suppose I was ungrateful for her saving my life; but the pointed truth of it was that my life would not have been endangered at all if it hadn't been for Iris.

"You have to be more careful, Nate," Iris said. "What does she look like?"

"She's a redhead," I said, just blowing smoke. "Pale as the moon. Tall. Was wearing white. Spoke with an accent I couldn't place."

"I don't know her," Iris said. "Maybe a transient. You have to watch yourself."

She wasn't worried or concerned for me; I couldn't hear that in her voice. Rather, it was just an admonishment—like saying "Bad dog."

"This is why you should be the one hunting, not me," I said. "I've become a target. Captain Howdy, all of that."

Iris smiled at that.

"Captain Howdy. What's that from?"

"*The Exorcist*," I said.

"What's that?"

"A movie," I said. Iris knew almost nothing about movies. She was probably too busy sucking people's blood in theaters to actually watch movies.

I sat down on the sofa where the Latina Rosamunda had been. And Iris sat down across from me, crossing a leg, resting her chin on a couple of her pale, slender fingers.

"What am I going to do with you, Nathan Sharp?" she asked.

The weird thing was that in that moment, I didn't want her to make me into a vampire. The prospect of being even more in thrall to her was just nauseating to me. I didn't know how much was genuine irritation and revulsion, and how much was Joliette, me being in thrall to her, instead.

"You have to stop this bad habit of not disposing of the bodies, Nate," Iris said. "That's really what this comes down to. It's like what Stalin said—'no person, no problem.'"

Her quoting Stalin amused and horrified me. Did she know him? Iris was effectively apolitical; I couldn't imagine her tooling around in Russia back in the day. Here's the thing, though: Stalin never said that. I looked it up.

I could see her looking me over, speculating.

"World War II was vampire heaven, Nate," Iris said. "The whole world was aflame, death everywhere. It was a feast. And with the mandatory blackouts? Roving death squads? Sieges? Strategic bombing? All of that? Paradise. The only thing we didn't like was the firebombing. Hated that. But the rest was nice. We all fed well back then."

"Were you back in Europe then?" I asked.

"For awhile," she said. "It doesn't matter. Alexei had talked me back to Europe for a bit of a sabbatical, a kind of walk down memory lane, to see how much the place had changed. And it was weird, I suppose, because to me, it seemed almost the same. Europe was Europe. Even the totalitarian ideologies infecting it felt retrograde to me, a giant step backward. But it was odd, like children playing with the same toys they'd always used. A death camp might as well have been a gulag. Only the industrial application of slaughter expanded the scope of it—the motives and players were largely the same. I wasn't a fan of the firebombings, of course. But you already know my feelings about fire. So, he took me around, tried to get me enmeshed in European politics again, like it had been in the old days, but my heart wasn't in it, anymore. I had made a name for myself in the New World, had enjoyed my primacy there. Of course, by the 20th century, there were plenty of emigrants; I wasn't the only old one there, anymore. But it hardly mattered; I had my place, and it wasn't in Europe. Alexei eventually saw that."

Another of Iris's stories, as evocatively told as any of them. I sighed, wondering how I had even fallen for her. Nature abhors a vacuum. That's how it happened—I was sucked into the void that she represented. I tried gamely to fill in the blanks, to make sense of the senseless. How very human of me.

"You get some rest," she said. "When you're better, we can talk about what your duties are around here."

She turned into mist and seeped out the window, leaving me alone with my thoughts.

My phone rang. It was Jennipher.

"Yeah?"

"Hey, Nate," she said. "Whatcha doing?"

"Resting," I said.

"Where are you?" she asked.

"Why?"

"Just wondering," she said. "I wanted to thank you. Let me tell you what I've been up to lately...."

And she did. Jennipher talked my ear off for like an hour, about hunting in the clubs, and being really careful, and just nipping a bunch of people a little bit, and how delicious everybody was, and how she first thought that sucking blood would be kind of gross, but how she just pretended everybody was like a smoothie—that's what she called 'em, "Smoothies"—and that made it better, and how some people tasted spicy, and some tasted sweet, and she just feasted on a ton of people, just little bits here and there, and she wondered whether vampires could get fat.

"No," I said. "You'll look like you do forever."

"Awesome," she said. "That is so reassuring. Because I was having an awesome time, and I didn't want to gorge myself or anything."

"Please," I said. "Be really, really careful. Because there are these vampire bosses around—Constance, Rosamunda, Alexei, Iris, Lucinda, and an Asian guy named Woo—and if they catch you freelancing, they'll fucking kill you."

"I'm being really super careful, Nate," Jennipher said. "I love the nightlife! It's such a blast. I can just talk to people and they just kind of zone out and then I'm like 'I have to try them!' and I do. And they don't even remember. I think I can put 'em into a trance."

"Yes," I said. "Your eyes can do that."

"How awesome is that?"

"Very," I said, rubbing my temples. "I'm really super tired, Jennipher. I'm gonna crash, alright?"

"Okay, Sleepyhead," Jennipher said. "We so have to get together sometime, though, okay? I want to see you."

"Alrighty," I said. "Bye."

I went upstairs, plugged in my phone, let it recharge, and conked out on my bed. I didn't wake up until midday the next day. Some crows were cawing. I didn't even know what day it was, checked on my computer.

I took a shower, got scrubbed, and then walked around the place, looking for Iris, my usual ritual. No secret doors, no hidey holes. I knew she was in here somewhere. But where? Where the hell was she?

I pocketed my phone, then went to the sporting goods store in my neighborhood, bought three wooden baseball bats and some canteens. I went to a department store and got a backpack, a headlamp flashlight, three cans of pepper spray, and some Christmas ornaments, the glass bulbs—couldn't believe they had Christmas stuff out already, since it wasn't even Thanksgiving, yet. What the fuck? I went to the grocery store and bought up a ton of garlic, got some garlic powder, too, a big bottle of it.

"You doing some cooking?" the clerk asked. "Sure you got enough garlic?"

"Yeah," I said. "I think so."

Then, heading back home, I snuck into St. Michael's and nicked some holy water, filled my canteens. Then I went back to Iris's place and lopped off the handles of the baseball bats and went about sharpening them carefully, until I got nice points on them. I put these in the backpack with the garlic cloves and the holy water. I carefully poured the holy water into the Christmas ornaments, sealed the tops with a spool of duct tape. I put a ball peen hammer and a pry bar in my backpack, and then I went out.

I was going to pay Alexei a visit. He deserved some payback after voting for my fucking death. And once he was gone, Woo was going to get it, too. It was the least that I could do.

-X-

CHAPTER 18

I stood across the street from Alexei's place, sizing it up. I'd been careful to put a baseball cap and shades on, not wanting to be conspicuous to the various cameras and such that were in the area.

The steel door, the supposed entrance, looked too daunting. I saw that there were three dogs in the side lot, now, including Blackface the Wonder Dog. I went around the block, checked out the service entrance.

Then I saw that the neighboring building, this old, dark three-story Victorian house, was built very close to Alexei's bunker, the way Chicago buildings sometimes were. There was a narrow space between the two, narrow enough that if I pressed my back against the brick wall of the Victorian, I could put my legs against Alexei's place and actually walk my way up it, one step at a time. So, I did just that, with the backpack on my lap as I went.

Since Alexei's was only a single-story place, it wasn't much of a slog at all—I just worked my way up and then realized when I got to the top of Alexei's place that I should have put my back against his wall, instead of against the Victorian. I tossed my backpack onto the black roof of Alexei's, then lunged for his place, barely getting hold. I brought a leg over with a wheeze and rolled onto the roof.

Then I put on the backpack and looked around, in case there were guards around or something. The absence of guards made me more than a little nervous. I pulled a ski mask from my pack and pulled it down over my face.

As I'd hoped, there was a service entrance to the roof, and I took out the pry bar and broke into it, after I was reasonably sure there wasn't an alarm rigged to it. There was a great big air conditioning unit on the roof of this place, whatever it was.

I went down the stairs, turning on a flashlight, carefully creeping. My heart was pounding as I went to another door, an inner door, and listened to it. I couldn't hear a thing.

This door was locked, too, so I took the pry bar to it and forced it open.

Inside was a large room full of iceboxes. The iceboxes were like coffins, arranged in neat rows. I went to one of them, opened it.

Within the icebox, shrouded in haze, were full packets of blood. Each icebox contained them.

"Blood bank," I said aloud, my breath fogging. It was cold in this whole place.

I stalked around in there, front to back, and didn't find anything that looked like Alexei. No bodies, nothing. Just blood. Lots and lots of blood.

I went back out the way I came, not sure if I'd set off any alarms or not. If Alexei was hiding in there, I'd not found where. That was the irritating thing with vampires—they were really good at finding little secret hiding places like that.

Coming out on the roof, I could see some cars pulling up to the entrance of Alexei's covert blood bank. Sleek, black sedans.

Silent alarms. Wonderful.

I jumped from the bank to the Victorian building next to it, landing on a balcony, and not a moment too soon, for I saw some big guys in dark suits speaking what I assumed was Russian or Ukrainian as they ran down the alley below.

I tried the window behind me, found it sealed tight, painted shut. Cursing, I hunkered down on that little balcony, while Alexei's goons combed his blood bank.

When it looked like it was clear, I elbowed the window, cleared the glass, and crawled in. The goons would eventually see where I'd come in, would likely trace me to this building.

Inside the shabby Victorian building, I looked around. While the thing wasn't much to look at from the outside, inside, it was stupendously opulent. I'd landed on a thick, blood-red oriental rug, and all around me was furniture that looked like mahogany and teak, with old paintings on the wall, none of which I recognized. It was opulent in a way that I expected Iris's place to be, and that's when it hit me—*this* was Alexei's lair. The blood bank was just close at hand, without being explicitly connected to this place.

It had to be, because the Victorian was crammed with amazing antiquities, and not just anything, but fucking Russian stuff—nesting dolls, painted eggs, even what looked like it could have been some Faberge eggs on the mantelpiece. There were weapons everywhere, on the walls. Swords, sabers, spears, halberds, pikes, axes, crossbows. It was an incredible homage to armaments, covering a millennium of mayhem, right there on his walls.

I was in some kind of second-floor drawing room, it looked like. And there I saw them, plain as day: a pair of portraits.

A Velázquez from 1629.

Here was a more measured Iris, stately and formidable, posing with Alexei in what I presume to be an allegorical drawing room, with the Venetian lion represented in a tapestry as well as the Russian two-headed eagle in a flag. Alexei was wearing an armored breastplate of gunmetal gray that held his moon standard in relief and pantaloons of black and silver, bearing a fine rapier of silver. Iris wore red and yellow, a dress of rich detail, brocaded and textured. They mirror each other—Iris with her black hair and red dress, and Alexei with his red beard and dark clothing. There was a naturalism to the portrait that breathed life into them both. I wondered if they had gorged themselves before the sitting, because their flesh was perfectly pink, altogether human.

The second painting was a Hogarth from 1734.

It was almost comic, with Iris and Alexei regarding each other from opposite a table that has a place setting for two on it, but no food. They gazed not at one another, but in some unnamed middle distance. Alexei looked like a kind of gentleman squire, and Iris looked like his lady wife. Over a century after the other painting. They were in a well-apportioned home, filled with trinkets and antiquities, were illuminated by lanterns. There was no love between them. I could see this. Or, more accurately, no love in Iris for Alexei. His own eyes betrayed exasperation, and an almost unfathomable loneliness.

I heard somebody moving below. Someone was coming upstairs, and I had nothing but a bunch of vampire-killing gear. I hid behind the entry door, as Oksana came through the door and walked over to the spot where I'd jumped through, the broken glass. She gasped at the sight of it, and I rushed her before she could turn around, tackling her and taking her to the ground. Before she could cry out, I gagged her with a bandanna, and then took out one of those zip-tie plastic bonds the police use for riot control. I pulled it tight and positioned Oksana so she wouldn't be able to see me.

She'd been wearing blue jeans and some pointy-toed boots and a nice purple blouse patterned with little yellow flowers. I peeked at her neck, and saw bite marks on either side.

Then I began to go through the place, room by room, listening to see if there was anybody else in the place. A grandfather clock intoned the hour with measured, genteel restraint: 2:15. I had plenty of time.

I was crazy for doing this, I understand that. But I was also crazy-pissed at Alexei. I went through every inch of that place, knowing that I had to find him, because if I didn't, he sure as hell was going to come for me and kill me for breaking into his blood bank and tying up his babe and breaking into his place.

There was no going back, and I knew this better than anybody.

The place was riot of colors, of forest green and gold, of red and yellow, and blue and white. Those were the dominant colors, with the third floor being mostly red and yellow, the second floor blue and white, and the first floor green and gold.

The armor and weapon motifs varied by floor as well, with the archaic weapons on the third floor—the maces, shields, swords, axes, spears, crossbows, suits of armor and so on lived there. The second floor housed things mostly muskets of many varieties, as well as some sabers. The first floor was more modern weaponry, things that were probably from the 19th century onward. The entire collection would have been great in a museum. Why Alexei kept it all at his place, only he knew. Sentimentality? Nostalgia? I was sure that he'd used every weapon he had on display, which conjured up all sorts of colorful images.

Where there weren't weapons, there were paintings of various sizes. The portraits were the exception—landscapes seemed more to Alexei's liking, particularly sunlit places I did not recognize, by artists that I did not know. It was odd, seeing the sun valorized in the artwork of a vampire's lair.

And, given Alexei's longevity, I felt that there must be other holdings in Europe and beyond, that this American lodging in Chicago was only a small part of his estate. I imagined castles somewhere. If the Nightlord had ranged as far and wide as Iris had indicated, then who knows where else he owned property?

Alexei wasn't anywhere upstairs, not that I could tell, despite searching everywhere. So I went to the basement, which was locked, of course. Then I ran back upstairs, dug keys out of Oksana's pockets, while she squirmed and strained to get free. But I had her trussed up tight. I dug out her cell phone, fished through the list of contacts. But it was all written in Russian or Ukrainian, and none of the names looked like "Alexei" to me.

I pocketed the phone and ran back down to the basement, while the grandfather clock tolled 3:15.

The door to the basement was steel, and it had a deadbolt on it. It was as good as any place to start. I was sweating, going through the keys. The minion had a half-dozen keys on the ring, and I went through them all. None of them worked. I ran back upstairs, and frisked Oksana again, muttering under my breath. She had a necklace on, a gold thing, and I fished that out while she squirmed and protested beneath the gag. On it was a key. I yanked the necklace off her while she struggled, then went back downstairs, breathing hard.

That key opened the deadbolt, but the door wouldn't open. There was a lock on the inside. Cursing, I dug out my pry bar and went to work on the door, which took about 45 minutes to force open, just because it was a very sturdy door, and I wasn't sure what the hell I was doing. It had quieted down outside, at the blood bank. I wondered if any of the goons who showed up would come here.

The door finally yielded and I opened it carefully, turning on my headlamp, so I could see. There were no steps leading into the basement. It was a fucking straight drop down, and I could hear something down there, a squirming.

"What the fuck?"

Shining my light, I saw that the floor of the basement was absolutely covered with rats. It was an unbelievable number of them, climbing all over each other, squinting up at me and my light, a zillion little red eyes. They were crawling all over each other, a mass of rodent bodies and tails, in constant motion.

"Fucking hell," I said. I had not been prepared for that. "Fuck fuck fuck fucking hell."

Then I was left with a choice, whether to go down there, or whether there was another hiding place.

I went back upstairs again, and grabbed Oksana, hoisted her onto my shoulder, and took her down there.

The grandfather clock tolled 4:00. I was cutting it close, goddammit.

"Where is Alexei?" I asked her, leaning her into the gaping mouth of the basement. She didn't protest, didn't do anything. "Is he down there?"

But she wouldn't say, and I wasn't going to go Gitmo on her or anything; I tried to reason it out. Either the basement was a trap, or it actually led to Alexei. Oksana had a key to that door, which meant that, in theory, she could open it to get in. But the door was bolted from the inside, which meant that somebody on the inside had access to it.

Once down in there, however, could I get back out? I fished around in the place, in the kitchen, lowered a chair into the basement. And then another one, and another. Just in case. Glancing at the digital clock on the oven, I saw that it was 4:15.

I took out my duct tape and wound it around my pants legs a dozen times. Fucking hell. Then I went into the kitchen and looked for something that would burn. I took a thick wooden candle holder and wrapped a towel on it, knotted the thing at the top. Then I soaked the towel in cooking oil, just got it completely drenched, and then put it over the stove and ignited it, created my makeshift torch.

It was 4:30.

This was all kinds of bad. I was about to go into a master vampire's rat-filled fucking lair, with a mind to kill him. Part of me was still of a mind to turn back now, to get out of there and hope that Alexei didn't come to kill me for the effrontery I'd shown in invading his home in the States.

And, frankly, I was surprised at how comparatively modest this place was. It was a comfortable abode, but was hardly a grand, imperial Russian kind of palace I had imagined Alexei would have preferred. I imagined him in the suburbs, living with a massive retinue of adherent-worshippers, a decadently civilized khan-like existence, somehow fitting his Russian autocratic nature.

But this place, while comfortably and marvelously well-appointed, was almost humble by comparison. Maybe Alexei had left his castles back in Europe. I didn't know.

What I did know was that if I didn't find him and kill him, I was a fucking dead man, or an undead man; he'd brick me into a wall and I'd live out my endless days mourning the bad decisions I'd made.

The lit torch in my hand, I had to decide for myself whether this was a con of Alexei's, whether he was actually down there, or whether there was another place I'd missed. That was the thing about vampires—it could go either way. Maybe all of those rats were down there as a deterrent Alexei had arranged, to ensure that only the most desperate and/or foolhardy of vampire hunters would actually delve down there and look for him. And maybe he actually was down there somewhere in that monstrous mass of writhing rodent flesh.

Or, and this was because of my years with Iris—maybe this whole rats in the cellar thing was just a deathtrap, something Alexei had arranged knowing that a vampire hunter looking for him down there would risk it and would find himself dead by thousands of rat bites. It all depended on what kind of vampire Alexei was.

To me, he was simply an asshole, but how deep did that assholery run? He was a soldier, a warrior. To me, that spoke of valor in combat, and a certain directness—nobody could accuse Alexei of not being direct. To my mind, it made me think that, yes, Alexei was down there somewhere, and this mass of rats was intended as a kind of living moat, specifically designed to keep vampire hunters at bay, or to lure the idiotic and desperate ones to their doom.

I could have put his home to the torch, but that would not get at Alexei, I knew. It would only alert him that I'd come for him, and he'd be on me in a heartbeat.

No, it was a moat. I had to find Alexei's castle. I had to cross this moat of rodents. Shining the headlamp down, I could see them crawling all over the chairs, some of them looking up at me.

The other question was what they would do when I got down there. What had Alexei instructed them to do? Would they rush me and attack and kill me, kind of like how Blackface the dog had probably intended to do? Was that how it would go? Because I'd have to be a jackass to venture into a rat-filled basement just sporting a torch. But I was, in fact, a jackass.

It was 4:45.

I took a breath and lowered myself into the basement, landing on the ground with a grunt, turning my headlamp this way and that, swatting at the squealing rats with the torch, swinging this way and that. The noise they made was kind of incredible, this many of them like that. I whacked them back with the torch, using it as a kind of club, while they squirmed and ran for me.

I'd have to get shots for typhus, for plague. Good fucking God, yes.

I kicked at the nearest chair, shaking rats loose from it, then forced it ahead of me, into the mass of rats. Then I climbed atop it, kicking at the rats, who were already trying to climb my legs. I'd strike at their bodies with my torch, the soft thump of them making me flinch with each hit.

Digging into my pocket, I pulled out a can of pepper spray.

There was no talking—I am a firm believer in Tuco's Law. If you've ever seen *The Good, The Bad, and the Ugly*, the epic spaghetti western, well, then you'll know about Eli Wallach's character, Tuco, the Mexican bandito.

In it, Tuco's caught apparently off-guard by this cowboy who he'd wronged early on, and the guy talks at length about how he's longed for this chance to get his revenge on Tuco. And then Tuco shoots him dead, without a word, having gotten the drop on him, saying "If you have to shoot…shoot; don't talk."

Ever since then, I have been an adherent of Tuco's Law, and you'll find that, in instance after instance, Tuco's Law always holds up. Point being, when being confronted by thousands of rats in a 1000-year-old vampire's basement lair, there's really no point in talking, there's really nothing at all to say. I sprayed those rats with pepper spray—held my torch in one hand, while I coughed on pepper spray fumes, grateful that I didn't have asthma, and had a fairly strong stomach.

The rats recoiled from the pepper spray, and I kept spraying it in circles, comical atop my chair, like some mad housewife caricature, whirling like a dervish. I hunted around for their master's coffin, keenly aware that the clock was fucking ticking, and I would be a dead man if I was too late.

There was a boiler room with a shut door, this roomful of rats, but no Alexei, no coffin.

I sprayed a peppery path to the boiler room door, gave that door a hefty kick. I wanted to give the rats a place to escape to, if that was their inclination, in the wake of my attack.

They were all around me, and I could see that I would be nearly knee-deep in rats, if I'd actually tried to wade through them. The boiler room door flung open, and rodents rushed in there, eager to escape me and the pepper spray, which I kept spraying. I had three cans of the stuff, was not sure if it would be enough.

Many of the rats did rush into the boiler room, eager to escape the burning, choking fog I'd created with the pepper spray.

I used up the entire first can trying to create a perimeter, while trying to look around me, finding Alexei's hiding place. When it was empty, I tossed it aside, fished out another one, even as some of the rats rebounded, biting my thighs and my shins and my forearms, trying to scale me to get at my face.

Coughing on the pepper spray fumes, I shook them off, remembering a Rembrandt painting of a rat catcher. Hadn't the man worn armor? Carried a sword? In the old days, rat catchers did wear armor, they did carry swords. They did so because they had to. It was in the nature of the job. Iris was right about me: I was a fool.

I stumbled back out the way I'd come, climbed back out of the basement and went upstairs, gasping in the sweet air above, cursing myself for wasting time.

It was 5:00.

Then I rummaged through Alexei's armory, found myself some chainmail and a helmet, put that shit on, and then I put on some gauntlets, mindful of the bloody burn of the rat bites I'd already gotten. I could only imagine the antiseptic arsenal that would be employed on me, should I survive this.

The fucking helmet made it hard to breath, harder to see, so I chucked that. But I grabbed a sword from the wall, decided that would have to do.

It was 5:15 before I went back into the basement.

The rats were definitely taking advantage of the open door to the boiler room, although there were still thousands of them in that main room, all pissed off, all looking up at me, now. Could Alexei see them? Was he commanding them, even now, in his slumber? Was it like a dream? Did vampires even dream?

I tossed the torch into the pit, and jumped back into it. Was it always this way for vampire hunters? Resolute in the face of absolute horror? Grimly determined to get their way against unnatural odds?

I could have kicked myself for wasting valuable time in my first foray, but felt stronger, now, buttressed by the jingling weight of the chain mail, the clink of the gauntlets. What an unwieldy, unheroic vision I was—pepper spray in one hand, sword in the other, jingling armor and a backpack, duct-taped pants and rat-bitten thighs and a headlamp aglow on my sweating forehead.

The pepper spray was my shield, and I sprayed it to throw off the rats, and swung back and forth with the sword, hewing my way through the rats, amazed and disgusted at how readily the sword parted their flesh.

Despite it all, I felt a bizarre kinship with the little pests—we were bonded in mortality and in our service to the undead. The rats didn't ask to be what they were; they were only doing what their master had commanded them to do. And I was doing what I was doing because I had been little better than a rat in the service of my own mistress. In the choking fog of that basement, I was reclaiming my humanity, or I would at least die trying.

Hacking this way and that, without elegance, but only determination, I understood something else about this moat Alexei had built around himself—it was perhaps only intended to waste my time, to delay me. It was succeeding.

It was 5:15.

I had one hour left to me before Alexei would awaken. One hour left to live. Back and forth, I hacked and slashed with the sword, spraying with the other hand, while rats scrambled and leaped at me, their teeth taking nicks out of the gauntlets, their squeaking and squealing cacophonous in the low-ceilinged confines of the basement.

It was taking too long to make my way into this place. I was sweating and was chilled, sharing space with this mass of fur and rat flesh, all around me, a black sea, while I emptied my second can of pepper spray, barely able to breathe, now, eyes burning and tearing, mindlessly slashing at the rats, this way and that.

There was no possibility of retreat, no respite for me; I could only press on and pray that I had found Alexei before sunset.

Swinging a sword is work, by the way. For all the cinematic dandies and their swashbuckling, it took something out of you, cutting that way, and my heart was hammering in my chest, my arm, unused to this kind of exertion, was aching.

"Where are you, Alexei?" I said, more of a groan than anything else, a lamentation. There had to be something somewhere. I had to think like a vampire. One as old as Alexei had seen everything before. More experienced hunters, less idiotic than me, had surely gone after Alexei, and they had all failed.

In the welter of movement around me, the squirming multitudes of rats, I saw and understood. A vampire would go where a man would not.

It was 5:30.

I sprayed around me in a circle, trying to create a perimeter, to push the rats at bay. Although the things were savage, any that closed with me met the blade, and soon the floor was slick with rat blood. I resisted the urge to gag, shoved aside the rodent bodies around me, tried to find something below me, something in the floor, itself. It was the only thing that made sense.

The pepper spray had kept the rats away, and the sword was there for any who were still coming for me. I banged the butt end of the sword against the floor, trying to sound out whether there were any hollow spaces there, a place where an ageless bloodsucker might hide. I tapped every spot where there wasn't a rat, mindful of the blood that was everywhere, now.

The floor seemed solid everywhere I struck. Maybe I was wrong about that. I had thought for sure that hiding beneath a curtain of rats would have been a perfect hiding place for a vampire, but what did I know? Maybe Alexei hadn't done that since the Black Death.

Then I could see the faint outline of a door in the floor, a door without a handle. It was only visible because the rat blood had seeped into a hole no larger than a pencil. It was something that I might have otherwise overlooked.

Without much time to spare, it was good enough for me. I raised the pry bar and smashed it against the door, which must have been very thick to evade my checking to see if it was hollow.

I hammered at the door with the pry bar, but could not breach the seam. There wasn't time to do major construction on it; I didn't have the tools to break the door. I glanced at my watch.

It was 5:45.

I was beginning to get terrified and desperate. I marked the hole with the torch, leaving it beside it. Then I ran back to the entrance of the pit, shook off the gauntlets, and clawed my way back upstairs, went to Alexei's liquor cabinet, grabbed everything that was flammable that I could carry, and went back to the basement, and proceeded to pour every bottle of vodka, brandy, whiskey, and cognac that I'd taken down that little hole, until I imagined Alexei (assuming he was down there) was bobbing in sea of alcohol and fumes. Then I ran back upstairs and looked for anything else liquid that would burn. I found some acetone-based nail polish remover, a trio of kerosene lamps, and a half-dozen bottles of cologne. I ran back downstairs and poured those in the tiny hole, as well.

It was 6:00. Fifteen minutes until dusk.

I wasn't sure what would happen, but I put the torch to the hole and backed away from it. In a millisecond, there was a whoosh and an explosion, and the hidden door blew clear off its hinges, smashed into the ceiling overhead, powered by a blue-orange column of flame.

Something in the pit let out a horrible howl, and I saw Alexei emerge from the hole in the ground, consumed with fire, his eyes flaring orange, his fangs bared. From the sight of him, vampires were marvelously flammable, and the alcohol and acetone bath I'd given him had accelerated that.

Because the sun had not yet set, Alexei was not in full command of his powers. And I was not about to give him time to recover them. The rats that were not aflame or incapacitated by the pepper spray leaped at me, biting.

I jumped to my feet, shaking off the effects of the concussion from the detonation, and brought the sword down on Alexei, who managed to block it with a withering, burning limb. The sword sheared off his hand, which turned to ash the moment it separated from Alexei's body.

"Boy," Alexei said with a cry barely audible over the crackling flames. *"Sheya, ili nichego!"*

He halfway toppled, and I struck hard with the sword, detaching his head from the rest of him. The moment my blade found its mark, what was Alexei vanished in a column of dust and ash, and the rats went from a writhing mound of belligerence to a disorganized pile of rodents. Disgusting, to be sure, but not moving with singular purpose, as before. They began to scatter.

I had wanted to say something so bad, but Tuco's Law was still in full effect, most especially because this was Alexei. I wasn't about to get all action hero-grandiose and say something so that Alexei could stop me. No, I was here to fucking kill him, and that's exactly what I did.

"Eat it, *Bolshoi*," I said, at last.

He was so very old, living on so much borrowed time. His body just dissolved, went from its flesh tones to a sandy color, then more waxen, as the flesh boiled off him, layer by layer, and then went to sinew and muscle and bone, and then to nothing at all, like he had never been.

I poured holy water onto the dust, and was treated to smoky hisses as the stuff boiled against the dust.

It was kind of a logistical challenge—where his head had been, there was just dust. Did I scoop up that dust and toss that into the furnace? Would that do it?

What was the protocol for that kind of thing?

Fuck it, Alexei was dead.

I had beaten that fucker. He'd been on top for so long, Alexei had lost the capacity to imagine himself imperiled by anybody. Simply put, nobody was stupid enough to go after him.

I scooped up some of the dust where his head had been, a big handful of the stuff, and I threw it on the escaping rats. Let them scatter him on their backs. Then I took several handfuls from where his body had been, and made separate piles. Then I took a handful of the dust and put it on the ground, poured some ancient cognac on it. I ignited it, sat there, while the grandfather clock tolled 6:15.

Sunset.

I watched that bit burn, and then I poured cognac on the other piles of dust on the ground.

Then I went back into the crypt, where the flames were already subsiding, and poured the rest of the cognac in there, got it burning nice and high again. I saved the last swig of the stuff for myself, took a drink of it, felt the stuff almost evaporate on my tongue. I didn't know how old it was, didn't care. I was alive. I had prevailed.

I tossed all of the empty bottles from Alexei's bar into that flaming hole in the ground, watched the room clear itself of rats. I would have to go to the hospital, for sure, to get treatment for all of the fucking bites I'd received.

Satisfied, or at least figuring that I'd done as much as I could, under the circumstances, I then took two of the chairs I'd tossed into the basement and used them to climb out of there.

Then I cut Oksana's bonds, and tossed her into that basement. She'd never seen my face; I was careful as hell about that.

I shut the door to the basement, then walked around Alexei's place. I took one of the Faberge eggs off the mantelpiece, pocketed it. Then I peeked out the window I'd come in. The goons weren't there.

I grabbed a bottle of vodka from Alexei's bar and poured it on all of the rat bites I'd received, wincing at the pain, imagining what bacteriological horrors had been inflicted on me in that fucking basement. I'd probably catch plague. I was getting sick of things fucking biting me.

I went to the bathroom and found a medical kit, cleaned and bandaged each and every wound, then I went back to the balcony. In the basement, I could hear Oksana screaming something in Russian or Ukrainian. She was wailing and shrieking, calling out for Alexei. The anguish in her voice gave me pause, made me feel bad about what I'd done. I hated to hear that much pain in someone's voice.

Climbing out onto the balcony, I worked my way back down the space between it and the blood bank, sweating, grateful for the shadows that had come with sunset. I didn't stand out nearly so much.

Reaching the bottom, I walked out toward the alley behind the building, avoiding the street. Then I caught a bus, after walking a few blocks out of my way, hell and gone from Alexei's place.

Only while sitting on the bus did I allow myself to breathe. I couldn't believe what I'd done. I'd bumped off Alexei. The top vampire in the Chicagoland area. Maybe Alexei lived inconspicuously enough, maybe he thought he was unassailable, or had made enough arrangements to feel that he had no enemies left. I don't know.

All I knew was that I'd found him, and I'd killed him. It had been messier than I thought it would be.

My hands started shaking.

I'd killed Alexei.

My phone rang. Iris.

"Nate," she said. "I woke up, you weren't here."

"Yeah," I said. "Getting an early start on the evening."

"I'm hungry," she said.

"So, eat," I said.

"Bring me something back?"

"No," I said.

"Come on, Nate," she said. "Where are you?"

"On my way back," I said.

"Do not come back empty-handed," Iris said, and hung up on me.

I wonder what she would say if she saw the egg I'd stolen from Alexei's place. I figured it would be better not to show her. Keeping secrets was always the mark of the end of a relationship, anyway. Once those walls came up, the rest of it came down.

My phone beeped. It was Clementine, texting me:

Hey, Nate. What's shakin?

Nothing. On the bus. What are U up 2?

We should hang out.

Yeah? And?

Do stuff.

Like right now?

Sure.

Mmmm….

Tempting?

Oh, you know. Where RU?

Home. Just got.

Just got what?

Just got HOME, Silly.

I paused, thought about it. Not going to see Iris would really tee her off. I could just imagine her going off to see Alexei and finding him not there. That would be so worth it.

I'll be there.

K. When?

Tomorrow.

Fab! OXOX

I closed my phone and pocketed it. I'd have to show Clementine the egg. I wanted to show somebody. I'd tell her I won it on eBay, or found it in a thrift store. Something like that. I didn't even really get a chance to look at it, yet, was afraid to in public.

Even now, I wondered what Alexei's people would be doing—Oksana was likely sifting through the ashes, no doubt wailing forlornly with his dogs, wondering why Master had not come back, yet. Or maybe she was on her cell phone, calling in favors, wanting to put a hit on whoever had done this. That would be a very Russian thing to do.

And while Alexei appeared not to have crafted a vampire *mafiya* for himself (bad move, old boy), he likely had his share of everyday people on his payroll—some corrupt cops, some businessmen, that kind of thing. Maybe part of his blood network. Alexei seemed like too much of an asshole to delegate much to his underlings, or to stomach any kind of competition in his ranks.

I really expected him to have a basement full of bloodsuckers, not just him down there. But the blood bank maybe told the tale—Alexei was just out for Alexei, wanted a steady supply of blood he didn't have to worry about getting.

That made me wonder, as I bumped around in the back of the bus. Alexei had other priorities than merely hunting—the blood bank meant he didn't want to be distracted so much. So, what was he up to?

Iris, for all of her longevity, had never thought to bank her blood. Had never cared enough to do that.

Lazy-ass.

I went to Mercy Hospital, told them that I'd gotten attacked by rats, needed to get checked out. The attending physician looked over my wounds and asked me what the hell I was doing. I told him I was exterminating pests. He examined the wounds, drew my blood, gave me some antibiotics and a couple of shots, told me that I'd be better off leaving that kind of work to the professionals.

I couldn't have agreed more.

-X-

I rightly figured Clementine's was a booty call, nothing more. She was happy to see me, and communicated that to me with her mouth and her thighs, and I was glad to see her, too, demonstrated that with my cock.

She saw all the bandages and asked me what the hell I'd been up to. That was an interesting kind of question for me to answer. What to tell her, exactly? I tried out the truth, just for the hell of it.

"I was out hunting vampires," I said.

"Wow," Clementine said. "Sounds dangerous."

"It was," I said.

"No, seriously, what were you up to?"

"I told you," I said. "Hunting vampires."

"These look like animal bites," Clementine said.

"They are," I said. "It's a long story."

"Dude," Clementine said. "That is messed up."

"Tell me about it," I said.

I showed her the Faberge egg, which felt like a tombstone in my bag, now, after my battle with Alexei. The egg was burgundy with gold crisscrossing it, and, inside was a golden coffin that sat beneath a platinum apple tree, from which were set tiny ruby apples. Tiny pearls and diamonds were piled on the ground like snow and ice. The whole thing sparkled.

"My god," Clementine said. "It's so beautiful, Nate."

"Yeah," I said, feeling sick to my stomach. "Gorgeous."

"Can't believe you got it off eBay," she said. "It has to be a fake."

"Sure," I said, knowing that it wasn't. I carefully closed it. It had to be worth millions of dollars, easily. Just holding it made me tremble. Alexei's egg.

I put it back in my backpack, then carefully set the backpack down.

Clementine laid her head on my chest, listened to me breathe. It was such a natural, human gesture. And I stroked her hair. She'd put orange sheets on her bed, so between her orange body, and the orange bedding, and that great orange painting on the far wall, I felt like I was experiencing retina burn.

"You are definitely boyfriend material, Nate," Clementine said. "For sure. You don't talk too much, you're so, you know, deep."

"I'm shallow, not deep," I said.

"No," she said. "You're the strong, silent type."

"The skinny, silent type, more like," I said.

"Skinny but strong, Nate," she said. "Let me talk."

"Alright."

I could just see the top of her head, feel her jaw move as she talked.

"The world is full of noise, and so when you're quiet, you stand apart from all of that," she said. "I ride the bus, I see everybody on the phone, or on their iPhones, or texting each other—and, you know, I do that, too—but it's still noisy. They're not talking out loud, but somehow, it's noisy. Whereas you are genuinely quiet—and it's powerful. Sexy."

"Hah," I said. "Maybe too quiet. Maybe I don't have anything worth saying."

"That's not it," she said. "You're haunted. I can tell. I can tell when somebody's haunted, and you are. Haunted people are quiet people. What's haunting you, Nate?"

I didn't want to tell her; she wouldn't understand. Nobody would. I don't know what I had expected in going after Alexei, but it had been grim and horrible work, worse than anything I could have imagined. The things I'd seen down there, the things I'd done, the knowledge of undeath that I possessed—after my years with Iris, I should have been inured to it, but I wasn't. It had been a horrible thing.

Clementine laid her orange face on my chest, listening to my heartbeat. Vampire hearts didn't beat, not in ways that human ears could hear, anyway. When I really thought about it, the profanity of vampirism leaped out at me.

Having Clementine there, warm and alive and breathing against my chest, me breathing, too, and warm—there was a beautiful communion there. We're the living. The world belongs to the living, not the dead, and that's what made it a wonderful place, a garden, and not a graveyard.

I stroked her hair a little.

"What's haunting you?" Clementine asked again, turning her chin up, looking up at me. "Dude, you can tell me."

"I'm being quiet right now," I said.

My phone rang, and I peeked at it. Iris, of course. I let it go to voicemail.

"Your mom?" Clementine asked.

"Yeah," I said. "She's one of those helicopter parents."

"God, I know," Clementine said. "My folks are like that, too. It felt like they went to college with me. I lived with them my first couple of years out of school, too, just because I couldn't get a job, that kind of thing. But it wasn't like anything I wasn't already used to—I mean, my folks have always been there for me. They bought this place for me, too."

"Nice place," I said.

"Yeah," Clementine said. "I mean, how else could I afford something this big? But they love me, they want me to be happy."

"Are you happy?" I asked.

Clementine nodded.

"You're not," she said. "I can tell. I'm psychic."

"Yeah?"

She nodded. "I knew you were going to say that."

I stroked her hair some more.

My phone rang again.

"Your mom is persistent," Clementine said.

"She hates when I don't answer," I said. "I'll get like a half-dozen voicemails from her."

I turned off the ringer, turned off the phone, put it aside.

We sat there and breathed awhile. You have no idea how welcome such a simple thing was—when you're around someone who doesn't breathe, you hold your breath as well. Her breathing reassured me of her human-ity, and her humanity reassured me of my own. How simple and lovely a thing that was.

"Do you believe in monsters?" I asked.

Clementine laughed softly. "Sure, why not? I mean, bad people are everywhere."

"I don't mean people," I said. "I mean things."

I heard her pause for a moment in her breath, like thinking about it.

"You mean actual monsters? Like the Bogeyman?" she asked.

I nodded.

"When I was a girl, I used to think there was a monster in the base-ment," Clementine said. "I would go down there and play, because we had a pool table and a pinball machine in the basement, and a bar—my dad had that kind of rec room thing going, and I would take pool balls and roll them on the table, just rolling them around and knocking them into each other. I'd love playing in the basement, even by myself. But then, when I'd have to go back upstairs, I'd have to turn off the lights, and so I had this system where I would turn off the lights in stages, and run to the next row of lights, so I wasn't ever in the dark. But the worst one was the last row of lights in the basement, because the switch was in a spot which meant that I had to be in the dark before running up the stairs. And I had this fear that this monster was waiting under the steps to trip me and grab me and pull me under."

"Bloody Bones," I said.

"Huh?"

"It's an old English bogeyman," I said. "What they called that kind of bogeyman—Rawhead and Bloody Bones."

Clementine peeked up at me, kind of flummoxed. "Was it a team?"

"No," I said. "One monster."

"But he's got two names," she said. "Rawhead AND Bloody Bones."

"It probably sounds tighter in English," I said, mimicking an English accent. "Mind your pease porridge, Clementine, or Rawhead and Bloody Bones'll have a go at you!"

I made it a Cockney accent, dropping the "h's" wherever I could.

"Besides, I think it's a package deal—like he had a bloody head and a pile of bloody bones nearby," I said. "The point was he lived beneath the stairs."

"Whatever," Clementine said. "You're weird. Anyway, I would sprint up those steps as fast as I could. And I did it every time, which was funny, because I loved playing in that basement, but only with the lights on."

"Yeah? So what's that got to do with monsters?" I asked.

Clementine sighed. "I just said that. That was the only monster I ever faced."

"But you never faced it," I said.

"That's the point, Dude," she said.

"So, you're saying you don't believe in monsters," I said.

"Mobsters are monsters," she said. "Some, anyway; there's only one letter of difference between the two."

Thinking of Iris and her inky eyes, emptied of vitality and humanity, an oceanic blue so deep and absolute that you could lose your soul to it, her body full of stolen blood, hundreds of thousands of lives taken.

Alexei bedding down beneath a sea of rats, emerging from his hole in the ground, burning brightly, fangs bared, eyes wide and insane with reflexive pain, his immortal flesh immolating before my very eyes.

Clementine poked me, smiled into my eyes.

"Hello in there?"

"There's no such thing as monsters," I said, patting her on the head, kissing the top of it.

-X-

Leaving Clementine's left me feeling rejuvenated and alive like I'd not felt in years. Sure, getting laid was absolutely part of it, but being with somebody alive was, too. Clementine, for all of her orangeness, was a fucking person, versus the walking cadaver that was Iris.

It honestly did leave me feeling happier and healthier than I'd felt in years. Everything sang to me—the city traffic seemed imbued with gleeful significance, the trees rustling in the wind, the lights—absolutely everything crackled.

Seeing life in motion, being a spectator to it, even postindustrial urban life in 21st century crumbling, imperial America, it was beautiful to me.

Then Iris called again, harshed my buzz.

"Yeah?" I said, answering.

"Where are you?" Iris asked.

"Walking," I said. "Not far."

"Alexei's dead," Iris said.

"Wow," I said. "What happened?"

"I don't know," she said. "We can talk about it when you get here. Are you bringing me anything?"

"No," I said.

"No? That's going to be a problem, Nate," she said.

What did I know? It was a conversation I didn't need to be having with her, shouldn't have even had to have with her.

"Iris, you have to do this," I said, glancing at my bag of tricks, my tools, my stakes. "You need to get some food. Or you can feed on me."

"Nate," she said. "Don't even bother showing up if you haven't brought me anything."

Right there, in front of a bus, I put a garland of garlic around my neck. Dug it out of my bag and just did it, stuck it under my coat. A gal standing nearby, waiting to board, with mint-green Doc Martens with yellow laces and ripped-up black leggings and a black and white striped minidress covered by a fuzzy jacket, looked at me like I'd whipped out my dick.

Yeah, I'm wearing garlic. Fuck you.

"I'm right around the corner," I said, hanging up. Not quite true, but close.

I walked to her place, wondering what she'd even say or do. I walked in through the outer gate, and there she was, on the top step, the entrance to her place, looking sharp in a black skirt-suit with a red blouse, arms folded.

She wrinkled her nose at the sight of me.

"Don't you even dare," she said. "Garlic? You're actually wearing garlic?"

I nodded.

"That is just so insulting," she said. "I can't believe you'd even do that."

"I needed insurance," I said. "Wasn't sure if you were going to attack me."

Iris rolled her eyes. "I was. But there's no way I'm letting you set foot in my place dressed like that."

"I just came to get my stuff," I said.

"Your stuff," she said. "You're serious?"

Of course I was serious. I wanted out of there.

Away from it, away from her. Away from all of it.

"With Alexei gone, I'm IT," Iris said. "I'm top dog. Do you even have an idea of what this means, Nate? For me?"

I shook my head, kept my hands in my pockets, paced on the rocks below, while she stood there, arms folded, statuesque.

"For 500 years I've had to put up with his bullshit," Iris said. "I've been under his thumb for that entire time, more or less. Part of the reason I came to the States was to get away from him, and then he showed up around 1929, as if we'd never been apart, as if he could simply show up and we'd pick up exactly where we left off. I stopped loving him a hundred years after he made me, learned to hate him the centuries afterward, tried to ignore him the centuries after that. He'd always lorded it over me, minded me, haunted my steps. And now he's gone. I've been promoted. I would have loved to have seen his face when it happened, when they got him."

I wondered if I should even tell her. I wanted to.

"Everybody who matters is going to have to pay homage to me," Iris said. "I'll have a seat on the…oh, well, no point in telling you, you don't care. The point is that you are picking an absolutely terrible time to try to fly out from under my wing, Nate."

"I did it," I said. "I killed Alexei."

Iris looked at me for a moment, before laughing, showing her fangs. "I know you did, Nate," Iris said. "I wanted you to."

"Huh?"

"I wanted you to," Iris said. "Don't you see how I set you up? Got you to really hate Alexei, made you feel jealous?"

I refused to believe that I'd somehow been a pawn in one of Iris's games. I just couldn't go there, wouldn't consider that.

"I didn't think you'd pull it off, honestly," Iris said. "I thought you'd end up dead, or even bitten, stuffed into one of his walls."

She watched me grinding gears in my head, trying to sort that all out.

"You think I didn't know you might try something stupid like that, Nate?" Iris said. "I know you. I knew what you'd do. I wanted you to do it. I chose you because I knew you'd be just the type to go do something like that, eventually. I mean, I couldn't hope to hurt Alexei, myself. He knew me top to bottom, front to back, inside out. He knew that I chafed under his leadership. He knew that drove me crazy, but he wouldn't let it go, wouldn't let me go. I don't think he counted on you, though. And I was prepared—if you'd failed, I would have just said that you were madly in love with me, and your jealousy drove you to try something insane. Maybe he would have believed it; maybe he would not have. It hardly matters, now, because you didn't fail, amazingly enough. You actually pulled it off. Tell me, how did you do it?"

I was still reeling at this. Had she played me that way? Was this how vampires worked, playing subtle games with each other that way? I told her how I did it, and she listened, attentive in a way that I had never seen before. She looked more alive in those moments than I'd ever seen her before.

"I didn't do it because of you," I said.

"Yeah, right," she said. "Nate, honestly, you need to get your head on straight, because as of this night, Chicago's mine. His seat on the Council's mine. Alexei never knew what to do with all of his power. He was actually trying to, I don't know, talk me back from the brink, whatever that even is. He actually made me feel guilty about feeding—part of the reason I would send you out was because of him."

"He had a blood bank," I said. "He didn't hunt."

"Yes," Iris said. "He did have a blood bank. How did you—?"

"I saw it," I said. "While hunting for him."

Iris walked down the steps, one at a time, deliberately, watching me closely. Then she laughed, actually looked skyward and laughed, this cold and empty sound, like bat wings brushing tombstones.

"Nate," she said, as if, despite herself, she was still trying to believe it. "I just knew you had it in you. You're a killer, after all. Love will do that to a person."

She said it like love was something she'd never seen before, like she was trying to recall an unfamiliar flavor, or a name of something she'd long forgotten.

"Do you know how many men have tried to do that and have died?"

"I don't," I said.

"A lot," Iris said. "Alexei and his damned rats. He loved using rats. Very old-school."

"It wasn't easy," I said.

Iris composed herself again, was back to her usual opaque self—enigmatic, deadly, ineffable.

"You hand me Chicago on a platter, and then you're going to blow it by leaving me?" she asked. "You'll miss out on absolutely everything. Like that little bitch pet princess of his, Oksana? I killed her. Took off her head with a swing of my arm and drank her down.""

I winced at the thought of poor Oksana, finding a speedy death at the cold, dead hands of Iris, and my own part in it. Even in this, I was her accessory, her accomplice.

Already, some of the vampire courtiers had turned up, bringing gifts. I didn't recognize the vampires, but their look when they caught scent of me with my garlic garland told me everything. Three had turned up, each with a glassy-eyed victim. Iris looked at them, and at me, and smiled.

"Go on in and get your stuff, Nate," she said. "Don't touch anything else. I'm feeling gracious right now."

I walked up the stairs past her, while Iris received these gifts, while the locals paid their respects. Inside, my head was reeling. I hadn't actually thought that through, what that meant, like me accidentally promoting Iris. All I'd wanted to do was stick it to Alexei; I hadn't really thought through what that had meant. Just as I hadn't really thought through what it meant, giving Iris the heave-ho.

For one thing, it meant having to pay rent somewhere, which would suck.

Still, as I gathered up my laptop and threw my cloths in a gym bag, it was worth it. Just getting out of there with my skin intact counted as a major victory, as far as I was concerned. I tucked the computer under my arm, and the gym bag on my other shoulder, and went back downstairs. After five years, it's all I had to show for my troubles.

Iris was receiving some more supplicants, and I swear to you, her living room was filling with glassy-eyed "gifts," these young women standing there, victims of the damned gaze of the vampires.

She saw me looking at them, and smiled at me. "Looks like I won't have to go out tonight after all. Can you believe how nice everybody's been?"

"Amazing," I said, walking out past her.

"Goodbye, Nate," Iris said.

"Bye," I said. The vampire bootlicks just looked me over like I was fucking insane, until they smelled the garlic, and then they just looked at me with raw disgust. To them, and surely to Iris, I was passing up a major opportunity. To be the minion of a vampire was, at least in their view, the highest a human could aspire to, and with Iris's ascension to the position of head bloodsucker in Chicago, it meant I was passing up a lot of power-by-proxy. No doubt any number of them were trying to figure who would get to be her number two go-getter. They were welcome to it.

I turned at the gate, saw Iris watching me, saw the cold amusement in her gaze, remembered what she'd said about visiting me at my funeral, and I walked out of there, past the growing parade of supplicants. It was like her empty, lifeless home had become a thriving nightclub that evening, thanks to me.

One thing I didn't see were the other big players—Woo, Constance, Rosamunda, Lucinda—none of them were there. No doubt they'd have a proper sit-down with Iris, versus having to come like these nobodies.

I wondered how Iris would handle it, her newfound power, what it would mean for her, to her, for Chicago.

For me.

Walking down the street, I saw Jennipher in line.

"Omigod," she said, seeing me. "Nate!"

"Jenn," I said. "What are you doing here?"

"Word has it that your boss is the Boss Lady, now," she said. "I'm paying my respects."

It amazed me how quickly word got out. I had only just killed Alexei the other day, and here it was, all these people turning up, kissing the ring.

"I'm done with it," I said. "With Iris."

Jennipher was wearing silver jeans and sparkly silver heels and a rhinestone tube top that was striped black and silver. It was cold out, but she was surely not feeling it, just wore a sparkly silver scarf. More club kid camouflage for her.

"Is that wise? I mean, Dude, she's the Queen," Jennipher said.

"Whatever," I said. "Enjoy being on her chain."

Jennipher reached out and put a hand on my forearm. Not as fast as Iris could have, but fast, all the same.

"Be careful, Nate," she said. "You're alright, you know that? You reek like garlic, but you're okay."

I smiled, but was feeling about as far from "alright" as a guy could be. I was glad to be walking out on Iris and still breathing. I thought of poor Oksana, wondered if she'd dared to confront Iris about Alexei's assassination. I suppose I should have counted my blessings.

"Clean up and give me a call sometime, Nate," she said. "Or I'll call you."

"Sure," I said, walking away. The line of supplicants and sycophants went around the block. I wonder what people in the area thought. Lord knows. All I knew for sure was that I was now officially homeless.

Something about the whole thing was nagging at me. I hadn't had the chance to really hash it out with Iris, like her and Alexei, what he'd been trying to do. But given the tongue-lashing I got from Alexei for being out and about, it felt like maybe Iris's block party would not sit well with Alexei—or marked a real departure from the past.

That's what it was. With Iris running the underworld in Chicago, who knows what the hell would happen? Nothing good, though. I understood this. If being a vampire was, at heart, an exercise in evil (and let's be honest, here: it is), then a vampire was forced to either act against their condition, or to embrace it. Those were the moral choices available to the bloodsucker. Alexei seemed conflicted by it—hell, maybe he even wanted to die.

That was another thing that hadn't occurred to me. Maybe I had gotten in there as easily as I had because, deep down, or maybe even not that deep down—Alexei craved death. Maybe he courted it. But maybe nobody who knew what Alexei was would have dared to risk going after him. That made a kind of sense to me, because cowardice must always be at the heart of evil—cowardice is to evil what courage is to good. Nobody was stupid enough to go after Alexei directly, so even if he wanted to die, there was nobody out there willing to kill him.

At least until I came around. I had been the perfect cat's-paw for Iris.

Walking through the neighborhood, it knocked me for a loop. Alexei would have been too chickenshit to take his own life, and everybody else had been too chickenshit to go after him, either. Only me, a jealous wannabe striver, had done it, had dared to do it, had been dumb enough to try.

Which meant, however, that I was responsible for Iris's ascension. I had broken the chain of collective cowardice that had kept Alexei in power in Chicago for the past 80 or so years.

My phone rang.

It was Joliette.

I answered.

"Hey," she said. "Come see me."

I felt the tugging in me, that pull that came from that bite she'd taken out of me last time.

"I'm only barely better from the last time you sucked on me," I said.

"C'mon," she said. "Get over here."

You can't know what that feels like. Maybe you do, if you've ever been in love. It's like a full-body craving. I don't know how that manifests—were there Joliettocytes swimming in my blood? Vestiges of her infection in me, compelling me? Was it like malaria, maybe?

"I'm covered in garlic," I said.

"Eww," she said. "Now why would you do something stupid like that?"

"Iris," I said.

"That's gross, Nate," she said. "Really, really gross."

"I'm gross," I said.

"You're delish," Joliette said. "Why don't you get yourself cleaned up and get over here?"

"You suck," I said.

"Oh, for sure," she said. I hung up on her, sweating all over. I mean, I really, really wanted to see her. But I knew if I did that, she'd probably kill me.

And that was the funny thing about it—I had a sure thing with Joliette. I could get turned into a bloodsucker right then and there, it was something I'd wanted from Iris for five motherfucking years, something she pointedly refused me. But with Joliette, I could get made this evening, no questions asked, no doubt about it.

But I didn't want to. Seeing Iris again, it was like a bucket of water in my face. What she represented, what Alexei was (good or bad), what it all meant, I wanted no part of it. Joliette was a newborn, a babe in the vampire woods—she didn't know what she was doing, didn't understand the costs of the nightlife.

Me, on the other hand, I knew. I understood this. It wasn't just a matter of entering the underworld and knowing that Iris was Queen Bee of Chicagoland—that she'd have Joliette and me dispatched in no time flat. Rather, it was an understanding that there was no future in vampirism.

That doesn't make sense, I know—vampires are immortal, so all they have is an endless future, and an ever-growing past. But that's exactly the problem: it's an empty forever.

What's that law? Parkinson's Law—work expands to fill the time necessary to complete it? If being human meant having limited time, it meant making the most of the time one had, burning brightly and burning briefly. But if all one had was time, then the requirements of existence were forever on the horizon.

Maybe that's how vampires earned their cowardice—the promise of immortality, even immortality bought with blood and lives—it kept them from ever having to face the requirements of their own morality, kept them stunted. There was too much at stake (pun intended) to risk true moral investment in anything they did. They valued their immortality more than anything else, would do anything to keep on living forever.

Maybe that's what vampires craved in their association with us pesky mortals. They thirsted for our drive, our fleeting, incandescent spirits.

I stopped by a pizza place and got a mushroom pizza, called up Clementine.

"Hey, I'm getting a pizza, you want to split it?"

"Yeah, alright," she said. "Where are you, anyway?"

"Down the street from your place," I said.

"Get some wine?"

"Sure," I said.

There was a grocery store nearby, so while they were making my pizza, I went in and got a cabernet in a paper bag, and picked up my pizza, went up to Clementine's place.

She was waiting for me in some orange yoga pants and a plain white tee. Her toenails were apricot-colored, look like they'd glow under a black light. Against her tanned skin, they looked luminous.

"Hey, Nate," she said. "Mmmm, that smells good. Holy shit, are you wearing garlic, Dude?"

"Yeah," I said. "My hands were full."

"What do we need all of that garlic for?" She asked.

"Seasoning," I said, nodding to the pizza, giving her a wry grin. She just shook her head, smiled at me, hand on her hip.

I took off the garland and laid it on her kitchen counter, and set the pizza box on the counter while she fished out some wineglasses and got out a corkscrew. I opened the bottle and let it breathe, noting the deep color of the wine, and, of course, thinking of blood.

She took out some orange plates and put some pizza on them, serving some for each of us.

"We can sit over there, if you like," she said, nodding to her living room. I went over with her, and we ate, chewing and gazing out over the lake.

"Cool," I said. "Look, can I maybe crash here? Just for a night or two?"

Clementine looked at me down the end of her nose with more than a little amusement. "What happened?"

"Oh, I got evicted," I said. "Literally everything I own is with me right now."

"For real?"

I nodded.

"Wow," she said. "Late on rent payments or something?"

"No," I said. "Dispute with the landlady."

"Intense," she said. "Sure, Nate. You can crash here for a day or two. But you're going to have to pay rent to me sexually."

"I can do that," I said. "What do I owe?"

"Let's just keep the meter running," Clementine said.

"I don't think rent is measured that way," I said.

"It is here," she said, grinning.

She smiled at me around a pizza slice, creases at the corners of her eyes I hadn't seen before. With all of her sun worship, she'd be a wrinkled prune in no time. Five years, ten for sure. My time with Iris made me keenly aware of the passage of time.

Clementine was younger than I was, but was probably aging herself faster with all the tanning. In no time at all, she'd probably look older.

But not yet. I hushed that thought. I was thinking like a vampire.

-X-

Sometime during the night, Iris appeared at the foot of the bed. She just coalesced out of mist, wearing a black shiny overcoat and sunglasses, hair up, hands in pockets, lips painted red. I woke up and she was just fucking standing there. How long had she been there?

Her face was flushed. She'd been feeding most of the night, by the look of her.

"Hey, Nate," she said.

"Jesus fucking Christ," I said, glancing at Clementine, who was snoring, laying there on her back, the sheets down about midway on her, so her breasts were exposed. Iris saw me look at her, and looked at me, cocking an eyebrow.

"This is the one?" she asked.

"The what?"

"The girl you went out with the other week?"

"What do you want?" I asked, getting out of bed, throwing on a pair of boxers.

Iris gave a backward glance to Clementine, then sat down on one of the orange chairs in the living room. I sat across from her.

"How did you find me?" I asked.

"It's easy," she said. "I could have found you any time I liked, Nate. I fed on you enough times. It's like GPS for us. A homing instinct. We know what's ours."

She was radiating warmth, was more than pink; she was flushed. I'd never seen her so gorged on blood. She may have been drunk on death, if such a thing was possible for a vampire.

"Why are you here?" I asked. "I figured you'd be busy getting your ass kissed by everybody in the underworld."

"It only took a few hours," Iris said. "Absolutely everybody brought gifts. Tribute galore. Felt positively medieval. I felt like royalty."

To see her like this, it was more disturbing than I'd ever seen her before, in her most ghoulish state. She was almost glowing.

"You didn't come by to have me clean up the mess, did you?"

Iris shook her head. "I came to make you, Nate."

"Now? Why now?"

She looked at me like I'd asked something fucking idiotic of her, just sat there motionless and radiating blood-heat, which her ageless body was, even then, consuming in its mysterious way, drawing life and sustenance from it.

"Why not?" Iris asked. "Because I want to. Because you've whined about it for years. Because your stupid, recklessly human fit of jealousy handed me the key to the city, exactly the way I'd hoped it would. You know, Alexei would be so offended that it was you who did it. He hated you. Or, more to the point, he hated what you represented.'"

"Why?"

Iris shrugged. "I don't know, Nate. Alexei was unhappy with me, has been so for the last couple of centuries. He didn't approve of my approach to things. You were, in his view, just another manifestation of my failure."

I didn't even know what that meant, but Alexei had been so old, it was almost impossible for someone like me to know what he might think, or why. Iris seemed to sense my confusion.

"He tried to get me to be a blood banker like he was," she said. "To not send you out to hunt for me. His own minion, he kept her around, I don't know—like a pet, maybe. He would always keep his minions safe. So, when he saw me sending you out hunting for me, he got up in arms about it. And here you go and kill him. The irony of it amuses me, will amuse me for the rest of my days. He worried about the harm the life-style was inflicting on you—he actually worried about that—and here you killed him. For me."

Iris laughed. She really laughed, her shoulders shaking. I peeked over my shoulder, to see if Clementine heard, but she hadn't stirred.

Then something just struck me, like a stake in the heart. It made me dizzy to think about, but the goddamned blood bank made me think that, the absence of other vampires there.

Alexei gave a fuck.

Oh, shit. Alexei *wasn't* a bad guy?

Was that even possible?

I hardly knew the guy, but my interactions with him had always been sour, and, perhaps, had been set up that way by Iris—I had thought it was some kind of personal vendetta against me, and had taken umbrage at that, without seeing her pale hand in things.

But what if it really wasn't me he was irked with, but, rather, with Iris? What if I was just, in his old, old eyes, a symptom of his disappointment with Iris, his spawn?

Fuck.

I hadn't even thought about that. I mean, before I'd gone into that bunker, I had really thought it would be packed with vampires, or with dead people hung from hooks like meat. Something ghastly like that. I didn't expect a goddamned blood bank.

The sea of rats, okay, that was fucking disgusting, and would have me waking up from nightmares for the rest of my days, but it was really just a deterrent on his part, something that would keep all but the most determined of vampire killers at bay.

Iris had visited Alexei. I had been so damned jealous, it hadn't occurred to me. Maybe Alexei was trying, in his lifeless way, to wean Iris from her need to hunt and kill.

What had I done?

"Shhhit," I said.

"It's just so funny, Nate," Iris said. "How did you do it?"

"I burned him," I said. "I just crept in there and burned him. You were always going on about fires, and it occurred to me that vampires had to burn really well."

She leaned forward in the chair, resting her arms on her knees. I'd never seen Iris more attentive and amused. "You'd never be able to do that to me," Iris said. "Not in a million years."

The way she said it, it was unclear whether it was a statement of literal fact, or one of emotional security—that I would not find it in myself to be able to kill her, or whether I would simply be unable to find her.

"Sure," I said.

"Now," Iris said, baring her teeth. "Shall I make you, Nate? It's the least I can do. You gave me everything; I can give you something."

You have to understand that this was all I had ever wanted. I mean, this was it. But in that moment, I didn't want it. I didn't want anything to do with Iris.

"What's the matter, Nate?" Iris said, mockingly. "Cold feet? I'm giving you the golden ticket, here. Just like you always wanted. Immortality. Power. Grace, even. Do you even know what grace is?"

I know what part of it was. To have her be my sire, I would be subordinate to her for the rest of my days. Her reward to me for freeing her from her sire was to offer to become my sire. Just like how Jennipher was standing in line, waiting to pay her respects to Iris, compelled by a blood pulse inside her, like a tug on a leash, so would I be forever bound to Iris, just as she'd been bound to Alexei. I would be fatally compromised.

So, while you could look at what she was offering as a gift in response to my slaying Alexei, it could as easily be seen as a ploy by Iris to get me back under her thumb, another move in her endless game of chess.

"What is it?" she asked. "Why the hesitation? I mean, I'm asking you. I didn't have to. I could've made you when you were sleeping next to Little Miss Tangerine Dream in there. I could have taken you both, could have killed both of you while you slept. I'm offering you immortality, Nate. What you've wanted, Darling."

"I don't want it," I said. "Not anymore."

She smiled at me, her lip half-raised.

"Really? Why the change of heart, Nate? I mean, I had to listen to you whine about this for years. The least you can do is tell me why not."

I shook my head.

"I don't know. I'm not ready to die, yet, I guess."

"A reason for living? Love? Lust for life?"

She leaned back in the chair, absently played with an orange bocce ball that was in a bowl beside the chair, on a tiny glass table.

"Thanks, but no thanks," I said.

Iris sneered at me, the cold contempt competing with the bountiful blood meal she'd enjoyed earlier in the evening.

"This is just like you, Nate. I offer you what you've claimed to want, and you turn me down cold? All I ever do is be nice to you, and this is how you repay me?"

"You look like you've had enough to drink tonight," I said.

"Oh, this? Yeah, I had a dozen people tonight," Iris said. "I took my pick. So many people brought someone. It was very sweet of them. It felt good to let go a little, to indulge myself, instead of holding back, like I used to, like I had to, to keep Alexei off my back. Frankly, I liked it. Are you seriously passing me up, Nate? Because this offer only comes once. Consider it a once-in-a-lifetime deal, so think very carefully before you turn me down."

"Then I pass," I said.

Iris looked genuinely amused and piqued by this. She stood up, smoothed her outfit with her hands, and went to the window, looking back at me. There was no orange in her eyes, only indigo, her darkest gaze behind her shades, though not a trace of emotion touched her face, which remained the mask that it ever was.

"Alright, then, Nate," she said. "I guess this really is goodbye, then. I can't believe you'd pass up immortality with me. We could have watched the world end together."

"You'll find someone else," I said.

"You're right," Iris said. "I will. I'll see you on your deathbed, Nate. Just like I promised I would.""

She disappeared into a mist, and flowed out of the window, through a crevice. Seeing her do that, even thinking about her having found me, unnerved me all over again. Because in this moment, she was communicating to me that she could find me wherever I went, whenever she wanted. It was the only time she ever went looking for me.

I leaned on my elbows, took a breath. I was glad I had resisted the temptation she offered, but in truth, coming from Iris, there was no true temptation—the price of her gift was too high, and I just couldn't accept it, even if it meant being a kind of undead dauphin in the city's underworld.

Was it strength or weakness, courage or cowardice? I don't know. Maybe I'll never know. It could be argued that I'd already taken a moral swan-dive the moment I entered into Iris's service. But that would be wrong; I hadn't known what I was doing, early on, had been under her spell. No, my moral freefall was likelier measured from the time that I knew what I was doing, and did it, anyway, out of love for Iris. The romantic might say forgive that, but maybe others wouldn't. Or perhaps when I killed Alexei, and unleashed Iris more fully onto the world.

But, to me, what mattered was that I did not take her up on her offer—had I done that, then I truly would have fallen into the abyss, never to emerge. Maybe it was that last free step I would have taken, and it would have cost me absolutely everything that was left of me at that time.

What can I say? I'm not a philosopher. To me, though, evil is the negation of choice—that which is evil must invariably be something that violates Man's capacity to choose. If we measure morality through choice—hah, if we choose to measure morality through choice—then all evils can be traced through the denial of that choice. That's what makes a tyrant a tyrant, isn't it? They rob everyone else of the ability to think and act for themselves, and reserve that right only for themselves. That is tyranny.

The great evil of human existence is our mortality—we can't choose not to grow old, to weaken, and to die—it simply happens, whether we want it to or not. From a human perspective, life is a struggle between those margins of birth, maturity, and death. It is unjust for us to grow old and die, but it is part of our existence, and is, in the end, a natural thing. And since we are creatures of nature, it is ultimately necessary. A world without death would fundamentally hijack the natural order of things. And that was Iris, an endless, insatiable appetite who lived on borrowed time, stole the lives of others, and would continue to do so.

I wasn't a philosopher, but I could do the math. I'd already said that Iris's vampirism alone had cost anywhere from 100,000 to 500,000 lives, and that was only so far. Stretch her out to a thousand years and it would be likelier around 1,000,000 lives. A thousand years further, and it would be 2,000,000 lives. And so on. The body count would grow and grow, and for what? So that Iris could continue indefinitely? Iris, of all people? What would she be in a thousand years, if what I saw of her now was what was left of her? She'd be a monster that would dwarf what she was, now. She'd be completely inhuman, a goddess of darkness, eager to make the world bend the knee to her in the shadows.

I knew her. I knew what she would do, could imagine temples built in her honor, the reshaping of society to ensure a steady blood meal to her. She was a parasite, like all vampires ultimately were, living on borrowed time and stolen lives.

There was a choice to be made, here—I could pretend I didn't know where it was going, could live the rest of my short years in that knowledge, and see Iris gloating at me over my deathbed, knowing that she had won. Or, I could redeem myself and make the choice that I knew was the right thing to do, and put an end to Iris, once and for all.

I got up and went back into Clementine's bedroom, just to check on her. She was on her side, now, the sheet still not covering her breasts. I took the comforter, a cream-colored thing, and pulled it over her chest, covering her. She was, thankfully, breathing. Iris hadn't killed her. It was something I had to worry about; Iris was that way.

Then I got into the bed, and Clementine rolled over and snuggled with me in her sleep, muttering something I couldn't make out.

Laying on my back, I thought about Iris's visit, and her offer. She had looked almost swollen, so infused with blood had she been. The thought of her taking me filled me with revulsion. It was so apparent and visceral, it gave me goosebumps.

Something else came to me, too. There would be no escaping Iris. She would be with me until my dying day. She would not be able to resist looking in on me from time to time. I knew her. She had a morbid curiosity, and probably always had.

I imagined her walking the streets of plague-wracked Venice, centuries past, finding her dead family, bodies swollen, flies and rats everywhere, and exulting in her own immunity from such concerns, grateful that she had escaped that fate, thinking that a pair of fangs, endless hunger and hiding from the sun was a small price to pay for escaping mortality. I can see her throwing her lot in with Alexei and thanking God that he had come for her and taken her away from all of that. As plain as day, I could see it, could see her laughing in the streets of Venice, beneath the light of the moon, the beginning of her long, dark joke on the world.

And without Alexei to hold her back, Iris would indulge herself in the worst way. It came to me in the belly of the night, as steady as a heartbeat.

I would have to kill Iris. There was no choice.

Morning came, the sun came blazing into Clementine's place, and she sat up, yawning, stretching, getting up, looking at me sleepily, nakedly, gorgeous and young and delicious.

"I had weird dreams last night," she said. "You were talking to a vampire."

"Yeah? What was I saying?"

"Can't remember," she said, mixing herself some Tang. "Something about stuff."

"Can't believe you drink that shit," I said, watching her stir it.

She smiled, licked the spoon, then drank it down, watching me as she did so. It was a funny image, conjured up Iris gaping at me over the neck of one of her victims, drinking them down. I actually shook my head, sought to banish that image.

"It's yummy," she said, finishing it, setting the glass down with an authoritative thud.

"Tang is so pre-Internet," I said.

Clementine finished it, licking her lips, looked at me like I was a nut.

"I don't even know what that means, Dude. Pre-Internet?"

"Retro," I said. "Old-school."

"I know, right?" Clementine said. "I think NASA invented it, Dude."

"That's the point," I said. "Let's say you wrote on your Facebook this morning 'I love Tang.' What do you think people would say?"

Clementine laughed, a snorty kind of thing.

"Yeah, okay, so what's your point?"

"My point is that Tang is ill-suited to the Internet age," I said.

"People are juvenile," she said, grabbing a white robe. "I will not apologize for my love of Tang, thank you very much."

I was right, though. The nature of the Net, and of social media in general, had impacted our language and what we thought about things in so many ways. It came up all the time, so often that perhaps people didn't even consciously notice it.

Anything that possibly could be misconstrued would be misconstrued.

Sharp's Law. That's what I'd call it.

"So, are you going to work from home or what?" Clementine asked, nodding to my laptop.

"Thought I would," I said. "Hey, do you want to help me kill a vampire?"

Clementine laughed, grabbing an orange bath towel.

"Yeah, right."

"Just asking," I said. I still had keys to Iris's place. She hadn't thought of getting them back from me. Or maybe she thought I would be back. Or maybe she didn't care. Or maybe she knew I would be back. How well did she know me? Odds were perhaps equally good that she might just have forgotten, or she counted on me coming back, so that the one living person who really knew just how horrible she was would return, and she'd fuck me up royally.

With Iris, anything was possible—no, that wasn't really true. With Iris, only bad things were possible. Iris sucked (pun intended). But it's true. The one constant in her otherwise multivariate and endless existence was that Iris truly sucked. She sucked as a person, and, in many ways, she even sucked as a vampire—she was lazy, selfish, greedy, vain, arrogant, manipulative, narcissistic, murderous—that may have made her an excellent vampire, a great monster, or it may have made her an incredible pain in the ass. Evil was either grandiose or it was completely ordinary. Evil spoke to the very worst in all of us, like a malevolent BFF who would whisper in your ear that you could suck as much as you wanted, but you were still awesome.

That's exactly what it was. Evil never asked questions of itself, never doubted itself for a moment, never chose anything but to be exactly what it wanted to be, regardless of the consequences.

Evil sucked. And that's exactly why it sucked. And Iris was a whole big pile of suckage. It sucked getting older, it sucked to die. But what sucked worse was to become a lifeless thing like Iris, sidestepping mortality and the confines of her human life and becoming a monster, and taking as many lives as it took to keep the reaper at bay. And it sucked to live in a world where those things stalked the shadows, where Mankind found itself to be nothing more than meals, or, at best, diversions or pets for these things. That really sucked, let me tell you.

You know what didn't suck? Being free.

Clementine went into the shower, and I grabbed my laptop, did a little day trading. It made me laugh, being a day trader with a night life, having served the Queen of Darkness, herself.

I had an advantage in hunting Iris, in that I had already combed her place top to bottom, so I knew where she wasn't, just because I had searched so many times. It freed me up to concentrate on places I hadn't looked, where she could be. And Iris was lazy enough, arrogant enough, proud enough to think that I'd never figure out where she hid.

That was the problem; I'd looked everywhere. Unless there was some kind of secret door I wasn't aware of, I had combed that place up and down, had searched every nook and cranny of that place.

Clementine was singing in the shower, some tuneless thing I didn't recognize.

What had I overlooked? What hadn't I seen? Where did she go?

Now that she'd ascended in the underground, it would be harder than ever to find her. Now was the time to act, while she was still sinking her claws into the city, before she'd properly protected herself, before she got into a routine.

I'd drop by there today, see what I could see.

I got dressed and shut down my laptop, put it with my stuff, left Clementine a note on a circular orange notepad:

OUT HUNTING VAMPIRES. WILL BRING BACK DINNER.
  —NATE

I grabbed my bag of tricks and went vampire hunting.

The city by day looked the same as it ever did. There weren't bodies piled in the bushes, wasn't bloody graffiti on the walls. Chicago was Chicago, would always be Chicago. The same waves beat the same gray shores, the same trees shook their arms at the sky in the ever-changing winds. I walked to Iris's place, keyed right in.

It was that easy. Inside these protective walls, there was blood. There was blood on the pavestones, in the garden. Drops of it, splashes. And bodies. There were three bodies strewn there—pretty people, two women, one man, like ragdolls. People always say bodies were like ragdolls, but that's what they look like, the way they're dropped, arms going every which way, their faces going this way and that.

I didn't know them, didn't recognize them. They had bites on their necks, they were dead. Iris had killed them. Or her friends had. Dead was dead. Undead was undead. These bodies sat in the shadows. At some point, the sun would find them, and they would burn, once whatever it was that made victims into vampires had its way with them.

I walked across the courtyard, keyed in. Inside, it was worse. There were a dozen bodies in the living room. Everybody dead, not a soul breathing. They were piled up.

Everybody was beautiful. Iris had a taste for that, a lust for beauty, or, at the very least, a greed for it, which was not the same as an appreciation of it—it was, rather, a desire for the beautiful to be at her mercy, to serve her. Iris was indifferent to everything that wasn't Iris.

All of the victims here were women. Some had dozens of bites on them. I wondered if they were all Iris, or if others had joined in. How would that play out? What would the sorry bastards do when they became undead? Who would they serve?

Had Iris been careful to destroy the bodies only because of Alexei? Clearly she was being a slob. I walked into the kitchen, where a young woman's body was on the butcher's block, flat on her back. She had bites on both sides of her neck, and severe blond bangs. Her face was peaceful, square-jawed, beautiful. She wore skinny black jeans and a gray blouse, had a scarf that somebody had playfully tied in a bow around one of her hands. She gazed at the ceiling sightlessly.

I went to the fridge and it was empty, as I expected. Iris was not the type to bottle her blood; it just wasn't her style.

"Can I help you?" came a woman's voice. I turned to see this skinny, fit, young woman in a white leather suit, standing there. Young woman, pretty, black hair cut in a rockstar shag, eyes like ice. A hint of a tattoo at her shoulder. In her hand was a gun. "You're Nate, aren't you? Iris told me about you."

"And you are?"

"Moxie," she said.

"Moxie," I said.

"She said you might come creeping around," Moxie said. The gun was a Glock. The black of it stood out against the white of her suit.

"Yeah?"

Moxie nodded. "So, why don't you give me the keys?"

The way she held the gun, just at her side, tapping it against her hip, tapping it to a beat only she knew. But I knew what that beat was: it was Iris in her veins. I knew the tune. She looked at me, leaned on a hip, leather suit creaking, and I could see it at her neck, the bitemarks. Just a taste.

"What'd she tell you to do if I didn't give them to you?" I asked.

Moxie smiled at me. "She said I should shoot you."

"Yeah?"

Moxie nodded. "So, how about you give me the keys, so I don't have to?"

From this distance, what did one do? I mean, that was it. She was too close to me. Some people see a gun, and their brains shut off. The implied death that is a handgun just freezes them. "Look out, she's got a gun!"

But having a gun, and knowing how to use it, were two different things. Moxie had a gun, but there was more to a gun than simply knowing which end to point at somebody. And she wasn't pointing it at me.

And worst of all, she'd broken Tuco's Law. She should have shot me; instead, she talked.

The question was whether I could reach her before she brought that pistol up and blew my face clean off.

I drew out the keys and held them out for her to take. Moxie looked at them, and at me.

"You look like a model," I said.

"I get that a lot," Moxie said. She reached for the keys, and for a split-second, her eyes were not on me, but were on the keys. At that moment, I rushed her.

And when I say I rushed her, I mean that I threw everything that I was at her, with both hands grabbing her gun arm, holding it fast, while she cursed and tried to free herself of me. I brought my left elbow up against her throat, while fighting to get the Glock free of her hand, twisting the pistol upward, breaking her trigger finger as I turned the gun sharply upward. Moxie cried out at the breaking of her finger.

I pried the pistol free, shoving her to the floor. Moxie grabbed at her throat, cursing at me.

"You crazy fucker," she said. "I'm telling Iris about this tonight."

"Yeah?" I asked.

I shot her in the head, without another word said.

Tuco would have been proud of me.

-X-

CHAPTER 23

I know that seems cold-blooded, right?

Don't judge me. You don't have a clue about it.

You have to understand that when you're in the business, someone like Moxie was someone like me—or what I used to be. I knew what she was, what was required of her, what to expect from her. I mean, Moxie was in that place with a dozen dead bodies, victims of Iris. She had made her bloody bed, and was rolling around in it.

You might think it was an act of jealousy, but it was really just a matter of survival. Moxie was the enemy. She was the dog of the enemy. I fished through her pockets, found a phone, and took one of the twist-ties from my bag of tricks and put it around her wrists.

In a few moments, Moxie recovered. She had fed from Iris, and the blood Iris had given her gave her unnatural vitality, which she was using up right now to save herself. She gasped and expelled the bullet, which rolled bloodily on the floor. She gazed at me with naked hatred, her one eye blood red, thanks to the trauma of the bullet.

"Motherfucker," she said, spitting up blood. "You shot me."

"Yeah," I said. "Used up your borrowed blood, didn't I?"

"Fucker," she said. She was straining at the bonds. "You are so dead."

"No, I'm alive," I said. "Iris is the dead one."

Looking through her phone, I saw Iris's number in there. Then I dialed up Iris, wishing I'd thought of it sooner. The phone rang somewhere in the place.

I started walking through her lair, trying to trace the ringtone. There were bodies on the stairs, bodies on the next floor up. The place was a mess. What the hell was Moxie doing in here, anyway? What could I expect? She was a dog, not a maid. Too busy being high as a kite on borrowed blood to really think through what she was experiencing, here.

What I assume was now her room was what had been my room. Not much in there. A couple of wardrobes, a big queen-sized bed, some dumbbells. A katana on a nightstand.

"What the fuck?"

I walked over to that, picked it up, looked at it. It was a beautiful weapon, with a rosewood lacquered scabbard and a white pommel wrapped in plum-colored braiding, with a white and purple cord on the scabbard. It looked very old. Half-drawing it, I looked it over. It looked antique, a gorgeous sword.

What, had Moxie wanted this and Iris gave it to her? The thing was fantastic. Okay, that pissed me off even more. Iris never got me anything. I took the katana with me, tucked it under my arm. Finders keepers, Bitches.

Then I dialed up Iris again, kept following the ring, trying to isolate it. I could hear it, but couldn't tell where it was, where she was.

After about five minutes of dialing her, I had found Iris's hiding place. She was in the ductwork. That's why I never found her all those years.

The fucking ducts. It made sense. She could turn to mist and secret herself in there, where I'd not be able to reach her easily.

Of course. Nothing was ever easy, where Iris was concerned. I went back downstairs, checked on Moxie, who was trying to free herself, snarling at me as I passed.

"Gimme back my fucking sword, you fuck!"

"I'm taking this," I said. "I'm so taking this."

"Thief," she said.

That made me want to laugh. After all that I had seen and done, that was the least that somebody could say to me. She was such a newbie to this game.

I went out to the garage and picked up a ladder.

"What are you doing?" Moxie asked, when I came back in.

"I'm visiting Iris," I said.

She kicked at me, actually caught me in the shin with one of her stray kicks. I backed out of her reach and went back upstairs, putting the ladder where it was closest to the sound in the ducts.

The ringing seemed to come from the main bedroom on the third floor, which had nice, high ceilings. There was a vent in that high ceiling, dead center, but it was far too high for the ladder to reach.

"Fuck," I said.

I took off my shirt, had only a t-shirt on. I put my garlic garland on, and a canteen of holy water. I had no place to put a stake, and, besides, no way was I going to be hammering while in the ducts. I stuffed the pry bar into my pocket, and took out a pair of leather gloves, which I slipped on.

I walked over to a section of the ducts I could reach, down on the second floor, and pried open the vent for it. She was on the third floor. I'd have to climb for it. I was a good climber. I could get there, although I worried about getting stuck.

Turning on the LED headlamp I'd pulled from my bag of tricks, putting that on my head, I squeezed my way into the duct, which gave a metallic groan of protest. I was skinny, sure, but I wasn't insubstantial. The thin metal of the thing was not designed for a person to creep through. No doubt this was what Iris intended.

Once I got myself in there, I did an Army crawl, pulling myself along with my elbows, the tightness of the ducts making it hard to breathe, even though I wasn't claustrophobic, or at least didn't think I was.

Not yet, anyway.

The sounds played strangely in there, the shiny metal acting like a drum, as I moved through it, bending and distending it. I came to one of the vertical passes, and looked up, letting the light shine. I'd have to slither like a fucking snake. It was ridiculous. I regretted even thinking of this.

I wanted out. I could feel that, too, in shortened breaths, and plenty of sweat. And, almost on cue, the furnace in the basement kicked on, and some hot air came blowing up from below, catching me in the face.

Turning onto my back, I inched my way forward, stomach muscles trembling, as I reached that vertical duct, and then tried a variant of what I'd done at Alexei's—basically pushing out against an opposing surface while climbing.

The duct creaked in protest, the metal giving way, which made it that much harder for me to wend my way up, and gravity went from meek mistress to bitch goddess in a pile of heartbeats, pulling me down, urging me to plunge into the basement, where I'd either get wedged or would burn up or suffocate.

No. I squeezed and inched my way upward, what felt like an impossible distance, an endless ascent. When I reached the top of the duct, I threw my arms out to either side of me, so I could just kind of hang there a bit. Then I fished out the phone and called Iris again, to try to get a sense of where I should go.

It sounded like I should head to the left. So, that's the way I went, wriggling, slithering, until I'd packed myself into the tight horizontal duct, toward that vent that I'd seen. I had no idea what I was going to do if and when I found Iris, nor any idea of how to get out of there. There were grates that opened into the rooms, but I was unsure I'd be able to generate the necessary leverage to pry them open.

Fuck leverage.

Fuck everything.

I was hunting vampire.

I was a motherfucking slayer. It occurred to me that, with my past, I was an almost perfect vampire hunter. For most slayers, I imagined, there was a period of adjustment, of transitioning from the sunlit, happy-go-lucky world of ordinary human misery and mayhem; so, when you took on the living dead, there was likely a sense of horror at seeing the ghastly things you encountered.

But, for someone who had served as a vampire's minion? Water under the bridge, man. I could face anything a vampire could fling at me and not be surprised, startled, horrified or stunned by it, frankly. Sure, Alexei's room o' rats was gross, but I'd gotten over it, hadn't it? I took care of it. Once you understood what a vampire could really do, knew what they were capable of doing, it let you just sort of shelve that and concentrate on slaying them.

My elbows were sweaty-slippery, so it took some effort to wriggle my way down the passage, toward where I thought Iris, or at least the phone, was.

I reached that grate and peered out, could see the floor below. Far, far below.

And above me, behind me, was another grate. I shined my light into it, and saw that it led to a secret room. There were no doors to it, and certainly no windows. The only way into it was through the grate.

I worked the pry bar into the grate, straining, turning it this way and that, bending the metal. In my years at Iris's lair, I'd never suspected that there was a little secret room like this, something that had been built when the building itself had been raised, likely to Iris's own specifications. It was ingenious—there was no way to get into it except through the grate. Safe from the sun, safe from me.

It took me at least 15 minutes to pry off the grate, and then I carefully pulled myself into this dark room. It was a tiny room, too, like a little built-in coffin, not some cavernous thing. I could get around it on my elbows, kept bumping my head as I moved. It was stuffy as hell in here; I could hardly breathe. But Iris didn't have to breathe, wouldn't have felt any discomfort, here.

I peered around me, saw a pair of feet.

Shoes.

Heels.

Holy shit.

Now what? I had no fucking idea.

It was horrible, sharing a tiny space with a dead person, and even worse, sharing it with an undead person. My own breathing echoed in my ears, contrasted by Iris's own utter silence.

I reached up and touched her foot, gave myself the willies. I had never seen her like this. She would have hated to know that I had seen her at all in repose, had finally discovered her hiding place.

But, truly, what was I going to do? No way in hell would I be able to inch back the way I had come. And the room was intentionally small. Iris had been living here since, what, 1871? So, this little room had been her lair for over 140 years. She'd been thinking ahead. Nobody would have found this place. She'd probably killed whoever designed it.

The scent of garlic filled the duct, which, along with the warm air and my own sweat, made me want to gag. I imagined she'd not like that one bit. Would that be enough to rouse her from her slumber?

I didn't know.

I hoped not.

There was really only one thing to be done. I started straining against the duct, using whatever I had left in me to try to burst the thing. For all of its groaning and buckling, the ductwork seemed to hold together, even as I tried to bring my knees up, pushing out against the thing.

I kept straining, trying to break something in that damned grate. The thing was that it had likely been painted over a dozen times over the long life of the place, so I was competing with that, too. Paint was powerful.

Back and forth I rocked, throwing my shoulders into either side of the dimpling duct, while pushing hard with my knees.

Finally, there was a rending sound, and by my feet, below my ass, the grate gave, and a tear formed in the ductwork. I got my feet in there and strained further, trying to widen the thing, while also holding on with my arms, so I didn't go plunging the 20 or more feet to the hardwood floor below.

The duct ripped out beneath me, and I strained again, holding on with my arms, and heaved myself up into that tiny room. Now I had a real challenge—I had to somehow pull Iris out of there, then drop her to the floor, then get myself down there and stake her before she rose.

She was in torpor, since it was daytime. I had to deal with it right now, because I'd never get a second chance at this. The same dynamic in place with my hunt for Alexei was in play, here. Act fast, act decisively. He who hesitates is fucking lost.

When you hunted vampires, you had to play for keeps, because they absolutely would come after you. You had one good shot with a vampire; blow that, and you were dead. Sooner or later, you were dead.

It was kind of like rock-climbing, which I'd played around with a bit in college; I braced my legs on the broken ductwork, braced one arm at the lip of the grate leading to the tiny room, and, with my free arm, pulled Iris toward me. This was awkward as hell, but that's as Iris had intended. Vampires always made it a pain in the ass to kill them, at least the master ones did, the ones to be reckoned with. Experience taught them to be pains in the asses.

I pulled her to me, mindful of her body against mine, the dead weight of it, grateful that she was comparatively small, and was in a torpid state, although how much jostling would she take before she arose? Would the exposure to even ambient daylight wake her up?

Iris would be infuriated to know that I had seen her hiding place, seen her asleep, was prying her body out of her hidey hole, and was planning to drive a stake through her heart. She'd be so pissed.

I managed to free her from her hiding place, and she collapsed against my shoulder. Between bracing myself in the ducts and carrying Iris against me, I was sweating like a pig. I could feel her cold lips against my neck, did not dare look her in the eye. The stink of garlic from my garland was heavy. That alone might stir her.

I had to be swift. Iris was motionless, lifeless, cold, and heavy. A corpse, eyes staring, the previous night's lipstick red on her lifeless lips.

Gravity had to be my accomplice in this. I let Iris drop to the floor with a ghastly thump-crack of her body and skull striking the floor. That started to wake her. I could hear her react.

She was wearing a black gown with a red scarf, and long black heels. I was unused to seeing her inert like this. I kept expecting her to get up and say something, but she just murmured and stirred.

Taking a deep breath, I dangled there from the ducts by my arms, having pulled my legs through the hole I'd made. And then I dropped, myself, landing on my feet, on the ground, trying to dissipate the force of my impact, sending pain jolting up through my legs. Thankfully, nothing broke, but I hit the ground hard enough to make me feel like the arches in my feet were going to fall.

I dug into my backpack and pulled out one of the stakes, the mallet. It had been easier with Alexei, because I'd fucking hated Alexei. Rightly or wrongly, I did. But Iris? What was I going to do?

I held the stake over her heart, hesitating, as Iris stirred.

Tuco's Law.

Always, Tuco's Law.

Moxie appeared at the doorway, carrying her katana, which she'd drawn. Her wrists were raw and bleeding, from where she'd slipped free of the bonds.

"Step away from her," Moxie said.

I held the stake over Iris's heart.

"This needs to be done," I said.

"Not by you," she said. "Not now. Not ever."

She stepped into the room, and I raised the mallet. I think we both knew that I couldn't possibly stake Iris with one blow.

"I should have shot you a couple more times," I said.

"Shoulda, woulda, coulda," Moxie said. She was winding up with that sword, and I was sure she'd lop my head off with it. So, I dropped the stake and hefted Iris, held her up in front of me, an inhuman shield. Her head lolled, while Moxie fought to get into position, to get me.

It was weird, facing down Iris's latest plaything, with the dried blood down the side of her head from where I'd shot her, her chafed wrists from where I'd bound her, her hands on that old sword Iris had given to her. Moxie was nimble.

I dug out the Glock from my waistband, pointed it at her.

"Back off, Killer," I said.

"Not a chance, Has-Been," Moxie said. "I told Iris she should've killed you. You know, she still cares about you?"

Moxie and I stalked each other in the room, a slow, deadly dance. We both knew the stakes in this, so to speak. Iris was continuing to stir, trying to rise. Thank the gods that the torpor was not the same as sleep, but really was a kind of semi-death.

I pointed the Glock at Moxie's leg and fired two shots, catching her in the thigh. Moxie cried out, knocked off her feet by the shot, half-spinning away. She fell to the ground, but hadn't dropped the sword. Her white leather slacks were now bloody as fuck.

I dropped Iris and took careful aim.

"She loves you," Moxie said. I wondered if Iris had told Moxie to say this. I didn't think Iris planned that far ahead, but didn't entirely put it past her. That kind of mindfuck was right up her alley.

"Look, no offense, Moxie," I said. "But you're in the way, here. I know why you're here. You're a guard dog, alright? I don't know what Iris offered you, but I can take a guess. Because whatever you think you got from her, it's nothing, okay? You're nothing."

"In three days, all those people she bit are going to get made," Moxie said. "This place is going to be crawling with vamps. And we're all going to come after you, Nate. How do you like that?"

"Looks like my work is cut out for me, huh?" I said, glancing at Iris, who remained in a lifeless heap in the center of the room, but had managed to move an arm, scraping at the wood on the floor with red-lacquered claws. At the sight of her mistress moving, Moxie became distracted a moment, and I saw my chance.

I leaped over to Moxie, who tried to swing at me with her sword, but the wound in her leg was causing her too much pain, and the blow missed. I kicked her in the face and pinned her sword arm with one of my shoes, and managed to pry the sword away from her, kicking it away.

"Just fucking shoot me already, you crazy fucker," Moxie said.

Frankly, I was worried about even having taken any shots. While Iris had the place fairly soundproofed, enough gunfire was sure to attract the police. Maybe that's what Moxie intended.

I picked up the katana.

Iris moved her other arm, an unnatural, almost spiderlike kind of extension of her limbs, her head still unnaturally planted against the wood floor, her eyes, unseeing.

"I'm sparing you because I feel bad for you," I said. "I've been there. I know this dance. You think she loves you because she picked you, out of all of those club kids or whoever she had here? She doesn't give a shit about anybody but herself."

Talking it up, it got me going, got my blood up. I walked over to Iris, raised the katana.

"No," Moxie said. "God, please, no. Take me, instead."

"You've known Iris, what, 24 hours already? And you're ready to lay your life down for her? You don't know what you're up against, here," I said.

"Nate," Iris said, stirring. Slow and sluggish, not graceful. I'd never seen her move by day. She propped herself up on her hands and knees, fought to raise her head.

"Sorry, Iris," I said.

"Nate, don't do this," she said. Her voice was guttural, a croak. "You stupid bastard."

She managed to get her head up, to look at me, but I averted my gaze, would not look into those radiant eyes. Even behind those droopy lids, her eyes were blazing.

Her hands were claws. She was trying to bring herself to her feet, but in the light of the day, it did not come naturally to her. She was so groggy.

"Mistress," Moxie said. "He's here to kill you."

"Nate!" Iris shouted, taking very bit of herself to say it. "You love me!"

My heart breaking, in one smooth motion with the katana, I took off Iris's head.

It was like playing golf in Hell—I just took a swing and the sword connected with her flesh, and Iris's head came clean off, rolled away, and her body spewed its harvest of stolen blood. She was a gusher, the blood spraying Moxie from across the room.

Just like that.

Moxie wailed at the sight of it. I mean she fucking howled, like an animal thing.

With her head detached, Iris's beautiful, ageless little body immediately crumbled into dust before our eyes. We watched as young Iris became old Iris, and dead Iris, and long-dead Iris, and bones Iris, and then dust Iris. It took moments, but the transformation felt like eternity.

"You monster," Moxie said. "You fucking monster."

"I'm no monster; I'm a slayer."

I walked out past Moxie, went through Iris's place, and I beheaded every one of those baby bloodsuckers. I just went from body to body and took their heads off with the sword. No drama, no weeping or wailing; I just handled it. The sword was perfect for this. Each time I made the cut, the katana seemed to sing.

Not to say it didn't affect me, because it did. I felt dreadful doing this—but, on the other hand, it was really just an extension of what I'd been doing for years, thanks to Iris. I knew how to dispose of bodies. I understood this.

There were 26 victims in her place, counting the three in the garden. I killed all of them, took their heads. I actually went into Iris's place and I got out a couple of big Hefty bags, and I put the heads in those bags, just went through and piled them in there. I even tied off the bags, once I was through. I put Iris's head in last. Okay, not so much a head, anymore, but a pile of dust. Just a couple of handfuls of dust that Moxie had been trying to put back together when I came back to the room. What a sight she was, blood-covered club kid taking white handfuls of dead vampire and trying to put it into a pile, weeping all the while.

That was the odd thing about it—for all of their powers and their grace and their charm and their vibe and their menace, once they were dead, all of that just ceased. The nothing that they were would come rushing back like a wave, and you were just this sweaty guy in a room, bloody, breathing hard, and carrying a bagful of severed heads.

I tied off the bag, looked over at Moxie.

Moxie watched me do this with incredulity, just sat there, weeping and bleeding. The mascara around her eyes had run, and she looked pretty ghoulish, herself, her hands white with Iris's dusty remains.

"I'm going to tell the police that you did this," Moxie said. "I'm going to rat you out, you fucker. I'll tell them you're Captain Howdy."

"I am Captain Howdy," I said. "You know, there's still some room in my bag, here."

Moxie hitched and wiped her nose with the back of her hand. Her fingernails were painted purple.

"I can't believe you killed her," Moxie said. "You just came in here and you fucking killed her."

"Yeah," I said. "See, that's the thing with vampires, Mox—you really have to play for keeps. I mean, if you want to win. So, what's it going to be? You going to keep mum about this, or do you go in the bag?"

"I promise," Moxie said. She stared at me with horror, like I was the monster. Like she hadn't been slaughterhouse-sitting for Iris, doing whatever she was doing before I came in. Tiptoeing around the bodies, tripping on the blood Iris had shared with her, thrilled at her good fortune that Iris had taken her in.

That's the problem with knowing what I knew; after years of Iris, I could tell when somebody was lying. Somebody would fry for this, and Moxie was damned sure that it wasn't going to be her.

"I won't tell a soul," Moxie said.

"I know," I said, and I cut off her head.

Don't judge.

I know it's terrible.

I know this.

That's why we're called "slayers."

There's a reason why most people don't become vampire hunters.

There's a reason why they had Buffy make it look so easy—kung-fu chops and vampires vanishing in puffs of bloodless ash the moment they got a splinter.

It's because it's not like that at all; it's bloody, ugly, horrible work. Nobody's got the stomach for it. You can't ever really get the stomach for something like that. Not for real.

And the worst thing about it, you are taking a life. Yes, it's a life that should have gone its merry way centuries before, it's a life built atop the lost lives of many thousands of other lives, but there is still that awareness that this link with the past becomes severed, that all of that experience bound up in that vampiric life becomes lost. It's like taking a folio and throwing it on a bonfire. It may not even have been a compelling read, or a particularly good book, but there remains a loss as you consign it to the fire.

I wasn't so shallow as not to understand this, and not to feel it strongly as I contemplated what I'd done, here. I had put an end to Iris Augenblick.

Here Lies Iris Augenblick, Venetian Courtesan and Vampire, 1492–2012, killed by Nathan Sharp, Slayer.

I stuffed Moxie's head in the bag, and I dragged the bags downstairs to the garage, shoved them in the trunk of the MG. I just stuffed them in there, and what else I couldn't fit, I put in the passenger seat.

Then I took that car out for a spin, not entirely sure where I was going to go, only knowing that I would drive very carefully. The last thing I needed was to be pulled over with a trunkful of severed heads. Detective Davis would have a field day with that.

As I was driving, I thought about Iris's "daughters"—Lucinda, for example, who lived in the city, who I had yet to meet. Would she be happy to be free of her sire? Or would she be angry? Had I incurred the wrath of the Augenblick Estate in taking out their founder? Was I in for a whole world of pain and suffering?

I didn't have any answers to this. I only knew that I had done something approximating the right thing by killing Iris. Had she continued doing her thing, the city would have been imperiled. Absolutely nothing good would have come from Iris continuing to do her thing. That much was a certainty. The body counts would have risen, her control of the city would have become ironclad, and nobody would have been able to breathe in peace, had she been allowed to have her day.

Although nobody would know it, the city had me to thank for this. The question I had would be whether Iris's daughters would be thankful to me, or would seek revenge. I had no way of knowing. And I didn't have it in me that day to actually try to hunt down Lucinda and find out, myself.

I drove the MG to the river, and tossed all the heads in there, for lack of a better place to put them. The city had the river flowing backwards, so I figured that was the way to go. Down they went, tumbling into the disgusting water. I watched them bob for a second, before sinking. Then they were gone.

I took the Hefty bags and stuffed them in a city trash can, then got back into the MG and drove back to Iris's place.

Then I went down to the basement and went through Iris's stuff. I took all 14 of her portraits—hell, yeah, I did—and put them in the MG. I rifled through her stuff. There was a trove of antiquities, here. For all of the things that were sitting at the Augenblick Museum, there was still a lifetime's worth of treasures, here.

Wasn't it Oscar Wilde who said that a man's face was an autobiography, and a woman's face was a work of fiction?

I don't know whether to believe that or not, because Iris's face told the story of her life before her life, something I was only barely able to cobble together, as she wouldn't talk about it. She was such a taker that she wouldn't even give me her life's story, not the whole story, at least.

I wanted to take all of the paintings and put them in a museum, the Augenblick Museum of Vampirism. People wouldn't even believe if if they'd seen it; they'd think I had created a conceptual art piece around this subject.

Of course, the more I thought about it, the more I liked that idea. Why not do something like that, when all the dust had settled? Why not make her into an exhibit?

But then again, that would surely bring me to the attention of Lucinda, and whichever other Augenblick daughters cared to come calling. I would never be able to show those paintings off, without immediately revealing that I was the slayer who had killed Iris.

Even if they didn't care for her, they would take umbrage at a mortal absconding with what was, ultimately, their property. I knew vampires, and knew they would not like that one bit. And I assumed that every one of the daughters with "Augenblick" as her surname was, in some fashion, beholden to their mutual benefactor, had bought into the Faustian bargain Iris had made with them in centuries past. They would not appreciate having one of their own felled, especially because of the threat it implied to them. If Alexei and Iris could fall, any of them were fair game.

I was thinking like a vampire, again—a murderer, thief, schemer, and a scavenger, right? How foul am I? Look, Iris was already dead. She was living on stolen time. And killing those other newbies spared the city from a glut of new bloodsuckers. That's what happened. I saved the city. With Iris gone, I didn't know who would be next in the underworld hierarchy. Woo? Constance? Rosamunda? Lucinda? I didn't know. Maybe I'd go after them, too. Maybe I'd have to.

Once you realized that they were out there, what were you supposed to do? Look the other way? Ignore them? Join up?

I couldn't. What was I supposed to do? Did you wish that I'd tried to talk Iris out of her evil ways? It wasn't possible. Iris was poised for bigger and better things, which in vampire terms, meant bad and worse things. She was a monster, and was embracing her monstrosity with glee, and would have ballooned it up into a parade float if she'd been able to. Iris was proud of what she was, felt nothing but enjoyment of her lifestyle. I deprived her of her opportunity to have a monstrous debutante ball. That was my crime.

There was a lifetime's worth of stuff in that basement. Treasures galore. And, upstairs, there were a couple of dozen headless bodies. Also her handiwork. She killed them, not me.

I took an armload of things from that basement, made several trips to the MG, loaded up the trunk, the interior of the car, then went upstairs, got that katana and the cool stand that came with it, and I also put them in the MG. Me and 14 priceless portraits of Iris, some bric-a-brac, and a katana. That was so very me.

Using Moxie's phone, I dialed up the Augenblick Museum, told them that Lucinda Augenblick should visit Iris's place, that she wanted to donate the contents of the basement to the Museum. When they asked me who I was, I said I was the executor of her estate, and hung up.

I swabbed my fingerprints off the phone, left it on the butcher's block.

Then I turned on the gas inside Iris's place, figured I'd let God and the pilot light sort it out, one way or another.

I got out of there, drove away in the MG.

I got Thai for dinner.

Clementine was thrilled.

-X-

CHAPTER 24

I had killed the Number 1 and Number 2 vampires in Chicago.

So, naturally, Number 3 came calling, once Iris's place blew up and burned down, and the firefighters labeled it arson and the police found two dozen headless bodies in there, burned beyond recognition. And the police found over two dozen heads in the Chicago River, and there was rampant speculation that the heads in the river matched the bodies found in the old Augenblick building.

It was Rosamunda who came.

She found me downtown, pulled up to me in a limousine packed with Latin bravos. All young men, all bloodsuckers. They looked at me with a mix of amusement and contempt, that look that the undead so often have for us mere mortals.

"Nathan," Rosamunda said, gesturing for me to join her. I didn't have much of a choice, judging from the looks on the faces of her goons.

Once inside, she had the driver take us downtown. Her young men hovered nearby, no doubt wondering why the hell the Mistress wanted to talk to a nobody like me.

"You killed Iris, yes?" she asked.

"Maybe," I said.

Rosamunda smiled.

"And Alexei, too, I gather? You are ambitious, Nathan."

In the dark of the car, her face took on deeper planes and shadows.

"Are you insane?" she asked.

"Uh, no," I said.

"Because one might think you have a vendetta against my kind," she said.

"Only Alexei and Iris, for different reasons," I said.

"That's good," Rosamunda said. "Because I would not want to have to worry about you, Nathan. I do not like to worry. There is no room in this town for a Slayer."

Of course, Rosamunda taking me for a drive and talking with me made me kind of irritated.

"Alexei and Iris were easy targets, in many ways," Rosamunda said. "Alexei because he was too confident, and Iris because she was too complacent. You'll find me to be neither of those things. I am both well-organized and well-defended."

She glanced at her boy bravos, who just looked at me with mute malevolence, a sea of pale, fanged faces.

"Why bother telling me this?" I asked. "Why not simply kill me, just to be safe?"

Rosamunda smiled at this, like I'd made some kind of joke. But I was serious.

"I don't have anything against you," she said. "And you have nothing against me. In fact, your rather rash acts of late have benefited me enormously, and I am not so ungracious as to overlook this fact. One does not live as long as I have and not forget the good deeds of another."

"What do you want?" I asked.

"None of my clan," she said, gesturing this way and that. "Do you understand me? I don't much care if you go after Woo or Constance or Lucinda; no doubt they'd be happy for you to come after me. You're getting a bit of a reputation in the underworld. You snuffed out 1500 years of vampire history in two deadly strokes. This is not to be taken lightly."

I could see her bravos were impressed by this, by glances they exchanged. They wondered how a skinny nothing like me had even done such a thing.

"Like I said, it was personal for me," I said. "Not business."

"I understand," Rosamunda said. "Really, I do."

I wondered how old Rosamunda was. It was impossible to know. She had to be younger than Iris, which put her at below 500 years.

"How old are you?" I asked.

"I am 350 years old, Nathan," she said. "I was made in St. Augustine, Florida."

"Wow," I said. I didn't think much of Florida, honestly. "Is your sire still alive?"

"She is," Rosamunda said. "But she is far away."

"Lucky you," I said. I did the math in my head. "1661. You were made then."

"Yes," Rosamunda said, nodding. "I have seen a lot, and I have seen nothing like what you have done. Never before have I seen someone so young go after anyone so old. I would laugh and call it beginner's luck, but you were not, in truth, a beginner, no, Slayer?"

Oh, the looks of her bravos, the jealousy and resentment, to have earned the praise of their sire.

"Can I be assured of my safety from your boy toys, here?" I asked.

"Yes," Rosamunda said. Then she said something in Spanish to them, looking at each of them in turn.

"*No sufran daño alguno a esta joven,*" she said. "*O puedes encontrar respuesta a mí.*"

"*Sí, Señora,*" they said, almost in unison.

"*Este cazador de vampiros sin embargo, puede resultar útil para nosotros, Hermanitos,*" Rosamunda said, in that speedy way Hispanics spoke.

"*Sí, Señora,*" they said, again, although they looked like they hated even saying it.

"Alright," Rosamunda said. "We have an understanding, Nathan. I am successor to Alexei and Iris. Our paths need not cross again, unless you wish it. I owe you a favor for this opportunity, but if you come for me, it will not go well for you."

"I understand," I said.

Rosamunda smiled, leaned forward and held out her hand, upon which a ruby ring sat. Her nails were painted red.

I kissed the ring, unsure what else to do. Rosamunda seemed amused by my gesture.

"I'm not the Pope, Nathan," she said. "I was just going to shake your hand, my young friend."

Embarrassed, I shook her hand, which was warm to the touch. Warm with stolen blood.

"Where can I take you?" she asked.

"Take me home," I said.

She dropped me off at Clementine's, by my request.

-X-

We were eating curry chicken and rice, chilling at her place. I'd told her everything about vampires. Absolutely everything I knew. She didn't believe a word of it.

"I so don't believe in vampires," Clementine said, drinking a big glass of Tang that she'd spiked with vodka, called it a "Screwtop," claimed it was a cocktail she'd invented. "I mean, seriously, Nate."

"They're real," I said. "You do not want to get on their bad side."

That was the thing I kept thinking about, like that sit-down with Rosamunda. Part of me really wanted to go after her, just because of the implied threat she represented. I mean, that's what she did—she politely threatened me.

It was like dealing with a gangster, I imagined. Going after Rosamunda would open up a huge world of hurt for me, likely get me killed. Maybe I had been lucky with Alexei and Iris; or maybe I was actually good at killing vampires. There was only one way to really know, and that was a road that would get me killed.

I likely had enough to worry about with Lucinda and the other Augenblicks, should they come after me, once they found out I was the one who axed Iris and burned that old brothel to the ground.

There were really two ways to go with it—vampire hunter, or vampire apologist. I mean, once you allowed for their existence, that is. That's why it was great for people like Clementine, who didn't believe in them, or never thought about them. But suppose Clementine went out one night and ran into one of Rosamunda's boys, and he bit her? How would that make me feel?

I'd be pissed. Now, maybe I could go to Rosamunda and cash in that favor, and say "Could you not go after Clementine?"

And Rosamunda, being a player, would agree to this, and my one favor would be cashed in. But suppose Clementine and I broke up, and then I was with some other girl, and some vampire went after her? And, say, I killed that vampire, who happened to be in Rosamunda's ranks?

Then I'd be back where I started, in a sit-down with Rosamunda, bartering for my life if I was lucky, and maybe something far worse, if I was not.

Rosamunda's operation was well-organized, was full of agents and confederates. I doubted I could get anywhere near her without there being an immediate counterattack. And that's what it came down to, ultimately: self-preservation.

That kind of clarity of thought stuck with me in the wake of the bloodshed I'd perpetrated. I'd let Rosamunda be, for now, and would go after the other big players in town, one by one. I'd shut them all down, or die trying. That at least felt like integrity to me, after my moral compromise of the past years as Iris's dog.

I'd run into some of Rosamunda's bravos from time to time, and they'd call me *"El Matador,"* as a kind of half-mocking, half-respectful salute. I just took that in stride, although I had no idea what being a matador had to do with being me.

My phone rang.

It was Jennipher.

I let it go to voicemail. Lord knows what she wanted. But then I knew, of course: she wanted me. The prohibition Iris had placed on biting me had died with her, and Jennipher was likely looking to have a go at me. Jennipher wanted me.

What about her? She hadn't asked to become a vampire. It seemed unfair to go after Jennipher, who had only been a victim of Iris's whim. I wouldn't go after the rank-and-file ones, I decided. Unless they were assholes or evil or crazies. Then I'd get them.

Instead, I'd go after the big fish, the big players, the ones who played the big game, who did the greatest harm, felt they were safest from harm.

I imagined turning the tables on what I'd done with Iris—she'd used me as bait to bring in victims. What if I were to troll for vampires, with the intention of killing them? That was something that hadn't occurred to me until that moment.

One thing that vampires counted on, I mean the real assholes, was that you didn't know what they really were, didn't see them coming, so they could go after you in peace, prey on you without fear of consequence or retaliation.

So, what if I went out there with a big "Bite Me" sign on, to draw vampires to me, and counted on my intimate knowledge of them, my experience with them, to give me the drop on them, and to spike them? A deadly dangerous game, but not without some appeal.

It was compelling, and might offer me a way out of my predicament, because the vampires that were inclined to hunt indiscriminately were the very worst of the breed. I mean, if a vampire hunted assholes, that wasn't necessarily a bad thing, right? But a vampire that just went after anybody was little better than a terrorist. And a vampire that actively went after good people was a real asshole. So, maybe that's what I would do. I'd turn the tables on those bloodsuckers and when they thought they just had another easy victim, they'd end up staked.

Of course, all vampires would ultimately reach that bullshit point of no return, when they simply accepted their monstrosity and gave in to it, became consumed by it. And when that happened, I'd be there for them, ready for them. It made sense. I could respect it. I could look at myself in the mirror in the morning and know that I had done the right thing. The moment I couldn't stare myself in the face would be the moment I knew I'd failed.

"Well?"

"Nothing," I said. Clementine gazed at me with a kind of guileless glow. "Forget I said any of this."

She smiled at me, made a whistling sound, mimed something passing through her head.

"In one ear and out the other, Dude."

"You must think I'm nuts," I said.

Clementine smiled at me. "A little. But I like it."

"Yeah?"

"Hell, yeah," Clementine said.

She leaned in and gave my neck a playful nibble.

CHAPTER 26

I had taken all of the portraits of Iris and had bundled them together in a crate. They weren't something I could just whip out at Clementine's: "Oh, here's a bunch of priceless paintings of my vampire mistress done by painters you've probably heard of. Would you mind if I put them up on your walls?"

No, that wouldn't do, and I was trying to be considerate, after all. So, I just crated them, along with the other bric-a-brac I'd taken from that basement. I put them in storage, figuring that'd be as good a place as any, until I got my own apartment. It might be a good thing to do, too, since Lucinda or the other Augenblicks might come looking for them. Better for them to think that they were lost in that fire than to realize that poor, lanky Nate Sharp was holding onto them. I sure as hell made sure that the storage place had good climate control, though.

I kept that katana with me. I liked it. That sword and I had been through things. And the egg. I kept that out, too. I put it on Clementine's dresser. The egg and the sword. Seeing them comforted me. Souvenirs, Bitches.

Jennipher called me again that night. Clementine was at a step fitness class, so it was just me there, at sunset. I answered this time.

"Nate! Where are you? I have been trying to reach you, like, for forever," she said.

"I'm around. What's up?"

"Iris is totally dead," Jennipher said.

"For real?" I asked. It was so easy playing dumb.

"Yeah," Jennipher said. "Her place burned to the ground. I thought maybe you were burned up in there, but you're not."

"No, I'm not," I said. "I'm a-okay."

"We totally have to get together," Jennipher said.

"And what?"

"You know," Jennipher said. "Like talk and stuff."

I glanced at the sword on Clementine's dresser, imagined taking that over to see Jennipher. But I couldn't do that; I just didn't have that in me to do that to her. Not yet.

"Are you being careful?"

"Really super careful, Nate," Jennipher said. "I need to see you."

"Why? What did you do?"

She laughed. I wondered how long it would take for Jennipher's bubbly kind of spirit to be stilled by the passage of time.

A decade?

A century?

How long did it take a person to die, anyway?

"Nothing," she said. "You were present at my, you know, rebirth. That matters to me."

"Alright," I said. "But I'm telling you, if you try any tricks, you're in for it."

"Not me, Nate," she said. "Come by my place."

I grabbed my trusty garland of garlic and put that around my neck and went to visit Jennipher. The doorman just looked at me mutely, watched me go in.

When I got to her place, Jennipher answered, was wearing a navy blue striped track suit. She was barefoot, and her toenails were painted navy blue, too. She had some club music playing, this throbbing, pulsing stuff that called to mind many-colored lights and matching pills, electronic ecstasy.

"Ohmigod, is that my garlic?" she asked, wrinkling her nose.

"Yeah," I said.

"You cannot come in here with that," she said. "Disgusting, Dude. Didn't you trust me?"

"Meh," I said, holding up my fingers to give her a pinch of my trust.

Her place looked about the same to me. I came in and closed the door. I don't know what I expected.

Jennipher sat down on her sofa. She had her hair down, her own hair, and looked gorgeous. Vampires did know how to work it, that whole monstrous charm they possessed. I avoided gazing into her eyes, of course.

"How have things been going for you?" I asked.

"Great," Jennipher said. "But I get lonely."

"Yeah," I said. "That happens."

"Nobody gets me," she said. "I mean, there are my friends, who think I'm still me, but nobody else. Just a parade of strangers. And, like, with my friends, I know I'm not me, anymore. And I can't tell them that. They totally won't understand. And no way would my parents even get it. What do I tell them?"

I thought about it a little, gave her my best guess. "Parents need to be kept on a low-information diet, for their own protection. You don't want to frighten or confuse them, right? So, you just give them big brush details, without the other stuff. So, you tell them, 'Hey, Guys, I've been having a great time with my friends. I love the city, there's always something to do.'"

"That works?"

"Sure," I said. "Just leave out the details."

"What if they want me to go to their summer beach house?" Jennipher asked.

"Just tell them you've got something else going on, can't make it," I said. "Come on, this is easy. And if they push, tell them that you don't want to get skin cancer, and you're staying out of the sun because, I don't know, the magnetic poles are shifting, creating weaknesses in the ozone layer. Pin it to something about health and they'll probably happily detour on that, and you're in the clear."

She brightened at that, nodded. "That's brilliant, Nate. Thanks."

"Happy to help," I said.

"What about family reunions? Won't they notice that I'm not getting any older?"

"Okay, so, for that, you just make sure you feed before you go, so you have good coloration—you don't want to go in there looking all pale," I said. "Or they'll think you're on drugs. At worst, you could just look them in the eye and mess with their heads, tell them whatever you want them to think. That's like the vampire fallback position."

"I just feel guilty," Jennipher said. "I'm the only one who's not going to die. Like in my family. Everybody else is going to die."

Vampiric guilt? I was not going to get stuck giving therapy to a vampire. No way in hell.

"Have you talked with your therapist about this?" I asked.

Jennipher sighed. "They're not going to understand my problem, either."

"What problem? You're immortal, now," I said. "The one great problem people everywhere face is solved for you."

Jennipher leaned forward, looked at me, kept trying to catch my eye, and I kept dodging it, not wanting to be enslaved to her hypnotic gaze, even if she wasn't consciously trying to do it.

"Nate," she said. "Vampires suck. You can't talk to them."

I wanted to laugh; she was dead serious. But I also understood what she was talking about.

"I know, I've tried," she said. "I've tried to have conversations with them, and they just look at me like I'm nuts. Is it because I'm a noob? Is that the deal? They just throw this vibe my way."

What could I tell her? Vampires did suck.

"Your sire was Iris," I said. "She was very strong. So, even though you're new, you are likely far stronger than they are. The power of the sire matters, near as I can tell."

"Okay," Jennipher said. "So, they're, like, scared of me?"

"I don't know," I said. "At the very least, they'll view you as a competitor. Some will see you as a threat. The nature of the nightlife is going to drive a lot of that vibe. Vampirism is like a never-ending game of chess. Learn chess, and you'll understand how they play their games. But understand that their games never end."

Jennipher sighed. "I just want to be friends. To have friends. I mean, we're all in this together. But they see me, and it's like they've seen a ghost. It's not like when you and I talk; you get me."

It was my turn to sigh. I didn't know what to tell her.

Vampires did tend to travel alone. Even if Iris had succeeded in packing her place with progeny, she would still have been walking alone. Something about the nature of the affliction compelled it, or the demands of survival. Rosamunda had her legion of bravos, but she was as alone as Iris was, I imagined, had to always be looking over her shoulder, wondering if there was another vampire lurking, wanting to displace her.

"I wish you were a vampire, Nate," she said. "You'd understand. You'd be my friend."

"I am your friend," I said.

And I meant that.

It seemed to cheer Jennipher up, just a little.

"But you're going to get old and die one day, and then I'll be all alone again, Nate," she said. "That'll really suck."

I looked around her place. It did not yet look like a lair, still looked like a home. At some point, that would change, and it would become a lair. Or she would move out of this place and find herself a lair, a place to be safe. There was a difference between a home and a lair—a home was a place where you felt safe; a lair was something else, something sinister. A place where you evaded capture, or a place that was a trap for the unwary.

"Let me make you," she said. "We can go through this together. We can look out for each other."

It was more tempting than Iris's offer, since I knew that Jennipher really did care for me.

"We could snuggle up by day, and hunt together by night," Jennipher said. "It'd be sweet. We'd be, like, *the* vampire couple. Like Becks and Posh. And you already know more about vampirism than, like, anybody I know. For sure more than I do. You're practically one already, Nate."

She grinned at me, those fangs in evidence. She looked vulnerable and exotic in a way that Iris never did. There was warmth, there, and it was very tempting.

"Here's the problem, Jenn," I said. "You make me, then you're my sire. I'd not be your friend, anymore; I'd be your, I dunno, subordinate. Your sidekick."

"Sidekick?" Jennipher said.

I nodded.

"It'd spoil our friendship," I said. "Guaranteed. You'd come to view me with contempt, and I'd view you with resentment."

"It's like sex with friends, yeah?" Jennipher asked.

"Sure," I said, although I really had no idea what it was like, exactly.

"That sucks," Jennipher said. "I mean, that really sucks, Nate."

"Yeah," I said.

"So, I'd have to get somebody else to make you, then, right?" Jennipher asked. "Then we'd not be stuck in that weird place? Then we could be real friends?"

"Whoa," I said, holding up my hands. "Then I'd be subordinate to that person."

"So, we'd have to waste that other vampire," Jennipher said. "So that you could be free."

I held up my hands. "Whoa, there. You don't want to go that route, let me tell you."

Jennipher bit her lip in frustration, actually drew a bit of blood, a single trickle, which she mopped up with her tongue without a stray thought.

"It's so totally complicated," Jennipher said. "I'm going to figure it out, Nate."

"You do that," I said, getting up. "You have all the time in the world. But if you do figure I out, please don't turn me into a vampire when I'm an old man, okay? I'd hate that."

Jennipher rose, coolly, smoothly, with that lithe kind of fluidity that vampires had in their movement without even having to think about it.

She gave me a hug, despite the garlic—I could tell how much it bothered her, but her hug was strong and long, and when we parted, she gave my arms an extra squeeze with her fingers.

"I'm here for you, Nate," she said. "Forever."

I knew she meant it.

-The End-

Interview with the Author

D.T. Neal: Vampires are both great and horrible. I'm not the sort to revere or soft-pedal vampirism. I mean, vampirism by its very nature is pretty terrible. When I was younger, I absolutely devoured (heh, pun intended) Anne Rice's Vampire Chronicles, among many other classic works. Vampires will always fascinate on some level. They speak to the Romantic imagination in many ways—who wouldn't want to be immortal and broodily beautiful?

When I wrote *Suckage,* it was definitely a reaction to the whole Twilight series, which I felt had pulled the fangs on vampires. I wanted to give them their fangs back, to basically reveal them to be terrifying and alluring monstrosities and take it where the story led me.

NP: Terrifying and alluring?

DTN: Of course. With both the Wolfshadow Trilogy and with *Suckage,* I tried to kind of deconstruct some iconic monsters. With the former, it was a response on my part to how werewolves just never got the attention they deserved, so I just ran with it.

And with *Suckage,* in addition to the sugarcoating of vampirism, there was this sense of vampires as the popular kids in monster school, and me wanting to take them down a few pegs. Or, more precisely, to really lay bare just what they are all about, the full implications of vampirism.

What does it say about our society that people still dig vampires? It doesn't take a political scientist to extrapolate the parasitic relationships we're forced to endure in the world as a form of vampirism. So, Suckage was my attempt to play with that, to show what it's like to be in a parasitic, emotionally draining sort of relationship. Quite literally, in the case of poor Nate and his dealings with Iris.

NP: Tell us more about Nate. What's his deal?

DTN: Nate comes to the reader in a transitional place. I feel like the *What We Do in the Shadows* comedy series touches on it so well, like how much it, well, sucks, to the minion of a vampire.

I had that covered in *Suckage* years before that movie and series came out, but the sentiment is the same—vampires are about the worst bosses a person could have. My sympathies were always with the minions, because it's far easier to be a vampire. You just glide in gracefully and inflict yourself on everyone. You're used to getting your way, and if things get too bad, you either mesmerize people into oblivion or you kill them or you float away. At the end of the night, you're still sucking people's blood and sleeping in the darkness, away from the sun.

That's something I hammered home with *Suckage.* They're monsters in human form, and that can't ever be forgotten. Even the most well-mannered, worldly, and cosmopolitan vampire is still a monster. People get distracted and dazzled by the vampire glamour, and I didn't want that to happen with *Suckage,* at least not completely.

NP: What happens to Nate after the book ends? Where does he go?

DTN: I get people asking me that, like "Does Nate become a Slayer?" It's a great question, because I definitely see the book as being kind of the evolution of a Slayer. Like you have Nate starting out as potential prey, then becoming a minion, and then becoming a Slayer.

Vampire Slayers intrigue me because, Buffy entertainments aside, it's a rough gig. It takes a toll on a person. It's like a never-ending war. Once you decide you're a Slayer, you've crossed a line from normalcy into perpetual paranormality. Not to bring up more Wolfshadow stuff, but it's something I explore with the *Synowie Srebra,* the Sons of Silver. They're a group of Polish Slayers, basically. They see their mission as being one of taking down werewolves and vampires. They're normal human beings who see the existential threat and they go after it.

NP: Does Nate join the *Synowie?*

DTN: Hah, I don't think they'd take him. They'd appreciate his work from afar, what he accomplished, but I don't think they'd trust him to bring them in. They'd see him as a talented amateur, or a bit of a paranormal tourist. Nate brought it to the vampires in *Suckage,* but it takes more than that to join the *Synowie.* The *Synowie* are lifers—they are in it for the long haul, through thick and thin.

With the *Synowie,* they understand that you only have one chance to get it right when taking down a supernatural creature, so they make sure everybody on their teams knows their stuff. The learning curve is steep. You play to win or you end up dying badly.

NP: Does *Suckage* take place in the same world as the Wolfshadow Trilogy?

DTN: It really feels like it should, right? Set in Chicago, roughly around the same time. However, the chronology doesn't quite mesh up, so, the answer is a reluctant "no" from me on that.

I mean, Nate's story wraps up in 2011, which would be about four years after all the crazy stuff in *The Happening*. So, there's really no way I can imagine Nate stalking around Chicago, hunting Iris and her minions, while all hell is breaking loose because of the werewolves. Nate's clueless and myopic to some degree, but I would think even he'd notice the chaos the Infectives inflicted on the city by that time.

That's not to say there aren't vampires in Wolfshadow and werewolves in *Suckage*. I mean, Iris disses werewolves at one point in Chapter Four, so they're clearly aware of each other. She calls them messy. She's not wrong.

Anyway, in Suckage, the vampires are very clearly large and in charge, despite Nate's best efforts.

NP: What's your favorite vampire movie?

DTN: The original *Fright Night* (1985). I mean, it's so good. It captures so much of what makes vampire stories so fun. Chris Sarandon was stellar as Jerry Dandrige, and, of course Roddy McDowell was perfectly cast as Peter Vincent, with William Ragsdale as Charley and Amanda Bearse as Amy and Stephen Geoffreys as Evil Ed epitomizing the youthful innocence going up against the eternal evil of vampirism. It captures everything fun about vampire stories, and is just a classic 80s horror movie, with that chaser of camp that makes it all work so smoothly. There are so many vampire movies, and they play it all sorts of ways, from darkly humorous to very serious.

For example, I really like *The Hunger* (1983), which plays with everything vampiric in a highly stylish and stylized manner. Although it's a far more taking-itself-seriously type of vampire movie, devoid of humor, it's lovely to watch and evocatively conveys the challenge any immortal is going to face in terms of relationships. Beautiful people doing horrible things—that's always at the heart of a lot of the sinister charm of vampire stories.

NP: Do you see yourself doing more stories in the world of *Suckage?*

DTN: Not truly. I wrote an (unpublished) vampire short story called "Bait" that takes place in a semi-apocalyptic future Chicago, where there is clearly a vampire doing their thing. I like that story, but I think it's one of those stories that's too long to find a home in any periodical but isn't (yet) long enough to become a novella. Maybe one day it'll live as a novella, we'll see.

But as far as Nate is concerned, his story is narratively complete. Any revisiting Nate would diminish him. It's better for Nate to kind of ride off into the sunset (or the sunrise, maybe? Hah!) and disappear. Kind of like Aaron Paul's great portrayal of Jesse Pinkman in *El Camino*—he gets his own sort of happy ending, well-earned after all that he endured throughout *Breaking Bad.* Nate gets his own ending in *Suckage,* and I'm fine with that. And with all that Nate had to deal with, the last thing he'd want to do is push his luck with more confrontations with other vampires.

I have another story idea set in the far future, a kind of vampiric dystopia in the manner of Richard Matheson's *I am Legend,* but we'll see if I give that one life or whether I'll be tied down to other writing projects.

NP: Would you say you have a love/hate relationship with vampires?

DTN: I don't think I hate vampires, but I don't love them, either. I'm probably in between those two poles, at least in terms of fictional vampires. In the real world, I'd be very anti-vampire, because they're elitist and predatory, and I wouldn't like that. In fictional contexts, though, I find them amusing and entertaining.

Suckage was a necessary project for me, owing to dealing with emotionally draining people, the toll they take. It's why the dedication was to victims of vampires.

NP: Werewolves or vampires? You have to choose.

DTN: Oh, man. Werewolves are more comprehensible on human terms than vampires. I mean, the duality of man, wrestling with our animal natures. That motif is understandable from a human perspective, even though werewolf life has to be rough. Werewolves are like serial killers on steroids. Exhausting!

Vampires are so otherworldly, being immortal. It defines them and keeps them far above us. Hard to relate to that. An actual vampire would be so terrifying, and the older they get, the more out-of-touch they become. That aspect turns up in *Suckage,* the burden of longevity. So, I guess I'd have to choose werewolves. That certainly reflects the number of werewolf books I've written.

NP: What's next for you, in terms of horror stories?

DTN: I have a few more lined up in my head. I worry that the horror I write is perhaps more cerebral, literary, and philosophical than the fans of the genre are willing to accept. I can only write the stories that I write, and hope people enjoy the ride. I can say that a couple of the future projects (likely 2022 and 2023, in terms of writing them) will almost certainly be novellas. There's something very appealing about novellas, not just for me as a writer eager to chase down an idea, but also for readers. They're quick, fun reads.

ACKNOWLEDGMENTS

I would like to thank all of my readers, who offered their time, attention, and opinions to the writing and revision of this novella. I would also like to thank Christine Marie Scott of Clever Crow Design Studio in Pittsburgh for her wonderful cover art and her invaluable assistance with the layout of these pages.

ABOUT THE AUTHOR

D. T. Neal is a fiction writer and editor living in Chicago. He won second place in the Aeon Award in 2008 for his short story, "Aegis," and has been published in *Albedo 1*, Ireland's premier magazine of science fiction, horror, and fantasy. He is the author of *Saamaanthaa*, *The Happening,* and *Norm,* known collectively as the *Wolfshadow Trilogy.* He's also written the vampire novel, *Suckage,* as well as the Lovecraftian cosmic horror-thriller, *Chosen.* He has written three creature feature/eco-horror novellas, *Relict, Summerville,* and *The Day of the Nightfish.* He continues to work on several science fiction, fantasy, horror, and thriller stories.

THE WOLFSHADOW TRILOGY

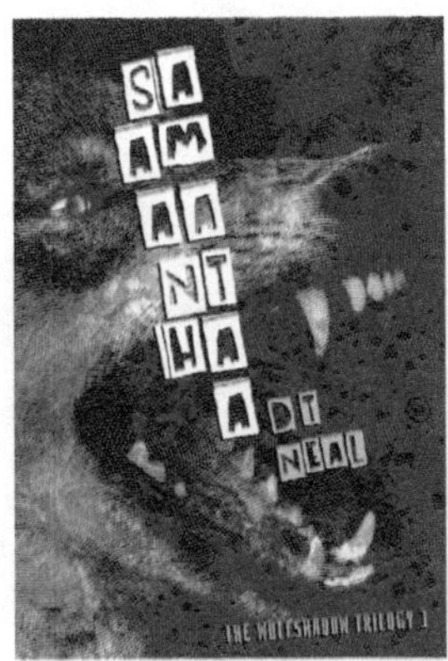

The Wolfshadow Trilogy by D.T. Neal features three werewolf novels, SAAMAANTHAA, THE HAPPENING, and NORM. Starting with a fateful interaction with the werewolf, Ansel Rupino, the title character of SAAMAANTHAA becomes infected with lycanthropy, which she eventually sees as a means of unique artistic expression. This view causes chaos, bloodshed, and death in her life, particularly among her closest friends. It also leads to the infection of Zooey Hummel, who gleefully starts a lycanthropic insurrection in THE HAPPENING. Her infectious revolution tears through both Chicago and the country at large, eventually reaching a climax in NORM, where vicious lycanthropic factions secretly vie for power and influence in a world ravaged by the Lupine epidemic, and Ansel fights for redemption for all the trouble he's caused, while the title character seeks to end the lycanthropic epidemic for good.

The Wolfshadow Trilogy runs wildly in a world of darkly comic horror, scathing social commentary, pop-cultural references, and horror-thriller territory that will dazzle both casual readers and thrill fans of werewolf fiction everywhere.

LUPINA
The Selected Poems
of Polly Drinkwater,
2007–2015
A WOLFSHADOW BOOK

Something's rotten in the Pennsylvania town of Ludlow, or, more precisely, deep within the Mercy River that flows through it. Chosen serves up a paranoid and terrifying vision of an undead epidemic in the form of the cult of the Brethren, uniquely lifeless-yet-sentient apparitions who seek to take over the town, with only a small band of survivors fighting for their lives as they try to stop them.

NOVELLAS

Four leisure travelers boat their way to Palmer Atoll, deep in the inky heart of the Pacific Ocean, hell and gone from anywhere, not guessing that they have stumbled upon the lair of something ancient and terrible. It watches them from the tropical waters, a lurking evil with an endless appetite: a monstrous, many-armed thing, a species of a bygone age with a golden gaze. Set in an exotic, remote island purgatory-paradise, "Relict" is a hybrid horror novella that grips you tightly in its clutches and won't let you go.

A young chef-in-training and self-styled culinary adventurer is transported by tasting the savory food fad, nightfish, at a top-notch hotel in Thailand with his rich girlfriend. Nobody can tell him what nightfish actually is, and his quest for the elusive and enigmatic nightfish takes him across half the world to the unassuming town of Gunwale, Rhode Island, sole producer of nightfish. Here, he works his way to get aboard one of the Blackfin Fishing Company boats, the Amanda Luce, for an unforgettable and horrifying seagoing adventure, where he gets far more than he bargained for.

Three friends set out to find casks of 150-year-old brandy at the bottom of a South Carolina river, not knowing that they've walked right into the clutches of a growing evil in the ghost town of Summerville.

NOSETOUCH PRESS

Nosetouch Press is an independent book publisher
tandemly-based in Chicago and Pittsburgh.
We are dedicated to bringing some of today's most
energizing fiction to readers around the world.

Our commitment to classic book design in a digital
environment brings an innovative and authentic
approach to the traditions of literary excellence.

*We're Out There™
NOSETOUCHPRESS.COM

Horror | Science Fiction | Fantasy | Mystery

Supernatural | Gothic | Weird